PUCK YES

_____

LAUREN BLAKELY

Lauren Blakely Books
powered by Ingie

ABOUT THE BOOK

When my ex trades me out for a better model—my boss—I don't take getting screwed over lying down.

Instead, I get a glow up, not only landing a new job with the hockey team but also scoring the city's hot new hockey player as my plus one to my ex's wedding. Then, the sexy team captain starts flirting with me, too.

But one night after a win, I accidentally marry that intense new guy after the captain dares us to say *I do*. One dare leads to another, and I'm experiencing double the pleasure as I say *puck yes* to both players sharing me on my wedding night.

In the morning, when hubby and I are on our way to get an annulment, the team owner spots our rings and invites the new *it couple* to attend her upcoming charity golf tournament.

Looks like I have to fake it as Mrs. Hockey for the hockey season and the wedding season. There's only one problem.

We're not just a couple. Both guys want more of me.

And pretty soon I've got a bigger problem – I'm falling for my fake husband and my secret boyfriend at the same time.

DID YOU KNOW?

To be the first to find out when all of my upcoming books go live click here!

PRO TIP: Add lauren@laurenblakely.com to your contacts before signing up to make sure the emails go to your inbox!

Did you know this book is also available in audio and paperback on all major retailers? Go to my website for links!

To all the girls who got glow ups, are getting them, or will get them. YOU deserve the best!

MY HOCKEY ROMANCE BOOK #2

AN MFM FAKE MARRIAGE SPICY HOCKEY
ROM-COM STANDALONE

By Lauren Blakely

TIMELINE NOTE

Hello! I thought you might find it helpful to know this story takes place a few months *after* the final epilogue in Double Pucked. (If you haven't read Double Pucked, never fear! You can read Puck Yes since both books are standalones).

But if you've read the Double Pucked bonus scene, this story takes place about four months *before* that scene. Thank you and I hope you enjoy Puck Yes!

SAN FRANCISCO MAP

Ever wonder where all the places in the books are located in my version of San Francisco? @Makeit-bookish designed this "town map" for my stories! Enjoy!

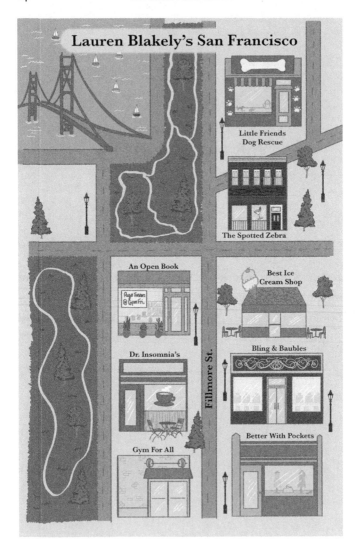

Lauren Blakely's San Francisco

PUCK YES

MY HOCKEY ROMANCE BOOK #2

A Fake Marriage MFM Hockey Rom-Com
By Lauren Blakely

1

A PINOT GRANDE

Ivy

Things I didn't have on my bucket list till right now—watching a hot guy strip naked on a rooftop while watering his eggplant.

It must be my lucky night, though, because my bestie just nudged me and handed over his bird-watching binoculars, whispering: "Free dick."

Jackson and I are across the street from the show, hanging out on the rooftop patio of our new favorite neighborhood bar, The Great Dane. Usually when I'm here, I enjoy a glass of white and a view of San Francisco. Tonight? I'm enjoying an eyeful of peen with my pinot gris.

Oh, excuse me. Let me revise that drink. "Did I actually order a *Pinot Grande* tonight?"

"Full-bodied, no less," Jackson says as I peer at the sight unfolding on the top of the building at the end of the block, where Jackson and I share an apartment. And where, on the penthouse roof, the gardening stud of my dreams has whisked off his gym shorts.

Hello, new neighbor.

The side view leaves little to the imagination. The strapping man is dressed in nothing but big-ass head-phones, sunglasses, and slides, and he's sporting a very nice hose to go with his hose. "Gotta love his commitment to gardening," I say approvingly, getting a kick out of the show.

Then, the naked gardener turns our way, and all the air escapes my lungs.

He's going full-frontal fiesta in the sunset, strumming an epic chord using the green hose as his guitar. "This is not a drill. *This* is a sign that tomorrow I'm getting that promotion," I whisper. Since I'm nothing if not a good friend, I thrust the binoculars back at Jackson. "Don't ever say I don't love you."

"You love me madly." Jackson jams them against his eyes while whistling a happy tune. After a few seconds, he lowers the binoculars with a satisfied sigh. "Show's over. He went inside. Aubrey is so going to curse her bladder for having missed this," he says, nodding at the hallway leading to the restroom.

"She is." I lean against the stone railing, gazing at the pink and lavender sky. "Also, I apologize for ever mocking you for carrying pocket binoculars."

Jackson gives a stately nod, conferring his royal pardon. "You're forgiven. It's your night." He sips his mocktail. "I can practically taste the promotion you're getting in the morning. That gardening striptease was like your *pre-ward* for it."

No one celebrates things that haven't yet happened better than Jackson, and I'm all in with this pre-ward evening out. After three shitty post-break-up months—cheating exes who insult you can suck it—and late nights busting my ass for Simone, my fashion influencer boss, I have a good feeling about tomorrow morning's meeting. I've been angling for my own channel under her online fashion umbrella, and she's been dropping hints that she has something big to share with me tomorrow.

My fingers are crossed.

I'm lifting my glass when the quick click of heels on the concrete heralds Aubrey's return. She charges at us, waggling her phone, nostrils flared, auburn hair flying.

"Your ex," she hisses when she reaches us.

Prickles of worry slide down my spine. What the hell could that philanderer have done while Aubrey was in the little girls' room?

"What about Xander?" I ask, not quite alarmed but definitely concerned.

Aubrey shoves the phone at me, her face a cocktail of anger and empathy. It's open to a pic on her social feed. Grabbing the phone, I squint at the picture, hold it close, hold it far, and then show it to Jackson for a second opinion on everything wrong with this picture. My heart pounds and races, and my blood goes from a simmer to a boil.

He recoils. "Why is your boss blowing your ex?"

"That's a very good question." I'm shaking with...is this shock? Rage? Betrayal? Actually, it's *all* of the above.

"Well, at least it's a mock BJ," Aubrey points out. The photo is clearly staged. My ex—also a fashion influencer, The (self-proclaimed) Dapper Man—is decked out in a pastel blue ruffled suit and posing against a redwood tree as he gets his knob polished. The woman in the punk rock bridal dress, kneeling on the mossy floor, is the same one I'm meeting for breakfast tomorrow morning.

The same one who consoled me and took me out for mojitos the night Xander broke it off. He'd told me he'd fallen for someone who was more popular online, thus *better future-wife material.*

I guess better future wives suck dick in the forest.

Fine, Xander's dick isn't technically in Simone's mouth in this shot. You can't even see his schlong, since he's wearing pastel blue briefs with that pastel tux jacket. But—and I can't believe I have to say this, even in my head—*faux fellatio is hardly better than real fellatio.*

I grip the phone until my thumb cramps, reading the caption. *Xander Arlo and Simone Vega have been blown away with a whirlwind courtship and will be tying the knot in two months. Hold the date—our wedding is going to be a blowout bash.*

I nearly blow a fuse. "My ex cheated on me with..." I stop, take a deep breath, then hiss, "my boss, and he's marrying her."

"So when he *infamously* told you he was upgrading," Aubrey spits out, "he meant to the woman who signs your paychecks."

I nod, slow-mo, then turn to Jackson. "Simone always updates her look books on Sunday night. Can you drive me to the office?"

"Say less."

We're out of there in seconds.

* * *

I fume as I thrust framed photos of my family into the standard *I'm quitting* box, then stuff in my collection of *Kindly Fuck Off* and *Eat a Bag of Dicks* mugs I won at book club. Finally, I drop my hot pink New Day planner on top. This planner is too good to have even visited this office. I add my favorite pens with a loud huff.

Oblivious to my ire, Simone sings under her breath at her nearby desk. Pretty sure that tune is Tiffany's "I Think We're Alone Now," and what used to be quirky and fun to me—Simone's love of eighties tunes—is beyond cloying in this moment.

"Hey, girl," she calls out. She's one of those *hey girl* people. Every woman beneath her is a *hey girl*. "Can you grab those samples from Charlotte Everly? I want to do a whole vid on retro meets chic."

"Oh, so sorry. I'm fresh out of fucks," I say dryly as I jam a succulent in the box.

Missing the sarcasm, she says, "Okey-dokey. I'll do it myself."

What the hell is wrong with her? Does she think it's okay to diddle my ex-boyfriend while telling me what a social-climbing jackass he was for leaving me on account of his "girlfriend upgrade?" What happened to the *sister solidarity* she espoused? The *we girls have to stick together* mantra she spewed when Xander said he wouldn't settle for me?

I stuff another plant in the box then scan my workspace. There's nothing left to pack, so I march to Simone's desk, where she's twirling a strand of her bright blonde hair that's held back in a Rosie the Riveter-style bandana.

"Hey, girl," I say, faux upbeat.

She looks up with a grin, still clueless to my mood, and wiggles her fingers at me. "Hey, girl to you too."

She is too much. They both are too much. A blowout bash? *Please.*

But when her big, Barbie-blue eyes linger on me, I see her put two and two together. Her smile falters and she points to the box. "What's going on?"

I don't have a job, don't have a plan, and don't have a parachute. But I still have one thing—*my pride.* "I have exciting news, and it's all thanks to you."

"It is?"

"Absolutely. You've been such a great mentor. I've looked up to you so much and truly relished the chance to write for your social channels," I say, winging it. "And since you were always so encouraging of my work, I finally decided to start my own channel and newsletter."

I mean, technically I'm rage-quitting, but I don't need to spell out everything for her.

"Oh, is it fashion for average girls?" she asks, like

that's not fucking insulting. She's five ten to my...well, *not* five ten at all.

"It's everything," I say. I have no clue what my schtick will be, but I know this—regular girls rock.

"And you're doing it so soon?" She sounds devastated.

"Well, the timing seemed...fortuitous," I say, swallowing all the *how could yous* that I want to unleash.

But I won't. My deadbeat father was wrong about most things, but he imparted one useful life lesson—*don't let anyone know they hurt you.* If I tell Simone why I'm really leaving, she'll think I'm a wounded little bird. She doesn't get to enjoy that privilege.

Her lips part in an O, followed by a long, "Oops."

This is an *oops* situation? Like oops, she just accidentally sat on his dick for three months while commiserating with me over the most insulting breakup ever?

I can't even speak, but I don't need to. Simone grabs her phone. Her fingers scroll-fly over the screen, then she winces. "Shoot. I'm so bad with social, Ivy, and you're so good with it. I meant to post that engagement shot tomorrow morning at six a.m., not at six tonight."

"AM and PM can be hard," I say with fake sympathy.

"Right?" She pops up from her chair, smoothing a hand over her rockabilly dress patterned with red roses that match the tattoos snaking down her bare arms. "And listen, I planned to tell you at breakfast tomorrow. I figured I'd soften the blow with avocado toast." She grins sheepishly. "Your fave, right?"

Oh god, that's a pity smile. A worse realization hits me right in the gut. Tomorrow was a sympathy breakfast. She wasn't going to promote me. She was going to tell me about her upcoming wedding, letting me down gently with the avocado-and-chia-seed special.

"Yeah. It's, um, great," I say, trying to figure out what the hell my next move is.

"I'm sure it must be hard for you," Simone says with a too-kind smile. "So I totally get why you'd need to move on and do your own thing. And you know I've always supported you." Oh, there's the *sisters in solidarity* bullshit that was missing when she was on her knees giving my ex a faux blow job.

Then, her eyes widen, her lashes blink and her lips round in an exaggerated O. I know that look—it's her *light bulb moment* face. "I just need one tiny thing from you before you go," she says.

"What is it?" I ask, armor on.

She gives a helpless grin. "Can you cover my wedding? You're the best fashion writer I've ever worked with, and I need someone good to cover it for my socials. And you can cover it for your own little channel too. Obviously, I can't do it, and it's a great opportunity for you. You could bring a plus-one, of course."

She truly thinks I'd want to go to my cheating ex's wedding? Where he marries my backstabbing boss? That I'm up for pretending her forest wedding is some sort of fairy tale instead of two trend-chasers dappering it up with choices that will be dated by next week?

It's going to be a train wreck.

Wait.

Holy shit.

It's absolutely going to be a fantastic freaking train wreck, and she just offered me a front row seat. I *can* use this to launch my own fashion channel at last. I've been writing about the business for others for the last few years. Now it's my turn.

I smile and take the invitation for what it is—a *pre-ward*.

"I'd love to," I say.

Jackson and Aubrey are waiting for me when I leave the office. I slide into the back seat of Jackson's ride, equally livid and delighted. "You're so not going to believe this," I say.

"Try us," Aubrey instructs.

I spill all the tasty tea, finishing with, "And somehow, I have an invitation to cover their wedding. Everyone who loves fashion will want to see them tie the knot. And, bonus, I won't even have to *try* to make her look like an asshole; she'll do it all by herself."

Jackson hoots as he navigates his matte black electric sports car through Sunday evening traffic in the city. "So when is the wedding? What are you wearing and *who* are you bringing? There are rules, obviously. First, you never show up at an ex's wedding solo."

In the passenger seat, Aubrey nods vigorously. "Second, you must bring someone hotter, richer, and more fabulous than said ex."

I give them the upcoming date then smile, patting Jackson's shoulder. "I know just the guy."

Jackson and I have been friends forever. Our older brothers—both of them star hockey players in this city, Ryker Samuels and Chase Weston—were best buds growing up. Our moms are best friends, so Jackson and I became besties too. "You have to come with me and be my emotional support hottie," I say.

Over the years, he's been my perma-plus-one, and I'm his. It doesn't occur to me this time would be different.

At the light, Jackson glances back with an apologetic smile. "You know I love being your fill-in man, but I can't go, sweets. I have an animation job in Los Angeles then."

All the air leaks out of me. I slump in the back seat. "Where am I going to find a decent plus-one?"

"We have time," Aubrey assures me. "We'll get on the apps, Ivy. We'll talk to Trina." Trina's her longtime bestie, and after she started seeing my brother over a year ago, she's become my friend too. "We'll get the book club gals involved. We are women, hear us roar." Aubrey adds a bestial sound effect. "We'll find someone so much better."

She's right. I'll have to start a manhunt as well as a job hunt. Starting my own channel isn't going to equal instant income. Finding a gig, freelance or otherwise, as a fashion writer won't be easy. Neither will finding a fantastic date.

"I don't know where I'll find him," I vow, "but with the Goddess of Fucked Over Girls as my witness, my plus-one will be perfect. And I will show up at that woodland wedding with my head held high, my mighty pen ready, and a Mister Perfect by my side." I take a beat. "And after that, I'll just have to, you know, find a new freaking job."

"You're about to start your own newsletter," Aubrey points out.

I rub my thumb and fingers together. "Mama needs a side hustle till it makes me some money." Until then I'll be busy, too, trying to find any openings covering the fashion industry. "The *only* job opening I'm even remotely aware of is one Ryker mentioned a few days ago, but it's not quite in fashion. It's more fashion adjacent."

"How adjacent?" Aubrey asks, arching an eyebrow. She knows my flair for the dramatic.

"Tangentially adjacent. I mean, it involves costumes, so there's that."

"Then, Ivy," Jackson declares, "it's glow-up time in every single department."

We drop off Aubrey then head to our building, where Jackson lets me out in front so he can wrestle the beast that is San Francisco parking. Clutching my quit-my-job box, I head inside and across the lobby. At the elevator, I spot a stranger with a newly familiar profile. Dark brown hair, a little messy in the front, just enough stubble to look the right kind of dangerous, and muscles for days.

It's my new neighbor—the naked gardener.

2

COMING IN HOT

Hayes

No matter how tempting the brunette beauty standing next to me in the lobby might be, I shouldn't flirt with someone in the building.

Especially not the night before I start a new job. I've got a schedule to stick to for the rest of the evening. I already went for my run this afternoon, then I watered the rooftop garden, and I'm about to chow down on this takeout I picked up for me and my landlord.

Besides, this spicy coconut grilled chicken and eggplant dish from the food truck a couple of blocks over smells just as good as the dark-haired beauty mere feet from me.

Lies, sweet little lies.

I draw a furtive inhale of her. What kind of perfume wizardry is that berry and candy scent wafting off her? Is it shampoo? Bodywash? Lotion she rubbed over her soft, bare, wet skin moments after she emerged from a shower?

Not helpful either, dirty brain.

Best to stick to my sked for the night. Eat dinner, do some yoga, and get to bed early. Tomorrow, I hit the ice for my first practice with the Avengers.

Being the new guy isn't easy. You'd think I'd be aces at it since this is my fourth team in a fourth city in four years. But I loathe first days. I shudder at the thought of getting to know teammates, coaches, and trainers only to find out—surprise!—I've been traded again. This team's a double challenge. I'm close with the captain since we played together in college, but I don't want to ride his coattails.

As I wait for the molasses-slow elevator, candy-berry girl heaves a sigh. I steal another glance at her. Her brow is furrowed, and those dark blue eyes look lost in thought.

She's holding an open box with a couple of framed photos sticking out. They're snuggling up against a stack of artsy notebooks, a whole mess of pens, and a pink planner thingy with whimsical illustrations on it.

Oh, shit. Those are the telltale signs of someone who either quit or got canned. I can't say *nothing*.

I clear my throat. "Rough night at the office?"

She whips her gaze toward me. I take her in. Full red lips. A pert nose. A round face, and so much long, wavy hair—perfect for tugging on. Three tiny silver earrings line her right ear—a rose, a skull, and a dangly thing. Pretty but fierce. Like her eyes, with fire in those sapphire irises. They're flecked with gold that seems to flicker like flames.

"You could say that," she bites out, her gaze locked on me instantly. "I quit my job about, oh, thirty minutes ago. Well, I rage quit, only my boss somehow missed all the context clues that I was rage quitting."

And someone is coming in hot. "Why did you rage quit?"

"Because tonight I found out that my boss is marrying my ex-boyfriend. What's the big deal there, you're wondering?" I don't have to wait for her answer. "That same guy dumped me three months ago because he wanted a"—she stops to sketch air quotes with the hand not precariously balancing the box of office accouterments—"girlfriend upgrade."

"Ouch," I say with genuine sympathy. Also, disgust. "What a dick."

She spills a few more details, then nods to the elevators that still haven't arrived. "These are the world's slowest elevators."

"Not the worst thing right now," I say. I'm not really flirting. Just keeping up the volley. Besides, I *don't* want to come across as aloof, like my ex said I was.

"Gives me time for some show and tell. Want to see a pic?"

My head spins from her rapid-fire chatter, but she seems to need to unload. "Definitely," I say as the elevator lights up again.

She fishes around in her back pocket for her phone, but the box she's juggling slides down an inch. I dart out an arm and grab the edge so it doesn't fall. "Let me," I offer, one hand still holding my food.

"Thank you. That has all my new idea pens in it," she says.

"I'll handle it with care." I take the box, brushing her hand as I do, my thumb sliding over her fingers.

For a few seconds, her gaze strays down my body, but then she jerks her eyes back up. She holds her head high, almost regally. She's very specifically looking anywhere but *down* at me.

Okaaay.

That's odd, and maybe a sign she felt zero spark when we touched. But whatever. This isn't a date.

She busies herself with her phone, unlocking, scrolling, then shoving it at me right as the elevator doors open for us.

My eyes pop as I scan the shot. "That's a—"

Well, I know what *that* is. One of my favorite things to receive and also to direct. But while I'm not afraid to say blow job out loud—or to tell a woman how I like it —an older lady with crinkled eyes and silvery hair toddles out of the elevator, so I zip it. She ogles the shot, then rolls her eyes. "Kids today," she mutters.

The brunette's expression turns to *oh shit.* "That's not—"

"They're all afraid to show the full salami," the older woman continues, shaking her head, then flicking a dismissive hand at the pic. "Just show some balls, for crying out loud."

Chin up, she ambles on through the lobby, not the least bit self-conscious about her BJ photo feedback.

Closing my dropped jaw, I hook my thumb back at the lady. "Did that just happen?"

"You mean, did she just chastise our generation for not being...bawdier?"

"Evidently." I stick out my arm to hold the elevator door open for the woman who quit her job to make a point. Which kind of makes her even hotter.

"Thanks," she says as she steps inside. "You're a gentleman."

"Sometimes," I say evasively. *Not in bed. Not one bit.*

I follow her in. "What floor?"

"Eight," she says.

I punch that button, then pause before I hit the penthouse one, hoping she doesn't think I'm a douchey prick for living on the top floor. I'm renting it from my buddy. I don't need strings in real estate or romance.

"Penthouse, I bet," she says, and when I turn to meet her face, there's a sly smile spreading on her lips. One she erases in a flash. "I just mean, you look like a penthouse guy."

A hint of pink tinges her creamy skin, spreading across her cheeks. I half want to ask what that's about, but I also want to know what she thinks a penthouse guy looks like? I'm wearing jeans and a gray T-shirt from my college.

I don't get to because she keeps going, filling the silence. "It's a good thing. A compliment. That's all. You look like you belong on the top floor."

I decide to take the words at face value, pushing the button for my floor too. "Thanks. I like it there. There's a rooftop garden from the prior tenants, so I'm learning to take care of...the veggies," I say, since *take care of the eggplants* sounds like I jack it on the roof.

She sucks in a breath. "Gardening is great. I love gardening. My grandma loves to garden," she says as the doors shut. "Cucumbers, carrots, asparagus."

Maybe I should invite her to plant some veggies? Ask if she wants to water the fava beans or the cucumbers? Those all sound like cheesy come-on lines.

Hey, baby, come play with my cucumber.

But she's still clutching her phone—the screen has locked now to an image of a little dog wearing a bandana—and I'm a big believer in finishing what I've started. I return to the topic of the first photo, although I'm curious about the fashionable dog too. "So you found out about the wedding via the world's tackiest engagement photo?"

"Yes, and this pic is also...wait for it...the invitation to their wedding. And want to hear the real kicker?"

"I do."

She pokes her finger against her chest, diverting my attention to—oh, hell.

Cleavage.

Tempting cleavage thanks to some kind of twisty neckline on a light blue flowered shirt.

I force myself to look at her face, which is no hardship.

"I'm invited to their wedding. To cover it," she bites out. "For my new fashion newsletter and social channels."

"Sounds more like a righteous quitting than a rage quitting to me, then."

She gives an appreciative smile. "But the cherry on the screwed-over sundae? I need to find a date for this event." Her long, frustrated sigh sounds like she's running out of steam, and she shrugs. "So that's my night. I'm out of a job, and I need a plus-one for a wedding," she says, naming the date of the nuptials. "I don't know which will be harder to find."

For the first time tonight, she sounds sad. Maybe a touch desperate. Whatever *wholly necessary* anger she displayed earlier has faded.

I study the button display on the elevator, taking a beat or two to give the situation some thought. While I can't help with the first dilemma, the second one is up my alley. I run through my schedule. I don't have a game that day. I'd be a dick if I didn't help. My ex sure thought I was a jerk—*cold and unfeeling* were her exact words—but would a jerk rescue a damsel in wedding-date distress?

As the elevator slows at her floor, I turn my gaze back to her. She's not looking directly at my face. She's taking another furtive tour of my body.

Enjoy the view, sweetheart.

After she travels the scenic route, she raises her eyes to mine, blinking, looking the slightest bit caught. It's a hot fucking look, so I seize my chance. "I'll take you."

Possibly I say it in more of a commanding bedroom tone than I should. But I don't regret it when a slight tremble seems to run through her body.

Her lips part, and she's quiet for a few seconds, her eyes glittering and her chest flushing. She bites the corner of her lips, and as the doors open on the eighth floor, she says, "Yes."

"Give me your number."

That's said like an order too. One she seems to like since we're trading digits on our phones before she says, "I'm Ivy."

"Hayes. Also known as...*your wedding date*," I tell her, then hand her the box I've been carrying.

She takes it then steps out of the elevator. But before she leaves, she turns around, a sly grin coasting across her lips. "Good. Because otherwise I was going to call you...*the eggplant guy*," she says, and she strides down the hall.

I'm enjoying the view too much to think on the nickname. I'm cataloging the shape of her round ass, savoring the swing of her hips, memorizing the swing of the dark hair cascading down her back. It's not until she disappears into her apartment that what she said fully registers—*the eggplant guy*.

Why did she say that like it means something?

3

THE GOOD TIME GUY

Stefan

Just one more good screw. Almost done...There.

With the screwdriver in hand, I climb down from the stepladder and peer up at the rail lights above the kitchen island. I'm appraising my fantastic handiwork on the brass fixture when the door unlocks and swings open.

Hayes walks in, then groans loudly. "You're *still* here?"

"I believe you mean, '*Thank you so much for all your amazing handyman skills, which are only superseded by your stick skills.*'"

"Things I will never say. Also, you take forever." Hayes strides farther into the kitchen, a bag of food in hand.

"No one ever complains about my stamina." I fold up the ladder and tuck it into the hall closet along with the tools. "I could have a second career as a carpenter."

"As long as you don't trip on your ego."

I join him at the counter, eyeing the bag. "Smells good. I presume you got enough for me?"

He flashes me a familiar *you're an asshole* smile. "Did you *want* to share?"

"Aww. I always love sharing with you," I say.

An eye roll comes my way. "Yes, I got enough for you. I'm thoughtful like that."

"Also, you're welcome—I replaced the smoke alarm battery in the bedroom and fixed the lighting fixture so it doesn't fall on your head. I didn't even have to. That's just how generous I am."

"You own this place. You literally *do* have to," he points out as he takes cartons out of the bag.

"Details." I gesture to the railing lights that the interior designer picked out when I bought this investment property a year or so ago. "But admit it, I do everything well."

Hayes stares at the ceiling, asking the heavens, "Why did I accept the trade to this city?"

"Because you missed me," I say, clapping his back. Then, we tuck into this chicken eggplant dish, and it is pretty fantastic.

I know my buddy needs his beauty sleep. He'll be stressed about tomorrow, worried about meeting the team, and he'll never let on. I also know he'll never forgive me if I mention that aloud. So I make myself scarce once we finish. "I need to check on The Great Dane," I say, devising a reasonable sounding excuse.

"Thanks again for the rental," he says.

I leave the building and walk through the city as night falls, taking pictures on my phone as I go. Just like I did in Copenhagen, where I spent the summer with my parents and my brothers and sisters. Too bad it's not raining in San Francisco. Nothing makes for a great black and white photo like a rain-soaked street. A puddle. A shop with a closed sign in the window.

But as I glance up at the night sky there's not a rain-drop in sight. Shame.

Then I realize I'm lamenting the weather as I haunt Fillmore Street, looking like a fucking tourist, snapping random photos of shops and shit to pass the time. As I turn the corner, I thumb through them. These slice-of-life shots are, objectively, excellent. Well, of course they are. *I* took them. I don't believe in doing anything half-assed. Hockey, school, sex, handiwork, partying—a man should go all in or not fucking go at all.

But my photography hobby doesn't excite me like it used to.

Maybe because you have a career you like, you asshole.

Oh good, now I'm talking to myself. Shaking my head, I put my phone away and circle all the way back to the building that houses the restaurant-slash-bar I bought a few months ago. The elevator whisks me up. I was here last night, but my father always said it's a good idea to check on your investments. Plus, employees move a little faster, work a little harder when the boss is around.

I push open the door and find the place is bustling with energy. There's a sense that things could happen here—deals, dates, hookups. With an open kitchen and a full bar, the vibe is modern and sleek, but the wall is lined with quirky caricatures of a big dog—lounging at a table, chatting with a canine bartender, bustling through an eatery holding plates on its paws.

After I greet the hostess, I weave through the crowds. Mere seconds later, I spot Yasmine, the manager, marching my way, determination in her eyes. She reaches me and arches a skeptical brow. "You don't trust us," she says, teasing.

That's not it. "I just like to know what's going on."

"Or maybe you have nothing better to do," she says pointedly, and ouch. She can't know how true that feels lately.

But I won't let on, and I flash my party boy smile. "Please. My nights are packed."

The bartender catches her eye, and Yasmine takes off. *She* has plenty to do. I cruise through the tables, heading to the patio, parking my elbows on the edge of the balcony to gaze at the city.

Yasmine's too damn right, and it pisses me off. I'm the team captain, the bar owner, and an amateur photographer. I can count friends across the world, and here in town, but I'm still lonely. Have been for the last several months. Ever since things...ended.

Not that anyone can tell.

But with hockey having started up once more and my friend in town again, I can throw myself into the game and ignore the feeling that something's missing.

I know how to put on a good face. I'm the good-time guy, after all. And maybe with one of my former teammates, Ryker Samuels, just traded to our cross-town rivals a few days ago, I can see about a girl I've been curious about since the end of last season.

His sister.

Didn't she move into his apartment when he moved out a year or so ago? A handful of hockey players bought in that building, and I'm pretty sure she took over her brother's place. I saw her around a few times, but she was with some jackass who wore fedoras. Never liked that guy.

The thought of her gives me a plan for the rest of the night. I head to the place I call home, a mile away, and settle into the endless living room with its expansive view of the bay and pour myself a glass of scotch.

With the drink in hand, I conduct a little recon to see what she's up to these days. Like whether she's finally kicked that asshole to the curb.

4

I LIKE YOUR DICK

Ivy

The struggle is real.

Do I write about sustainable fashion for my first newsletter post? Or talk about DIY trends in a video for social? Mostly, though, what the hell do I call this brand-new venture?

I groan as I set my laptop on the table while Roxy finishes breakfast in the tiny kitchen. "I didn't think I'd be flying solo so soon," I say to my Chihuahua-Beagle mix, but she's enrapt in her morning devotional to kibble.

Grabbing a hair tie from the coffee table, I loop my long hair into a messy bun as I talk to my dog's butt. "Was I supposed to be doing my own newsletter thing on the side sooner? As insurance and all for the back-stabbing?"

My short-haired, cinnamon-colored girl wags her

tail, but doesn't turn around. She's selfish like that—totally immune to my inner turmoil while there was any chance of a speck of dog food dust left in the bowl.

I know what she'd tell me though. I should have expected to be blindsided. You can't rely on anyone but a dog. Or a German Shepherd of a brother. Ever since our terrible dad took off when I was ten, Ryker's looked out for my mom, my sister, and me. He paid for my college, and he pays for my sister's college now. Katie's off in New Zealand having the time of her life in her semester abroad.

But I've been determined to make it on my own since graduation four years ago, which is why I gobbled up every freelance fashion-writing gig I could find before I took the assistant job with Simone. I was logging twelve-hour days, which made it hard to build up my own name. No one is looking for Ivy Samuels' opinion.

Yet.

I swallow my pride, open my texts, and type.

> Ivy: Hey, Ryker! Any chance that gig is still available? LMK!

I put the phone away and grab Roxy's gear from her dog clothing basket by the door. Once I snap on her hot pink harness, I show her two bandana options. "The one with watermelons or the one with palm trees?"

With her bossy snout, she nudges the Hawaii-themed one, so I fasten it on her little neck. I head to the door with my five-pound, senior pup—adopted by me when she was twelve years old.

But as I grab the knob, I stop and pluck at my blah outfit. What if I run into Eggplant Guy in the elevator again?

I fly to my room, shed the sweats, and tug on a pair of denim cut-off shorts instead—ones that say *I'm fashionable, but I'm not trying too hard.* I trade the loose shirt for a cute crop top then swipe on some blush and lip gloss. Just a primp here and there, and it's like I rolled out of bed looking all casual and cool. I head to the elevator, nerves jumping in a good way. Maybe I'll see Hayes. Maybe I'll get to know him more. Find out what he does for a living with all those muscles and that fancy apartment in the sky. Probably prints money, then carries big bags of it around to grow his biceps.

But when the doors open, it's empty, and I'm a tad disappointed. It's for the best though. I don't have room in my life for a crush, especially when I'm trying to figure out my career.

Still, I *should* probably make plans with him for the big day. Out on the street, Roxy strutting by my side, I start to draft a note with the details of the event when my phone pings.

Oh. It's Mister Penthouse. This text from him feels like a pre-ward for my good intentions.

Hayes: What do I wear to the wedding?

What you had on yesterday, say, around six p.m.

I don't write that, though, because I'm classy.

Ivy: I'm interpreting this note to mean please tell me the guest wedding attire isn't retro-ruffle themed like that engagement photo.

Hayes: It's like you can read my mind.

Ivy: Just standard attire for a woodland wedding of course.

Hayes: Funny, I don't know what that is.

Fair point because I don't either.

Ivy: The wedding of two fashion influencers probably has a specific dress code. I'll find out.

Hayes: Thanks. I aim to please.

With a furrowed brow, I study his reply as I head up Fillmore. He sounds sort of...just friendly.

What did you expect? You poured out your tale of woe to a stranger in the elevator, and he took pity on you.

I wince, realizing that Jackson was right. "I bet he's one of those guys who always wants to save the day," Jackson had said last night when I told him what happened.

"That's not bad, right?"

"It's perf for a wedding date. Bad for bed, though," he'd said sagely. "Nice guys are never any good in the bedroom. Maybe you need two dates—a nice guy for public and a bad boy for private."

"Who said I was taking him to bed?" I'd countered, but I kept wondering—is Hayes a nice guy or a bad boy? The whole time in the elevator, I couldn't stop thinking about him naked. It was hard to look at him with the weight of all that cock knowledge on my shoulders. What if the wedding's like that too? It only seems fair to lead with honesty.

Especially after what Xander did to me.

Then what Simone did.

And what my cheat of a father did to my mother years ago.

So, I dive bomb into the truth.

> Ivy: So there's something I have to tell you. About eggplants.

Hayes: This could go any number of ways.

He's so dry he's almost hard to read. But I speak deadpan, so I keep going.

Ivy: Do you know that bar across the street from our building?

Hayes: I haven't been there, but I believe in its existence.

Ivy: Well, to make a long story short, my friend Jackson and I were there last night on the rooftop patio at sunset. We saw someone on the rooftop of our building taking off his clothes, and Jackson whipped out his binoculars, and I took them from him and maybe possibly checked you out while you watered your eggplants and strummed the air guitar. On your hose.

I hit send before I can second-guess myself. Then I add one more word.

Ivy: Sorry.

There's no reply for a whole block as Roxy struts, tail high, head whipping back and forth at all the people she passes, both two-legged and four-legged. My neighbor is going to think I'm a very dirty girl. He's probably going to ghost me. Or worse. Report me to... the rental board? Oh, shit. Is there some sort of San Francisco housing authority? Maybe he'll register me as a balcony peeper.

But before I can double apologize, I spot the owner of Better With Pockets adjusting her chalkboard side-walk sign in front of her store. It's my favorite dress shop in the neighborhood, and Beatrix Martinez has built her business with an irreverent social media strat-egy. *One I'd like to be a part of.*

Her lip ring glints brightly in the morning sun, but her expression is unreadable as I tell her I struck out on my own and that I'd love for her to keep me in mind.

"Cool, email me some ideas," she says, and I don't know if that means she actually needs help or she's just being nice, but I'll take it either way.

"I will," I say, hopeful she'll actually read her email, then continue on my walk, returning to my phone, where a text blinks at me.

Hayes: Are you sorry though?

Oh. *Oh.* He's not irked. He's...intrigued. I can work with intrigued.

. . .

> Ivy: Actually, I meant to say...Sorry, not sorry.

> Hayes: Good answer. Also, this explains a lot.

My cheeks flame, even as my fingers fly with my question.

> Ivy: What do you mean?

> Hayes: I noticed last night that you tried really hard to look only at my face, Ivy.

Something about the way he writes my name out in text feels...commanding. Like an order. Maybe he *is* a bad boy in bed.

> Ivy: I felt bad for having seen you naked and you not knowing.

> Hayes: Why would you feel bad?

> Ivy: Because I'd seen you naked!

> Hayes: I'm still not seeing the problem.

My cheeks go hotter. He's kind of...sarcastically flirty.

> Hayes: Or do you feel bad because you were trying to get another look?

I chew on my lip, debating. But...what do I have to lose?

> Ivy: Look, all I'm saying is if the Emoji Association ever needs a spokesperson for the eggplant, it should be you.

There. I pretty much said *I like your dick.* There's silence on my phone for a few minutes until an image lands.

You can't see his face. You can't even see his torso. The photo is a tight shot of a man holding an eggplant against his shorts. And I sway closer to the screen, squinting. I'm pretty sure that's the outline of his cock right next to the veggie. And...he's half-hard. I stare so long I become a danger to traffic. Then, I force myself to read the note.

> Hayes: Just thinking of you.

He's not white-knighting me after all. But I'm not going to send a similar shot. Well, I *am* out on the streets. Instead, I write back asking for something else—info.

> Ivy: I have to know, why were you naked on the rooftop? Was it Naked Gardening Day?

> Hayes: That's a thing, right?

> Ivy: I googled it but it's in the spring. Is that your kink though? Naked gardening?

> Hayes: Is voyeurism your kink?

That's an excellent question. In the moment, yesterday's rooftop entertainment felt like good old spectator fun. Like, why not check out some public, non-sexual nudity? But now it sparks questions I've not considered before. Like, if I'd been alone at the bar, would I have watched longer? Or if I saw that man stripping off his shirt through my apartment window, would I stare?

I'm noodling on a reply when another text lands.

> Hayes: Because if it is, tell me when you'll have those binoculars out next.

The hair on my arms stands on end. With excitement. With possibility. I don't even know what he's offering. To strip for me? To touch himself on the rooftop? Something else? This is next-level text flirting, and I'm not entirely sure what to say.

I don't have this sort of experience. My ex wasn't a sexter. The guys I dated before him sent messages that were more of the *hey* variety.

Hayes doesn't wait for my answer before he sends another text.

> Hayes: Or...the next time I get dirty while gardening and strip off my clothes on the roof before I head to the shower, I'll just stay out there longer. A lot longer.

And I have my answer. If yesterday's show had shifted from fun to sexy, I'd have watched more.

> Ivy: I think I need a shower now.

> Hayes: I just got out.

This is another chance. To find out if I do like sexting. I was bold last night when I quit my job. Might as well be bold now.

Ivy: Prove it.

The man doesn't make me wait. Another photo lands seconds later. It's a sliver of his abs. I can imagine water sluicing down those carved muscles and into the top of the white towel cinched around his waist. He's strong, but not perfect. There's a small, horizontal scar on the right side of his stomach. It's an inch long, white, practically translucent, like he's had it for a while. I want to trace that scar then run my finger along those star tattoos on his hip.

Ivy: That's my favorite kind of evidence.

Hayes: Good. I'd keep this up, but I have to go to work. But don't check out any other rooftop gardeners today. Got it, Ivy?

Holy shit. Did he just give me an order to stay away from other guys? He sure did, and I like it.

Ivy: Yes, sir.

* * *

After a long, hot shower, I get dressed, then force myself to fire off an uncomfortable email to Simone. I ask about the dress code, hit send, then shake off the ick to find a text from my brother. He tells me he called the marketing department and they desperately need me for the gig.

I thank him profusely, then turn my attention to the job hunt, reaching out to the publications I used to freelance for. Then, I plan some outfit-of-the-day ideas for Beatrix's shop and send those along to her. After that, I write my first post for social, picking the handle YourScrappyLittleFashionistaFriend and writing what I call the "Look The Part" fashion rule. In short, since you never know who you're going to run into, be it a colleague, hookup, or client, don't leave home looking like you just changed the cat litter. I finish it with this line: *You never know when you might run into that certain someone you've got a thing for.*

As I'm leaving for my meeting, my phone pings with a comment on my post. I'm unreasonably excited as I click it.

The handle is Number18. *I'm following this advice today.*

The comment has a masculine tone to it. I'm not sure why, but it just does. I reply with a cheery: *Glad I could be helpful!*

Seconds later, there's a response.

Number18: There's a certain someone I might run into today. I'm thinking a nice Henley.

YourScrappyLittleFashionistaFriend: You can't go wrong with a Henley!

Number18: Yeah? You approve?

YourScrappyLittleFashionistaFriend: It's one of my favorite looks.

Number18: Noted.

YourScrappyLittleFashionistaFriend: Let me know how it goes.

Number18: I definitely will. I'll report back if I see her. Call me a hopeful guy.

So I was right in my assumptions. Something about him seems confident, too, and a little cocky. It's a good combo.

YourScrappyLittleFashionistaFriend: Good luck, hopeful guy.

5

NEW GUY, TAKE FOUR

Hayes

My car probably wants to know why we're cruising through the streets of San Francisco and *not* downtown Los Angeles. Four months since the end of my season there, I'm heading to the Avengers facility a week ahead of the new season here. I've got a Stone Zenith rock anthem turned up and doing its damnedest to drown out an annoying hint of nerves and a definite case of *here we go again*.

I grit my teeth, refusing to give in. Eventually, I'll meet a team that wants to keep me. No idea if it'll be *this* team, so all I can do is keep my head down, play well, and avoid trouble.

I hang a right onto Van Ness on instinct, grateful I don't have to learn a new city this time. I grew up in San Francisco, and even though I've bounced between Toronto, Seattle, and Los Angeles, I'm back home now.

That means I'll need to arrange for tickets for Dad and his girlfriend so they can come to my first game. Not my mom. Never my mom. And...that's brought to you by *all the things I don't want to think about.* I turn the music up until I can't hear a damn thing in my head.

The chorus thrums in my bones as I pull into the players' lot and cut the engine. I glance around, scanning for arriving teammates but seeing none. I can't coast on the fact that I know the team captain. Don't want to look like the popular guy's friend. I've got to do this myself. I looked up everyone online, memorized the roster, and matched names to faces to try to make this transition easier.

Here it goes: New Guy, take four.

* * *

The Avengers PR guy waits for me inside the players' entrance. Oliver looks exactly like his photo, right down to the purple dress shirt—the Avengers team's color. With neatly combed brown hair, freckles that stand out against his pale complexion, and a warm, welcoming grin, he looks every bit the PR guy.

I stick out a hand, eager to go first. "You must be Oliver Redwood." He's emailed me a few times since my agent dropped the news of the start-of-the-season trade a couple days ago.

"And you're the new star left winger," he says as we shake hands.

That merits a small grin, but I don't let it linger because he's a PR guy and that's a PR thing to say.

"Thanks, but check back with me in a couple weeks and we'll see if that fits." Humility goes a lot further than braggadocio.

"No doubt it will. We're glad you're here. You're only going to be the subject of, oh, say, all the media coverage for your first few games, so I figure we'll be seeing a lot of each other."

"Bring it on." The media doesn't scare me. I've had four years to sell the same line—*I'm just happy to be here.* I don't let the media see anything I don't want them to see.

With a smile, Oliver gestures to the corridor in front of us. "Love that attitude. Let me give you the tour."

An hour later, I've seen the trainers' room, the workout rooms, the video review room, and, obviously, the ice. I've met the general manager, the ops manager, the equipment manager, and the equipment manager's assistant. Violet, Jamal, Mike, and Doggo. I caught that his real name is Doug, but Doggo works for me. I've also met Parvati, the social media manager and Oliver's right-hand woman.

As we walk down a swank corridor with cool blue lights and Avengers logos plastered over the walls, Oliver tells me, "This might all change soon. We're likely changing our name this season."

"Oh yeah?"

"Well, a certain movie franchise has made searching for the team name a fruitless mission."

"What options are in the running?"

Oliver places his finger on his lips. "I'm under strict orders."

"Fair enough," I say. I catch the click-clack of heels on concrete, growing louder. The sound is sharp and purposeful, and it can only signal one thing.

The owner is here.

Oliver glances behind him and then straightens like he's a ruler. "That's Jessie," he whispers out the side of his mouth. I stand straighter too. "Don't let the sweet name fool you."

Jessie Rose is one of three female owners in the NHL and an absolutely fearless competitor. The Texas native is a former tennis star who made millions with a wicked backhand and then turned those millions into billions. She's said to love winning more than she loves Louboutins.

I turn to greet the boss. She's polished and poised in a dark pink suit, with tight, shoulder-length curls, warm brown skin, and deep brown eyes. She stops in front of me, and in a twang familiar from post-match interviews, she says, "Hayes Armstrong. At last, I finally got you." Her pink-lipsticked grin spreads as wide as her home state. "I'm so glad we convinced you to join us."

"Thrilled to be here," I say, shaking her offered hand. But I don't let her compliment go to my head. I'm sure this is stuff that she says to new players.

"Cade and I watched you play last year when we were in Los Angeles," she says, referring to her shark of a sports agent husband. "And I sure hope you saved some of those goals for us."

Translation: *you better stay good*.

"I've got lots in the tank, Ms. Rose."

"Good, because I've got a bet going with my besties on whose team will go farther this year, and I don't want to lose to Lacey or Hannah. You're not going to let me eat crow, are you?"

She says it with a straight face, and I answer like a good soldier. "No, ma'am."

"Play hard and get me some wins, and we'll get along just fine." The smile vanishes, and she stares sharply at me. "Because I didn't trade to be disappointed." She checks her watch and the smile flashes back on, full wattage. "Don't hesitate to let me know if you need a single thing."

I won't need a damn thing, but still I say, "I will. Thank you."

She heads off, click-clacking down the hall in a cloud of expensive perfume and the confidence of a Bugatti.

When she's out of earshot, Oliver lets loose a huge breath, then shudders. "I want to grow up to be just like her," he whispers.

I laugh. "I get that."

Oliver rolls his shoulders like he's shaking off an encounter with a lioness, then resumes his pace, guiding me down the hall, chatting more about the potential new team name, some of the plans for the contests, and Jessie's hope that the new name won't become the next big *damn movie franchise*.

When we reach the locker room, I brace myself. This is a bigger test than meeting the owner. Oliver swings open the door, and inside it's boisterous. A tune from Muse blasts from someone's speaker. There's a game of cards in one corner, a debate over the best barbecue in another. I scan the faces, matching them with the names I've researched.

Oliver clears his throat for attention, and the noise lessens a bit. "This is Hayes Armstrong. Last season with LA, he had twenty-nine goals, sixty-three assists, and ninety-two points. We just traded for him, and he's going to do great things."

The praise is embarrassing. I don't want to come across as a guy who buys his own press. My stats aren't bad—they're fucking awesome. But they are better than the guy they let go in free agency last season—Alf Nilsson. The team brought up a left winger from the minors to replace him but word from my agent is he wasn't ready. So, here I am.

Nobody acts too impressed as Oliver talks me up. No one except the right winger, who whistles when the PR guy is done. Brady Clampett is from a hockey dynasty in Vancouver. His dad and brother played before him. "Let's call him Hot Shit, then," Brady offers with a lopsided grin.

Ah hell. The nicknames have begun already. *Please don't let Hot Shit stick. Pretty fucking please, universe.*

Over by his stall, Stefan rips off his Number Eighteen jersey with his name, Christiansen, on the back, then turns around. "Nah, I vote for New Alf. What do you like better, New Alf?"

I rein in a grin. Stefan loves to stir the pot. Plus, he's not treating me like his kid brother, which I really fucking appreciate.

Of course, he can joke. He *has* a bad-ass nickname —The Viking. But the star forward from Copenhagen has earned it. He's three years older than me, but we played together in college. He's fearless on the ice.

My nickname in the last few years of my college career was my favorite—The Iceman. But nothing gets you labeled a prima donna faster than trying to pick your own nickname.

"Whatever works for you guys." The less I say the better.

"Let's call him...*him*," someone shouts. I turn to the deep voice and see the goalie, a guy named Devon Ryland, but goes by Dev. He's from Minnesota by way of San Diego—born by the beach, raised in the snow, he's said. What matters most is he's a brick wall in the net. Well, a flexible brick wall.

And he has some good ideas. I can work with *him*.

But Dev shakes his head, dismissing his own idea. "Nope. I'm wrong. That's gonna get confusing." He scratches his jaw, then a slow smile spreads. "Hey, you," Dev says, droll enough for the desert.

Stefan's brow pinches. "Hey, what?"

Dev points at me. "That's his nickname. *Hey You*."

Stefan nods a few times, then tests it out. "*Hey You*." He gives me a onceover. "Yeah, I fucking like that."

The captain polls the crowd, and nearly everyone seems to agree. Stefan turns back to me. "New guy, you're now...*Hey You*."

That beats Hot Shit.

* * *

During practice, I play fast and tight as we take turns shooting into the open net, then Dev moves in front of the goal and does his damnedest to stop us. He's a brick wall, all right. We take turns shooting puck after puck, but eventually I slide one past him.

Then another.

Some might say it's only practice. But this time on the ice with a whole new team is absolutely critical to fitting in. And to staying. I've got to be at my best at all times.

Every team has its own rhythm, its own routine. But after changing teams so many times, one of my greatest strengths has become adapting. I have to. I don't have any other choice but to fit into their style.

When practice ends and I skate off the ice and into the tunnel, Stefan shouts to Dev, "*Hey You* is handling the laundry, right?"

"Yeah, and that's perfect," Dev says to Stefan. "Because he can deal with the mascot thing then."

Let the errand hazing begin. This is a good sign. I bet *the mascot thing* is related to the possible name change.

After I shower and get dressed, a former Avengers player strides into the locker room. It's Ryker Samuels, one of the top defenders in the league. *Huh. Wonder what he's up to.* But he says hi to his former teammates, who are still clearly his friends, then grabs some shirts from his locker before he catches up with Dev and Stefan.

"You don't even work here. Why the fuck are you here?" Stefan says.

But I don't catch his answer. A minute later, Ryker says a quick hello to me and nods to the laundry cart. I grab it and push it into the hall, both Ryker and Stefan following behind me. "*Hey You*, here's the deal," Ryker says, and I'm glad they gave the ex-Avenger my nickname. He gestures to the end of the hall. "Gotta separate the whites. Don't forget Christiansen likes the lavender dryer sheets."

"Wrong, Samuels. It's the daisy ones I dig."

Ryker claps my shoulder. "Don't fuck up the captain's laundry," he says, then he rattles off ten more laundry specs, it seems.

"And make sure to fold everything neatly and leave it by the stalls," Stefan adds.

I don't expect I'll actually be washing anyone's gear, but I understand how hazing works. I repeat the instructions and start toward the laundry room, but Ryker clears his throat. "And one more thing. You have to get the mascot costume. It's being cleaned. Thank fuck."

His relief sounds specific enough to make me wonder, "Why 'thank fuck?'"

Stefan answers. "The last guy got busted for renting his sorry ass out to after-hours parties, making appearances in costume, then dealing drugs. Someone snapped a pic of him taking off the head of his costume to snort a line."

I blink. "That's a choice, I guess." A bad choice.

"New one just signed on. For a couple months," Stefan says. "Take the costume to Equipment Room A."

"Got it," I say and try again to leave.

But neither the current nor the former Avenger is done with me yet. "And listen, you'd better be a nice fucking guy when you bring it to her." Ryker's tone is stern. "And don't hit on her."

Stefan snorts, and I laugh in surprise at the idea of hitting on someone at work. "Not a problem."

"No, seriously. Don't," Ryker says, staring sharply at me.

Stefan's laughter grows louder. "Oh, man. We don't have to listen to you anymore on that count, Samuels."

I'm pretty sure I'm missing the joke, but I'm not going to let on.

They send me on my way, and when I enter the laundry room, Doggo shakes his head in amusement. "Why are you bringing me the laundry I was about to go collect? It's literally my job, and no one takes Doggo's job."

"Wait till you hear what they want done," I say.

Doggo rolls his eyes. "I can only imagine."

"And I'm supposed to get the mascot costume," I add.

"Yup. Let me grab Blob." It takes me a beat to realize Blob is the name of the outfit. He rounds the corner and hefts a large, furry, purple thing into his arms, carrying it to me. "Here you go, kid."

Kid.

That's not bad. Well, from a guy twice my age.

"Thanks, man," I say.

Carrying it down the hall, I run into Dev, who's scrolling on his phone. He looks up and nods at the purple blob in my arms. "You taking Blob to Ryker's sister?"

Um. I have no idea. "Does she work here?"

"She's the new mascot," Dev explains, then returns to his phone.

The *don't hit on her* comment makes a lot more sense now. But when I reach the equipment room and see the woman waiting outside, I know it's too late.

I've already hit on her. And now it looks like I'm working with her.

Yes, universe, the joke is on me.

6

MASCOT PATROL

Ivy

I gape at the dirty texter who stands frozen in the doorway of the equipment room, a purple furball of a costume in his big arms. "What are you doing here, and why are you bringing me Blob?"

I'm praying he says, *I'm here from Mascot Patrol to seize this costume on account of it being hideous.*

But Hayes stares back like he can't believe his bad luck, either, "You work here too?"

Too. I deflate. There goes my hope he's the Mascot Patrol.

"You play hockey?" That explains why he has all those muscles. Why his chest is so broad. Why he's the height of a tree.

Of all the jobs in the city, why does my hot neighbor have to work with...*me*?

Having answered my own question, I answer his. "I'm the new Avengers mascot. You're...?"

"Hayes Armstrong. I was just traded here from LA," he says, tone as flat as the fur on Blob.

"I didn't know you were a hockey player."

"And I didn't know you were a...mascot." His gaze drifts to the heap of material in his hands. Before I can launch into the whole story of how I became the mascot, approaching footsteps and voices from the corridor grow louder, and I glance around for an alternative location to continue this personal chat.

Hayes shifts the costume to one arm and pushes open the door to the equipment room. Then he sets that hand on my shoulder and spins me around. "In there," he says in a firm voice.

He's got a firm touch too. He slides his free hand down my spine as he guides me. His hand is big and strong.

Hayes follows me inside and kicks the door closed. He flicks on the light and strides deeper into the room where there's an empty shelf labeled *Mascot Costume* with masking tape and marker. He looks stupidly good in those jeans, and his T-shirt that shamelessly hugs his biceps and shows off his trim stomach. I can't stop watching his ass, his back, his legs as he advances past a wall of sticks to set the blob of fake fur in its place.

I'm supposed to try that on and then join the Avengers Ice Crew in ten minutes for our own practice. But I want to sort out this whole mess first.

As Hayes returns to me, his eyes lock on my face. I back up against the concrete wall, needing something for stability, something to rest against under the weight of his lusty stare.

I'm pretty sure this turn of events means putting a lid on the flirting, yet he doesn't look like a man who wants to stop dirty texting me.

Then, in a heartbeat, he seems to shift gears, shaking off the desire. "This would be a bad idea," he says, resigned.

"A very bad one," I echo in the same tone.

He's quiet for a beat, then says, "The universe has a funny sense of humor."

"I'm not laughing."

"Shame. You have a pretty laugh."

"I thought you said this was a bad idea," I say, but I suppose I'm not stopping either.

"I did say that. But you still have a pretty laugh. And," he says, his gaze meeting mine, "beautiful eyes."

My skin tingles. His compliments are so simple, but so welcome. My ex doled out compliments like a miser. "So are your star tattoos. Beautiful, that is."

He lifts a brow. "You noticed."

"Well, I spent a lot of time with that picture."

His smile is deservedly smug. Leaning closer, he parks his right hand on the wall behind my head, pinning me but not quite pinning me. I'm *almost* caged in. "There's no point in keeping this to myself now. You should know I was absolutely planning on asking you out tonight," he says.

The tingles become full-blown sparks. "You were?"

"Yes."

I'm giddy hearing it, especially when he adds, "I definitely wanted to see you again."

"Same," I admit, still feeling fizzy. But there are probably rules or at least guidelines against a workplace romance. We'd need to tell HR or something. Both of us are new here. Is a date worth it? I don't know, especially when the Ice Crew members are supposed to be brand ambassadors for the team. Pretty sure hooking up with a player is not the *fan engagement* skills they want in a mascot.

Blinking off the haze of lust, I stand taller, then circle back to the first question—the *you're the team mascot* one. Does he think I misled him last night about my job situation? Maybe he thought I was flexing.

"About the mascot thing. I landed this job today, but it's just a stopgap. I work in fashion, and I started up all my social channels this morning, and a newsletter. I used to write about fashion in college on my own blog, and now I'm just doing it again as a freelancer and on social."

Do I sound defensive? I hope I don't sound defensive.

Hayes lets go of the wall, holds up his hand like it's all good. "I didn't doubt you. I was just surprised. It's not exactly a job anyone can get. Especially in hockey."

I tense, the echo of Xander's constant mascot jokes ringing in my ears. He'd always teased me about having been one. He'd even said when I got the job with Simone that I was leaving my *little mascot days behind me and finally growing up.* "I was one in college," I explain tightly.

Yep, that definitely sounds defensive. I don't like men belittling me. Heard enough of it as a kid when my dad did it to my mom. Heard so much of it I decided to protect my little sister so she wouldn't hear it too.

Hayes's brown eyes sparkle with laughter. "That's pretty cool."

Okay. Maybe he's not like Xander. Still, we're going nowhere, and probably not even to the wedding now. "I guess I need another date for the wedding," I say with a sigh.

He seems to give it some thought. "You're my neighbor."

"Right."

"We met in the elevator."

"True," I say, as it becomes clear he's telling the public story.

"You told me what happened with your shitty, no-good ex and your terrible boss. I offered to go." He gives a *no big deal* shrug. "So that's that. It's platonic. I'll take you to the wedding as your new neighbor."

Platonic is officially my least favorite word as it relates to this man, but I get it. And I appreciate the extra descriptors for Xander and Simone. *A lot.* "Are you sure? I can go solo. I don't want to cause problems," I say.

"I made a promise. I keep my promises. I'm a nice guy."

I hear the echo of Jackson's comment. *Nice guys are never any good in the bedroom.* The bedroom's not an option, but I can't resist one little flirty remark. "Will you be a nice guy at the wedding?"

Hayes's smile is confident. Strong. "If being a nice guy means no one will know what I really want, then yes."

I have to know. "What do you really want?"

With his eyes on me, Hayes takes his time, leaning in close then closer still. He runs his nose along my neck, slowly, sensually, lighting up every inch of my skin. "I want to see you slide those fingers between your thighs like you did this morning after I sent that picture."

"Oh," I gasp, as my thighs clench and my stomach swoops.

"Is that what you did, Ivy?"

He can read my thoughts so easily. It's such a thrill. "Yes."

"I thought so," he says, as he pulls back, looking far too pleased.

The air between us is charged, and we hold each other's gazes for a hot second. But there's a rap on the door.

My heart explodes. Hayes rips himself from me, jumping away. I shouldn't do this. I shouldn't be sneaking around in an equipment room. It's the first day and I'm already going to get in trouble.

"Be right out," Hayes says immediately, his voice still a little husky.

"This is your captain speaking." It's Stefan, and I relax some. "I'd like to welcome you to the Avengers arena, where we're expecting temperatures on the ice of fucking freezing. But that's ice for you. If the weather continues to cooperate, the new mascot should be able to practice any second."

I breathe a big sigh of relief, so glad it's not Oliver or the team owner demanding to know what I've been up to in here.

I imagine *getting turned on* isn't a good answer.

"Almost ready," I call, then hustle over to the shelf with the heap of fake fur lumped on it.

Stefan is the playful, outgoing team captain I've spoken with several times over the last few years when my brother played here. The handsome Dane has ice-blue eyes, a dusting of stubble, and a panty-dropping smile, and the times I was single I would have loved to be asked on a date with him—but he also has a gorgeous fiancée from his hometown who he gave a sparkling, four-carat diamond to. I might have noticed her ring on social media and in person when I met Annika at last year's Christmas party. She's basically perfect—she speaks three languages, happens to be a brilliant young climatologist for the world's leading think tank studying climate change, and is legit a nice person. I can't even hate her. I just like her.

"Just trying on the costume," I say. Like I was supposed to be doing ten minutes ago. But I'm trying it on with Hayes in the same room. That looks bad. "Over my clothes," I add quickly.

There's a pause, then a clearing of a throat from the other side of the door. "Well, it sounds like more fun is being had in the back of the cabin than the cockpit."

Hayes dips his face, laughing silently into his hand,

and I realize my faux pas. "Of course I'm trying it on over my clothes. That's how you wear it."

No wonder Xander needed a girlfriend upgrade.

"I'm sure there are many ways to wear a costume," Stefan calls back, and he sounds...amused.

Great, I'm embarrassing myself in front of the new guy and the team captain. *Real smooth, Ivy.*

Hayes watches me, seeming to catalogue my every move as I wiggle into this purple furball that's supposed to be an *A* but resembles more of an ink splotch. Once I shove my arms into the costume, I tug it up to my neck, then zip it. With Blob on—though not the head—I spin around and hold out my arms. "How do I look?"

His smile is slow and sexy. "Somehow even hotter."

The weird thing is I believe him.

But since I don't need to parade around the arena in a costume, I take it off, then head to the door with the costume under my arm, and my *just a friendly neighbor who's also a wedding date* by my side.

When I open the door, Stefan's shooting a casual smile my way as he runs his long fingers through his bedroom-style hair like I bet Annika did mere hours ago. His sandy-brown hair has golden streaks—like he somehow, incongruously, plays hockey in the sun—and it always makes him look freshly fucked.

It's a good look.

The corner of his lips hook up in a grin.

He's wearing a Henley.

7

MY LIFE MOTTO

Stefan

Since I'm a lucky guy in general, I figured I might be fortunate enough to bump into Ivy some morning when she was walking that little dog around the neighborhood, the one I saw on her social when I did my Ivy recon last night. Or I guessed that I might run into her in the building when I popped by to see Hayes.

Sure, I *could* have DM'd her. But why DM when I'm great in person?

But then look what karma served up this afternoon —I get to work with her. I swear, fate loves me. Possibly, there are HR guidelines about asking out someone you work with. I'm not concerned though. I'll deal with those *after*.

Something about Ivy hooked me a few months ago when I ran into her at the Hockey Hotties calendar fundraiser in the park. We chatted for a while about

Denmark, and she peppered me with questions about the country I'm from. She was especially curious why I didn't have an accent. Well, when your diplomat parents move to the States when you're young, you tend to lose it, I told her. They've since returned to Copenhagen, and so have my brothers and sisters. I didn't tell Ivy I miss them terribly.

Instead, I entertained her with stories of the pranks my friends and I got into on the houseboats there once upon a time, then listened as she told me all the places she wanted to travel to in the world. Ivy was easy to talk to, fast, and clever with her mouth, and witty girls get me every time. It didn't hurt that she had a certain mischievous look in her midnight-blue eyes the whole time we chatted. What can I say? I like mischief. Even though she's Ryker's sister, I still looked her up that night after the event, since I was single for the first time in years. But I learned she was dating some douche named The Dapper Man. I mean, who else would call himself that but a twat?

And now she's not dating him, and she's not a teammate's sister.

The runway is all clear.

With flushed cheeks—perhaps from changing into that costume quickly—she's standing next to Hayes, adjusting Blob under her arm. I flash her a smile. "I don't get a preview of the costume too?"

"You'll have to wait till I hit the ice," she says and sticks out her free hand, adopting a more business-like persona. "It's good to see you again, Stefan."

This is how we're doing it? All professional? Fine,

fine. It's still contact and that works for me. I take her
offered hand and shake. Her skin is soft, and her palm
feels good in mine, but as much as I'd love to read into
a handshake, I don't. I believe in winning women over
with the total package of me.

When I let go, she steals a glance at Hayes, and
something seems to pass between them. I file that away
for later, then focus on the *now*.

I gesture to the costume. "I'll carry that for you."

"Thanks," she says, taking me up on my offer and
handing me the thing.

I tuck Blob under my arm. "Oliver had to take a
phone call. So he sent a responsible adult."

"And you qualified?" Hayes says dryly.

"That's debatable," I say.

"Are any of us really though?" Ivy adds.

"Questions I ask myself every day," I say, then
gesture down the hall toward the ice.

When Hayes makes no signs of leaving, the three of
us walk together, my teammate and I flanking Ivy.
Doesn't bother me that he's here. Just makes things more
interesting as I try to read the room with her. She seems
to be doing the same with both of us, looking from him
to me with questions in her pretty blue eyes rimmed
with gold. "I guess I have two escorts to the rink," she
says, seeming a little amused we're both with her.

"The mascot is a very important job," I say.

"We can't have anything happen to you," Hayes
adds.

"This is Mascot Protection Service then?"

"We're all about the full-service treatment here at the Avengers," I say.

Out of the corner of my eye, I catch Hayes stifling a grin. Cheeky fucker. After he clears his expression, he says dryly, "Yes, it's our specialty."

It's my turn to hide a smile and I do it by shifting gears, focusing my attention briefly on my teammate. "*Hey You*, you better have my fresh-as-a-daisy jersey for me very soon."

"*Hey You*?" Ivy asks.

With a grimace, Hayes grumbles, "My nickname."

Ivy snickers.

"Don't laugh," he mutters.

"Too late," I say.

Ivy's brow furrows as we turn the corner, and once again she looks from him to me. "I'm getting the vibe you two are friends? And not of the *we just became besties when Hayes joined the team today* variety?"

"We skated together in college," I say.

Before I can add that we've stayed friends ever since, the social media manager rounds the corner, then brightens when she spots my new teammate. "Hayes, can I borrow you to show you this picture we took of you at practice before I post it?"

"Of course," Hayes says, and huddles with Parvati.

Since Ivy's due at the ice in a few minutes, the two of us continue ahead without him.

"You must skate. Are you a hockey player as well? Or did you figure skate?" I ask. She must have done one or the other. The mascot doesn't only dance in the stands. The mascot straps on skates and races around the ice in between periods.

"No to the first, yes to the second. I took lessons, but never competitively or anything. Just for fun. I spent enough time at rinks when I was younger, and I didn't want to sit on the sidelines."

I don't, either, when it comes to her.

In the months since Annika called off our engagement, I've been lonelier than I want to admit. I miss interesting company, and that day Ivy and I chatted in the park was the first time I've sparked with someone. I don't know where it will lead. I don't want to sit on the sidelines, either, when it comes to her.

"That's my life motto, too, Ivy," I say, keeping it simple.

She quirks a questioning brow. "Did I say it was my life motto?"

"No. But that's what I heard." We pass a series of framed photos of Avengers all-stars over the years, including yours truly.

She's quiet for a beat, as if puzzling something out. "Maybe it should be."

"I highly recommend it," I say as we near the tunnel that'll take us to the ice. If this convo keeps going well, I'll use this chance to tell her I saw her pics on social and that I'd love to take her out for a drink.

Maybe then the long months ahead might be a little more interesting.

8

NUMBER18

Ivy

In the tunnel, I replay the last few things The Viking said. I thought we were discussing skating, but then it seemed like he was flirting.

Is he the Henley guy from earlier? The hopeful guy? A Henley's a broad qualifier though.

The bigger concern about Stefan is, oh, you know, *he has a freaking fiancée.* My jaw ticks with irritation. Is this how Xander romanced Simone? Did he flirt with her while he was dating me?

"Are you still enjoying Pacific Heights?" he asks as we near the ice. "We were talking about a new Turkish café on Fillmore that you wanted to try when we last spoke."

You were with another woman when we last talked.

But I bite back the words. I can't be pissy with the team captain. That's not a good look for the new mascot. "The café is great," I say, with false cheer. I mean, the café *is* great. "And how's everything with you?"

Maybe that will remind him he's involved.

But his smile is pure flirtation. "I can't complain about a thing. How's your dog? Is she liking the neighborhood as well?"

That feels flirty too. He says it like we're on a date. Like he's checked out my personal social and all my pics with Roxy. What's his deal?

"She's a big fan." It comes out cold, and that's no good either. I try to let go of my annoyance at, well, men. "She's practically the neighborhood mascot."

When his crystal blue eyes meet mine, they glimmer. "A mascot and a mascot. I like that very much," he says, full of charm but also something subtler. A late-night charm. A late-night gaze too.

Maybe he's just being friendly. As the team captain, he's the face of the team, does a ton of press interviews. It makes sense he'd want to chat with the mascot since I have to work the promo angle hard. I fasten on a professional smile. "Thanks again for the mascot protection services. They were much appreciated."

"Anytime. I'd be happy to help," he says. "Speaking of, would you—"

A deep, Barry White-esque voice calls from the rink. "Oh good, you're here."

I snap my gaze to a lithe man in a purple turtleneck and leggings who's skating to me at the edge of the rink. "I'm Moses, head of the Ice Crew. You must be Ivy.

There are skates for you on the bench. Lace up and come join us."

"I'd love to," I say, then I turn back to Stefan, ready to put my uncertainty and frustration behind me. I can't make enemies. I need this job. When he hands me the costume, I take it with a smile. "Thanks for walking with me."

"I'm here for all your needs," he says in a smooth, sexy voice that has me questioning everything.

Especially since he's already walking away in that damn Henley.

At home that night, I try out a baked feta pasta recipe that Aubrey sent me and try to make sense of this afternoon at the rink. Going from Hayes to Stefan felt a little like whiplash. One guy was all *I want you but can't have you*, and the other was *pure charm.* As I set the dish in the oven, Roxy stares forlornly up at me, attempting to use cuteness to sway me to enlist her as a taste tester.

"You can't do that to me. I have no willpower when it comes to your face," I say, then tell her to "strike a pose."

She turns to the side, giving me her best three-quarter profile. "There. Now I'm not spoiling you," I say, then give her a tiny piece of cheese. "This is just compensation for the user experience you provide."

She wolfs down the treat, then as the dish bakes, I retreat to the couch with my phone. Roxy follows me, wagging her tail hopefully. I peel off my sock and toss it her way.

Excitement flashes in her doggie eyes, and she grabs it from the floor, then scampers to the bedroom to drop it in her sock collection. She trots back, sockless, and I scoop her up so she doesn't jump and miss the couch. Her little legs aren't as strong as they were. She curls up next to me with a sigh that suggests she had a long, long day and is so relieved to finally relax. Well, being a spoiled Chihuahua-Beagle *is* hard.

Jackson's out with some friends, but instead of catching up on my book club reading, I turn to my texts, sending a quick note to check in with my sister Katie. She tells me she's learning so much, and loving every day, so I bring up my group chat with Trina and Aubrey. I need some girlfriend time.

> Ivy: I was today years old when I discovered I now work with the guy I secretly saw naked last night.

My phone lights up seconds later.

> Trina: I'd like the dick details, please.

After I give the rooftop striptease debrief, Trina replies.

> Trina: Well, that's a lot to unpack.

Ivy: Yes, it was a lot.

> Trina: And did you say that when you saw him at work?

> Aubrey: Or did you add a personal touch? Like, That's a real nice cock. Can you smack me in the eye with it tonight?

Cracking up, I dictate a reply.

Ivy: I didn't hit on his dick at work. Or him.

> Aubrey: Try harder next time, please!

> Trina: Also, which player was it??? I need to know.

Trina knows pretty much all the hockey players on both the city's teams. She's not only involved with my brother; she's with Jackson's brother, Chase too. More than a year ago, they fell in love with her, and she fell for both of them. They all quickly moved into Chase's place, and I moved into Ryker's here in this building—

at a bargain basement price. All I needed to do was give my brother a kick in his pants and tell him to go after his unconventional arrangement.

Their throupling has garnered a lot of attention amongst hockey fans and romance lovers alike. It's unconventional, but it works great for the happy three-some. They're living their life out in the open, and it's seriously refreshing to see—and refreshing how far the media and the sports world have come in their acceptance of them. At events, photographers post pics of Trina and her two NHL superstar boyfriends, tagging and captioning the pics just the same as they would any other player and a significant other. As it should be.

The three of them have also become passionate advocates for rescue dogs, and they work together to raise money for several shelters. No doubt some people shake their heads behind closed doors at their arrangement, but that's people for you. For the most part, the boys have paved the path by living in the public eye with Trina as their girlfriend.

Ivy: Hayes. The new guy.

Trina: Oh, I thought you were going to say Stefan, since he owns the penthouse in your building!

Huh. But that makes sense. I've seen him around from a distance a few times.

. . .

Ivy: Is there nothing you don't know?

Trina: When you go to hockey events for two teams, you learn all the details. Also, Hayes is hot, but so is Stefan... and did you hear the news about him?

Ivy: Tell me.

While I wait for her reply, I spot an envelope icon winking at me. Maybe it's a response from one of the editors I queried about fashion writing. Or maybe a designer with a marketing opening.

Instead, it's a notification that I have new comments on my post about today's fashion rules. Well, that's good too.

The first is from a user I don't know, saying *This is why I shower before I leave the house.*

I laugh, then reply before I open the next one, which is from my grandmother. Her handle is Card-Shark, and she writes: *Same rules apply in the place where I live too. What if I run into the cute widower who can still drive at night? A lady can't shuffle around in her jam-jams. Linen is my friend, as my granddaughter taught me.*

I smile, grateful for her support. The next one is from the hopeful guy. Intrigued, I click on it.

Number18: The timing wasn't right. But I'll try again.

YourScrappyLittleFashionistaFriend: Timing is everything.

Number18: Timing is the *only* thing.

YourScrappyLittleFashionistaFriend: Truth.

Number18: But I love a good challenge. And I'm up for one.

Well, someone is definitely confident. And while the last thing I need in my life is an online flirtation with a stranger, I write back anyway.

YourScrappyLittleFashionistaFriend: And you know how to dress for one. In a dark green Henley.

Wait. Shit. Did I just post that? Stupid subconscious. I meant Henley of an unspecified color. I edit my faux pas quickly, then close out of the comments. No more flirting with anyone.

Speaking of flirts, I decide to follow up on the Stefan situation. I need to know if I should secretly loathe his philandering ass or not.

I look him up, poking around on his social, checking out his recent pics. There are some moody city shots of San Francisco. Some others of Copenhagen. He's in one of those pics, a shot of him at a river, Scandinavian buildings in the backdrop, and Stefan, with his typical Nordic complexion, fitting in perfectly.

I jump to Annika's social.

Oh. *Ohhh.*

They're no longer following each other. She no longer lives here, having returned to Copenhagen. And she's no longer wearing that gorgeous rock on her ring finger.

Then, I go back to Stefan's bio and team photo, and I gasp.

Holy shit.

How did I miss it?

He's Number Eighteen on the team. Did he wear that Henley...for me? Am I the certain someone he's been hopeful about?

I fly back to the group chat in time to read Trina's newest note.

Trina: His fiancée broke it off last season.

9

MY FAVORITE SPORT

Hayes

A month ago, I was strapping on skates for Los Angeles during training camp. Now, I'm grabbing a stick for San Francisco and jumping into the action in our first game of the season.

In the rink, I don't dwell on existential shit like where I've been or where I'm going. I focus only on where I want to be on the ice—in sync with my team-mates. We're five minutes into the first period. My heart pounds as I dodge Arizona players in the line change, and then I'm moving toward the puck, picking up speed as Stefan races down the ice into their zone, shoulder to shoulder with the enemy. When the defender gets too close to him, the captain deftly passes the puck to me.

The prize is mine, and for a flash of a second, there's a clear shot to the net. But their goalie's a fast motherfucker. Just as quickly, there's no wiggle room there. I dart around the defenseman, then spot another chance. Yes, fucking yes. This is it. With a swift flick of my wrist, I shoot forward, a powerful shot.

Right into the Arizona goalie's outstretched leg pad.

There go my hopes of being a hero in my first play.

But games are long, and chances come around more than once. Near the end of the second period, adrenaline pumps through me as I fly down the ice, hunting for an opening, the crowd shouting for us to get going. They're damn eager for something other than a cipher on the scoreboard from the home team.

They're restless here in the Avengers arena, and I want us to give them something to shout about. But the Arizona goalie's a ten-foot wall tonight, and no one's been past him yet.

Stefan's weaving through their D-line, passing to me, then all at once, everything comes into sharp focus. The noise quiets, my vision narrows, and there's nothing but a straight shot to the goal.

I gear up to slap the puck in when an Arizona defender whips in front of me, but I eke out a pass to Stefan before the enemy can steal the puck. My teammate attacks in a flash, sending the little black disc on a one-way flight right through the five-hole.

The lamp lights, and so does my competitive heart. The score is tied now, and I get my first assist with my new team.

It feels like a massive victory even though it's only one point. But it's mine, and I'll take it.

When I'm on the players' bench during the face-off, I catch sight of a purple furball up in the stands. She's shaking her gigantic furry ass, waving her fluffy arms above her head, hyping up the crowd.

Then, she cups a furry hand—or is that a paw?—to her ear, urging the fans to make some noise.

Sounds like they're saying *Armstrong*.

A smile tugs at my lips.

But I don't let the sound go to my head. I don't let the smile finish forming. And I definitely don't let my focus go to Ivy or to my father in the stands. I don't look for the mascot or my dad for the rest of the game. I can't afford a distraction.

We win, two to one. It's a relief more than a thrill.

* * *

After a quick sesh with the press, where I sing the *just happy to be here* tune, I head down the corridor, headphones in, AC/DC cranked sky-high. I hope the head-banging music drowns out the emotions I don't want to feel around my dad. By the time I round the corner, I'm ready to see the guy. He waits for me, a smile on his face, a full head of hair on his head, a Vacheron Constantin on his wrist, and a woman twenty years younger on his arm. He's a smart guy, and his bank account would testify to his acumen when it comes to money management.

But his ticker's softer than a down pillow.

Mine must be made of lead because I can't be happy for him and his new squeeze. But...track records matter.

I take out my earbuds. "Hey, Dad," I say, giving him a quick clap on the back.

"Nice assist. How did it feel, your first game with the new team?"

"It was good." I don't want to answer truthfully in front of Cora, for no reason other than I don't trust her. But I do need to be polite. "Hi, Cora," I say to the woman who at thirty, is three whopping years older than me.

She flicks her ash blonde hair off her shoulder, looking as polished as my father. "You played so great tonight. Your dad and I are so proud of you," she echoes.

Because they're a unit. Because he's attached to her now. Just like he's been attached to every girlfriend and wife he's had since my mom left us many, many moons ago.

Me? No thanks to attachments. I tried it in Seattle with Tia, an art gallery manager. We dated for most of the season. But toward the end she kept telling me I was too focused on my career, that I needed to show up for more of her events even though most of them were right before my games. That made it a *little* hard. When I was traded to Los Angeles, she didn't even want to try long distance. "You're cold and aloof anyway," she'd said.

Well, thanks.

Tia's behind me, though, and San Francisco's in

front of me. Romance is not on the table for me like it is *always* for my dad.

"Can we take you out for dinner?" he asks as Stefan walks toward us.

"You're always hungry after games," Cora puts in, like she knows me. She doesn't. She just made a good guess.

But Stefan swoops in. "Good to see you, Mr. Armstrong, but I need to steal this guy away. Got to celebrate that win."

"Of course," my father says, understanding the benefits of teamwork.

I'm just grateful for the save. I'm even more grateful for the text from Ivy that lands as I'm walking to Stefan's car to head to dinner.

Ivy: How was the first night at your new job?

A small smile tugs at my lips. I feel like I can answer her honestly. Maybe it's because there's no history with her, no expectations. Or maybe because this whole thing started with her unloading all her job weirdness onto me. I do the same.

Hayes: Nerve-wracking. But weirdly fun too. How was your first night mascotting?

Ivy: Is mascotting even a verb?

Hayes: Now it is.

Ivy: Then I mascotted my furry butt off tonight. And it was…weirdly fun.

We trade friendly messages until we reach the car and I force myself to put the phone away.

* * *

"What's it going to be, *Hey You*?"

The question comes from my buddy Gage a little later as I scan the chalkboard offerings at Sticks and Stones, a bar he opened recently.

With a chuckle, Stefan offers Gage a fist for knocking, clearly delighted Gage is using the nickname he told him about when we arrived a few minutes ago.

I stare sternly at my longtime friend on the other side of the counter. Now my enemy. "Dude, *you* don't get to call me that name."

The smartass wiggles his brows. "Bartender rules. Someone serves up a story, I get to use it."

Stefan leans back in the stool, parking his hands behind his head as he casts a glance my way. "Just be glad I helped hand-select a good nickname for you. It could have been *Little Buddy*."

I groan at the reminder of my awful nickname from

freshman year. "Fuck you. Fuck you. And fuck you some more." I offer him the bird for each one.

"Why, thank you. That's my favorite sport," Stefan says.

"Yeah, mine too," I say.

With a smirk, Stefan adds, "I'm aware."

I shoot him a look. We don't usually talk up the things we've done with women in public. But he's not quite serving anything up. Still, privacy's privacy.

He returns my look with a reassuring one of his own that says *don't worry. I know the deal.*

I relax. I'm also seriously glad he didn't pick *Little Buddy*. A bunch of the seniors on our college team gave me that nickname because I was the freshman hotshot. It sucked, obviously, and it's not like I'm little. I'm taller than The Viking. When those jokesters graduated, I became The Iceman, which suited my style of play. Emotion-less.

From behind the bar, Gage grins. "I can start using *Little Buddy* though."

"I certainly hope you'll use it frequently," Stefan puts in.

I drag a hand down my neck, then throw in the towel with these two clowns. "You've got your pick of ammo," I say to Gage. "Now, how about a burger and a pale ale?"

"Coming right up, *Little Buddy*," he says, then sighs faux thoughtfully as he pulls the tap on the brew. "See? I just can't decide which one to use."

"I'm never going to live this down, am I?" I ask.

"I'm not sure why we'd let you," Stefan answers, then gives Gage his drink and food order too.

A minute later, Gage sets a mouth-watering glass of golden brew down in front of me, along with a stout for Stefan, then turns to the kitchen presumably to put our order in. Gage is a couple years older than I am, and I grew up living next door to him. He's the older brother I never had. Hell, he's the sibling I never had, and I love seeing his success. He worked his ass off managing a bar in Sacramento for several years while raising his kid solo after his wife died. He's wanted to run his own place for some time, and he recently opened this new spot that's teeming with people. I'm glad to see business is good.

When he returns, he glances around the joint, filled with sports memorabilia and dark wood, leather booths, and brass hardware. There's a youthful vibe too. If you don't want to watch sports, you can play Ping-Pong or pool. Fun and games for everyone. "Not too shabby?"

"Not at all," Stefan says, clearly proud of his fellow proprietor.

Then, Gage's green eyes meet mine straight on. "And you didn't play too badly tonight either."

"Thanks," I say, but I feel like I'm holding my breath. "I'll just need to do it for eighty-one more games."

Stefan sets down his glass and fixes me with a serious gaze. No bullshit this time. "And you will, Armstrong. You fucking will," he says, and that makes me smile for real.

"Thanks, man."

As Gage wipes down the bar, he gives me a chin nod. "So, other than winning your game tonight, how's your first week?"

Busy. Good. And frustrating. I home in on the latter. "Let's see. I met a cute girl in the elevator. Flirted with her. Turns out I work with her."

Stefan jerks his gaze to me with avid interest in his eyes.

10

FARMER STEFAN

Stefan

He might mean Parvati. Maybe he's referring to the general manager, Violet. Or possibly the new yoga instructor, Briar. But if I know Hayes's taste as well as I think I do, he's keen on our new mascot.

But I don't let on right away. I want to have some fun with this intel. After I take a drink of the ale and set it down, I shoot him a curious look. "Jessie? Really? I never pegged you for the type to go after the boss. But more power to you."

Hayes rolls his eyes. "Yes. I flirted with the team owner in the elevator. That makes perfect sense."

I clap his shoulder sympathetically. "She's married, my man. Maybe best to shut that crush down?"

"Don't think you fooled me right now. I know you know it's Ivy," Hayes says.

Well, cracking that case was easy. "Only because it's *that* obvious."

Gage cackles as he sorts some glasses. "This I have to know. Tell me how Hayes made his new puppy-love crush known to everyone."

Hayes drops his head to the bar. "Why did I come here?"

"Because it's better than The Great Dane," Gage says.

I let my jaw drop in over-the-top shock. "Those are fighting words."

"I know and we'll fight later," Gage says, then turns his focus back to Hayes. "Now. Spill."

Hayes lifts his face and turns to me, then Gage, looking dejected. "She's feisty, she's fiery, she's funny. She likes gardening and standing up for herself. And she's hot as sin. I'm starting to avoid my own building. I'll probably have to live here soon just to resist her," he says, gesturing behind the counter as Gage grabs some glasses from the dish rack.

"Cool, there's a sleeping bag under the bar," Gage says.

I take another drink, and already the wheels in my head are turning. This is better than I'd hoped for. This is fan-fucking-tastic. I had no idea he was into Ivy, but then I shouldn't be surprised. We've always had the same taste in women.

Excellent taste.

"So, why not pursue her?" I ask, feeling him out.

Hayes grimaces. "An office romance is not a good look for the new guy. Besides, I should focus on hockey.

Fitting in with the team." I know that matters to him. He wants to find a place to call home, though he'd never put it in those terms. I want him to, as well. "But she's...something else. We just vibed."

That explains the moment I saw passing between them in the hallway the other day. A twinge of jealousy curls up in me. I want that spark with her too, but she was a little cool with me. Or perhaps just professional? I'm not sure where she stands with me or if she's interested.

I'm the wild card here.

Hayes is into her. She's into Hayes. I'm into her. Would she be into me the way I suspected at the calendar event? And if so, would she be interested in us sharing her?

It wouldn't be the first time we've shared a woman in bed. Or even the second or third. But this is a delicate situation, being a workplace tryst and all. It'll require finesse.

But, like I told her, as Number18, I'm up for the challenge. And I'm particularly savvy with these sorts of arrangements.

I draw a deep, satisfied sigh. At last, I have a project to keep me truly busy. Flirting with Ivy, feeling her out, and laying the groundwork for a special night where my friend and I can introduce her to the most mind-blowing sex there is.

Doubling her pleasure.

With my plans forming, I return to the convo. "She's a cool one," I say of Ivy, subtly egging Hayes on.

"Always been fun to talk to. I can see why you'd be into her."

There. Step one. Make him see that it's *okay* to want a co-worker. Hayes can be rigid. He needs someone in his life who knows how to bend the rules.

He shrugs. "Win some, lose some. But it's no big deal. It's not like I was going to marry her. Or date her even."

Gage snorts, then flicks a dismissive hand at both of us. "Pretty boys are always trouble."

"Aww, you think I'm pretty," I mock.

"Please. I can tell who looks like a fuckboy, and that's you, Stefan." He points at my buddy, too, in accusation. "And you, Hayes."

I pat my cheek. "I can't help it. I was blessed with good *bone* structure."

With a smile, Hayes lets his gaze drift downward. "I was blessed with it too. *Everywhere*."

Gage mimes gagging. "Enough about your bones." He grabs another glass and pours from the tap. "Also, does this new crush mean you've put that Tia shit behind you?"

I shudder at the mention of Hayes's ex. "He'd better put Tia behind him. Because she was one hundred percent wrong in her assessment of him." No one messes with my friends.

"Dead wrong," Gage confirms.

"Yes, Tia's in the past," Hayes says.

"Sounds like Building Girl needs to be there too," Gage says.

Oh, no. I won't let him rain on my plans for a sex parade.

"I don't know about that," I say. "Sometimes Hayes plays hockey even better when he's...*happier*," I suggest, sowing the seeds for a night for three. Just call me Farmer Stefan.

Hayes acknowledges that with a nod. Yup. I'm right. "That may be true," he says, "But I don't need romance fucking up my head. Saw enough of that with my dad."

From what he's told me, it wasn't easy for Hayes to watch his dad jump from woman to woman, from hurt to hurt, from broken heart to broken heart. All the more reason for me to engineer a night of fun for my friend.

"Hayes, up for a run in the morning?" I ask.

"Always," he says.

And so it begins.

The four-mile run I've planned takes us through the hills of the Presidio then down to Lower Pacific Heights. We peel off miles till we finish.

Conveniently, we don't end our run near my three-story home at the top of Pacific Heights with its spectacular view of the Golden Gate Bridge. Instead, we're a mile away, off Fillmore, pulling up outside Hayes's building. I'm strategic that way.

And I'm also very, very thirsty. "I need some water. Help a guy out," I say, panting, sweat dripping down my

T-shirt. I might even need to take it off if my plan works well.

Carelessly, Hayes points to a nearby fire hydrant. "There you go. Or I could set out a water bowl for you."

"How generous." I ignore the offer and trot up the steps to the building's revolving door.

"And feel free to let yourself in," he deadpans.

"Don't mind if I do."

He comes through the door right behind me. "Let's get a drink then hit the weights in the building gym?"

"Fantastic." It's almost as if I'd thought of it myself. Once we're inside the penthouse, and I've guzzled a glass from the tap, I gesture to the winding staircase leading to the rooftop. "I'm craving a fava bean."

With his dark eyes, Hayes shoots me a look of disbelief. "Who craves fava beans before they work out? Who craves fava beans at all?"

I point to my chest. "This guy."

"Seriously?"

"Some men crave potato chips. I have a thing for fava beans. Don't judge me."

"I will judge you for your oddball craving as much as I want."

"Fair enough. But seriously, that garden is a major selling point. I need to check on it. When the Avengers lock you up, you'll probably go buy some mansion in Cow Hollow."

Hayes laughs dryly. "Yeah. Right. More like when you get the place back once they trade me."

This guy. My heart bleeds for him. He's on edge. "That's not what I mean."

He just shrugs. "But I should check on the veggies anyway. The previous tenants left a list of instructions, and it's fuck-all confusing."

"Eggplants are complicated. I understand," I say solemnly.

We head to the rooftop, and I drink in the gorgeous view of the city. "I should take some more pictures from up here. It's stunning."

"Yeah, the views are great," he says, dryer than usual. Then he points across the block. "You can see The Great Dane from here."

"And vice versa."

I spin around and head to the planters, pluck a fava bean, and pop it into my mouth while Hayes scans the gardening instructions left in the small shed, then stares at a gigantic green leaf, also known as kale.

His brow furrows. His gaze strays from the leaf to a weed, to the instructions and back again.

I'm practically holding my breath. *C'mon. Connect the dots.*

"What am I even staring at? Is that kale or a weed?"

And we're getting closer. But I'm not about to tell him. "No clue. Ask Google," I say casually.

He snaps a pic, then, presumably uploads it.

And shit. Fuck. Hell.

He wasn't really supposed to ask the search engine. "I think it's a weed," I say, before he tells me the results.

"You do?"

"Yeah. Definitely."

"Google says it's kale," he says.

"Well, do you trust Google or me?"

"What do you know about gardening?"

A lot. "Enough," I say.

"Enough to be dangerous," he counters. Then, finally, he follows my breadcrumbs and says, "I'll just ask Ivy. She loves to garden—said she got it from her grandma."

Brilliant. I turn to hide my face and how pleased I am. "Have her come up. Check it out in person. Easier that way."

I munch fava beans while he's busy on his phone for a few minutes, then he looks up and asks, "Can she bring her dog?"

I love it when a plan comes together. "Of course."

"Cool. I hope she's not bummed when she sees you, though," he says with a grimace, then a long sigh. "But she probably will be. I'd better warn her."

"And fuck you too."

With a smug smile, he taps out a message on his phone, then meets my eyes. "There. Let's just hope you don't scare her away."

I hope the same. But I can be very convincing. For starters, I strip off my shirt.

11

THE CERTAIN SOMEONE

Ivy

I read the last message from Hayes just as I shut the door to my apartment with my pooch, post-walk.

Stefan is with him. Why does that make my pulse race and my nerves skitter?

Because he's sexy, too, and I don't know what to do about that.

But I also work with them, so I really shouldn't think about either of them like that, neither a lot nor a little. I definitely shouldn't think about Stefan's admission as Number18—that timing is everything. That he'll try again. I don't even know for certain he was trying to get to know me the other day. That's a lot to think about. To accept.

I'll just help with the kale, then leave. With that decided and Roxy's leash still in my hand, I spin back around and open the door again.

"Wait."

Jackson's deep voice booms across the living room. He's striding through the apartment in his gym clothes, looking far too pretty to work out. But he always looks good. "Where are you going with that *Imma 'bout to get some* look on your face?"

I do my best to erase any pre-sex face, since we're not, not, *not* having sex. Not Hayes and I, not Stefan and I, not the three...

Nope. I won't let myself go there even in my thoughts.

"What look?" It comes out innocent. At least, I hope it does.

When Jackson reaches me, he draws an air circle around my face. "I can read you like that."

"So you're a face reader?"

"Yes, ma'am. And yours says *I'm getting some dick.*"

"Please. I'm going to see a guy at his place with a friend."

Jackson's eyebrows climb so high. "Let me amend that. Your face says I'm getting some...*dicks,*" he says, dragging out the plural.

"No, that's not happening." My traitorous pulse rockets.

"But it could be happening. Why have one dick when you can have two, as I like to say."

I hold up a stop-sign hand. The more he talks about two dicks, the more flustered I'll get hanging out with two guys. "I'm not looking for one dick, let alone two," I sputter, feeling caught. I know I should stay away from Hayes. *And* Stefan. For a long list of reasons, starting with—I find both of them attractive, and that's confusing to me.

Jackson wiggles his fingers at my phone. "Who's the man attached to the dick? Or the men, I should say?"

"Since men are attached to their dicks, more than the other way around?"

"I like to think of the man-dick attachment as a package deal. Now, let me see."

I huff then relent. "I'm going to see Hayes," I begin. Easier to focus on one guy right now. The thought of a pair is throwing me into a lopsided spin cycle.

Jackson's dark eyes twinkle. "Are you going to water his eggplant with your tongue?"

"No."

"Any reason you're *not*? Aside from the fact he has company, that is."

"I work with him," I say, insistent. "And he lives in the building. That would be doubly messy."

"Other things would be too."

I groan. "Stop."

But also, I don't choose well. What if I dated Hayes and he turned around and slept with my new boss? What if he subtly put me down and I barely realized it was happening? What if he dismissed my dreams? "Honestly, just not ready," I say, which is the truth too.

Jackson nods thoughtfully, giving up his playful pushing. "I hear you, hun."

"I mean, it's not even that I'm covering Xander's stupid wedding. It's just...I can't imagine anything going well with anyone right now. I'm not sure I know how to pick a good man." My heart's too tender, and my ego's too bruised.

"I get it," Jackson says gently, then rubs my arm with affection. When he lets go, his brown eyes twinkle again. "But you don't have to get your heart involved, if you know what I mean."

I slug his arm. "You enabler."

"Just think of me as your libido's wingman."

"I think of you as the devil."

"Same thing," he says, while Roxy yawns loudly from the floor, interjecting herself into the convo. Jackson waves at the little lady. "See? Your dog agrees with me. She thinks you should get some."

"No, she does not. She's coming along to protect my virtue," I insist, like she's proof of my innocent intentions.

Jackson tuts. "Your five-pound senior dog's not the cockblocker you think she is."

Fine.

Maybe I *am* using Roxy as a shield. If I have the dog to focus on, I won't be able to throw myself at Hayes.

Or Stefan.

But mostly Hayes, right? I'm mostly attracted to him. Which means I'll need to resist his charms more when I head upstairs. I'll activate a Hayes shield.

Jackson and I take off. He heads downstairs and my dog and I go up to the penthouse level. My stomach flips as the elevator rises, and I tell myself it's from the change in altitude.

It's not from the anticipation of the company.

A minute later, I head down the hall and rap on the door. "Garden patrol, at your service," I call out.

See? I can be friends with Hayes. And Stefan too. In fact, it's just good sense. I work with both of them. I should be friendly with them too.

When the door opens, Hayes is there, sporting a cocky grin and those damn gym shorts again—the ones I've seen him take off. They're blue and hang low on his hips, reminding me how easy they'd be to just. Push. Down. A gray T-shirt snuggles his pecs, his biceps, and his abs, and it's the luckiest piece of fabric ever. His smile is pure sex. He looks at me like he's undressing me. His stubble is a little thicker now too. Almost scruff levels.

Yes, he's the one I'm most attracted to. That makes sense. We're well past the *are we into each other* phase— we crossed that somewhere between *here's my eggplant* o'clock and *check out my shower towel*.

We've acknowledged, too, that we're sticking to being neighborly. Stefan? He's just a handsome guy I've known casually for years. He'll be easier to resist.

When my gaze travels to him, he's in the kitchen, leaning casually against the counter, hair mussed up, lips quirked in a grin. He's got a smattering of stubble, and his jawline is chiseled but imperfect thanks to a scar on his chin. A perfect imperfection I'd like to touch.

But there's no shirt in sight.

The man can wear the hell out of a Henley, and, I'm learning, out of nothing. His muscles glisten. A smattering of golden-brown chest hair covers his broad pecs. He doesn't have any tattoos, but there are scratches on his shoulders and a few bruises on his arms. His abs are out of this world. Long, carved, tight.

His running shorts hug his hips, and I try to look away. I swear I do. But it's one thing to think a guy with a fiancée is handsome. It's entirely another to find a single man thoroughly fuckable.

But I can't think that. Nope. I can't. And I won't.

Best to deny this lust blooming inside me. "Hi. I'm here to help," I say.

Roxy's bushy tail goes wild, faster than a metronome set to its highest tempo.

Hayes kneels in front of my cinnamon pup with her whitening muzzle. "Hey, girl," he says and offers her a hand for sniffing. My mutt rubs her face against his palm, then the shameless hussy stretches her paws up onto his chest.

Not satisfied saying hi to one, she scampers to Stefan next, looking up at him, and barks her hello bark. Her *look at me* bark.

He must speak Dog, since he's kneeling too, offering her a hand.

"Well, hello there," Stefan says, and that only makes my girl waggle her butt more. "Who's a good girl? You are."

Dammit. My chest tingles at those words. Can he please say them to me?

Wait. Do I want Stefan to say that to me, or Hayes?

Hayes is the guy I'm resisting, right? Stefan is just a handsome afterthought.

But am I his certain someone? The one he

mentioned in his comment on my post? *There's a certain someone I might run into today.*

Has he been into me since before I showed up at work the other day?

I don't even know what to think as Roxy taunts me, stretching against Stefan, getting a double pawful of his pecs before sliding her greedy mitts down his bare stomach.

"Sorry," I say. "I hope she doesn't scratch you."

Stefan lifts his face, his eyes locking with mine. "I don't mind a few scratches." Heat flickers in his eyes, and I swallow roughly.

Hayes drags a hand through his thick, dark hair. "Yeah, nothing wrong with a scratch mark here or there," he says in that sexy voice before he joins Stefan in the kitchen.

"Such a good girl," Hayes says to Roxy, and yes. That sounds delicious too.

The double good girl.

My stomach flips, and my mind goes fuzzy. I can barely think straight as Hayes rewards the pup with more pets and chin rubs.

And she takes them all.

Hayes gestures to the bandana she's sporting, black lined with chili peppers. "Fashion statement or a warning she's spicy?"

Huh? Did he ask me something?

Oh, right. A dog question.

"Both," I say. I try to clear my head and focus on my visit, not the view of two men lavishing praise on the little dog I rescued so she could have a home in her final years. So she could experience love. So she could be adored.

My stupid throat catches.

"Is that why you adopted her? Because she's fiery?" Stefan asks.

It's so seamless the way the guys trade off. And it's good, too, that they're asking about Roxy. Dog talk makes me emotional, but surely that's safer than desire.

I head into the kitchen where Roxy is bounding back and forth between the two guys. Yes, better to focus on my shameless girl.

"She is fiery, but mostly I got her because I felt like she needed me. Trina told me about her," I say, talking over this erratic beating of my heart, this quickening of my pulse. "Trina is Ryker's girlfriend, and also Chase Weston's from the Sea Dogs," I explain to Hayes, but he nods right away. Maybe he's heard about the throuple. "She volunteers at the shelter where I got Roxy from— Little Friends. But Roxy's a Florida girl."

The men are now sitting on the kitchen floor, listening attentively to me, like my rambling talk about my dog matters. They don't look bored like Xander was when I told him the story. Sure, Xander listened, but then he wanted to go shopping for new bow ties because his favorite vintage shop was having a sale.

These guys look legitimately interested, and it's irresistible to me. "Roxy's owner had been in hospice. But she didn't have a family. When she passed away with no one there except the hospice workers and her dog, she'd left a note to the shelter that said *please take care of my girl*." This part of the story always chokes me up, and I stop to breathe past overwhelming emotion. Stefan pops up, grabs a tissue from the counter, and hands it to me. I dab at my eyes. "Sorry. That note always makes me sad."

"Of course it does," Hayes says gently. "You feel for the person and the pet."

My heart warms. "Yes, exactly."

"Reminds me of my grandmother," Stefan adds, his tone serious, and it's one of the first times I've heard it that way. "She was in love with cats. I think cats were her soul mates. She was very concerned about what would happen to them when she passed."

"What did happen?" I ask, a touch alarmed for the cats.

"My mom took them in," he says simply. Like, what other choice was there?

"I'm glad to hear that. Does she still have them?"

"Yes. She cooks them dinner every night."

"So, they're her soul mates now?"

"Absolutely," he says.

Stefan sits down again, and I join them on the floor, leaning in close, getting in on the Roxy love. "I get that," I say. "As for this girl, I just felt for both of them. For this dog who'd lost her person and the little old lady who had no one in her later years but a dog. Little Friends helped the Florida folks facilitate the rescue, and when I saw their video about Roxy, I basically busted down the door to Little Friends, demanding, *Let me have her*." I swallow the hitch in my throat. "I just felt this intense desire to make her mine. To slather her in love and kisses and attention and bandanas throughout her golden years."

Hayes's smile grows bigger. "You're the reason, then, that she gives a lot of love."

My heart glows a little more, and I tell myself it's just the dog story making me emotional. "Maybe," I say. "But I think it's also her personality."

"I think she found the right person," Stefan says, his voice warm now.

"I like to think so, too," I say. "Someday, I want to donate a bunch of money to the two shelters and get a plaque for all the dogs waiting to be adopted, and it'll say Roxy's Playroom, and all the dogs will get homes."

I try to shake off the emotions. I certainly don't need to get teary-eyed in front of two strapping hockey studs who called me up for my kale expertise. This isn't my personal therapy hour, where I bare my soul about my feelings about family, and taking care of other people, and trust, and support. "I'm just glad Trina tipped me off about her. She has a dog from the same shelter—a three-legged Min-Pin named Nacho. We call them cousins."

"Found family includes dogs," Hayes says.

"Definitely. And they're lucky pooches," Stefan adds.

My head swims with even more questions. How is it that they both understand my overly emotional attachment to an animal?

I tell them more about Roxy and Nacho, how she stays with Nacho when I have to travel for work. Like this weekend. The mascot doesn't travel with the team

—whipping up the crowds is solely a home-arena job —but the team asked me to travel with them to Vegas for a promo stunt the Sabers want me to do with their mascot.

Will it be weird to travel with both of these guys? With the one man who got me hot and bothered in the equipment room and this other one who's growing on me now? Of course, I probably won't even see them on the trip. They're the players. The stars. I'm just a girl who puts on a sweltering, fluffy costume and trips on the ice on purpose.

A girl like me, trying to hold onto her side hustle, can't afford to fall for one co-worker, let alone two.

Shake it off.

I stand, smoothing down my crocheted top, centering myself. "About that kale…"

They get to their feet, and Hayes, leads me up a winding staircase to the roof, Roxy in my arms, Stefan behind me. "Does she have a whole collection? Of bandanas?" Stefan asks.

"Of course." I toss him a guilty-not-guilty grin. "She's a scrappy little fashionista. Like me."

It's the first time I've acknowledged my handle in front of Stefan, and a realization clobbers me.

He didn't come across my newsletter by accident. He searched it out. He commented on it. He tracked me down. I am the *certain someone*.

"And she seems to enjoy the attention," he says, his blue eyes locked on mine, like he knows a secret.

"Maybe she does," I say evenly, trying not to give too

much away. Just that he doesn't have the upper hand. "Number Eighteen."

It only seems to delight him more that I've put it together. Hayes looks at his friend curiously, assessing, but doesn't seem bothered that Stefan's flirting with me.

That surprises me. Hayes gives off possessive vibes, like when he told me not to talk to other rooftop gardeners. Is he unbothered because he already backed off? Is this some sort of hand-off from one guy to the other?

My head hurts, and really there's no point in trying to puzzle this out. My guy radar is out of whack.

My plant radar is not though. It's hot again on the roof, the sun beating down. As Hayes strides to the planters, he reaches for the hem of his shirt and peels it off.

I was not expecting that.

He shoots a confident glance my way, his dark eyes glinting a message. *Two can play at the shirtless game.*

With the same swagger he's shown since he announced he'd take me to the wedding, he turns back around, like he doesn't even care if my eyes are on him.

The sexy, cocky fucker.

I do care. I care so much that I sway. The man's muscles are insane. He's long, strong, and toned everywhere.

As I stare at him unabashedly on wobbly knees, Stefan reaches out a hand and steadies me, grasping my elbow. "The view can be dizzying," he says with an amused smile.

I roll my lips together and nod, sealing up my sighs.

Yes, the view is dizzying.

Two toned, strong, shirtless men on a rooftop.

I don't know what I've gotten myself into, accepting this invitation to the garden, but I can't seem to resist stepping into temptation with Hayes. And now, it seems, with Stefan.

But is it that I can't resist either of them? Or both of them?

* * *

Forty-five minutes later, my girl is stretched out on the patio, frog-dog style, back legs splayed behind her and her eyes closed as she sunbathes. Nearby, there's a telescope—the stargazing must be amazing from up here on a clear night.

I've thinned some carrots, and now I'm showing the guys how to weed the kale in the big metal planter in the center of the rooftop garden. Gardening is much safer than talking about dogs or the fact that I can't keep my eyes to myself. "My grandma loves to garden. She taught me everything I know. And she won gardening prizes."

"Mine taught me to sail. Not quite as useful," Stefan says dryly.

Hayes laughs. "Dude, that's so bougie."

"Yes, that's my grandparents for you," he says to Hayes. "Not everyone's grandparents teach them how to pitch a tent or build a campfire."

"Did they teach you to play polo too?" his friend asks.

"I feel like there's no good answer to that," Stefan says.

I smile, relieved that their banter dispels some of the tension. "You harvest the leaves from the bottom of the plant," I explain, running my finger across a leaf. "Like this."

The sexy new guy on the team moves next to me. "Got it," he says as he reaches for a leaf.

Hayes is so close I can smell his woodsy soap, mixed with sweat. The scent drifts into my nose and fills my head, lighting up my senses.

"Did you just work out?" I ask, distracted. Then his scent mingles with the equally alluring smell of clean sheets and powdery snow as Stefan steps closer, reaching for a leaf too.

"We went for a run a little while ago," Hayes answers, and I picture the two of them pounding the pavement, looking strong and virile. I stifle a whimper.

"And we're hitting the gym after this," Stefan adds in a casual tone, but one that lingers at the end, like he's inviting me to picture them at the gym.

And I do picture them. Pumping iron. Doing push-ups. Lifting weights. *Unfair, brain.*

I focus on the kale, tugging gently on the leaf. "You don't want to damage the bud in the center, so you snap from the bottom," I say as I pluck off a leaf.

"Does that hurt the plant?" Stefan asks, running his fingers along the stem like he's concerned for it, but he does it in such a slow, sensual way that I'm concerned for my panties.

"No. The kale likes it," I rasp, then I shake my head

quickly. "I mean, the plant is fine." *Focus, girl.* I reach for a leaf to demonstrate. "You pull it down and out."

Stefan reaches for a plant next to me, his smoky voice next to my ear as he repeats, "Down and out."

It's not the words but his tone that sets my skin to scorching.

It's the warmth of the weather.

It's the mix of masculine scents, each unique, each intoxicating.

I'm not sure I can handle being so close to them when I want to put my hands on one, then the other. When I want to lean back against Stefan's chest and let Hayes stalk over to me. I've never thought this before. Never pictured anything like it. Now I can't stop, and it's driving me batty.

I flap a hand at the kale on the other side of the planter with urgency. "You guys should do the ones over there," I say, giving an order they'd better follow.

My amateur gardeners comply, moving to the other side. Good. I have some breathing room. I won't be subjected to their pheromones making me...feral.

I focus on weeding, getting into the rhythm of gardening, feeling like I can survive this newfound attraction. When I look up several minutes later, Hayes is pulling a leaf, but his eyes are on me, and they're heated. His lips curve up. "You looked like you had fun on your first night as a mascot." There's a beat, then he adds, "Riling up the crowds." There's a touch of innuendo in his tone. But I can't go there.

"I tried. I was a cheerleader in high school." This is a safer topic. Easier.

Hayes tilts his head. "You?"

"A cheerleader?" Stefan seems surprised too.

"Yes. Me. A cheerleader."

Hayes lifts a dubious brow. "You don't give off cheerleader vibes."

I raise my chin, a little defiant, taking back control from them. "I contain multitudes, gentlemen."

Hayes turns to Stefan, faux confused. "Gentlemen? Who's she talking about?"

Stefan holds his hands up in surrender. "No idea. Not me."

"Definitely not me either," Hayes says.

Whew. Things lighten up as they banter. We return to gardening, and Hayes looks me over once more. "You give off indie girl vibes."

"Explain."

"You seem...more punk rock. Like a girl who wears motorcycle boots and a black leather jacket. A girl who probably once dyed her hair pink. A girl who has a..." His gaze drifts down my chest.

Oh. Oh god.

He's staring at my tits, and I swear I can see the thought bubble over his head—*Do you have a nipple piercing?*

But you know what? I think I'll keep that intel close to the vest. "That's classified, boys," I say, like I'm playing an ace.

They stare at me like they're salivating.

Everyone's quiet for several sultry seconds. Hayes has a naturally quiet side, an introspective aspect to him. But this might be the first time I've seen Stefan speechless. He's like a cartoon character who got the wind knocked out of him.

By Hayes.

And maybe by me surprising him too, so I add, "And who said girls who dye their hair pink—it was magenta streaks, thank you very much—can't be cheerleaders?"

Hayes gives a *you've got me there* nod. "Nice," he says.

Stefan recovers the power of speech. "Multitudes, Ivy." It comes out thoroughly seductive.

And with my name on his tongue, the power shifts once again. I drop my gaze and focus on the last kale plant and not on this cat-and-mouse flirtation. Hayes works on his, pulling the leaf, grunting slightly. The sound has me thinking of him in bed. "Did I do it right?"

"You did."

He's doing everything too right. But so is his teammate. I'm confused, completely off-kilter.

Until yesterday, Hayes Armstrong was the most sensual man I'd ever met. In all our brief encounters, he's radiated sex. Every instant with him has been charged with electricity. We've barely touched, and Hayes has ignited a spark in me, a desire to explore my own fantasies.

The trouble is those fantasies are now intertwining with thoughts of his team captain. I feel trapped in a spell they're weaving.

They're both unfairly handsome and tremendous listeners, and they're both looking at me like I'm some kind of answer.

I don't know what the question is though.

But I know this—I really shouldn't be asking it.

I stop, brush one palm against the other, and say, "And that's how you tend to a garden. Now I have to go...write and answer emails."

With that excuse, I scoop up my dog and hustle off the roof.

A day ago, I only had to resist one guy at work. Now, I have to resist two.

12

NO GENTLEMEN

Ivy

I successfully avoid both guys at the next home game.

It's not hard. I don't need to go into the locker room, or the media room, or the workout rooms. I don't need to get my hammies stretched, or my sore muscles worked on with a trainer.

And I'm never on the ice at the same time as the players.

I avoid them both in the building too. Stealth Ivy is in the house. I keep busy writing for my newsletter and posting on social, including a piece on the best finds in secondhand fashion, and another about clothes that make you feel strong. I'll need an outfit to do that when I have to face Simone again soon. She emailed asking me to meet about her wedding coverage, so that date at the end of the month looms on my calendar.

Planning my clothing armor helps, so I use my new idea pen to write down possible outfits of the day in my notebook with the woman in the old-timey red evening dress on the cover.

I plan to avoid the guys on the plane to Vegas, too. Books are truly a girl's best friend, and I've brought a paperback, a Kindle, and the aforementioned notebook. A triumvirate of Do Not Fucking Disturb signs.

At the airport, I keep busy, chatting with Oliver at the gate. He tells me about the plan to test out new names for the team soon after we return to San Francisco. Marketing has selected two new options for the Avengers and is working on a third. I sincerely hope the costume for the mascot is better than the ink splotch I wore in the first two home games.

We board together, and I don't gawk at the size of the seats or the legroom. I'm cool Ivy too. But damn, those seats are big. There are three in each row, and Oliver points to the first of them. "Grab a seat by the front. The guys take freaking forever to deplane. You don't want to deal with their shenanigans."

"I'll consider myself warned." I claim a seat in the second row. The window seat.

Ha. Men don't like middle seats, so no one will sit next to me.

Just try, motherfuckers. Try.

"And mum's the word on the new names," Oliver whispers from the aisle.

I mime zipping my lips. "I'm a vault," I say as I toss my imaginary key away.

As he grabs a spot in the third row, I settle in,

busying myself with my phone and the latest pick for Trina's book club that we'll discuss when I return. It's a small-town romance set at a lavender farm, and the blurb promises the couple will bang in the bushes. Bring it on, bangathon.

I'm no less than ten seconds into the heroine learning the handyman she's been daydreaming of is actually the farm owner when a big man is parking his ass next to me.

I groan privately. But when I look up, I give a genuine smile. "Hi, Dev."

"Not gonna miss my chance to bond with Blob."

I close the chapter on my phone. "Yes, team bonding with the mascot is sooo important." I arch a skeptical brow. "Ryker sent you, didn't he?"

Dev feigns shock. "Why would you think that?" He gives me a conspiratorial wink and I laugh. "Seriously, how's the new gig treating you? Are any of the guys being jerks?"

"Ryker definitely sent you."

"Of course he did."

"So why do you assume they'd be jerks?"

He scoffs. "Because I know pro athletes."

"Are you a jerk? Is Ryker a jerk?" I counter.

Dev hums as if weighing the question. "I plead the fifth...So, is anyone being a dick?"

Stefan strides past the galley and into the aisle with Hayes right behind him. Hayes is wearing the hell out of a slate-blue suit that's just a touch tight in the arms. Stefan's is a dark gray, the color of a stormy sky, and it makes his blue eyes look even brighter. I swear whoever made the rule about pro athletes wearing suits when they travel did not have to endure the view. I fight the urge to undress both of them with my eyes and focus on answering Dev's question. "Gentlemen all around," I say.

Stefan must have heard me. He stops at our row, scans behind him, then up ahead. "Nope. No gentlemen in sight," he says, lifting his cup of coffee like he's toasting to his own brand of trouble as he meets my gaze and holds it. My pulse skips one beat and then another when Hayes shoots me a knowing grin.

"Especially not the guy you're talking to," Stefan adds, eyeing Dev.

Dev raises his middle finger above his head, not even looking Stefan's way.

"Aww, it's Dev's love language," Stefan says.

"It's my *only* language," Dev adds.

But Dev's a lover, not a fighter. Goalies don't fight often, after all. Plus, he's a fun guy, so I know he's just teasing.

Hayes is quiet through the exchange, his expression more serious. I get that—it's his first flight with his new team. He probably just wants to blend in.

Dev stands and stretches. "All right. Don't cause any trouble for Ivy or I'll have Ryker after my head. That goes for you, Viking. And for *Hey You*."

"Will do," Hayes says, taking Dev seriously. Stefan just laughs.

Mayday! Where is Dev going? He was supposed to be my goalie.

"Enjoy the tenth row, aisle seat," Stefan says to him.

Hayes lifts a brow. "He's superstitious?"

"Like you've never seen before," Stefan says, then shrugs. "But I'm not."

Stefan drops down into the aisle seat. Well, someone is staking his claim on me. Hayes gives a chin nod. As the new guy, I doubt he wants to get into a seat scuffle. But Stefan pats the middle seat for Hayes.

The taller man scoffs. "I'll find an aisle."

I roll my eyes, unbuckle, and stand up. "I'll take the middle."

I'm a regular girl, after all, and I don't want Hayes to feel uncomfortable.

Hayes's lips curve up. "Yeah?"

"I don't mind," I say.

I don't want to be rude and leave. What reason would I give anyway? *The two of you give off hungry wolf vibes and I want to be your prey, so I need to run to the back of the plane to avoid your dirty, flirty gazes.*

The flight's only about an hour.

I can handle the tension. Because it's just that— tension. Hayes has already made it clear that we'd be a bad idea. Stefan seems more persistent but does that matter?

Besides the obvious problems with anything more than flirtation when we all work together, I don't trust my judgment with men. My dad had treated my mom badly, and I'd missed the same signs in Xander. Even before he cheated on me, Xander didn't value me or appreciate my attempts to include him in my life. But I didn't see his critical comments for the put-downs they were. I foolishly thought he was being constructive and encouraging when, really, he was judging me and undermining my confidence.

My throat tightens. I liked him so much when we were together. Without my rose-colored glasses, I see the flaws in my judgment. It strengthens my resolve.

I can handle lust when I remember I'm not getting involved with either of these guys, so sitting with them is no big deal.

"Off we go to the city of sin," I say, making small talk. "Will you play the penny slots in your free time, Stefan? Bet it all on black, Hayes?"

Hayes dips his face, smiles softly. "I'd definitely bet it all. I love to gamble, more than I should."

"What about you, Ivy?" Stefan asks after he takes a drink of his coffee. "What's your Vegas poison? Black-jack? A show? A roller-coaster ride? Late-night clubbing?"

I tap my chin as if considering. "You left out staying in and ordering room service."

Hayes chuckles. Stefan scoffs.

"What? You don't believe me?" I look from one to the other.

Stefan tilts his face and locks eyes with me, holding my gaze. "I'm calling your bluff," he says in a smoky voice that makes my insides melt a little.

I fight back against these feelings, sitting up straighter, trying to keep my cool. "Fine. What do you think I like to do?"

But Stefan doesn't answer. He looks *around* me at

Hayes, tipping his forehead to his teammate. "What do you think?"

With a soft hum, Hayes tilts his face toward me, studying my expression. He takes his time roaming those soulful brown eyes over me, like he's undressing me, body and mind. It's sexual and also…knowing. Like he's both looking at me and wanting me. It's unnerving, but in an exciting way. Warmth flows through my veins. My chest swoops with each second his eyes linger on me. And everything feels a little fizzy, a little…hazy. Like I'm caught in a mirage between two men.

"I bet she'd like a show," Hayes says, as if he knows my secrets.

And really, he does.

But only some of them.

I have other secrets now. Like this one—I'm attracted to two men at the same time, and I don't think either one of them is bothered by that.

Especially when Stefan says, "Is that so, Ivy? Would you like that?"

My shoulders rise and fall. My breath comes faster. What are they doing to me? Is this on purpose? Are they flirting with me? Toying with me? Is this just how they are? Are they just the type of guys who exude sensuality like it's their cologne?

Suddenly, this middle seat feels smaller than it was before. One shoulder brushes against Hayes; the other is pressed against Stefan. I'm sandwiched between them—and something sparks in my chest, the start of a sizzle.

I swallow, look to Stefan, turn to Hayes, then at last

answer them with a shot of courage. "I guess you'll have to find out."

I close my eyes as if I have the upper hand when really, I'm just treading water, trying to get control of my heart that's beating far too fast.

Normally, the team flies in and out quickly to nearby cities, but since they're doing a charity breakfast tomorrow morning for a youth hockey organization the Avengers and the Sabers both support, everyone is staying overnight. I don't have to go to the breakfast, but I still get to stay since I'm traveling on the team jet. Which means I get time to myself in the morning. Translation: I'll wake up early and work on content and chasing freelance gigs.

After I check into The Extravagant hotel later that morning, I cruise through the casino on the way to the elevator, rolling my bag behind me, running through the PR stunt the Vegas team wants me to pull off tonight. It's not hard, and I'll have time to practice it, but I'm a little lost in my head when a pretty voice hits my ears with its Texas drawl.

"If it isn't the Scrappy Little Fashionista?"

The team owner knows my handle? I stop and turn around to say hello to the towering and powerful Jessie Rose. "Hi, Ms. Rose."

"Good to see you, Ivy," she says, then, wincing, she gestures to her red-soled shoes. "Personally, my Louboutins make me feel strong, but boy, do these suckers hurt. But what's a gal to do when she needs some power pumps?"

"Actually, I have some ideas," I say as a Star Trek slot machine next to us disappoints a man in a Hawaiian shirt.

Her deep brown eyes sparkle with interest. "Do tell."

"Lily Greer," I whisper, passing on the name like it's a secret. "She makes seriously comfy alternatives that look just as good."

Jessie looks like I just gave her the Holy Grail. "Where do I find these ruby slippers?"

"Online. I'll send you some links."

"Today, please," she says, a clear order. Then, she gives me a quick appraisal, eyes landing on my leopard print top. "Hmm. Leopards? Do I want leopards as a possible team name?"

"Leopards are pretty amazing hunters. Very stealthy," I say. "Plus, it'd be a cute mascot costume."

"That is true," she says, humming thoughtfully as if she'll consider it. But before she goes, she lifts a finger, like she's just remembered something. "By the way, your brother and his partners are coming to my golf event in a few weeks. They'll be seated at my table. I've just loved watching their love story unfold."

That warms my heart. "Thanks for letting me know and being so supportive."

"Of course," Jessie says, like there's no other way to be.

When I'm up in my room a few minutes later, I send

the team owner—the freaking team owner!—shoe suggestions.

With that done, I sit on the bed, grab my laptop, and use the next hour I have free to write for my newsletter about the best alternatives for established brands.

That calms me. I know fashion. I give good fashion tips. I'll keep doing this and building my name, and I'll move on from the Simone and Xander fiasco. I'll use their wedding to grow my name, that's all.

I quickly check my email and speak of the devil. There's one from Xander, and one from Simone. Their wedding is key to my career goals. With a pit in my stomach, I open his first.

Simone told me you're covering our wedding. I'm seriously proud of you! What an opportunity! You'll do great!

I stare at it like it's a message from a Martian. Who says those things? With so many exclamation points too. He's proud of me for landing this prestige assignment by quitting?

I keep reading.

Maybe we can meet up soon, and I can tell you about some of my new business ventures?

Ohhhh. Of course. His email makes sense now. He wants me to mention his new ventures in their wedding coverage.

And the ick gets ickier. While I'm crawling with it, I

click on a reply from Simone to my dress code query. *Dress code is festive,* she writes. *Can't wait to share more details when we meet soon!*

I don't actually want to read more about my ex-boss and my ex-boyfriend right now. I'll come back to these later. I'm about to close out and get ready to head to the Sabers arena when I spot a new email.

Oh! It's from one of the editors I wrote to.

The editor.

It's from Birdie Michaels. She runs *Your Runway*, a popular site about adapting fashion trends and making them work for you. Holding my breath, I open it.

Dear Ivy,

Your pieces are sharp. Can you get me a story about the top five new looks in sustainable fashion by Wednesday?

Birdie

I light up like a neon sign on the Strip as I reply with a most enthusiastic yes. I text Trina and Aubrey and tell them the good news. I've been obsessed with her site for months. Their replies are bursting with exclamation points. I'm in the best of moods when I change and head to the Las Vegas Sabers arena.

* * *

Several hours later, the Avengers are winning, and I am tripping. And falling. And flailing.

All on purpose.

Good thing I wore knee pads under Blob. As circus music plays, I crawl along the ice in my purple costume, heart pounding as the Vegas tiger mascot skates circles around me on one leg, his other furry leg sticking out behind him.

The tiger looks all tough and tiger smooth while I look like, well, like a bulky letter A about to get demolished. But at the last minute, I comically—or so I hope—scramble to my feet and awkwardly—also on cue—rush off the ice with the tiger chasing me like I'm his last meal.

I finally make it to the tunnel, arms flapping, the crowd booing me off. Then, their mascot thrusts his orange and black striped arms in the air and glides around the oval, whipping up the home crowd.

I'm panting as I "escape," finding Oliver, who high-fives me, palm to paw. "Good job," he says.

The crowd loves it.

But it doesn't do the trick of riling up the home team, since we destroy them.

Ha! Take that, tiger.

One of the guys I sat next to on the plane scored a goal. So did the other. I'm especially ecstatic for Hayes, since he wants to prove himself, but I'm thrilled for Stefan too, which is a new feeling. I've been to countless

Avengers games over the last few years, rooting for my brother's team, and I've witnessed plenty of Stefan's goals. But the goal the captain scored tonight gave me a little zing, especially since it came right after Hayes's goal, and I was already on a high. It became a double high.

Or maybe a triple high since I'm still giddy about the *Your Runway* assignment. But there's nothing to do with these feelings but bottle them up.

After the media session, I've packed up my costume and given it to the equipment manager, and I'm ready to flop down on my big bed in my hotel room. On my way down the corridor to the exit, I spot Hayes and Stefan.

They're huddling by the corner, dressed impeccably in their suits once again, and I wish Hayes and Stefan didn't look so good.

But...suits.

They aren't alone. They're with Dev and Brady. A woman with sleek black hair stands next to Brady. She's sporting a matching ring.

"It's Blob!" Dev calls out, even though I'm two feet in front of him. "We're taking New Guy out to celebrate."

He grips Hayes's shoulder, like *atta boy*.

This is promising. I glance at Hayes. "New nickname?"

My wedding date shrugs, like it's no big deal. But there's the start of a smile on his face because it *is* a big deal. He's moving beyond his first nickname, and that's huge. He doesn't answer, though, and I understand not wanting to jeopardize the fragile shift in status with the team.

Stefan nods, then points at me. "Yup. And since you're the new guy, too, you're coming with us."

Wait. What? They want me to go with them?

"Captain's orders," Dev seconds in a tone that brooks no argument.

"Please come," the woman next to Brady pipes in. "Then I won't be the only estrogen there." After a quick pause, she extends a hand. "I'm Kana. Brady's wife."

"Nice to meet you, Kana," I say, but don't yet commit to being the additional woman.

I look to Stefan first. He leans against the concrete wall of the corridor, all laid-back and easygoing like he's just waiting for my yes or my no. But his blue eyes glint with something like...hope? Or maybe that's opportunity flashing in his irises?

For a few seconds, I'm sure he's up to something. Like "Captain's orders" means he wants to give...*other* orders. The kind he might give in the bedroom.

My stomach swoops, and a low, tender ache deep inside grows more insistent. I feel wobbly. Uncertain. But strangely excited too. I turn my attention to Hayes, hunting for confirmation in his eyes. Are there new guy orders, too, with this big group of hockey players and a wife? But Hayes's expression is unreadable.

It's up to me. Yes, I'm trying to avoid trouble of the man variety and that goes double for the double man variety.

I swallow, buying some time to figure out if I want

to do this—hang out with two tempting men I work with. I mean, *yeah*. I really do.

It's been a good day. I'm amped up from the good news about the writing assignment, and a night out feels like a reward rather than a pre-ward.

Plus, Dev, Brady, and Kana will be there as a buffer.

When in Vegas... "Let's do it," I say.

13

BIRTHDAY SUITS

Hayes

"And then I scored a goal buck naked." Stefan plunks his glass down on the wood table with tequila-fueled bravado as he finishes his tale.

It's nearing eleven, and we're in a corner booth at The Winning Hand off the Strip. Stefan says it's his favorite off-the-beaten-path bar in this city and claims no one will recognize his *handsome face* here—his words.

He's just told us the story of his wildest dare. One I don't believe. I shake my head since I know this guy. "Nope. You did not. No fucking way you skated naked at your hometown rink at the end of your first season."

Brady and Kana are playing pool in the other room. But Dev's here with us. Ivy too. She's on my side, shooting the captain an *are you sure about that* stare. "I'm with New Guy. I don't buy it," Ivy says.

Stefan scoffs, holding up his hands like he has nothing to hide? "I don't back down from a dare."

"You hardly back down from anything," I say.

"That is true," he agrees, looking from me to Ivy with a grin that's not quite private. Then he picks up his water glass and polishes it off—we switched from Patron to H2O an hour ago.

I've got a damn good feeling what Stefan's up to. Have sensed it for a few days now. I just didn't want to face it. I've kept my head down and pretended like I haven't noticed his...machinations.

But the moment he said, *"Multitudes, Ivy,"* on the rooftop, I had a hunch. On the plane ride when he asked what she liked to do in Vegas then threw the question to me, I was certain.

There's little Stefan loves more than orchestrating a good time. He arranged our first threesome after we won the Frozen Four his senior and my freshman year. We were celebrating our win at a party and had both been chatting with the same pretty blonde when Stefan pulled me aside. I figured he was going to call dibs. But instead, he said, *I know we're both into her, and I have an idea.*

His idea turned into the hottest night of my life.

Once I put two and two together on the rooftop, I knew the puppeteer had come out to play again. But I've said nothing for a few days. Mostly because I don't want to face the reality of this wild desire to have Ivy all to myself, or to ourselves. Sharing a woman was one thing when Stefan and I were teammates in college, and then when I first started in the pros, but this situation is different. She works with us. I don't want to mess things up for her, especially considering what happened to the last mascot.

Every time I think about it, there's this too tight feeling in my chest. A sense that one wrong move and everything could snap, like elevator cables under too much load.

I should ignore all these feelings, but Ivy's too tempting. The possibility that she *might* want both of us is addictive. And dangerous. I need to stay away, yet here I am, my mind swirling with possibilities I should not entertain.

One night in Vegas. No holds barred. Driving her wild. Giving her what I suspect she wants—to be overwhelmed with wicked pleasure.

What's the harm?

What happens in Vegas...

I force myself to focus on the group and Stefan's tale of naked skating, not on my dirty fantasies of naked Ivy.

Dev stabs his index finger against the table, meeting Stefan's gaze head-on. "Let me get this straight. Your Danish buddy says he doubts you have the balls to skate naked and the next thing you're free-balling on the ice in Copenhagen? Because a friend back home said you wouldn't?"

"It was a rink, not a lake," Stefan says offhand.

I shudder at the mental image, just like when he told the story. "Do you have a dick death wish?"

His lips crook up. "My dick and I are very attached, and I take excellent care of him."

Ivy snort-laughs, then raises her glass of water in the air. "To dick care."

"I'll drink to that," Stefan says.

Ivy considers the topic while country music plays overhead, a tune about a guy who lost his pickup truck. "It's important because proper dick care leads to pretty dicks."

Dev spits out his beer. "Dicks aren't pretty."

"Maybe you haven't seen the right dicks." Briefly she casts her gaze my way, a bit of flirt in her voice.

Is she thinking about the night I met her, when she watched me on the rooftop? That look in her eyes heats my blood.

Ivy takes a drink, then adds, "But dick aesthetics aside, I still think Stefan's story is highly suspicious."

The team captain parks his elbows on the table and deals her a hard glare. "Don't make me show you all the pics."

He's playing to win, upping the ante tonight, and I don't have it in me to stop him. It's too fun to watch him move chess pieces around.

Normally, I wouldn't think a naked skating story would be a come-on. But I have a hunch he's not leading with the goods but with his gusto. That's his style. Me? I'm subtler. A flirty word. A dirty look. It's our one-two punch.

Except...nope.

I'm not hitting on her tonight. I'm not pitching her on a threesome, especially with Dev here and with Kana and Brady in the next room. I'm just celebrating.

Ivy sets down her glass, shooting Stefan a dubious look. "Pics? Now I *have* to call your bluff."

"Well, I had socks on. I don't put on skates without socks," Stefan says, stretching his arms out across the back of the booth. "And yes, I have pics. My buddies took them." He grabs for his phone in his back pocket.

Dev laughs, shaking his head. "No one wants to see that much of your naked ass."

But it's too late. Stefan scrolls and then slaps down his phone, and...*oh shit.* That's some birthday suit on skates. I jerk back, covering my eyes. "Dude."

Ivy blinks. "Holy shit."

Dev drops his jaw. "Whoa."

Stefan smiles smugly. "Thank you." Picking up his phone, he regards the photos like an art appraiser. "It is a pretty dick, come to think of it."

I crack up. "That was not a dick compliment. I can't believe you carry that pic."

"I can't believe you showed it to us," Dev seconds.

"I can't believe you took the dare," Ivy puts in, each of us in escalating disbelief.

"Pictures don't lie," Stefan says, then shoots me a stern stare. "And since you doubted me, you can pick up the check here. I'm ready for a change of scenery."

Dev nods, big and long. "When you score an assist in one game and a goal in the other two, you gotta treat the vets, Hayes."

"No problem."

I don't mind footing the bill, especially considering what Dev just called me. I've gone from *Hey You* to *New Guy* to my name in one day with him, and he's the kind of athlete who sets the tone with the team. I'm glad, too, that I didn't need my longtime friend to be my cheer-leader. My skills led the way to this first sign of...acceptance.

I rein in a grin so it's not obvious to everyone that I'm stoked. I reach for my wallet and raise a hand for a server. When a man wearing an apron and sporting a goatee signals from a few booths away that he'll be right with us, I turn back to the guys across from us.

There's a gleam in Dev's eyes I can't read. He shifts his gaze to Stefan, but Stefan looks away, like he's delib-erately ignoring Dev.

Hmm. Not sure what's going on with them, if anything. But maybe the liquor's messing with my head. When the server comes by, I hand him my credit card and tell him we'll take the check.

"All right. I'll be right back with that," the server says and once he leaves, Stefan's phone buzzes. *The Great Dane* flashes across the screen.

He instantly switches to serious business owner mode. "I need to take this."

When he scoots out of the booth and heads off, Dev slides out a few seconds later. "Gotta call my girl."

They head in opposite directions, leaving Ivy and me to keep the table warm. She sighs happily then runs a hand through her lush hair. Turning her face to me again, she's all glowy, her smile soft and a little tipsy, but not much. She had two shots to my three. I don't like drinking more than that. Don't like feeling out of control. Also, working out the next day with a hangover is the worst.

"So, is this your Vegas poison?" I ask, circling back to the plane convo. "Hanging out?"

"Maybe it is," she says.

"Or do you still want to see a show?" I give her a long, lingering look. She's wearing jeans that hug her legs and a crocheted sweater with a red tank top under it. Mostly, though, it's her mouth and her eyes that I can't stop gazing at. Her lips are perfection, and I'm dying to know how they taste. The remnants of this tequila haze make me want her even more.

She twirls a strand of hair. "What kind of show?"

The thing is—I think she might want to *be* the show. "An after-hours one," I say, since this night has loosened some of my resolve. I'm not even sure what I want to have happen. I just don't want this evening to end.

But rather than answer, she sidesteps. "Do you like it with the Avengers so far?"

I follow her changeup easily. "It's only been three games, but yes, I do like it so far." I feel a little vulnerable with that admission but also like I can trust her with it.

"Three games to no nickname."

"You noticed that." Her candy-berry scent swirls around my head.

"And I noticed you liked it."

Heat sparks higher in me. "You have to stop noticing things about me," I say, feel-good endorphins flowing through me, making me want to wrap her in my arms and kiss the breath out of her and then fuck her senseless.

Those are things I shouldn't think. And yet, these dangerous ideas have me in a chokehold tonight. My dirty train of thought is only stopped by the goateed server, who I see heading our way now with the bill and some refills on the water.

He sets down the glasses with a cheery grin. "Here you go. And good luck for the rest of your stay."

When he leaves, I look around for the guys but lose interest in their whereabouts real quick when Ivy stretches, her chest rising and falling, her top pulling across her tits, the outline of a barbell teasing me. My resistance crumbles a little more.

I lean closer. "You have a piercing."

"Do I?"

"Do you?" I counter.

Before she can answer me, someone clears his throat. "New plan." It's Dev, and he's returned. Brady is next to him, sporting a grin. Kana looks like she's stifling a laugh. Stefan's not here though.

I sit up ramrod straight, jerking away from Ivy. "We were just—"

Dev adopts the biggest grin in the world. "So we have this tradition with the new guy, Hayes. You can't escape it. It's a rite of passage." He takes a beat, then, like he has a winning hand, he says, "You need to get married."

14

OFFICIALLY FUCKED

Stefan

When I return to the table, my head pops. Are they pulling this prank again?

All my best laid plans go down the drain with this idea. I was hoping to call it a night soon, then take Ivy and Hayes to the Rapture club back at The Extravagant. Indulge in some music, dim lights, and a seductive vibe, then pitch her on a night together with us taking care of her every after-dark desire. Here in Vegas would work for me. A night back in San Francisco would work too.

I had it all planned out solo—what to say in this proposal of sorts. I didn't ask Hayes in advance because I didn't want to come at Ivy with a full court press.

I had originally hoped to take them out after the game, but Dev and Brady roped me into drinks, and I couldn't say no to a couple shots with the team. But no way was I leaving Ivy behind. I insisted she come with us so I could keep her by my side until I could engineer a way out for the three of us.

Instead, I've walked back into the double-dog-dare shitshow.

Why did Yasmine have to call on a Friday night at eleven o' clock to ask about an unusual ticket? Why did I spend so much time talking to her and pacing outside The Winning Hand? I could have prevented this. But now, Dev and Brady and Kana are showing them *the pictures.*

"Did you see this?" Hayes asks skeptically as he points to Dev's phone. I sit down across from him, glancing at the shot of Dev and his girlfriend at the chapel down the street. A year ago, I'd issued the dare to Dev, who'd signed with the team in a mid-season trade the season before.

"Wait. I thought she was your girlfriend, not your wife?" Ivy asks Dev with a raised brow. She doesn't miss anything. *Please let her catch them on this.* A wedding will take hours. "You just called her."

With a *no shit* grin, Dev stabs a finger at the screen. "Yeah. Eva and I got married on a dare last year, then got it annulled, and, well, I'll probably ask her to marry me for real really fucking soon."

Great. He makes it all sound so plausible.

Brady clears his throat, waggling his phone and his pic. "Kana and I tied the knot here too," he says, then swings the screen around to a shot of him and Mrs. Clampett kissing in the same chapel.

Huh. I don't remember that one. But not my place to narc.

Hayes drags a hand across his chin like he's trying to make heads and tails of the dare. "So, how does this work? You get married, then have it annulled in the morning?"

"It's Vegas married," Brady says. "Tomorrow before the breakfast, you call it off. Or after, whatevs. It's fun. Just like the night we did it. "

Kana laughs then smacks a kiss to his cheek. "And I'd marry you in Vegas all over again."

Hayes's brow furrows. He's not quite buying their story, but he's not ready to back down either. He grabs one of the glasses the server left and knocks some water back. This night is a wash. Might as well just go along with the dare now. "Hayes, the record is an hour," I say, giving in. "I dare you to beat it."

"What record?"

Maybe I can move things along though. "The record for finding a woman here in Vegas to marry you," I add dryly.

"The marriage license bureau closes in one hour," Dev says. "Get cracking. You need to find a wife, stat."

Ivy rolls her eyes, then raises her hand. "I'll do it."

That's it. My plans are officially fucked.

15

FOOLS RUSH IN

Hayes

An hour later, I've got a marriage license in my hand, and we're in the foyer of a white roadside chapel while an Elvis impersonator runs my credit card. "Now, you be sure to tie that tie, son. You need to look real pretty for your bride," he says to me in that King-like drawl.

I glance down at my emerald-green post-game tie. It's a hot mess. Guess I was tugging on it all night at the bar.

I move to tighten it when Ivy reaches for the silk. "I'll fix my man's tie."

Those words—*my man*—go to my head. Hell, they go to my dick. I want to hear her say them after dark, when we're alone, when she's gazing up at me from the floor on her knees. I shake off that filthy thought. Don't need a bowling pin in my pants when I say *I do* on a dare.

Why did I agree to this Vegas wedding? Well, you don't back down from a dare from your new team-mates, that's why. Sure, I've only been with the Avengers for a few weeks, but already I'm feeling like I'm a part of them, like I've wanted to be since I was called up four years ago to Toronto. Like I've hoped to be on all the other teams I played for.

And hell, Ivy offered. As she adjusts my tie, she says, "You're my wedding date. The least I could do is return the favor and be your wedding date."

"At my own wedding," I say, amused.

As her nimble hands adjust the knot, she meets my gaze, but something's different in her expression. I study her for a beat, then I figure it out. "Your lips are red," I say stupidly. I can't stop looking at those slick, plump lips.

"I reapplied lipstick. You like?"

I want to kiss it off with my mouth. I want to wipe it off with my cock. I want to mess it up in every single filthy way. "Ask me in a few minutes," I say.

Elvis clears his throat. "A bouquet for your bride would be nice," he says, then reaches for some red roses on a mirrored table and hands them to her.

"Thanks, King," she says.

"Anything for you, sweetheart," he says, out of the side of his mouth.

Three minutes later, I join my teammates at the front of the tiny chapel, where Dev is nudging Stefan, and Stefan is nudging Brady, and they're saying something about how I'm a gamer, and there's nothing I've wanted to be more.

Elvis stands at the front of the chapel, decked out in his white sequined suit, big sideburns, and thick glasses. Next to him, a showgirl twirls a feather boa.

Kana strides in, playing the temporary maid of honor. Brady wolf whistles at his wife as she walks. When she reaches us, the music starts. It's not the wedding march.

It's Elvis himself crooning "Can't Help Falling in Love" and it's coming from a giant jukebox in the corner. As soon as the King warbles about fools rushing in, Ivy comes through the doorway.

Holy fuck.

She changed.

She's not wearing her jeans and that crocheted top she had on post-game. A white dress is tied at her neck and clings to her curves, teasing me with the swells of her breasts. The skirt is swingy, the fabric satiny. She looks prettier than she did the night I met her in the elevator, and that's saying something.

Next to me, Stefan lets out a soft *wow*.

I seize the chance for us to admire her together, something I fucking love doing. I lean closer to him. "I know, right?"

"She's gorgeous," he whispers. "Those fiery eyes."

"Those lush lips," I say, and a tension I wasn't even aware I was carrying lessens. This is our first spoken admission of the shared attraction, and while I knew he felt it, it's freeing to voice it to him.

"And her hair," he mutters, just for me. "Think she'd like it wrapped around my fist?"

"While I tell her how good she looks when I smack her ass," I add.

We're a chorus of praise for my temporary bride as she walks down the aisle. But also, I can't miss how my pulse spikes as the King sings about whether it'd be a sin to fall in love.

That won't be happening.

No room in my life for that. No way. But right now, as Ivy strides toward me, I'm having a hard time remembering why I'm supposed to resist her. Don't want to resist her tonight.

Stefan doesn't seem to want to either since he lets out a rumble of appreciation, unbidden it seems. I relax even more. At least I don't need to keep this secret. I *like* admiring a woman with him. It's risqué in ways I crave.

"How badly do you want her?" I whisper to him.

"More than anything," he says.

"Me too."

When Ivy reaches me, she's smiling—a warm, sweet glow that's part the memory of tequila and part laughter. She glances around like she isn't sure what to do with the flowers. Kana reaches for them. "I'll hold them, hun."

Ivy hastily thrusts the flowers at her and the music fades away.

"Dearly beloved, we are gathered here this evening..." the Elvis impersonator begins the affair, reciting a script he's no doubt performed hundreds of times before.

One minute later, he's saying to me, "Do you take this woman to be your wife?"

For a moment, I pause, considering my actions. I squint, picturing the photos the others showed us at the bar. Did they really get married or are they putting me on? Hmm. I have a feeling. But it doesn't matter. One look at Ivy and those red lips, and I make my choice. We'll untie the knot in the morning. "I do."

"And do you take this man to be your husband?"

Ivy grins. "When in Vegas, I do."

Dev hands me the ring, and I slide it on Ivy's left hand. Brady gives her one, and she puts it on my finger. I stare at my hand like it belongs to someone else. But when Elvis declares, "You may kiss the bride," *that*—a kiss—belongs to me.

That mouth. This woman. Those lips. This will be so fucking worth it. Anticipation grips me hard. Kana's been snapping pics and she gets one right before I lean in to kiss Ivy.

But before my lips touch hers, the chorus to "Hound Dog" blasts at a million obnoxious decibels, and we're all rubbing our ears and begging the King to turn off his phone.

"My bad, my bad!" The King holds up his hands in apology, sliding into a Jersey accent that's totally incongruous with his outfit. "Just an alarm that I have another wedding in ten minutes."

And that's that. My teammates are already moving onto the next thing. Dev's hooting and wrapping an arm around Stefan. "Let's get tacos," Dev says. "There's a place nearby that's still open. Meet us there after you get your paperwork and shit. I'll text you. And send me those pics, Kana."

"Count on it," she says.

"Your wife is the best, Brady," Dev says to our team-mate, then to the officiant, he adds, "And you're the man, King."

"Anytime," Elvis says, returning to his drawl once more, then Dev steers everyone out of the chapel. For a second, Stefan looks back at Ivy and me, longing in his eyes, before he goes.

Elvis taps his watch. "I've got another one to perform in ten minutes. You can sign the certificate, but first why don't you help her out of that dress and give it back to me?"

Well, that's not a bad idea.

Elvis exits, leaving Ivy and me alone in the chapel. She gestures to the white dress. "They had costumes, so I changed," she says, then spins around and heads to the door.

That won't do. Fueled by dares and desire, I stalk over to her and grab her hand, jerking her around so she's nearly flush against me. "Where are you going?"

"To change," she says with a pinched brow, like why would I ask?

I shake my head. "Not until I kiss my wife."

16

EYES ON US

Ivy

His eyes glimmer darkly. His jaw is set hard. He smells like lust and power.

A prickle of fear slides down my spine from the way he stares at me with such possession. I feel like borderline prey. And the strange thing—the new thing—is I like it.

"Take it," I whisper.

Let him figure out that I want him to punish my mouth. To claim my kiss.

He reads my wish, yanking me flush against him. He's not soft or sweet. He's not tender or gentle. There's something almost mean in his eyes, and it makes my heart beat faster.

My gaze slides briefly to the door, looking, wondering if Stefan's coming back. But I stop wondering when Hayes grabs my face firmly then ropes his other arm around my waist and grabs my ass. I gasp, but he shuts me up with one hard kiss. I stop thinking about the other guy.

Hayes's lips crush mine. They're demanding, determined, and I'm all too pliant under his touch.

His kiss is rough and greedy. A man with hard edges. He backs me up against the wall by the door. This is where I want to be. Pinned by him, like I was that day in the equipment room, when he gave me a hint of what he'd be like.

In charge.

Is that what I've been craving all along? Someone who kisses my mouth ruthlessly? Someone who grips my face like this? Someone who treats my body like it's his to play with?

This isn't how you kiss the bride. This is how you kiss a woman you want to pin down, tie up, and fuck.

There's just one more thing I want...

I look to the door again, but my brain goes blurry as Hayes devours my mouth mercilessly, his strong arms keeping me in place, his stubble likely leaving whisker burn. I can't move, and I don't want to. Not as his tongue plunders my mouth. Not as he lets go of his grip on my ass to wander a hand up my body. Not as the creak of a door oh-so-faintly registers in my mind. Hayes dives in and delivers more carnal kisses until we're panting and gasping for air. I'm so aroused I can barely think about the sound of the lock slipping into place.

But somewhere in my mind, a voice tells me to pay attention.

My eyes float open, and I feel like a bunny spotted by a wolf in the woods at night. My pulse soars as my gaze locks with Stefan's. His blue eyes aren't icy now. They're fire. His lips part as he stares at me.

This is what I want.

"I dropped my key card for my room," Stefan says, but there's no apology or shame in his voice.

Hayes barely pulls back from me. "How convenient," he deadpans against the skin of my neck as Stefan strolls down the aisle, turning away from me.

Is that all Stefan's here for? He's not even looking at me as Hayes dives back in, kissing my neck more, dragging his scruffy jaw against my skin deliciously. My pulse rockets with unchecked need as I watch Stefan walk—the cut of his shoulders in his dress shirt that stretches across his broad back, the shape of his ass, strong, rounded, and so damn muscular it should be illegal.

Most of all, his attitude.

Like it's no big deal to walk in on us. Desire coils in my chest, travels down my belly, then settles between my thighs in a sweet ache. Even as Hayes slides a hand down my arm, I'm watching Stefan while he grabs his card from the floor and turns around.

The smile he sends me is pure gamesmanship.

"Don't stop on my account," Stefan remarks with a casual shrug. "I'm here for the show."

My breath hitches. Yes. Yes. Fucking yes.

A wicked light shines in Hayes's eyes. "You want that, Ivy? You want to give him a show?" He tucks a strand of hair behind my ear.

I'm afraid to speak. Afraid if I use words this wild, daring moment will crumble. I just nod.

But that's not enough for Hayes. He grabs me tighter, rougher. He likes to manhandle me, and I think I love it. "Say it, or I'll tell him to get the fuck out."

His command thrills me. I want to obey.

"Watch us." Locking eyes with Stefan once again, I add, "Watch me."

He grabs a chair from the altar, spins it around and straddles it, parking his elbows on the back, his gaze rolling over me like a heat wave. He flicks a hand at his friend. "Kiss her again, Hayes."

Holy shit. He's telling Hayes what to do. A crackle of electricity roars through me. But Hayes doesn't kiss me. He regards me with firm, clear eyes. "Are you drunk?"

Only on the heady feeling of the two of them. I shake my head. "Not even tipsy." I married him on a dare, not a drink. My buzz has faded. "You?"

"Same," he says, then runs his knuckles against my cheek. "You want this?"

Like I've never wanted anything before. But I learned all sorts of things about myself as they've circled me this past week. And now, tonight as they've cornered me.

I've learned I like to play too.

With a tease of a smile, I say, "Find out."

He slides his hand down my cheek, over my jaw, curling his palm against my throat. He's not grabbing me. But he is holding me firmly.

He draws a deep breath, cranes his neck to the door where Elvis walked out, then turns back, his eyes roaming up and down me. "There's another wedding in five minutes," he says, and it's not an equivocation. It's the stakes.

"Better get on with it, Hayes," Stefan says, all laid-back and casual. "The woman needs to come, and she needs to come fast."

Letting go of my neck, Hayes sets to work, tugs up the fabric of my skirt, then slides a hand across the panel of my panties. My hips tilt. I need more. The look on his handsome face is pure devil. "But you're so wet, I bet it won't even take me that long."

"You're confident," I taunt, but I'm at the mercy of his touch and he knows it. I'm at the mercy of their words.

"You testing us?" Hayes demands as he pinches my clit.

Us. I get wetter as he says that. "Yes," I say, my voice wobbly from the sharp sting of pleasure.

"Put her hands up against the wall," Stefan commands from several feet away.

I don't even know how I'm standing, especially when Hayes says to Stefan, "Why don't you do it?"

I'm giddy with anticipation as Stefan rises, heads over to me, grabs my hands, and lifts them over my head. Gripping my wrists together, he presses them to the wood behind me. In a chapel, after midnight, in the city of sin, he puts me in position to be finger fucked by his friend. But Hayes doesn't slide a hand into my panties right away. Instead, he grazes the side of my neck with his fingers, then coasts them over my throat, then travels to the top of my breasts.

Hayes has less than five minutes, but he's taking his sweet-ass time while Stefan gently pushes waves of hair from my neck and whispers in my ear, "Don't worry, sweetheart. He'll get you there." Stefan dusts a feather-light kiss to the shell of my ear before he lets go of my hands. "Just keep her hands up, Hayes. I need a better view."

While Hayes takes over, Stefan retreats to his chair, straddling it once more. My brain is scrambling, and I'm breathing hard as Hayes pins my wrists with one hand and uses the other to travel down my chest again, palming one breast this time.

With a glint in his eyes, he flicks the barbell through the fabric of my dress.

I moan. Or maybe I'm babbling. Whatever noises I can make, I'm making them as he pinches my piercing, his smile so full of swagger and something else too—a dirty kind of joy. Like a man opening a naughty gift left under the tree at Christmas.

"Bet her panties are soaked now," Stefan says with filthy delight.

"I should check," Hayes remarks, offhand, then slides thick, confident fingers into my panties and across my slickness. I groan, arching into him.

"She's so fucking turned on," Hayes tells his friend as he strokes my wet pussy.

With a salacious moan, I arch my back, rock into his hand.

"Do more of that," Stefan urges Hayes. "She likes it."

"Because she loves being watched," Hayes says, and I feel unlocked.

"I do," I say, closing my eyes as pleasure crashes over me.

"Nope," Stefan orders. "Eyes on us."

A shudder rolls through me as I open my eyes. I'm unsure where to look. Hayes? Stefan? I don't know what to do with this assault of pleasure. It's slamming into me everywhere. My mind, my body.

Hayes strokes me and I'm so slick, so close. My nerve endings fray and I'm dying for release. "Yes, that's it. You've hit the spot," Stefan says.

"You think so?"

"She's a fucking mess. It's beautiful. You want to come, sweetheart?" Stefan asks me.

"Yes," I beg.

"Hayes, finish her."

Hayes cocks his head, regards me like he's just not sure he's going to follow the captain's orders. "Not until you show me how well you take direction, Ivy."

Eager to please, desperate to come, I ask, "What do you want me to do?"

Hayes stares at my mouth, lips quirked in a cocky grin as he fucks me with his fingers till I'm panting again. He lets go of my wrists, grabs the end of his tie, and raises it to my mouth. "Bite down on this."

He shoves the silk between my lips all while he strokes my clit.

"Now, shut the fuck up and come like a good dirty girl," he says.

I bite down. The pleasure is so intense I'm afraid I can't keep my eyes open, but I want to watch...Stefan. His hands are curled around the back of the chair, his knuckles white, and his gaze locked on me. "That's right, sweetheart. Eyes on me when you come," Stefan says.

Hayes strokes faster, and I can't speak. I can only scream silently against the fabric, rocking into his talented hand, seeing stars as an orgasm seizes my body.

When my knees buckle, my temporary husband catches me, holds me steady, then gently takes the tie from my mouth. I tremble in his arms for long, delirious seconds, my world still spiraling away.

When at last I can focus, Hayes says, "To answer your question...I like your lipstick."

The man I married presses a tender kiss to my mouth. When he breaks it, he glances down at me. I'm a mess—the skirt of my dress hiked up, panties twisted, hair likely wild.

And my world's been upended by two men. But when I look around for the other one, he's gone.

17

MY WIFE

Hayes

Adrenaline's still buzzing under my skin, and my brain has zero real estate for anything but Ivy.

I need to grab a minute to take the temperature with her. That escalated quickly, skyrocketing from hungry kiss to wild tryst. I don't know if she's done anything like that before, if she's going to freak. But I give her some space to change, pacing in the foyer, back and forth for a minute or two, replaying the hottest five minutes of my life.

When she emerges, dressed in her own clothes again, she runs a hand breezily through her waves then says, "Should we get those tacos now?"

My Spidey senses tingle. She sounds too chipper.

Is she out of sorts because we work together and messed around? Or because the *three* of us messed around? I can't get a read on her.

We exit the chapel at a rapid clip, and I'm about to ask if she wants to talk when Brady rounds the corner. He holds out his arms, like he's been searching for us all night long. "There you are."

"We're here," Ivy says brightly. "Took me a few minutes to change."

"Taco shop's closed," Brady says, hanging his head. The lack of tacos is evidently the height of devastation. "But there's a ramen spot in The Extravagant, and Dev wants to go there, so our Lyft is on the way."

It's odd that he came back for us. Most dudes would just text and let you find your own ride. "Kana made me come look for you," he says, and that explains everything. He's here on a mission to collect us on behalf of the mom of the group. He hooks his thumb toward the end of the block. "You can join us."

I've no good reason to turn him down, so even though I want a moment with Ivy alone, I find myself piling into an SUV with Dev, Brady, Kana, Ivy, and Stefan.

She's in the third row, wedged between Stefan and me, but she fiddles with one earring, then the other, then the third one higher up her lobe. As Dev gabs about some Vegas fan who was talking shit to them on the street, Ivy keeps her gaze fixed on the road like the lights of Vegas are the height of fascination.

We turn onto the Strip and my gut churns. This is bad. She regrets it and I don't know why. But I can't let her stew alone. I inch closer. "Hey," I whisper, checking. "You okay?"

She nods, then pastes on a smile, jerking her head toward me in a quick glance. "Yes. Totally. Absolutely."

My heart sinks with a thud. Three yeses is the kiss of death.

Stefan turns to her and parts his lips to speak.

"—Boom! Eight a.m.," Dev shouts from the row in front of us, then twists around, waggling his phone as we swing past the Bellagio, its fountains arcing gracefully against the dark night. "Who fucking loves you, Armstrong? Got you an appointment."

I furrow my brow. "For what?"

"For your annulment. C'mon, man. Keep up with us," Brady puts in.

Oh, wow. Right. I'm kind of touched they scheduled one.

"Thanks," I say, and I steal another glance at Ivy, but she's fixed on the windshield, rotating her earrings once again. If she's regretting what happened up against the wall in the chapel, I won't forgive myself.

"Also," Dev adds, wiggling his brow, "we photoshopped those pics tonight. The ones we showed you. We didn't really get hitched."

My jaw drops. "Are you kidding me?"

Stefan stares out the window, saying nothing.

"Well, Brady and I did," Kana puts in, an impish laugh on her face. "We were married before he was even drafted. But not in Vegas. At the Japanese Gardens in Vancouver. My entire family from Osaka flew in."

Wow.

I should feel fooled, but I don't entirely. I got something out of the wedding dare for one night.

Belonging.

Correction. I got belonging and the most mind-bendingly sexy five minutes of my life. The trouble is I don't know if Ivy got anything out of it.

A few minutes later, we pull up to the hotel, spilling out of the car at well past one in the morning, with Brady talking up the best ramen in the city as we head into the hotel.

But when they turn down the concourse toward the food, Ivy stops and says, "Hey! I'm beat. I'm going to call it a night."

After a quick goodbye, she whirls around the other way, taking off in a blur of chestnut waves and regret.

My heart clangs. I need to see her, talk to her, ask if she's okay. She's my neighbor and she's become a friend. But will I give us away if I go after her? I've got to protect her privacy, and she gave off a distinct *we're all just buds* vibe then.

When we reach the ramen shop and the guys duck in, I'm torn. I should go with them and do the whole unspoken team bonding thing. But I need to take care of Ivy too.

Stefan seems weirdly distant as well. He's quiet when he's usually not. He's so often the life of the party, but when he gets to the counter and checks out the menu, he just seems bored. He gives a shrug, like he's so over it. "Nothing looks good. I'm out of here," he says, then takes off before I can say a word to him either. Out of the corner of my eye, I catch him snapping pics of stores and shops as he goes.

Five minutes later, the guy behind the counter slides me a carton of noodles. As I carry the container to the table, this feels all wrong.

I don't need to be here with the guys. I need to see my woman.

I stuff the container in a to-go bag. "I'm going to take off."

I don't give anyone a chance to protest. I leave, calling Ivy as I weave through the slot machines to the elevator. "Hey. What's your room number? I need to see you."

A couple minutes later, I knock on her door. When she opens it, she's dressed in a loose cami, but she hasn't taken off her jeans. Her hair is pulled back in a cloth headband like she was about to wash her face.

But she's still got a wall up. I can sense it in her too bright eyes, her too peppy smile. Did she have to fake her emotions for someone in the past? A family member? A parent? She seems like she knows how to put on a good face, and it's almost believable. But I see through it. "Hey. I brought you ramen. I didn't know if you were hungry."

"I like ramen," she says in a tone I can't read.

I thrust the bag at her, and she takes it, but makes no move to let me in. "Thanks, Hayes. See you at—"

"—Can we talk?"

"Sure," she says, but like she's bracing herself for terrible news. Of course her guardrails are up. She's a woman who's been cheated on.

She holds open the door and I go inside.

I glance around. Her room is smaller than mine, and that's kind of irritating. But there's a couch, and when she sets her food down on the table across from it, I join her there on the sofa cushions.

She adjusts a strap on the cami. Is she avoiding eye contact again? Man, I fucked up tonight. Maybe I should have talked more before I pinned her against the wall. "Are you okay?"

"You asked me in the car. I said yes. I am."

"You took off right away though."

"It's late," she says, then sighs, like she's emphasizing how tired she is. "I should go to bed. We have a busy day and—"

"—That's not what I mean."

"What do you mean?"

There's no point beating around the bush. "Did what we did freak you out?" I ask it point blank, putting my cards on the table. "I don't want you to be uncomfortable. That's the last thing I want."

She sighs heavily, then meets my gaze. "Look, it surprised me. But it also didn't."

"Yeah?"

"I mean, I kind of got vibes all week," she says and looks down, then back up. Ivy's not usually unsure of herself but she seems off-kilter now. I've got to do something.

I reach for her hand, thread her fingers through mine. "Since the night I met you, I haven't been able to stop thinking about you. You're under my skin. You're in my head. I tried to resist you and did a shit job of it. Want to know why?"

Her lips twitch in the start of a grin. "Why?"

"Because you're fiery and fascinating, and you have a big heart. And you're so sexy it fries my brain and scrambles all logic. I've wanted you since the second I saw you, and the more I got to know you, the more I had to fight it. When I realized Stefan was into you too, the craving only got more intense."

Her eyes brighten. The smile takes over. "Really?"

"Yes."

"That made you want me more?"

"I like what I like," I say, owning it.

She nibbles on the corner of her lips, then draws a breath and asks, "Have you done that before?"

I don't know if the truth will make her run for the hills, but I owe her honesty. "Yes."

"With him?"

I've never admitted anything about our shared trysts before. I'm not ashamed. They're just private. We've only ever done hookups. We've never shared a woman we'll see again. "Yeah. A few times. It started in college."

"Oh," she says, but her voice pitches up. With intrigue. With avid interest. "You guys like it? Like, a lot?"

Understatement of the year. "Fucking love it," I say, opening myself up. "You couldn't tell?"

She dips her face, but she seems more flattered than embarrassed. "I mean, I could tell you both liked it," she says when she looks up again.

This girl. Man, her ex did a number on her. I scoot closer, thread a hand through her hair.

"No, Ivy," I correct. "I don't like turning on a woman with him. I *love* it."

Her shoulders relax. "This is new to me. I mean, Trina's in a throuple, so the concept isn't strange. I've just never personally done anything like that."

I turn the key question around on her. "Did *you* like it?"

She's quiet for a beat. "No. I fucking loved it."

When she uses my words on me, I groan, my dick jumping in my suit pants. But this moment isn't about getting off. It's about getting it right. "Seeing you so worked up feels almost illegal," I rasp out. "You're like magic. But if you had a good time, why were you so distant in the car? Because everyone was there?"

That has to be it.

She squares her shoulders. "Because I didn't know if you guys would want to do that again."

That's her worry?

Before I can tell her I want it so much it's suffocating, she adds, "And I was working up the courage to ask you." She points to her phone, and I'm on the edge of my seat, feeling like I'm about to hit the biggest jackpot in this city. "I've been typing out messages to you two since I returned to my room. Messages I didn't send."

"What would they have said?" I'm on the edge for her answer.

"I was going to ask if you guys would want to do that again..." She pauses then says the most beautiful word in the history of the world: "Tonight."

* * *

Ten minutes later, I'm marching down the hall on the tenth floor, powered by raw desire and Ivy's dirty dreams. I play out scenarios, desperately wanting to fulfill every single fantasy Ivy outlined before I left.

I clench my fists. I'm a high-wire tension line. My long legs eat up the floor as I stalk to Stefan's room. I'd burn down this hotel—no, this whole city—to give her what she wants tonight.

When I reach my destination, I pound on the door mercilessly.

Didn't text him I was coming. And I don't have the patience to wait much longer. I bang again, louder this time, my knuckles getting raw. I might wake everyone on this floor.

And I don't care.

"C'mon," I mutter.

Soon, I hear the shuffling of feet, then the unlatching of the lock. Stefan opens the door a few inches. He squints at me, his hair sticking up. "What the fuck are you doing here at this hour?"

"Open the door," I demand. "And get out of bed."

With a tired groan, he rolls his eyes. "I am out of bed. This is literally me out of bed," he says as he tugs open the door.

I storm past him.

He shuts the door behind me. You never know who might overhear, and this conversation is for him and me only.

I cross my arms and look him in the eyes. "I've got a question for you."

"What is it?"

I'm no longer in a rush. I take my time as I let a dirty smile curve my lips. "Do you want to fuck my wife?"

18

ROOM SERVICE

Stefan

Clothes are such a formality. But you can't walk around a Vegas hotel naked.

At least, you shouldn't.

Normally I'm sound asleep at a quarter after two. Hell, I was cruising toward the land of nod fifteen minutes ago. Now, I'm wide awake, teeth brushed, hair finger combed, dressed in jeans and, yes, a fucking Henley.

I lean against the wall outside Ivy's room as Hayes walks toward me. Like me, he's ditched the suit for jeans and a T-shirt.

I give him a chin nod. "Took you long enough to figure it out."

"Did you think I didn't know you wanted her?"

Actually, I did. For a while at least. "Well, no," I

admit. But then screw it. I'm not here to shoot the shit with Hayes. We're here for the woman.

I rap on the door. The seconds spread, each one growing heavier with anticipation, till the door opens, and Ivy's there on the other side.

Wow.

She's not wearing seductive lingerie.

She's not pouting like a pinup.

Not that I'd object to any of the above. She's simply wearing sleep shorts and a cami.

That. Is. All.

Her makeup is scrubbed off. Her skin is glowing. I want to devour her, but she seems to want to hold the reins for a bit since she checks us out with a fierce sort of determination. Purposefully, she looks me up and down, her eyes traveling freely in a way they haven't during our last encounters. Her gaze slides to Hayes, and she gives him the same treatment. "You two were wrong," she says.

A throwdown.

Did Hayes misunderstand Ivy's request? "What do you mean?" I'm a little concerned. I don't usually misread interest. My radar is finely calibrated.

"On the plane. You called my bluff."

My brow creases, and I try to remember the conversation's specifics.

"When I said I wanted to stay in," she prompts. "And order room service."

I remember now. Oh hell, yes, do I remember.

She licks her lips, then swings the door open all the way.

"Room service is indeed here," I say, then we go inside and seal out the world. I head straight for the couch and sit down. Sofas are such fantastic accomplices in a seduction.

"Come here," I tell her.

She follows my order, Hayes behind her. When Ivy reaches me, I tug her onto my lap. She looks nervous but excited too. My job is to help her relax so she can feel as free as possible tonight.

"Can I tell you a secret?" I say as Hayes moves behind her, standing, sliding his hands in her hair.

She gasps as he touches her. Yes, just as I suspected. She'll want her hair played with.

I stroke her cheek with the back of my knuckles. "I've been planning this for some time."

"That so?"

"Yes. I wanted to get you two alone. To make my pitch."

She curls her hands around my shoulders, and her touch makes my pulse gallop.

"So make it," she says.

Do I want to lay it all out right away? I look to Hayes, who's a little caught up in roaming his fingers through her hair. I think I'll tease Ivy a little. "Should I tell her? Or let her be surprised?"

"Bet she likes surprises," Hayes muses, then lowers his face, brushing his jawline against her cheek. "Do you, Ivy?"

She shudders, then rocks against my erection. "I do," she says, eager, a little breathy.

But there are good surprises and bad surprises.

There are delicious expectations, and there are disappointing misunderstandings. I want the former not the latter.

Yes, we've done this before, but Hayes told me she hasn't. He told me, too, the basics of what she wants. But the thing is, wants can change, and I need to hear them from her.

Quickly, I roll through a couple scenarios, and she tells us what's on and off the table tonight.

With that done, she locks eyes with me, then says, "I'm honestly a little bummed I didn't get to hear your big pitch. To see you at a table, holding court, ordering top-shelf liquor, being all seductive as you tell me why you two want to have me." She's sly and playful, revving my engine with how she paints the picture of me.

Yes, I do like holding court. "Why don't I cut to the chase now?"

"Do it."

"Here are my closing arguments," I begin, but I start with deeds, rather than words. I slide my thumb along her jaw. Not hard though. A whisper of a touch. It's soft. Subtle. When I reach the corner of her mouth, I tease it open.

"Mmm. Beautiful," I say, praising her as she swirls her tongue along my thumb.

She preens at the compliment, straightening her spine, all while Hayes strokes her hair. I run my other hand up her stomach, using only the tips of my fingers, a feather-light touch that makes her squirm.

She rocks a little faster against the outline of my cock.

"So here's the thing, sweetheart," I say.

"Yes?"

I move my face closer, but still inches away. Her lips part. Our girl is desperate for a kiss. "I haven't even kissed you yet, and you're practically begging for me."

She lets out a whimper. "That's your pitch?"

I shake my head. "No. That's why it's going to be so fucking fantastic when we make you come over and over again..."

She gasps, then rocks harder. I take my sweet time touching her face, teasing her body.

Earlier, Hayes led with power in the chapel. Now, I'll lead with seduction. I dip my face to her neck, lavishing open-mouthed kisses along her flushed skin as she trembles.

When I pull back, her eyes are closed. I cup her cheek. "Look at me."

She complies, her blue eyes glassy with lust.

"Here's my pitch. I bet we can make you come harder than you ever have before."

I press a hot, slow, tease of a kiss to her soft lips, taking my time as I pull away, watching her reaction. Her sighs, her gasps.

A quick nod to my teammate and he tugs on those locks then comes in for a rough kiss of her lips, almost bruising.

But he breaks it quickly. "How does that sound, sweetheart?"

She blinks. Centers herself. Collects her thoughts. "I dare you."

Challenge accepted.

19

THE SEX LOTTERY

Ivy

"I think I'll take care of her next orgasm." Stefan's smooth, seductive tone floats over me like warm honey. "But I wouldn't mind a little assistance."

"I got you," Hayes says to his friend, like a good teammate.

Pretty sure these men have already devised a script for me, and it looks like the next scene has Hayes by my side on the couch, shifting my hair to the side, exposing my neck.

A shiver runs down my back while the ache in my core intensifies.

Before I know it, Hayes is kissing my neck, Stefan is kissing my mouth, and I never knew kissing could be like this.

I'm like any woman. Hell, any person. I melt under a

good kiss. If a man can't kiss, he needs to be shown the door. Some men, though, kiss like they've been gifted with a secret, a precious knowledge they must protect, and it's this—most orgasms start first with a kiss.

My skin tingles as Hayes brushes his lips along my shoulder. My stomach swoops as Stefan explores my mouth, his tongue flicking against the corner, his lips traveling along mine.

He murmurs as he goes, a deep, masculine sound that thrums in my bones and makes me ache with need. I'm wriggling on his lap, hunting out more of the ridge of his thick cock, more of his mouth, more of this moment.

I never knew a kiss could be like this. It's like I'm cocooned inside it, and with each passing second, any worries, any awkwardness dissolves.

Soon, I'm panting, moaning. Then, shuddering and closing my eyes as Stefan slides his big hands up my stomach, under the fabric of my cami, heading straight for my tits. When he cups them, he slides a thumb over my piercing. But he quickly tears himself away, and I snap my eyes open. "What is it?"

Stefan's grin is wicked. "Hayes is a tits man. Since I'm a generous guy, I'm going to let him play with them first."

"Okay," I say, breathless.

"You'll probably come when you touch these beauties," Stefan says to Hayes, who growls against my neck, then bites down, nipping me like he can't help it. Like the mention of my tits is just too much.

"You think so?" Hayes asks Stefan, with filthy excitement in his voice.

"I fucking love them. Bet you jerk off and come on her back."

My head swims with dirty images. "That sounds so hot," I blurt out.

Stefan laughs, clearly pleased with the scene he's painting. "Yeah, I thought you'd like that. But have some patience, sweetheart." He tilts his head, regards me, like he's devising a new plan. "You're a little exhibitionist, aren't you?"

My lips part, but I say nothing. I feel caught. I'm just beginning to understand this side of myself. "I don't know."

"Let's find out," Hayes says, then drags his gaze away from me, turning his face to the floor-to-ceiling windows and the glittering lights of the city below. "Want to give the city a show?"

Hayes knows I do. I told him as much before he left to fetch his friend. But it's empowering to say it out loud.

"Yes. I want that."

Hayes lifts me off Stefan's lap then brings me to the windows. "Need this off now," Hayes demands in a gruff tone, grabbing at my cami, tugging it over my head. Stefan strolls over, stripping off his shirt as he walks. After tossing it on the floor, he unbuttons the top button on his jeans. When he reaches me, he tugs down my sleep shorts.

"Yessss," he says, admiring my panties.

I didn't come to Vegas expecting sex, so I'm wearing

basic cotton undies—a pair of sky-blue low-rise panties. But they're visibly wet. He kneels before me, sliding them down to my ankles, then off, while Hayes yanks off his shirt.

Hayes comes to my side, staring salaciously at my breasts, gaze lasered in on the right one with the silver barbell through it. "Been obsessed with this since the day I knew you had one," he says, flicking it.

I moan. The chain reaction begins. Another flick, and I gasp louder.

"You'll be obsessed with this too," Stefan says, then tosses my panties up at him.

Oh.

Well.

I wasn't expecting that either. Or for Hayes to bring my panties to his nose. He draws a deep, hungry inhale, then growls before he tosses them on the floor.

I'm even wetter, but I'm also the only one naked. And I feel...exposed. A little uncertain. They're so good at this, and I'm such a rookie. "What are we doing now?" I ask, glancing at the glass next to me.

The city is lit up after dark. Even though it's the middle of the night, cabs and cars cruise along the Strip, taking partiers to their next destinations, bringing others to the end of their evenings at last.

Across from us is the other tower to this hotel. Hayes spins me around. "Hands up against the window," he tells me, then positions me in full view of Las Vegas. Stefan moves so he's kneeling between me and the window.

I know what they're going to do to me, and I'm so wet it's obscene.

All of Vegas can see my naked body.

To anyone out there, I'm just another girl up against the glass. To me, I'm finally a girl who's *wanted* desperately. Anyone can see how wanted I am. Anyone can watch us. We're far away from prying eyes. I don't think peeping Toms could tell who we are—or that they'd care, frankly—but no doubt someone out there is walking past a window, doing a double take, calling over a friend or a partner, then whispering, "Hey, check that out across the Strip."

Then, they'll watch three people getting it on in full view.

Why does this idea excite me so much? Someone watching me? Have I always been an exhibitionist and didn't know it till I spotted Hayes on the rooftop? Till he asked me my kink? Till Stefan walked into the chapel earlier tonight and unlocked it fully for me? Have I subconsciously craved eyes on me this whole time?

I don't know the answer. But the possibility that someone in the city of sin can see how much *two men* want me is electrifying. That's not all though. I hope the world can tell how intoxicated I am on *them*.

Because I am simply drunk on this new desire.

Hayes moves my hair to the side of my shoulder and drags a finger down the back of my neck while Stefan kisses right above my knees.

"You're making it hard to think," I murmur.

Stefan dusts his lips to the inside of my thigh.

"Don't think. Just feel. Just let yourself be the greedy girl you are. That's who you can be with us. Be that girl."

God, I think I will. My whole body hums as Stefan kisses up my thighs while Hayes's big hands come around and cup my tits. The sound he makes is nothing I've ever heard before. It's a low, dirty rumble, masculine and demanding as he slides his thumb across my piercing, then bites out: "Do you have any idea how crazy this has made me since the equipment room?"

Did he see the outline through my shirt? I'm usually discreet in my bra choices. "You noticed it then?"

Stefan laughs from below, his hands sliding up my thighs, his face dangerously near my pussy. "Did it drive you insane?" Stefan asks Hayes. "I had a feeling you'd be obsessed with it."

"Obsessed barely covers it," Hayes rasps out, running his fingers along the metal.

"Why did you want me to have one?" I ask Hayes.

"Why *do* you have it?"

Feeling bold, I answer with, "Because it makes me feel so good when I play with my tits."

Stefan growls a *yes* against my center.

"Fuuuuck," Hayes grunts against my ear, then licks the lobe while pinching my pierced nipple.

Like they know exactly how to play their favorite instrument, Stefan presses a tantalizing kiss to my throbbing clit, sucking hard and making me grab his thick hair. But he stops abruptly, meeting my gaze with his hungry eyes. "You want me to eat this pussy, sweetheart?"

Um, yeah. "So badly," I gasp.

"Then, play with your tits too. It'll drive your husband even wilder."

As Stefan kisses the inside of my thigh with whisper-soft lips, I cover Hayes's hands and together, we play with my tits. Stefan is off to the races, licking right up my seam as Hayes squeezes my tits and devours my neck.

I groan, rocking against Stefan's face from the doubling of my pleasure. My tits are like a direct connection to my clit, so everything is amplified.

While Stefan eats my pussy, Hayes and I work together to fondle and knead, pinch and squeeze. The twin sensations of hands and tongue drive me wild. The man on his knees laps me up like I'm the best thing he's tasted in ages. But soon, the pleasure is too intense for me to concentrate on playing with my breasts, so I let go, needing desperately to hold onto Stefan again.

I grab wildly at his hair, jerking him against my pussy, rocking into his mouth. My tits are Hayes's playground, and he knows exactly what to do. He squeezes till the sounds coming from him, and me, and Stefan, are unreal. Groans and grunts, and animalistic cries.

My head is swimming with lust, my body pulsing, tensing. When Stefan draws my needy clit into his mouth one more time, I burst. I come so hard, it's criminal, calling in a rapid chant, "Oh god, oh god, oh god."

I'm sparking everywhere, barely able to stand as

Stefan devours my orgasm. I can't see straight. I don't think I can stand much longer. I grip Stefan's shoulders for dear life till my breathing finally settles and my pulse slows back down.

When I've recovered, Hayes scoops me up in his arms and carries me to the bed where he sets me down gently. He's surprisingly tender. Climbing over me, Hayes kisses my hair, my cheek, my lips. I'm still murmuring and coming down from the high when he lets go and smacks the side of my ass.

Hard.

"Now, get on your hands and knees," he orders.

Hayes moves off the bed, undoes his jeans and pushes them off, freeing his gorgeous cock. But I barely get a moment to admire his length or the ink on his hip that I've been wanting to check out in more detail since he turns to Stefan, who's busying himself grabbing a condom from his wallet in his jeans. "You almost ready?"

Stefan brandishes the protection. "Yup."

"Good. My wife is greedy for your cock. Don't deny her," Hayes tells him, gruff and demanding.

I nearly come again. I scramble to my hands and knees, arching my back for Stefan, offering him my body. "I'd never deny this beauty," Stefan says, stripping off his jeans now, his cock springing free.

He's thick, hard, pulsing.

I can't believe I'm having sex like this but in an *I can't believe I've won the lottery* type of way. Judging from these two, I've definitely won the dick sweepstakes.

I gaze up at the men standing at the foot of the bed. Feeling playful, I say, "I was right."

Hayes prowls closer to me.

"About what?"

"You both have very pretty dicks," I say with a satisfied grin.

Hayes grins too, then it burns off. "Shut up and take these dicks like a good dirty girl."

They might be the ones in charge, but I've always suspected Hayes liked it when I talked back over text. Does Stefan? I'd like to find out.

I lift my ass higher. "Do you like me like this?"

I have some ideas, but I'm not entirely sure what bedroom games we're playing. I don't think it's quite Dom/sub. It feels more boss-me-around good cop/bad cop style.

While Stefan climbs onto the bed, he answers, "With the whole city watching me get ready to fuck my friend's wife? Yes, yes, I do."

Standing in front of me, Hayes slides a hand down his cock, squeezing the tip as an offering. "Now lick the tip."

I dart out my tongue, flicking it against the drop of liquid arousal beading at the crown of his cock. I murmur because he tastes so good, salty and musky.

Stefan positions himself behind me, rubbing a gentle hand over my ass. "She loves sucking you, Hayes. Gets her even wetter than when I ate her pussy," Stefan remarks with pride, like he's admiring their twin accomplishments.

"I can tell. Just fucking look at her. She's so hungry

for our cocks," Hayes says, rubbing the head against my lips.

If I could come hands free, that would have done it. I'm gushing, and I swear there's a line of wetness trickling down my thigh.

Stefan slides his hand between my legs, catching it, groaning in approval as he feels how slick I am. "Yes, you're so ready for me, sweetheart."

"Please fuck me," I beg, rocking back, arching my hips, offering him my aching center.

I feel empty right now. Empty and pulsing and desperate as I swirl my tongue around the head of Hayes's cock while Stefan notches his against me.

"That's right. Take him, pretty girl," Hayes encourages, petting my hair while Stefan pushes in.

Hayes is telling me to take Stefan's dick, and when that awareness fully kicks in, my breath comes out in a harsh gasp. It's a wicked thrill when one man tells me what to do with another man's cock.

But as Stefan sinks farther into me, I drop my head, tensing briefly. I feel tight and full. It's been a while, and he's not small whatsoever, so I grit my teeth for a few seconds from the intrusion. Stefan presses a tender hand to the small of my back while palming my ass. "You're doing so well. Just a little more," he says, and I breathe deeply.

That and Stefan's words of praise settle my nerves.

I ease back, relaxing fully onto Stefan's dick. His hands grip my ass, tight. "She's so fucking slick, so fucking tight," Stefan says to his friend.

Hayes growls, then slaps his cock against my mouth

again. "Suck me off, baby," he says, and his voice breaks, his control fraying.

Nodding intently, needing him desperately, I circle my fingers around the base, then draw Hayes's dick into my mouth. His right hand is spread through my hair; the other is parked on his hip. As Stefan finds a tempo, a steady drumbeat of pleasure, I turn my eyes to the window, shuddering as I watch our reflection.

Stefan is on his knees behind me. He thrusts deep, then pulls back. Hayes stands in front of me, feeding me his cock.

But the best part? We aren't truly alone. Anyone could see these three people fuck.

"Bet someone is watching us. You like that, don't you, pretty girl?" Hayes growls, as if reading my mind.

I whimper around his shaft as I push my hips back, fucking down on Stefan's cock, shamelessly searching for another high of my own.

"Makes you greedy, doesn't it?" Hayes taunts. "Makes you want to come all over my friend's dick."

My brain fries. I'm a live wire, crackling everywhere. I have to speak. I drop Hayes from my mouth and hold myself up with my trembling arms. "I want everyone to see us," I say to him, the words rushing out in a confession before I pull his dick back between my lips.

"You fucking love the risk," Hayes says. And I really do. I love the thrill, the risk, the ride. I love the attention, the praise, the filth. I love that I can barely handle all this pleasure, and that I want to drown in it too.

I love the intensity of this night.

It's an overload of sensations, the raw power of

Stefan's thrusts as he fucks me mercilessly, the challenge of taking Hayes to the back of my throat, the swinging of my tits. The electrical charges running roughshod over my body.

I love it all. I need it all. I crave it.

"Anyone can see how dirty you are, Ivy." Hayes grunts as he fucks my mouth.

"Anyone can see how well you take me," Stefan adds with a deep thrust.

One man is fucking me, but they're both making me ride to the edge.

I cry out, letting Hayes fall from my mouth.

"That's right. Give us another one," Stefan orders and that feels true—I'm giving my orgasm to *them*. I shove one of my hands between my thighs, my search for pleasure reaching a crescendo. But it's the noise Stefan makes that trips all my wires. An incoherent grunt, followed by a strangled yes.

My vision turns blurry, but Stefan holds on tight, pistoning his hips to his own release. "Fuck, yes," he grunts, losing all control, too, as he comes with me.

One final demanding thrust, then a long, low grunt, and he stills inside my pussy. We're both panting, gasping for air.

It takes me a beat before I realize Hayes is taking care of himself. He's in front of me, stroking his own cock.

Before I can say a word, Stefan smacks my ass as he pulls out. "You've got to feel her, Hayes. She feels so fucking good. You need to come inside our girl."

What? Wait. They're both going to fuck me? I didn't

think we'd execute this kind of tag teaming tonight, but the second Stefan mentions it, I'm sure I really have won the sex lottery.

Hayes tucks a finger under my chin, makes me look up to meet his eyes. "You gonna let your husband fuck you too?"

I vibrate with desire. "Well, it *is* our wedding night."

In one swift move, he grabs my hips, flips me over, and pulls me off the bed. Then he bends me over it while Stefan flings him a condom.

In seconds, Hayes covers himself, then sinks inside me, slamming me back on his cock while Stefan heads to the bathroom.

But Stefan doesn't take long disposing of the condom. As Hayes presses a rough hand to my back, Stefan returns to the bed, flops down on the pillows, and parks his hands behind his head.

"Yes. I do enjoy a good show in Las Vegas," he says, then inhales deeply, smiling as he watches Hayes fuck me senseless.

Tonight will be my fodder for self-care for the rest of my days as Hayes drives into me harder, deeper, rougher, fucking me till he's grabbing my hair and then shuddering, groaning out my name.

I'm spent, thoroughly used, and I know I've experienced something I desperately want again—but can't have.

* * *

Fifteen minutes later, after I shower, I do want room service. But I have the ramen, so I eat it, sharing it with my two lovers on the couch.

When we finish, I'm not sure what will happen next. If we all go our separate ways to our separate rooms. But I'm sure of this: I don't want to be alone after the most intense and vulnerable night of my sex life.

If I asked to be fucked, I can ask for *this*. "Can you both spend the night?"

There's zero weirdness when they say yes.

In the morning, this will be over, but for a few more hours, I'm going to enjoy the night.

20

LUCKY NUMBERS

Ivy

Stefan stirs as the sun rises, his warm skin against mine. I'm used to waking up next to soft fur, a gentle paw, a lick of my nose.

I miss my girl, but I'll see her this afternoon. Right now, I'm enjoying Stefan's bare chest pressed to my back. He fits me well, all big and strong and a little greedy with his morning mouth, now coasting across my shoulder.

On the other side of me, Hayes is sound asleep, sprawled on his stomach like a starfish. "He's a bed hog," I murmur.

Stefan hums quietly against my skin, and, I think, peers over at his friend, as if checking my report. "Seems he is."

Have they done sleepovers when they've been with

other women? But that doesn't feel like a morning-after question. Or, really, one I should ask at all.

I say nothing.

Stefan presses more soft kisses to my neck, then asks quietly, "Do you miss your dog?"

Like a cat enjoying the sun, I bask in the attention —both the question and his touches. "Are you reading my mind?"

He laughs softly. "No, I just had a feeling."

"Why?"

He presses another kiss to my neck. Wow. He's affectionate in the morning. Come to think of it, he was pretty affectionate last night too. "Your social media," he answers. "There's a lot of your dog. And clothes. And friends. And pretty things like pens and notebooks."

"Stalk much?" I tease, but inside I feel glowy. He checked me out. Like, really checked me out.

"What can I say? I've had a thing for you for a while."

I go still, a little surprised by the candor. I'm not used to that. "You have?"

"Yes," he says, seeming undeterred by my reaction. "When I said last night I wanted to make my pitch, it was true. But you've also been on my mind since the Hockey Hotties event in the park."

That was in April, at the end of last season. "I had no idea."

"You were with that jackass," he adds quietly as Hayes's even breathing continues. Stefan runs his fingers along my naked shoulder, recounting the moment in more detail. "And Ryker was with the team. But that didn't stop me from checking you out online that night."

The idea of this confident, outgoing man being so taken he went home to look me up is like a shot of liquid gold in my veins. "And you developed a crush on my dog then too," I tease.

He chuckles. "She's cute. But it wasn't till your brother was traded and I saw you'd ditched the douche at the start of this season that I decided no one was going to ruin my chance."

I'm a little floored. But a little enchanted with him too. I turn to face him, searching for the full truth. "Really?"

His eyes are bright and honest. "You doubt me? Or do you doubt yourself?"

That's a good question. I give it some thought, and no, I'm not someone who thinks *oh god, why ever would that hot guy be into me?* But I don't think I'm doubting Stefan either. I doubt...men.

"It's not you. It's...people," I say, cautiously. "But I remember enjoying talking to you about all sorts of things. I remember thinking I liked that you had a sort of worldly charm about you. I didn't think anything more on it because of my boyfriend at the time, and then I just thought you were with Annika."

His sunny expression vanishes. "I was. And then I wasn't."

It's said crisply, like it stings. That worries me for him. "Does it still hurt?"

His brow screws up, as if he's really considering the

question. "It was months ago when she called off the engagement."

I'm dying to know why. Truly, the desire claws at me. I don't think it's my place to ask, but I don't have to because he keeps talking.

"I'd known her for years. Our families were close growing up. When she had a job opportunity in the States, she took it and we connected again, fell in love, got engaged. But she had an opportunity to return to Denmark, and she took it."

Something seems to be missing though. "There was no cheating? No bad breakup?"

"None of that. It ended because I was willing to try the whole two continents thing. She wasn't. That was that."

And that's what was missing. One person put in the effort. One didn't want to. "Ouch."

"Yeah," he says with a heavy sigh and a cloud passes over his eyes, darkening his whole expression. This isn't what I'm used to seeing from Stefan. He's normally so upbeat, so happy-go-lucky.

"That must have hurt," I say gently.

"It did," he says, staring at the ceiling. He's pensive for a beat, and I give him the time he needs till he turns to me. "But then you move on."

"Truer words," I say.

Even though last night feels distinctly like a one-night stand, this morning feels like a deep conversation with someone you want to see again. Especially when Stefan nuzzles me and says, "There you go again. Making me open up."

I laugh lightly. "I didn't make you."

"Yes, you did."

I swat his arm playfully. "I didn't!"

"You absolutely did. Just like at the party. You're too easy to talk to."

"Other people aren't?"

"There's this thing called questions. Most people don't ask them."

That's so strange to me. "How else would you get to know someone?"

"Excellent question. I have no idea, but most people I've met don't ask me all the things I like about Denmark, like you did that day, or if my grandmother's cats were taken care of, like you did on the patio."

I don't even try to hide my smile as I say, "You like to ask questions too."

"You got me there," he says, and he's light again, breezy again. "Though, come to think of it, you were a little standoffish that day at the rink the other week."

Chagrined, I admit the truth. "I thought you were still with Annika."

He rolls his eyes. "Woman, I was flirting with you. Was that not obvious? Do I need to up my flirting game?"

"Oh, I knew you were flirting. I just didn't know you were single."

He shoots me a serious stare. "I'd never flirt with you if I was involved with someone. I'm certainly not going to go out and flirt with another woman later today for that matter either."

Does that mean he thinks we're involved? Or just

that it'd be tacky to flirt with someone else after fucking another woman? Probably the latter.

"Good. Then I won't flirt with someone else today either," I say, then let my eyes drift to Hayes. "Except for maybe Hayes."

I say it to test the possibility. I truly don't know how far this sharing extends. Stefan's eyes twinkle, but then the man in bed with us stirs, shifting slightly under the sheet. Both Stefan and I go starkly quiet.

With one deep sigh, our bedmate is breathing steadily again, snoozing. I relax.

"Here's a question," Stefan says quietly. "What happened to Fedora Fuckface?"

A laugh bursts from my chest. Immediately, I slam a hand to my mouth so I don't wake Sleeping Beauty. When my laughter settles, I answer. "The jackass hooked up with my boss. Well, former boss."

Stefan's jaw drops. "Are you fucking kidding me?"

I flash a fake smile, one clearly meant for Xander. "I wish. But he also dumped me saying he needed *and* deserved a girlfriend upgrade. It turned out he was banging my boss while he was with me and while I was working for her."

I tell Stefan the rest of the story and with each successive morsel, his jaw drops farther. When I drop the tidbit about the blow job engagement picture, Stefan's jaw is unhinged. Then he's speechless for a long beat. "Holy shit. I always thought he was a twat with those stupid hats. But fuuuck. That's award-level douchery. I'd like to kill him for hurting you."

I smile stupidly. I shouldn't enjoy this caveman side of him. But I do.

"You'd like that?" he asks with a quirk in his lips.

I smile and shrug. "Maybe."

"He never deserved you."

"I'm sort of learning that."

"Also, his wedding sounds like a train wreck."

"They invited me to it," I say, and once those words come out, it hits me that I've still got to plan for this event. "It's in a few months."

He growls. "You laughed in their fucking faces, right?"

"Actually," I begin, then I tell him the story of how I landed a plum gig covering their wedding.

When I'm done, Stefan nods, clearly impressed. "You're brilliant, Ivy. I thought that at the event in the park. I was impressed by your quick wit."

"Thank you," I say, a little awkwardly. I'm not used to compliments from men that sound so genuine.

"Seriously. I mean it. You're going to do huge things. And even though your ex is a dick, I love that you turned this around into a chance for you. Your writing is fun and fresh."

"I like that you found my writing," I admit.

"Took you long enough to figure out it was me," he teases.

"Oh, excuse me for not memorizing your jersey number."

"Bet you won't forget it now." He tips his forehead to our bedmate. "Or Number Twenty-one."

"My lucky *numbers*," I add, feeling sassy with him, feeling confident.

His eyes twinkle. He likes this side of me. "They'd better be."

But before we get sidetracked with this flirting, I return to the wedding story, compelled to tell the rest of it. If I didn't, I'd be keeping something from Stefan and that seems wrong after last night, but mostly after what he just shared with me. "That's how I met Hayes—after the invite to my ex's wedding. I'd just found out about their engagement when I ran into Hayes in the elevator for the first time. I poured out my whole sob story to him. He volunteered to go to the wedding as my plus-one."

Stefan smiles with genuine affection for his friend. "That's very him."

"Is he a white knight?"

"He doesn't like it when people are hurting. He wants to fix things," he says.

"You like that about him."

"Yeah. I do. He's a good guy. I can always count on him." Stefan says all this with no jealousy, no weirdness —just a rock-solid understanding of who Hayes is.

Maybe good guys *are* good in bed. I can't wait to tell Jackson just how great some are. "He seems to be," I say.

"I'm glad he'll be there at the wedding. To protect you," Stefan adds, then glances at the clock. A reminder that it's ticking, and we both have places to be.

"What sort of threats do you think I'll encounter at a faux fairy-tale woodland wedding?"

With a shrug, Stefan says, "Bears, I suppose."

"He could protect me from a bear?"

"Yes. But here's a tip—if there's a bear, just run faster than Hayes."

I crack up, then I stop laughing when Stefan kisses me quiet. "Shh. Don't wake that bear."

"But I have morning breath," I whisper in protest.

"I don't fucking care," he says, giving me another kiss. "I've been wanting to wake up next to you for a long time. Don't you get it?"

He's thoroughly over his former fiancée and into me? I don't know that I do get it. I don't know that I understand what Stefan wants from me either.

Except I suppose I do know his actions and his words. Pretty sure he wants *more*. Maybe he even thinks we're *involved*?

What does *more* mean though? For him, for me, for my job, and for...the three people in bed? We still work together. I don't want to lose my job or my focus on rebuilding my career.

We kiss for a few more seconds till he pulls back with some reluctance.

He drops a kiss to my nose. "I should go. I have to make a few calls before this breakfast thing, and you have the annulment. But we should—" He cuts himself off when he looks to Hayes, then winces. "I should go."

I swear he was going to ask to see me again. And I want to say yes.

But I don't know how this works. Any of this.

Instead, I let him go with a soft smile and a *thanks for last night.*

When he's gone, I head to my suitcase and tug on a long T-shirt, staring at the gold band on my finger, then checking out the matching one on the man still in bed. They look so surreal. Both will be gone in an hour, and only last night's crew, an Elvis impersonator, and a showgirl will be the wiser. Yesterday, I felt surprisingly empowered saying *I do.* I wasn't the yes-woman I'd been to Simone for the last year. I was *yes-womaning* myself. I said goodbye to the person who wanted to please a boss who never truly cared about her. Let go of the woman who wanted to spend time with a guy who never truly saw who she was or bothered looking. I embraced the woman, the new me, who felt empowered enough to ask for two men in bed.

That daring night was like a fabulous outfit that makes a statement.

But like all good outfits, you can hang it up and tuck it into the closet once you take it off. As I grab some fresh clothes for today, Hayes stirs at last. Blinks his eyes. Scrubs a hand over his scruffy jaw. Meets my gaze. "Hey."

His voice is froggy.

"You're a heavy sleeper."

With a smile, he scratches his head. "Yeah, I am. Were you guys up for a while?"

"Just chatting," I say.

He hums. "That sounds nice."

There's no jealousy from him, and it's so fascinating. I don't know what to make of it. But I know *this*. Last night is over, and daylight has come.

He pushes up on his elbows and checks the time. "I should get ready for our..." He doesn't seem to want to say it.

"Annulment," I supply, just so he doesn't forget we have an appointment.

He winces like Stefan did before he left. Like this pains him. I feel off as well. But what, exactly, is making me sad? Is it the marriage ending? Or is it the ending of the unexpected connection forged between the three of us after dark?

I have no answers. I hunt for a pair of jeans. Hayes is laser focused as he picks up his discarded clothes. He tugs on his jeans and T-shirt, smooths a hand down his chest, and blows out a breath. That feels final too. "I'll meet you in the lobby in thirty minutes. Is that enough time?"

"I'll be ready in twenty," I say, resolute. I refuse to be someone who hangs on too long.

With a crisp nod, he leaves, and, missing my two men, I prepare for the end of my eight-hour marriage.

21

UNTYING THE KNOT

Hayes

I run a towel over my hair one more time, Outrageous Record blasting in my earbuds. Top volume drowns out the racing thoughts of what I have to do this morning, and now these text messages from my father.

> Dad: Great goal last night! Cora said she was thrilled for you too. You're on your game with the Avengers.

I'm in a terse kind of mood so I reply with a quick thanks. Don't want to jinx myself by saying how much I like playing on this team. But I don't have to since he moves on right away with another message.

.   .   .

> Dad: P.S. I'm considering asking her to marry me! What do you think?

My jaw tightens as I set down the phone, unsure what to say other than *dude, she's thirty.* Not like I'm going to say *Hey, I got hitched too. Isn't that cool?*

As I grab the toothbrush, I try to come up with a reply that's somewhat genuine when a new text pops up. It's from Dev and it's short. ***Here you go. Keep it safe.***

It's the pic of Ivy and me getting hitched, and something in my chest stirs as I stare at it. She looks...happy.

So do I.

I stare down at my ring, a heaviness taking over in my chest—a heaviness that doesn't belong. Saying *I don't* shouldn't have me so twisted up. Especially considering what the three of us did after my dare of an *I do.*

Good sex never fills me with so much angst the next morning. Hell, Stefan was right when he said sex makes me happy. Sex makes me play better. Why do I feel so down then?

My mind flashes to that moment at The Winning Hand, when it was just Ivy and me at the table, when she could tell it made me happy to be called by my name. Then back to the texts she sent after my first game with the team. My heart feels a little tender.

Grabbing my travel kit, I yank up the zipper and breathe out hard, trying to focus on the day ahead. Like I'm getting psyched up for a game, I blot out distractions. Like feelings, like frustrations, like the voice in my head of my ex saying I'm a jerk.

But there are other voices echoing too. Voices from long ago. From my mom leaving, saying breezily, *I'll be back next summer.* That was true enough, but it hardly mattered—her once-a-year reappearance in my life was like a comet that was gone before it even arrived. I can never find comets in my telescope anyway.

All these thoughts bombard my brain annoyingly as I get dressed for the charity breakfast. When I'm at the door, I check the confirmation I got a few minutes ago from the annulment place Dev hooked me up with. They're expecting us. With dread in my gut, I text Ivy.

Hayes: I'll call a Lyft now, K?

Her response is swift.

Ivy: Great!

It's the exclamation point that kills me. The excitement over the end. As I walk down the hall, I can't stop staring at the ring on my finger. The gold band is so basic. Just a simple ordinary band. I shouldn't care about it so much.

I head down a flight of stairs to Ivy's room a floor below me, but she's already left, and she's marching toward me at the elevator banks. She looks focused and ready.

"The Lyft should be here soon," I say, taking a businesslike approach to this uncoupling too. "It shouldn't take too long once we're there."

"Then you can get to your breakfast with the team."

"And then we'll just have that photo as a memory," I say dryly, trying to make light of this whole uncomfortable morning as the elevator arrives.

When we step inside, she turns to me, lifting a brow in a question. "What photo?"

"It's one Kana took last night."

"I want to see it," she says in a determined tone.

I click over to it, showing her the shot. It's not the almost shot. It's us saying *I do*. I want to look at it one more time too.

She bends closer, and I catch a hint of her scent. It wafts past me, blackberries and something sweet that makes me crave another night with her. One time did nothing to quench my desire, and I barely notice when the elevator slows at a floor. I'm inches away from Ivy, her long, dark hair falling in a soft sheet near her face, her scent intoxicating me, her gaze locked on the picture of us on the screen. I steal a glance at her face. Her smile seems to take her hostage. "That was fun, Hayes," she says, vulnerable and warm.

The dreamy sound hooks into my heart.

"Yeah, I liked marrying you last night," I say, right as the doors open and I look up.

At the face of the team owner.

22

IT'S KIND OF A FUNNY STORY

Hayes

Oh, shit.

Jessie Rose is shooting a closed-mouth smile at us. Her brow arches, and I swear I can see wheels turning in her brain.

"Good morning," says the polished, poised woman as her misses-nothing gaze strays to my hand, then Ivy's, then the picture splashed across my phone screen —Ivy and I pledging to love each other in front of Elvis and a couple teammates.

Jessie doesn't waste time with questions. "Congratulations are in order." She waggles her fingers at the phone. "I want to see the wedding pics."

Ivy is frozen in place.

Words are stuck in my throat like *we're not really married, that was a joke, we were drunk.*

But Jessie's not speechless. "The brand-new mascot and the new guy," she says, clearly delighted by this pairing, maybe even picturing how it might look to the press.

"Well, we're um—" Ivy begins, but then turns to me, her blue eyes saying *help me.*

I jump on the remark from the owner like it's a puck, and I'm flying down the ice, ready to slap it into an empty net. "It's kind of a funny story," I start because I can finesse this story like a play. Quickly, I run through my options. I'll say something about a dare. A good time. I don't have to say we were drunk. I'll just say it was a prank. Jessie won't be pissed about that, will she?

But my stomach churns immediately in answer. It's not a great look to be three games into a new team and getting annulled due to a whim or a dare either.

Jessie's faster than my attempt to devise an excuse. "I love wedding stories. I can't wait to hear. But hold on a sec." She taps her chin, her sharp brown eyes assessing. She glances at a diamond bracelet watch on her wrist, a gift from her husband, I'm sure. "In a couple weeks, Cade and I are sponsoring a charity golf tournament and luncheon for our foundation that gives scholarships to first-generation college women getting business degrees. You know, Ivy"—she turns to my not-so-easy-to-annul wife—"the one I mentioned yesterday. Anyway, a couple at our table dropped out, and we've already paid for it. I would love to have the two of you take their spot. You'd be perfect for it."

She's picturing how we look together like we're the new sweet couple.

"Actually," Ivy begins, apologetic, as she likely girds herself to tell the truth of our drunken dare.

But I'm hearing the story of the mascot who lost his job for after-hours parties. I'm hearing the echo of Oliver's voice saying the Ice Crew are the brand ambassadors for the team. I'm thinking of Ivy's horrible ex-boss and terrible ex-boyfriend screwing her over.

There's only one solution. I don't care about anything at all but making sure no one—not a single person on earth—screws over Ivy again. I won't let her take the fall for this. I reach for her hand, clasp it, and hold it tightly. "My wife and I would love to go," I say with a grin.

Ivy's hand freezes in mine, but Jessie smiles, a pleased, professional one as the elevator arrives at the lobby. We step out and Oliver's waiting by the elevator banks, his gaze connecting with Jessie's, then with us.

He's doing the math too.

"Oliver, look who I found in the elevator," Jessie says, beaming as she gestures to us. "A pair of newly-weds. Why don't you two join us for coffee? We can talk about the charity lunch."

Oliver's brow knits, like he's puzzling this out. His eyes say *how did you get married without me knowing you were even dating?* But then he rearranges his mouth into a PR smile, and he must just decide to go with it.

"Well, that's fantastic," Oliver says.

They step ahead of us and Ivy's no longer a shocked

robot. She whips her gaze to me, her lips a ruler, her eyes asking *what the fuck*, her hand squeezing my knuckles like she's going to break them.

I flash her a grin. Sometimes a man's got to protect a woman.

23

THIS FAKE MARRIAGE GAME

Ivy

On the bright side, Jessie is wearing a fantastic pair of Lily Greer pumps. Of course she was able to get some delivered overnight.

But on the not-so-bright side, what the fuckity fuck?

As we round the corner past the elevators, weaving through the casino behind Jessie and Oliver, I jerk Hayes's hand. Hard. I hope he has to see the trainer about some wrist pain. When we've slowed enough to get a smidge of privacy, I mouth, *What the hell?*

Hayes tips his forehead to the pair still walking ahead of us. "You saw how excited she looked. Imagine if we'd told her the truth," he hisses in a low voice.

I scoff, shooting him a dirty look as we pass a row of *The Wizard of Oz* slot machines, the witch cackling as we go. "Imagine when everyone finds out the truth."

"We can just pull this off for a little while," he says,

all brash and bossy, which was sexy in bed but is irritating now.

I burn. No, I seethe. Who is this man who's made this decision for me? "You just told the team owner we're really married. Now we have to pretend to be married for...I don't even know how long," I say, sputtering, but that's only the tip of the iceberg.

Something else is gnawing at me. Something that's far too vulnerable to even voice now.

"I was trying to help," he bites out, like he can't believe I'd be pissed at him.

But I'm livid. He gave me no say. This has shades of Xander all over again. Someone taking over. Someone telling me what to do.

I shove those vulnerable feelings deep down and stab my sternum. "I don't need to pretend to be married to impress the team owner."

Hayes's brow knits in utter confusion as we march past a man muttering *freaking pair of bananas* to a clearly disobedient slot machine. "The last mascot was canned for snorting coke. I didn't want you to lose your job for getting drunk after the third game."

Damn him. He makes too good a point.

I breathe out hard, fuming because he's right. It *would* look bad. "But you didn't even give me a say in this! And is pretending we're married the only solution? Couldn't you have stalled to give us some time to make a plan or something?"

Hayes gestures subtly to Jessie, click-clacking several paces ahead of us on the marble walkway, polished in a burgundy suit and brand-new shoes.

She's dispensing instructions to Oliver, who nods like an obedient soldier.

"Did you see her? The woman already put two and two together," Hayes says. "I didn't want to cross her. And I didn't want it to look bad for you."

I love that he did this for me. But I hate that he did this for me too. This is a whole new mess I need to deal with while I look for new gigs and try to sort out my life. I slow our pace even more. "You didn't just do it for me," I point out, since he wasn't completely altruistic. "You get something out of it too. You're the new guy on the team, and you didn't want to look like a fuck-up in front of Jessie either."

He blows out a breath of admission. "Fine. I get something out of it too."

I stare him down, glad he's admitted the truth. "She invited you and *your wife* to a charity event," I say, unfolding my arms to sketch air quotes. "It would have looked bad for you to say *hey, we were plastered*."

His eyes harden with a new intensity. "I wasn't drunk. I was barely buzzed in the chapel." This is important to him, this emphasis on his almost sobriety. "I didn't do anything last night because of liquor. I wanted *everything* that happened. The wedding because it was fun. I had a great time marrying you for fun." He drops his voice to a harsh whisper. "And I wanted the rest of the night desperately because I wanted...*you*."

I blink, taken aback by the strength of his tone and the reminder of his desire.

"And I still fucking do, so much it's driving me crazy,

so I'm sorry I made the decision for you, but Ivy, the last thing I want on earth is to hurt you. I don't want anything bad to happen to you. I wanted to fucking protect you."

A breath ghosts past my lips as I try to process what he's saying. What it means. Those vulnerable feelings rise up inside me in a rush, and I'm tempted to ask quietly *what's next*?

For the three of us...

But I already feel like I've let down my guard enough this morning with Hayes and with Stefan. I know how relationships go. I've seen it with my parents. Trust is a mirage. *You can only trust a dog.*

I hate that my cruel dad was right when he dispensed that little nugget of intel to my baby sister and me. I wish I were home, my pup curled up in my lap, writing articles about fashion trends, rather than stuck pretending I'm the Mrs. to his Mr.

There's so much Hayes and I have to sort out. Like how long we're doing this, what we're saying to friends and family, but most of all, what it means for...*three people.*

Because I can't stop thinking about Stefan *and* Hayes. I can't stop thinking about the way I felt with both of them. I can't stop thinking about how even though I know it's a bad idea, I want to see Stefan again.

And Hayes.

But now isn't the time to say *I want to see you and your friend a second time.*

I especially can't say that because the cheery face of Oliver pops into my field of vision. He waves a hand as if he's sorry to interrupt but has no choice. "Jessie has a packed day here in Vegas and she's meeting with some of the hotel owners later, so we should do that coffee now."

Translation: don't keep the owner waiting. And since we don't need an annulment now, I guess we're free to have coffee. Oh, joy.

"Of course," I say, and since Hayes can make a game-day decision, so can I. "But is there any chance we could keep the marriage on the down-low on the plane home? Our whirlwind romance happened so quickly, and we're obviously so wildly in love that we had to elope, but..." I stop, affecting an *oops* grin, "I need to tell my mom and grandma, since they obviously weren't there last night."

"Of course," Oliver says with a smile, understanding me completely.

As we head to coffee, I flash Hayes a *take that* grin. Two can play at this fake marriage game.

Benefits of not going to the breakfast that morning? Snagging the window seat in the second row and asking Oliver to sit next to me. Benefits of my second white lie of the day, the one I told to Oliver about wanting to tell my family? Tucking the ring away in my jeans pocket.

I don't know what Hayes did with his ring. I don't know what he told Stefan. I avoid them both as they board. I flip open my laptop and I don't look up as I research my piece for Birdie on the short flight back to San Francisco, my gut churning the whole time. Jessie's not on the same flight. Oliver mentioned the meetings she had in Vegas. It's a blessing that she's not here, but there's so much I need to deal with.

I don't even know where to start. How big this will be. What this means. Maybe Oliver knows. As the plane is landing, I turn to him and quietly ask, "The team isn't going to make a big deal of this, are they? I mean, I'm just the mascot."

He gives a sympathetic smile. "We won't post anything on our social unless you want us to."

Others might though. We can't possibly be that interesting. Can we? I sincerely hope the mascot and the new guy aren't a story.

When I peer over the seats, the guys are grabbing bags and phones, slinging trash talk, flipping each other off. Like it's a regular flight and one of their own didn't just get married to, well, one of their *adjacent* own.

I don't look at Hayes. I don't even try to talk to him. He's only texted me once since we left each other this morning.

> Hayes: Can we talk later today?

I responded with one word. *Yes.*

As I shuffle off the plane, making sure to linger well

behind the players, I chitchat with Oliver. I do my best to ignore the churning in my gut and the worries that bombard me over how the hell to navigate this new terrain. "We have your costume all made up and we'll debut it at the next game," Oliver says. "We're going to do a fan poll too. It's all set up, and we'll prime the pump by taking videos of you in your new costume skating and firing T-shirts into the crowd."

"Sounds fun," I say, trying my best to stay focused on my job. Admittedly, operating a T-shirt cannon does sound like a blast. "I ran one in college. I'm a certified T-shirt cannon expert."

And a liar.

But I'm also a dog mom, and once I get out of the airport, I text Trina, asking if she can meet me with my dog at a coffee shop, ideally with Aubrey too. I need girlfriend therapy. Badly.

24

FOOT MEET MOUTH

Stefan

Good thing I have cat-like reflexes, because I almost lose my footing on the treadmill later that afternoon when Hayes finally tells me why he's been a moody bastard all day.

"Are you kidding me?" I ask, as I grip the sidebars, steadying myself.

We're at my house in my state-of-the-art gym. From the treadmill next to mine, he sears me with a look that says he's not at all kidding. "I wish."

I catch back up to my pace, running some more, processing this turn of events. "That explains the sullen mood you've been in since the breakfast."

"I was not in a bad mood at breakfast."

"You were so."

He heaves a sigh as he runs even faster. "I tried to hide it."

"Try a little harder next time," I tell him, annoyed with him for one of the first times ever. I rarely get annoyed with friends, especially Hayes. Or anyone, for that matter. Life's too short for little grievances. At the moment, though, Hayes Armstrong is not my favorite person. "But back it up please. I want to get to the part where you're in the elevator with the team owner and have the brilliant idea to explain your shenanigans last night by saying you're still married."

I can't believe that was his solution.

"It seemed like a good idea at the time," he huffs.

I scoff. But I don't say *that was a dick move when I want us both to take her out on a date*. I'd be the asshole then, and I generally strive to avoid that. Instead, I say, "I can't imagine why that would be a good idea."

"I thought it looked better to be married than wasted and playing a prank," he explains, with some self-loathing in his tone. "I thought we could just do, you know, one of those stay-married-for-a-few-months-and-then-let-it-blow-over things. Like it's no big deal."

He hits some buttons on the console and slows his pace. I do the same since my workout is over. "And now you're going to be fake married to her for what? A few months? The season?" I ask, still trying to understand this hot mess.

I'm asking out of curiosity but also out of selfishness. I'd like to know what their matrimony means for me.

He stops the machine and hops off, grabbing his water bottle from the floor. "I don't know, man. I need to talk to her later. Figure out the details," he says, and I sure hope those details include me getting to enjoy some of the benefits of his hot wife. But I shut up about my wishes when he drags his free hand down his face. He's really beating himself up, and I don't want to pile on. "But she's pissed at me. I feel like a fucking idiot. I thought about it on the plane, and I thought about it on the drive home, and I thought about it my whole fucking workout. I need to apologize to her. And you." He shoots me a sincere frown. "I'm sorry."

There goes the last of my annoyance. It's out of the door and gone completely. What kind of friend would I be to stay pissed at him for something like this? "I get it, Hayes. Your mouth loves your foot."

With an eye roll, he flips me the bird.

I pretend to peer a little closer at his mouth. "There's a lot of room in there still. You wanted to test inserting the whole damn thing, right?"

"Fine, fine. I deserve that," he says, but then he fixes me with a serious look. "But do you really get it?"

I tilt my head in question. He's going to need to do some more heavy lifting. "What do you mean?"

"I don't know how to fucking do this," he says, raising his eyebrows importantly, like he's sending me a secret message. "I mean, we've done *this,* but we haven't done *this.*"

Fallen for the same girl?

I don't want to say that out loud. Don't want to give it air and breath yet, especially since I'm pretty sure my friend is in a different place than I am when it comes to matters of the heart. Honestly, I'm pretty sure Ivy is too. But I can take a step closer to Hayes. I can lead the conversation to where I think he's going.

"I'm not annoyed anymore that you're married to her, and I appreciate you telling me now. But I'm going to be blunt with you." This is harder than pitching him on a threesome, something I didn't even have to do. Hell, he pitched me. He's done the hard work so far. I can do the same.

I pinch the bridge of my nose and lean against the wall, then, like Ivy opened up to me this morning, like Hayes opened up to me just now, I do the same with my friend. "I don't want a one-time thing with her. I don't want last night to be like the other times we've shared a woman. I want to spend more time with her."

I take a beat and say something even harder. "I want *us* to spend more time with her." As his lips curve up in a grin, I beat him to the punchline. "I suppose what I'm saying is...I'd really like to fuck your wife again."

He cracks up, then shakes his head, blowing out a long breath. "Yeah, me too. But I'm pretty sure she's royally pissed at me."

I laugh like the cat who ate the canary. "And you're going to need to fix that and do it really fucking soon. Because I don't just want to fuck her. I'd like us to take her out."

He paces beside the treadmills, clearly puzzling through next steps. When he turns around, he's smiling like he's pleased with himself. "I have an idea for how to say I'm sorry."

"I want in on it."

"What do you have to say you're sorry for?"

I wave a dismissive hand. "Please. I don't need to say I'm sorry. I have other things I need to say to her. Namely, *come over tomorrow night*. So whatever you do, make sure it covers your sins and my request."

25

AN APOLOGY BOUQUET

Ivy

Fun fact. There is hardly a woe that a vanilla latte and girlfriend time can't cure. But big woes require big drinks, so I get a big-ass one.

With my drink in hand, I sink down into a comfy chair at a sidewalk table at Dr. Insomnia's and take a thirsty sip from the mug. It gives me courage.

So does Roxy, who's curled up in my lap at this outdoor table with me. When Trina brought my pup, she whimpered with excitement when she saw me, proving once again that dogs are a girl's best friend. I scratch her ears while Trina's three-legged pup, Nacho, sits on the sidewalk like a good boy, ears up, checking out lady dogs with avid interest as they walk by.

Well, he might be checking out boy dogs too. I don't really know his preferences.

Aubrey settles in with her mango smoothie, flicks

some strands of her red hair, and gives me an *I've been waiting too long* look. "Are you finally going to tell us about your wedding night?"

They already got the big picture details in text. Now it's time for the real tea. My stomach does cartwheels as I draw a deep, fueling breath. I start with the good news. "I have been introduced to the joys of a double dicking."

Everyone's quiet for several long seconds till Aubrey gasps, and Trina's green eyes pop. "Get it, get, get it," she sings, shimmying in tune, before she says, "With who? I want details. Do not skimp."

Aubrey lifts a finger. "Hayes and Stefan, I bet."

"Nailed it," I say.

"Sounds like they nailed *you*," she corrects.

"Touché."

Then Aubrey shoots me a frustrated stare. "Also, I hate you. That's not fucking fair. When do I get my turn on the double-dude merry-go-round?"

Trina points down the street. "There's a ticket counter at the fairgrounds. Just order two for the price of one and you're good to go."

"Thanks for the tip," she deadpans, then turns back to me. "Now. Story time. And start at the beginning."

"I will, but how did you guess who it was?"

She taps her skull. "They seem like the type who'd give a good dicking."

"You're not wrong. Also, who knew pleasure could be exponential when it's doubled?" I whisper.

Trina clears her throat, all over the top. Takes the time raising her hand.

Aubrey slumps in her chair, hands raised in surrender. "Seriously, what does a girl need to do to get in on the double-duty action?"

"It's not all fun and games," I say, since as good as the night was, now I have to deal with the mess during the day. "Have I mentioned that I'm stuck being married to only one of them while I still want to see *both* of them?"

Aubrey mimes playing a small violin. "Poor baby."

"Seriously, though. What do I do? I didn't sign up to be a fake wife." I take another drink.

Trina sets down her coffee and gives me a thoughtful look. "What do you want to do about it? Do you want to come clean to the team owner? That's a viable option."

I shudder, immediately and involuntarily. "Jessie's been good to me. I don't want to let her down. I don't want to draw more attention to myself either."

"There's your answer. You have to pretend," Trina says. "For a reasonable amount of time."

My gut swirls, but I know she's right.

"Do the charity event," she continues. "Then move on and it'll be fine. Relationships don't always work out. Maybe in a few months, you can quietly divorce. It's not like Jessie's going to say *you must stay married forever*. It sounds like you're just trying to get through a couple months to save face, to be honest."

I give that some thought as I take another drink. That sounds reasonable enough. This isn't forever. It's just for a short while. I can handle that. Hayes needs to focus on hockey and finding his footing with the team, and I can do this for him. He was helpful to me with his plus-one offer the night I met him. Maybe this is my turn to *white knight* him. I can be his plus-one. We'll do Jessie's golf luncheon so he can impress the owner. And we'll go to Xander and Simone's wedding so I can write about it for Your Scrappy Little Fashionista. Tit for tat. "You're probably right. I was so pissed earlier that he didn't check with me, so I've been stewing, and I hadn't really thought through those details. But a short marriage makes sense."

Aubrey taps a long pink fingernail against the iron table like she's thinking this situation through too. "Besides, is it really the worst thing? It sounds like you could enjoy some *benefits*, if you know what I mean."

I sure do, and I like how her dirty brain works. "I'm not interested in anything serious though. I don't want to jump into another relationship."

"Somehow, I don't think it'd be a hardship to enjoy the marital benefits, judging from what you told us about last night," she says dryly.

My chest flutters with nerves. Asking for what I want is a big hurdle. What if they reject me? What if one does, and the other doesn't? How does that even work? This is uncharted territory for me. "But how do I broach that? How do I say *can we keep seeing your friend while we are married*?"

"Say that," Trina says, like it's so simple.

"I hate putting myself out there," I mutter.

"It is hard," she acknowledges. "But sometimes that's what you have to do."

* * *

Later that night I'm pacing through my apartment, trying to locate the nerve to go upstairs and see Hayes, when there's a knock on my door. My heart races. Then it sprints when a voice says, "Hey. It's Hayes."

I'm still frustrated with him, but I'm also eager to just say what's on my mind.

I fling open the door and whoa...

My husband is standing on the other side holding a basket of artsy, illustrated notebooks in bright pink, soft lavender, and cherry red, along with...is that what I think it is? "Is that a bouquet of pens?" My voice squeaks.

"Yes," he says, clearly pleased. He hands me the pens, wrapped with a huge purple bow.

I must have ingested helium when I ask, "For me?"

He smiles and laughs. "Is there someone else here who has a thing for notebooks with women in vintage dresses on the front and beautiful colored pens for all her ideas?"

I reach my arms out and happily take the basket, hugging it close. "Thank you. I love it."

"Open the first one," he says, then hands me the notebook with the purple cover. On the front is a pencil drawing of a woman in a flapper dress. Gingerly, I open it, and the first line on the paper reads: *I'm sorry I didn't ask you first. If you forgive me, I promise to be the best fake husband there is.*

The apology is more than I expected. I close my eyes, letting a new, warm feeling flow through my body.

When I open my eyes, I vow to put my frustrations from this morning fully behind me. But I also need him to understand a few ground rules. "I don't want you to make decisions like that without me," I say, clear and firm.

He nods, understanding in his dark eyes. "I get that. I do."

"I'm a part of this."

"I understand. I should have handled it...differently."

"I know you felt like you were doing it for me, but it affects me," I add, gentler now.

He sighs, dragging a hand through his hair, his eyes full of regret. "I wanted to help. But I didn't do it in the best way. If you want to get an annulment now, I'll handle it all. I did some research. It's not that hard, and I'll just man up and explain it to Ms. Rose."

I set a hand on his arm, reassuring him. "I appreciate that, but you don't need to do it. I'll go to the golf event with you. You'll go to my ex's wedding with me."

"Absolutely."

I let go of his arm, square my shoulders, and say, "I just want to make a few things clear."

"Lay it on me."

Deep breath. *Say the hard thing.* "I hate to bring this up, but given what happened with my ex, I have to. I don't want to be made a fool. You can't see anyone else."

He blinks. His brow furrows. "Are you fucking crazy?"

I tense. Did I misread everything? "That feels reasonable to me," I say, standing my ground.

He rolls his eyes. "Don't you get it, Ivy?"

"Get what?"

"I want you. *Only you*. I tried to resist you because we work together, and a lot of good that did. So I'm standing here, still wanting you."

A smile takes shape on my lips, slow and easy. "Good. Then I only have one condition for us staying married."

The next night when I arrive at The Great Dane, I say hello to the hostess then add, "I'd like a table for three."

Well, I'm having a double date after all.

26

A DOUBLE DATE

Ivy

"Tell us."

The demand comes from Stefan, delivered in the smooth, playful voice that matches his whole easygoing demeanor. He takes up all the space in the chair, stretching an arm across the back and crossing his legs.

"C'mon, you know you want to," Hayes goads in a rougher tone, leaning closer. His stubble is filling in even more, the start of a beard coming in.

We're at a private table in the corner of the rooftop patio at Stefan's restaurant-slash-bar, and they're trying to pry a secret out of me.

I shake my head, adamant, my hair swinging back and forth. "Nope." I lift my bubbly water—no liquor for this girl tonight—and swirl it defiantly. A statement. "You're not winning this one. I refuse to give up team secrets. You'll find out next week." That's when the team will debut the first of three options for a new mascot/team name.

"C'mon," Stefan says, trying again. "You know the candidates before anyone else. It's only fair to give us a hint."

Hayes gives it his best shot. "We won't say a word beyond this table." He draws an air circle around the three of us as stars wink in the San Francisco sky.

I have a little fun with them. "Why do you even want to know? It's not like you have to wear new uniforms yet. As the mascot, I'm just testing the potential name."

Stefan sets down his wineglass amidst the remains of the dinner we just finished. "I bet we could get it out of you. *Later. In bed.*"

I like the sound of his seduction plans. "Is this another dare?"

"Smells like a dare to me," Hayes says, accompanied by forks clattering and glasses clinking.

We're far away from other diners, but I'm not worried about how this looks. We're just three people having dinner. But this is what I wanted—a night with both of them. My family knows the truth, and that was important to me. I didn't want to fool them, so over breakfast this morning I told my grandma and my mom about the marriage arrangement so they wouldn't worry if they heard anything on social. I texted with Katie too.

"Is this a new dating trend I need to know about?" my mom had asked when I'd told her.

"Because if it is, I'm out," my grandma had seconded. "It took me long enough to learn to like avocado toast."

"Fake marriage is not the new avocado toast," I'd reassured her. I'm lucky they're so supportive and didn't give me a hard time at all. But I left telling Ryker to Trina, since she knows how to handle him.

Now I'm just enjoying my evening with these two guys as they play the new-team-name-guessing game.

"I bet it's an otter," Stefan muses.

"It's not an otter," I say.

"What about a mustang? That'd be cool," Hayes says.

Stefan arches a brow at Hayes. "Does that even make sense? Then we'd be, what, horses on skates?"

"That's your issue? The realism of mascots? The other team in this city is called the Sea Dogs and you're pointing out that horses don't wear skates?"

"What even is a Sea Dog?" Stefan's brow knits as he turns philosophical.

"A seal," I answer confidently.

Hayes's irises twinkle with victory. "So that's what you'll wear? A seal costume?" He says it like he's cracked the code.

When he so didn't. "I took a mascot oath. I will not reveal the mascots we're testing." But the whole city will know at the next home game when I zip up the costume.

"We'll get it out of you later," Hayes says, all bravado once more.

"Speaking of later." I sit up straighter. We've been

having such a good time at dinner that we haven't even had *the talk* yet. But we can't put it off any longer. It's important. "We should talk."

Hayes glances around the eatery, full of diners but none close enough to eavesdrop, making sure the place is private. "Yeah, we should."

"Seeing as I'm Mrs. Hockey for a couple months, we should establish the ground rules. Any *situationship* needs them," I say, sketching air quotes.

"Situationship," Stefan says, clearly amused.

"Well, it seems apropos."

"If anything is a situationship, it's this. And rules are good," Hayes seconds.

Stefan gestures regally, bestowing the floor on me. "Have at it. I feel like whatever rules you establish, I come out ahead."

Such a cocky fucker. "How do you figure?"

The Danish man waves a hand at Hayes then me. "You two have to go to these events. Charity luncheon, wedding, whatnot. I basically get the fun end of things. Correct?"

Hayes rolls his eyes. "Yes, you do. What a shock."

With a casual shrug, Stefan turns to me, those ice-blue eyes sparkling. "I've got a packed schedule with the upcoming Sportsman of the Year award anyway. Meetings with sponsors and The Sports Network. I don't need more public events."

"Humble brag," Hayes says, coughing under his breath.

Stefan turns to me. "Besides, being your secret

boyfriend seems a lot more fun than being the public husband."

I blanch at that term. Secret boyfriend? I wasn't looking for a boyfriend at all, let alone a clandestine one. But I wasn't seeking a husband either.

Maybe I didn't hear him right. "Secret boyfriend?"

"Sweetheart." Stefan gives me *the look*. The confident one that says *don't argue*. "I'm your secret boyfriend and you know it."

Well then.

Arousal shimmies through me at his declaration and the certainty of it. *Secret boyfriend* seems reasonable.

"Fair enough," I say, hiding a grin. I like his possession. I didn't see it coming, but it's impossible to deny.

"As the captain, I've got enough on my plate with promos and whatnot," Stefan adds. "Seems I get to have my cake and eat it too—at night."

"Am I cake?" I ask.

His eyes pin mine. "Yes, Ivy. You're the cake."

Hayes tosses his napkin on the table. "I'm definitely ready for dessert then."

Me too, but there's one more thing. I hold up a hand. "So, we're doing this...*arrangement* for the course of the"—I glance around, lowering my voice more—"the marriage?"

"Yes," Stefan says, as surely as ever. But he shifts to legitimate concern when he adds, "if that works for you."

"Does it, Ivy?" Hayes asks, checking in too.

The man can learn. And I like it.

"Yes. That works for me." I'm no expert at group dynamics. I'm a total novice, in fact, but I wrote my top questions in my new notebook today. It's not in front of me now, but they were pretty damn easy to memorize. "Just a few things though. Little details."

"Hit us up," Hayes says.

I swallow, then begin. "How does it work if I want to spend time with one of you when the other's not around? Like, if I want to sleep with my boyfriend when my husband isn't around? Or vice versa?"

Judging from their faces—both pairs of eyes are blazing—I've asked the right question.

Stefan lifts a finger, a sign that he'll take this one. "Thanks for asking, but you don't need to check with me if you want to fuck Hayes. I don't want to check with him if I want to tie you up, kiss you slowly and sensually all over your delicious body, and make you come hard again and again. We're not jealous guys."

I'm a little caught up in the images, in the promises of pleasure. It takes me a few seconds to absorb this new world order.

"You're really not," I say, kind of amazed but still curious. "Why not though?"

"Why would I be? I like it when you're getting all the attention. That's what turns me on," Stefan says matter-of-factly.

"Same here," Hayes puts in. "I like getting you off. I like watching you get off. I like watching him get you off. It works out well for me when you're coming. *A lot*."

My cheeks flush, and I need to get out of here really

soon. "About that mascot deal," I begin, my voice feathery with desire.

"Yes?" Stefan asks.

"Three orgasms, and I'll give you a hint what it is."

"Deal," they say together.

27

A NEW COCKTAIL

Ivy

I have a sex plan for our second night together. Well, after I try not to gawk at Stefan's palace.

But I fail because...wow.

"It's good to be the captain," I say in awe, staring wide-eyed up at the massive ceilings, two stories high. A modern chandelier hangs down, all sleek lines and glass. My gaze swings to the windows on the far side of the massive living room—floor-to-ceiling ones that offer an uninterrupted view of the city, the Golden Gate Bridge in the distance, and the vast bay beyond.

"It's home enough," he says, and that *enough* is doing a lot of the emotional work in that sentence. I want to ask what he means, but Hayes's hands come down on my waist, and his body presses to my back. I file away that *enough* for another time.

"Mmm. The way you smell," Hayes murmurs, then

drags his nose along my neck. "Like berries and candy, and I just want to fucking eat you up."

"Patience," I murmur as Stefan turns around in the foyer and joins us, lining his big frame against my front. I'm sandwiched by these two teammates and my brain is already frying. But I'm not going to let them lead tonight. I shake off the lust. "There's something I want to do first. Can I be in charge?"

"What do you think, Stefan?" Hayes asks his friend.

"Sure. Give her fifteen minutes."

That ought to do the trick.

We don't bother with the bedroom. In the warm living room that belongs in a Scandinavian design showroom, Stefan busies himself with his phone, hunting for a playlist, while Hayes strips by a massive U-shaped couch, me standing next to him.

When I'm down to my black lace panties, I push Hayes's briefs off so I can say hello to his cock. My mouth waters at the sight of his ambitious erection, but first things first. "I didn't get to check out your ink on our wedding night," I say, sinking down on the couch so I can admire the artwork in person at last, tracing my thumb along the constellation.

Five finely drawn stars curve down his hip. "Did it hurt?" I ask, as I run a finger reverently over the blue ink right below his hip bone.

"No, but my dick will hurt if you don't give it some attention now."

I drop to my knees, straighten my back, and gaze up at him, a soft smile on my lips. He might like to give orders, but I know he likes when I talk back too. "Does this work for you?"

"Fuck, baby," he grunts, then runs a hand over my hair. "So fucking much."

Music fills the room, and it sounds like The Weeknd. "Do you want Stefan to watch me suck your dick?" I ask the naked man in front of me.

Hayes trembles. He actually trembles as he slides a hand down his cock, squeezing the tip as an offering. "Bet you'd love it more if he was jerking his cock at the same time."

A shudder racks my body from head to toe. I'm lit up with desire. "Yes."

"But you're not really in charge, Ivy," Hayes says in a predatory tone as he grabs my discarded bra from the couch.

He dangles it in front of me. "Tie her up," Hayes commands Stefan.

I gasp, then say, "Please."

"You heard her," Hayes says.

Stefan moves behind me, kneeling as he tugs my wrists together.

"I can't fucking wait," Hayes says, smacking my face with his dick as Stefan wraps the lacy straps around my skin, binding my hands. "Open up."

I comply, parting my lips as Stefan gives a final check of the restraint. "She's good to go," he remarks.

"Thanks, man," Hayes says amiably, then turns his gaze back to me, his eyes darkening. "Take it now,"

Hayes orders, his rough demand sending a jolt of pleasure to my core.

I dart out my tongue, catching the salty, musky taste of Hayes while Stefan rises and comes around to stand next to him. Stefan tugs at the bottom of his tight burgundy polo, pulling it up. Hayes ropes a fist in my hair as I put my mouth on his dick.

One man strips for me while another feeds me his cock. It's a feast for my eyes and my mouth. I draw the head of Hayes's dick past my lips with a loud suck.

"Look at you. Look at those sexy lips," Stefan praises, undoing his jeans as I show him how well I can suck his friend. "That's right. Do a good job, sweetheart, and I'll let you have mine too."

I squirm, feeling warm and pliant, eager for more. With only my mouth to use, I focus on Hayes, relishing his groans as I draw him deeper. His gaze is heated, dark flames in darker eyes as he watches me. "Those perfect lips were made for my dick," he growls.

I preen at the compliment, opening wider. Hayes pushes in deeper, watching my lips stretch around him. He's a big man with a hungry cock, and I want to please him. I arch my back so I can inch closer. Hayes reads my cues, and pumps a little harder, a little faster.

"You're doing so good," Stefan murmurs.

My gaze drifts to him, and he's parked on the couch in his naked glory, fisting his cock. God, it's a gorgeous sight, my secret boyfriend watching me suck off my public husband.

I feel good everywhere, goose bumps sliding over my skin as Hayes tightens his grip on my hair. His eyes squeeze shut. For a few seconds, he stays like that, almost frozen, as if he's trying to decide how hard to go next.

When he opens his eyes, there's coiled restraint in them. With a huff of his breath, he pushes my hair all the way over to one side and then thrusts. "Let me fuck your face hard, baby," he demands.

I tremble, nodding a fast yes, since I can't speak with my mouth full. But Stefan speaks for me. "Turns you on, doesn't it, worshiping his dick?"

I gush, nodding around Hayes's cock in answer. Turns me on so much that I want them to know exactly what I want. I jerk my face back, letting go of the cock in my mouth for a hot second to look up at Hayes. "Can you come on my face?"

With a carnal rumble, he hisses out a yes. "All over your perfect mouth, baby."

I take him back in.

As Hayes fucks my mouth, I'm drowning in lust, even when I cough, even when he asks if I'm okay and I nod a yes. I'm flooded with the eagerness to please him. Stefan shuttles his fist faster, stroking harder, watching my mouth work his friend's cock.

"Fucking beautiful, sweetheart. You're so fucking good at that. You look so lovely taking his dick," he says.

I want Stefan too. Desperately. But I won't let go of Hayes. Somehow, Stefan understands my unspoken wishes, since he tilts his head, then curves his lips. "Bet you want us both to come on that pretty face."

My eyes roll back in my head, and I nod savagely as

I suck, my eagerness stoked by how he understands my desires. How he fans the flames.

Then Stefan's up on his feet, moving next to me, his free hand wrapped in my hair too. There's one on each side of me. Both men are touching my face, claiming my hair.

While I'm on my knees with my wrists bound behind my back, my breasts bouncing, one man fucks my mouth while the other jerks his cock. Both of them use me for their pleasure.

This is what I wanted tonight. To be used.

I'm rocking my hips, too, aching for another high of my own. "Fuck, baby. You're so fucking dirty. You fucking love it, don't you?" Hayes rasps out.

So much it's obscene.

My panties are soaked as Hayes pumps his hips, grips my head, then draws a sharp, harsh breath. "Gonna come," he warns, then pulls out, his fist flying along his length. "Take it. Fucking take it."

I open my mouth, and seconds later, he's painting my face with his come, hot strands landing on my cheek, my lips, my tongue. His sounds are feral.

I'm shaking everywhere with lust, but I don't dare swallow as I turn to Stefan and stick out my tongue. He steps closer, gives a final jerk of his cock, then spills his release, too, on my waiting tongue.

Then, I look up at the men before me, roll my lips together, and swallow their pleasure at once.

A perfect cocktail of the two of them.

When I part my lips to smile, they both look like they're in a daze, drunk on me.

I'm drunk on pleasure, struggling to break free of my lingerie restraint. Hayes moves behind me, unbinds me. Immediately, I jam a hand between my thighs to touch my throbbing clit, but Stefan barks out a "no."

It's a stern order from the gentler one.

I stop, obeying.

"Clean her up," Stefan says to the other man.

Hayes leaves the room and returns seconds later with a wet washcloth. With tender hands, he wipes my face with it as Stefan rubs my wrists soothingly. When Hayes sets down the cloth, Stefan is firm again. This time, his tone is directed to me.

"Get on the couch, spread those beautiful thighs, and let your husband eat that sweet pussy. He hasn't had a chance to taste you, and that's just not fair, now, is it?"

"It's not," I say.

They strip off my panties and lay me down, my head in Stefan's lap, my body stretched along the big couch. Hayes crawls down the cushions, spreads my thighs, and brushes his stubble against my inner thigh.

I cry out, then I murmur as Stefan leans down, strokes my face, and brushes feather-light touches to my arms, shoulders, and breasts while Hayes kisses a hungry path up to my pussy.

When he reaches my slick center, he growls.

And one man eats my pussy while the other lavishes sensual attention on my face, my hair, and my tits, caressing me.

Stefan adores me while Hayes devours me.

Soon, I'm parting my legs wider, letting Hayes shove

my thighs apart with his hands as Stefan kisses me like I'm the star of the show.

And really, as pleasure pulses through me, swirling tight in my belly, I am.

I am kissed everywhere by them, my body aching with pleasure, with the promise of impending bliss, and soon I can't hold back. I cry out against Stefan's lips on mine, thrust against Hayes's mouth on me, and shatter into a million pieces from their filthy devotion.

I think I'm going to like having a temporary husband and a secret boyfriend very, very much.

* * *

Later, in bed, I feel fizzy and soft until I remember something. I sit up, alarmed. "Roxy!"

I need to go. Yes, Jackson's home, but she's mine, and I can't leave her. She hasn't even had her daily sock.

Hayes swings his legs out of bed, setting a firm hand on my stomach. "Stay. I'll get her."

* * *

Thirty minutes later, he returns, and the scrabbling of paws and the whimper of my cutie makes my heart expand. I toss her my sock. She grabs it and then whips her snout left and right, hunting for a sock hiding place. But she doesn't have one here yet, so she gives me a *help please* look. I scoop her up, wrestling the sock away. We get back into bed, and my little cinnamon love scampers across the dove-gray comforter. She gives a kiss to Stefan, then Hayes, then sighs contentedly and curls into a tight ball against my neck.

"Guess she likes both of you too," I say, then I add, "Think...San Francisco."

Hayes shoots me a *what are you talking about* look.

"That's your hint."

Stefan chuckles. "Ah. The mascot hint. But we didn't give you three orgasms."

I grin. "I said three. Not three for me. We each got one."

Stefan wraps an arm around me and kisses my cheek. "Hope you enjoyed dessert."

"I know I did," Hayes says, turning the other way to, presumably, sleep on his stomach.

I close my eyes, having enjoyed the marital benefits indeed.

28

A REWARD PLANNER

Stefan

In the morning, I'm up before Hayes, so I pad through my home, looking for my guest, since she wasn't in bed when I rose. I spot Ivy on the back deck, calling to her dog in the yard, urging Roxy to come inside. But the little critter isn't listening. The cinnamon pup is rolling on her back in the grass, soaking up the sun.

I try not to think too hard on how good they look here as I slide open the glass door. Since I learned she was officially single, all I've wanted is some company, some fun, and some good times. I'm here for that—to fill my empty nights with one woman. Okay, one woman and a friend. But a tryst, nevertheless.

"Girl, c'mon," Ivy calls out, a little desperate, but like she's trying to keep her voice low at the same time. She whips her gaze to me. "Oh, hi. Sun makes her drunk and defiant." Ivy gestures to the fenced in yard, hemmed by tall hedges. Roxy's wiggling around on the emerald blades, which catch the early morning rays.

"Understandable. I've done the same," I say.

Ivy shoots me a quizzical look. "Rolled around on the grass?"

"In a manner of speaking. Once you've gone through a Scandinavian winter, you soak up the rays whenever you get them." I nod to the dog. "She seems happy."

Ivy sighs but smiles as she checks out the dog lolling in the grass. Ivy's wearing just a T-shirt, and she looks fantastic in the morning. Just as I suspected, since yeah, I did picture this all the times I imagined a little *companionship* with her. She makes the empty mornings better.

"I should round her up soon though. I have things planned today," Ivy says, fussing with the hem of her shirt, like she's unsure about how we should interact in the morning.

Doesn't she know me by now? Touch is my favorite language.

I crowd her, wrap a fist around her lush hair, and gently tug it back while pressing a possessive kiss to her lips.

When I let go, I ask, "What's on your agenda?"

She takes a few seconds to blink and perhaps to absorb the kiss before she screws up the corner of her lips, then gestures to the house. "I'd better check my planner to be sure. Hayes picked it up last night when he got Roxy."

That catches the dog's attention at last, since she

scampers across the yard and up the steps, wagging her tail at Ivy, who scoops her up and peppers her head with kisses.

We go inside, sinking down on the couch with the pup. Ivy grabs her canvas bag from the table, then pulls out the planner.

"I guess size does matter," I say, kind of amazed at the scope of that thing.

She pets the front cover. "In planners, it does. This one is practically perfect."

It's pretty and feminine, with whimsical illustrations of shoes and dresses and clothes. When she flips it open to this week, the dates are filled with details about what she has to do.

She slides a pen from a holder on the side. "Hayes got me this one," she says of the silver pen, then shakes her head. "Wait. Both of you did."

"Good girl," I say, then run a hand through her hair as she shows me her plan for the week. Lots of writing and hustling, working on freelance pieces and creating her own content. "And then I reward myself for hitting my goals."

My chest warms and I rub a hand against my sternum, like I can hold onto this fizzy feeling. This is what I've wanted. To soak up all the details of Ivy. "What kind of rewards do you like?"

"A latte. A TV show. A bandana for Roxy. A slice of pie. A new book," she says, rattling off little pleasures.

"Hmm."

She turns to me, studying my face. "What's that hmm for?"

I meet her gaze, a smile tugging at my lips. "How about battery-operated gifts?"

She dips her face.

I tuck a finger under her chin. "Does that embarrass you? Because I don't think it does," I say, calling her out on the shy act.

"Why do you say that?"

"Because you told us in Vegas you like to play with your tits. I bet you like to play with yourself. *A lot*," I say.

She nibbles on the corner of her lips.

"You do, Ivy," I press.

She swallows, then shrugs. A subtle admission. And I plan on running with it. I lean closer, nip her neck, then point to the days of the week. "You might need to X out the evenings. We're going to keep you very, very busy."

"Are you now?"

That's what I've wanted. And now I'm getting it. "Yes," I say, then take her pen and add some items to her agenda so she knows that Hayes and I will be occupying her nights. Not gonna lie—that's a ray of sunlight, knowing I'll be busy in the best of ways. "We should meet at his place, though," I add, with some reluctance. I like having her here. I've wanted this for some time. But it's also...risky.

When she meets my gaze, waiting for me to say more, I add, "Just in case anyone spots you leaving in the morning. It seems wiser that you'd be seen leaving your hubby's home."

"Instead of my secret boyfriend's?"

That sounds too damn good on her lips. So I focus

on the calendar in front of her and making plans for the next few days. "What about Thursday night?" she asks since that day's blank. But she answers for me. "Oh, right. Game night in Phoenix."

"But you can FaceTime us the night before. And see us after the game if we don't fly in too late."

She writes an *O* on that day. "So this is officially a reward planner now."

I take the pen and add an *O* to every night. Then, a couple extras. "Yes, it is."

We give her plenty over the next few nights in person, then on FaceTime the night before the game. Well, I like to stick to the calendar too.

* * *

In some ways, I'm a lucky guy. I've had a good career for nearly a decade, but I don't take that luck for granted. I try to cultivate it and shape it. On Thursday morning in Phoenix, I do yoga at the hotel, order a kale smoothie, then stretch.

The better I take care of my body, the longer I can play. Hockey's a brutal game, and my body takes a pounding every time I take the ice, but it's still a game —and I love it as much now as I did when I was a little kid, strapping on skates in Denmark, then in Virginia where we moved when I started school.

That afternoon, we hit the opponent's ice for warmups, and I easily blot out the jeers of the opposing team's fans. That shit never bugs me. Never has.

Playing is a joy, and I'll stop playing when I can't do it or when I stop having fun, whichever comes first.

There are a few Avengers fans in the crowd, so after we stretch, I sign a couple pucks. But when the game puck drops, I'm all focus, racing across the ice, jostling against the other team. Right off the mark, I spot an opening and pass to Brady. He shoots but misses.

He mutters a curse, clearly frustrated with himself. When we reach the players' bench for a line change, I tap my stick to his skate. The dude is hard on himself. "Keep it up. There are plenty of chances."

"Thanks, man," he says. We find our chance at the end of the period, and we take it, and the goal.

"You were right," he says as we skate off.

"It's one of my many gifts."

"Humility isn't one of them," he says.

"And that's a good thing." Nope. I amend that. "A great thing."

* * *

During the third period, the score is tied, and I've been hunting for another shot on goal all night, but I've found none. As the clock ticks, I race down the ice. Hayes chases the puck, but he's crowded by two defensemen, so he slings a pass my way.

And it's all clear. I send a breakaway shot down the ice. It sails high, past the goalie's reach, and slams beautifully into the twine.

Adrenaline whips through me, and when I turn to the camera, it briefly occurs to me Ivy is probably watching us back at home. I flash her a smile, confident she'll know it's for her.

* * *

Later that night, sitting next to Hayes on the team jet, I open our group chat.

> Ivy: Nice teamwork. You guys deserve a reward.

Stefan: Is that on your planner?

> Ivy: It is now.

Hayes: I know what I want for my prize.

> Ivy: Do tell.

Hayes: You answering the door naked.

Stefan: Such a simple man.

> Hayes: Got a better idea?

Stefan: Yes, she'd look sexy in a Number 18 jersey.

> Hayes: Sexier in Number 21.

Ivy: Here's a better idea. How about Number 21 in the front and Number 18 in the back?

Cracking up, I raise my face from the phone and meet Hayes's eyes, which spark with mischief and dirty thoughts. "She's perfect," I whisper in filthy approval.

"I know."

When we see Ivy that night, she's not naked. She's not in a jersey either. She comes upstairs to Hayes's penthouse wearing a T-shirt and shorts and carrying her peach-bandana-wearing pup, who side-eyes me before she remembers she likes me.

Seems Ivy had the better idea after all. She looks incredible at the door just like that, here for us.

When she comes inside, the loneliness fades a little more.

* * *

On Friday morning, I run alone across the Golden Gate Bridge as the sun rises. On the way back up the endless hill of Divisadero Street, I spot a familiar silhouette ahead of me. Ledger McBride is one of the veterans on the Sea Dogs, the other team in town, and he's running a block ahead.

Well that's an opportunity if I ever saw one. Finding some in the tank, I rev my engine and race up the street. As I pass our rival, I flash a *sorry, sucker* grin.

He rolls his eyes, but a minute later, he catches up to me at the top of the hill. "Don't underestimate me, Christiansen."

"Did you miss the part where I beat you?"

"Did you miss the part where I caught up to you?"

"Seems I did." We jog down the hill toward Pacific

Heights together, shooting the breeze about the season so far.

"Are you still getting all the retirement questions?" I ask. He's logged well over a decade in the pros and gets asked on the reg when he'll hang it all up.

"If I wasn't having one of the best starts of my career, I would be," he says, then checks his smart watch. "A bunch of us are going out to play pool tonight. Want to join?"

I flash back to Ivy's planner. To the note I left her. To what Hayes and I have in store for her. "I'm busy tonight."

"I get it. Rearranging your sock drawer is important."

With a grin that comes from knowing what's on the reward agenda, I pick up the speed and leave him to chase my luck.

29

YOU CAN SHARE IT

Hayes

A few weeks ago, I was considering camping out at Gage's bar to resist Ivy.

Now I'm indulging in temptation.

On Friday afternoon, I hit the gym down the street for a workout, and when I leave, I spot a flash of dark wavy hair. My wife is walking quickly up the block. She's wearing a cute pink sundress that's temptingly short and high-top Converse sneakers. She posted a piece this morning about what to wear when you want to feel like your best self. Is that what she's doing right now?

Impulsively, I pick up the pace and draw up next to her.

"Hey. Did you just come from a meeting about a potential gig?" I ask.

"How did you know?" she asks, slowing her speed.

"This outfit seems to hit that mark. Like you feel like your best self."

A smile tips her lips. "I met with an editor for a fashion site. She might have some work for me." She crosses her fingers. Then she gives in to curiosity and asks, "You read my newsletter?"

"Yes. Every piece."

Her gaze softens more, her eyes dancing. "I didn't know that. I knew Stefan did."

"We both do," I add. "He just likes to brag about it."

She laughs then takes a beat, tilting her head, then surprising me when she says, "You have a telescope."

"That's random."

"It's yours, right? On the rooftop?"

The question seems important to her, like the answer will give her insight. I get an antsy feeling like I've drunk too much coffee. Like I need to pop on my headphones and blast music too loud to think. Things I feel when I don't want to open up.

But Ivy's eyes are wide with genuine curiosity. Another temptation I can't resist—giving her this piece of the puzzle. "I like stars. And planets."

"They go together," she says wryly.

"My granddads are really into astronomy," I tell her. That's the simple part. The rest is not. "My dad and I had a complicated relationship when I was younger. We still do. I spent more time with his parents than with him. I'm closer to them."

She only seems puzzled for a moment, then it clicks, and she asks, "Your dad has two dads?"

"Yes. Ryan and Bryan."

"That's adorable. Their matching names."

"They're adorable *and* ornery."

"What are they like?" she asks as we walk.

"They run an ice rink in Petaluma. I spent a lot of time there when I was younger."

"Did you drive a Zamboni?" She doesn't hide her excitement at that prospect.

"I did, and it's as fun as it sounds."

"I'm jealous. But tell me more about your granddads."

"They like to camp, and they took me with them a lot as a kid. They taught me everything I know about stars and planets and got me hooked on astronomy. Bryan is a sharp dresser and Ryan has horrible fashion sense. He wears white socks with sandals despite my efforts to stop him. I had to try again this morning," I say, shuddering.

She squeezes my arm sympathetically. "Hate to break it to you but that's trendy now."

"Really?"

"Yes, really."

"When I talk to them, I'm going to pretend you never said that."

"I'll back you up if it comes to it." That feels good, her support, even in a playful way. We chat more as we head inside our building then into the elevator. When it reaches the eighth floor, she says, "Thanks for telling me all that."

Something warm spreads in my chest. But I say nothing, just nod and give a faint smile.

"I should go write. But before I see you guys tonight,

I'll send you a pre-ward." She heads down the hall, leaving me wondering what these little moments will be like when this thing between us ends.

How awkward they'll be.

How uncomfortable they'll be.

Or if I'll see her around at all.

Until then, I go to my home and call my dad. I don't love chatting with him, but I should be a good son and touch base. As I straighten up the apartment, he tells me the latest on his proposal plans for Cora, and I listen, chiming in with *that's great*.

A little later, I take off to meet Stefan. We're shopping for Ivy's gifts, and as we're out and about, my phone pings with an artsy black and white shot from Ivy. Of the swell of her breast. The outline of her piercing. The curves of her torso. Then, the words, *You can share it*.

I show it to Stefan, and we admire it together in the store. "I want a whole fucking boudoir shoot of this woman," I say.

"Bet she'd love that too. We're going to have so much fun with your wife tonight," he says, satisfaction already in his tone.

"Yes, we fucking are."

We tell her as much in our group chat, and I count down the hours, trying not to think too much on how quickly I've gone from resistance to addiction.

30

TWO MEN AND A VIBRATOR

Ivy

I push on the door to An Open Book. A sign on an easel greets me. It's for the Page Turners Book Club. There's a lipstick-mark design on the sign. The book club has more than tripled in size since Trina started it a few years ago, and now she runs it both in person and on Zoom, with romance lovers signing in online from all over the world.

I head to the back of the store where she's setting up with the regulars, gals who have been part of the club since the start—Prana, Kimora, Aubrey, and a handful of others.

Kimora is shaking the peach-colored paperback with a couple drawn in latte art on the cover. "I'm telling you, if my brother's best friend saunters into my small-town coffee shop after breaking my heart years ago and peeling out of town, he's not getting my best latte. He's getting it in his lap," she says. She's brash and bold, but clever, too, as she adds, "But I'd make it look like an accident. I'd be all *I'm so sorry.*"

"But would you grab some napkins and awkwardly try to clean it up like every movie where someone gets a latte spilled?" I ask.

"No way," Kimora says with a defiant shake of her head. "I'd leave him alone with his spilled drink and turn to the next guy in line, and he'd be a handsome billionaire wanting to whisk me away on his yacht. He'd want me to photograph gorgeous ocean views around the world."

"And if he offered to have you quit your job and just shoot pictures all day, you'd say yes?" Trina deadpans.

Kimora fixes her with an *obviously* stare. "Do I look stupid? I'd say *hell yes.*"

Prana lifts a hand like *sign me up.* "When this billionaire walks into my store, I'm not saying *oh no, don't buy me things.* I'm like *please pay off my student debt for one date, K, thanks.*"

"Or the rent on my booth at the salon," Aubrey suggests.

"But only after he tells me he's been coming to my shop and ordering lattes every day because he likes the way I make them better than anyone, and he's finally decided to tell me, and now no one else can ever have me," Prana says wisely. These are some of the very important conversations we engage in here.

"Things romance novels have taught me," Aubrey adds.

"Someday we'll write a dating self-help book and

title it that," Trina puts in, then segues the conversation as she lifts a finger. "Let me steal my girls for a second."

Trina tugs me away from the crew, along with Aubrey, guiding me into a quiet nook of the store. "So, how's your own bangathon going?"

My cheeks flush as memories flash by of the last week with the guys. Trina smirks and before I can answer she asks, "So it's going that well?"

I smile nervously. "What's better than well?"

"You deserve this after your ex and your ex-boss. Truly you do," she says, squeezing my arm.

"There's nothing quite like karma deciding to sprinkle fairy dust on you in the form of two dicks, is there?" Aubrey asks with a wistful sigh.

"Now that should be our next book club pick. *Two Dick Fairy Dust*," I say.

"Has someone written that?" Trina asks, mock seriously.

"No, but I'm going to put it out in the universe and hope the universe returns it to me," Aubrey says, then crosses her fingers. "But in the meantime, one of my clients asked me out." Her grin grows wider. "Oh, have I mentioned he was my prom date?"

Trina smacks Aubrey's shoulder. "Is he the one who got away?"

Aubrey's eyes say maybe. "Aiden's someone my family knows. My dad always thought he'd be perfect for me," she says, then trails off for a few seconds, before she collects herself. "Aiden came back to town recently, and he started coming to see me. He has the most amazing head of hair and a fantastic beard, and we're going out next week."

"I want a full report on Aiden and his hair," I say.

"You'll get it...and I'm seriously happy for you."

Me too. Though I'm also realistic enough to know it won't last. That karma is simply sprinkling this glittery stuff for a little while and soon it'll end.

But I'll enjoy it while it lasts.

* * *

When I return to Hayes's penthouse that evening, I find gifts and a note. I follow the instructions to the letter. I slick on the red lipstick they left, then I slip into the white lace bikini panties and the demi-cup bra. Next, I slide on the thigh-high white stockings they bought for me.

I follow the first instruction.

Gaze at my reflection in the bedroom mirror for a minute.

I look...seductive. I look sexy. I look like someone who owns her pleasure.

I follow the second instruction.

Tease yourself with the toy before taking off the panties.

I return to the bed, turning on the vibrator to a low setting. I press it over my panties.

The pulse is subtle, a tease of vibration, but my toes start to curl. The tempting buzz tightens my belly. A door clicks open.

Two sets of footsteps echo against the tiles outside the bedroom, then slow and stop. My men fill the doorway. They don't move though. With darkened eyes, they watch me play with myself.

Hayes stalks over to me, yanks off my panties, then barks a command. "Bend over the bed. Now."

Electric from the order, I scramble to the foot of the mattress, lifting my ass, then I push the toy back between my thighs and inside me.

"You like that toy, baby?" Hayes asks.

I keep working the vibrator. "I do."

"Bet she'd like the real thing more," Stefan says, coming up beside me, stroking my hair, pushing it to one side of my face as he runs a thumb along my top lip.

I quiver as I ease out the toy, turning it off and tossing it on the bed. "Please fuck me."

They don't take off their clothes. They just take out their cocks.

Hayes covers himself, then notches the head against me as Stefan gets on the bed and kneels, shoving down his boxer briefs, offering me his thick cock. "That lipstick? Get it all over my dick, sweetheart," Stefan urges.

I lick the head of his cock right as Hayes bands an arm around my waist, then takes me with punishing thrusts.

I feel helpless to the lust. Bombarded by too many sensations. My brain flatlines and I'm no longer thinking about my life, my career, where I'm going, what I'm chasing, and all the things I've yet to work out.

I'm not thinking at all.

This overdose of pleasure blasts through my body

and mind. As Hayes works his fingers against my clit, I'm hostage to the exquisite torture of this new brand of sex where I can't speak. Where I can't think. Where I can only feel.

The insistent pulse, the intensifying build, then the brilliant explosion as I break apart.

It's not until later in bed that I think again. *This is going better than well.*

31

PICTURE THAT

Ivy

In my right hand, I hold up a high-neck, sleeveless halter top in a red sheen fabric. In my left is a flowy V-neck cheetah-print blouse. Both are from thrift shops. "Which one for the meeting with Simone?"

Stefan slices a banana at the kitchen counter and studies both options, then nods to the ruby-red one. "Very stylish," he says, then grimaces. "I think? Is that the right answer?"

I laugh from the other side of the bench. "You're the one who wanted to see what I was going to wear."

"When I said *give me a fashion show,* I thought I'd get to see you changing," he says, a teasing spark in his eyes.

"Pervert," I mutter.

From the tiled kitchen floor, Roxy seconds me with a bark before she returns to watching Stefan, with please-drop-a-slice-of-banana dreams in her doggy eyes. Stefan is wearing lounge pants and nothing else. I'm staring at him, too, but with *do me* in my eyes.

Hayes, naturally, is sleeping. He does not get up early. Which works for me because Stefan's become my morning companion. He's an early riser too.

"I like to think of myself more as an aficionado," Stefan says, switching to slice up some kale leaves, then adds, "of you."

This man. I swear he's some kind of feel-good elixir. It's Monday morning, and we're at Hayes's apartment. The guys fly to Detroit tomorrow, then to Chicago. By now, their teammates know Hayes and I *eloped*. That's what we told them, which is all anyone needs to know.

I'm meeting Simone later this morning to discuss wedding coverage, and when I told Stefan I'd wear something that made me look badass, he asked to see it, so I ran downstairs to my place to grab some options.

I set both shirts down on the stool, then adjust my little dress, a cover-up kind of thing. "For what it's worth, I like the red one too. It makes me feel...strong."

"You are strong. So it sounds perfect," he says, then holds my gaze for a beat as he drops bananas and kale into the blender. "Which means it'll make you feel great when you have to deal with an uncomfortable meeting."

I've been dreading today, and I told both men as much last night. "Thank you. I'll shower in a bit and then get dressed. Maybe I'll let you see it then."

"I'll finally get my fashion show," he says.

"If you're a good boy," I tease. My phone buzzes on

the counter, and I grab it. Oh! It's another email from Birdie. She already told me she loved my first piece when I turned it in a few days ago. "*Your Runway* wants another piece. This one is on secondhand fashion."

"That's your thing," he says.

"And that's her thing. They sponsor the Secondhand Fashion Show in LA every December. It's a bunch of designers mixing and matching their older pieces in new ways," I say, and when he asks more about it, I give him all the details.

"Sounds right up your alley," he says, then surreptitiously, or so he no doubt thinks, offers a slice of banana to Roxy.

She wolfs it down as he covers the blender and blitzes the ingredients for his morning kale smoothie. The machine grinds at top volume, and I shake my head, amused, when he turns it off. "I still don't get how he can sleep through that," I say, pointing at the bedroom door.

"It's his superpower."

"What's yours?"

He flicks out his tongue, giving me a salacious onceover.

"I walked right into that one."

He lifts a hand, brandishing his palm. "You can walk into this one again too, sweetheart."

I want that as well. But I've also been meaning to ask him something. "The first night I stayed at your house. You said it was *home enough*. What did you mean?"

He sighs as he pours some of his drink into a tumbler. "You noticed that." He sounds...grateful.

"It was hard not to."

He's uncharacteristically quiet for a beat, and while I could say *you don't have to tell me*, Stefan's an adult. He knows he can opt out if he wants. After he takes a drink of his smoothie and sets it down, he says, "Sometimes I miss home. My brothers and sisters. They're all settled in Copenhagen. My parents too. I miss the family gatherings, the big dinners, the bike rides along the water. Just the life I was used to there."

"That makes sense," I say.

"But I'll see them soon enough. They'll probably come here in December. My parents, I mean."

"For the holidays?"

He shakes his head. "I'll go there if I can. They'll try to be here for The Sports Network awards."

Ah. He mentioned those the other night, and Hayes teased him. But I can tell it's important to him to see his folks. Maybe even to make them proud. "You sound excited about that."

His lips curve in a slight grin, like he's not quite going to admit his anticipation out loud. "Well, I like them. It'd be nice if they were here."

"I hope they can make it." A new worry digs into me. Is he still carrying a flame for Annika? Do I want to ask? But we're temporary. This is an arrangement, so there's no harm in asking. "Do you miss your ex?"

I hold my breath, but not for long. "At first, yes," he answers. "But then I realized after we split what I missed was the connection to home. The familiarity.

She was from the same place as me. She knew the same people." He seems more clinical than wistful. "I was missing that more than anything. And then after a while I was missing...*someone*."

He locks eyes with me and holds my gaze importantly. Does he want that with me? A connection with *someone*? That's hard to fathom, given my speckled relationship history, so I sidestep even the possibility. "Do you want to go home and see your family? I get to see mine when I want, so maybe I take it for granted."

"Yeah, someday," he says, then knocks back some more smoothie. "You'd like it there." There's no question in his remark. It's a certainty that I'd enjoy his hometown.

"I would?"

"Yes." He beckons me with his finger, and I move around the counter and join him. "Because I'd take you to the river..." He presses a hot kiss to my throat. "I'd run my hands through your hair. I'd tell you how fucking sexy you are while I slide a hand under your skirt and fuck you with my fingers as the boats go by."

My pulse gallops. "Sounds like a good trip," I say, my skin buzzing with excitement.

"You'd like that," he says, then takes a quick break to scoop up my dog and bring her to the couch. Couches are her kryptonite, so she curls up in a dog ball. Stefan returns to me and pulls up the hem of my cover-up, inch by inch, revealing pink cotton panties.

"I'd fuck you on a boat," he says, then runs his thumb along the top of my panties.

I arch into his touch, wriggling against his fingers, asking for *more, more, more.* "You would?"

"Pull you onto my lap," he says, then lifts his other hand and cups my breast, squeezing it.

I gasp, then lean my head back, taking all his attention, relishing it.

"Make you straddle my cock," he muses. "Then I'd cover your mouth and tell you to be quiet while I fucked you by the river, my sweet exhibitionist."

Heat roars through me. "Show me." It comes out like a plea.

He spins me around. "You look good bent over the counter, so lift that ass," he orders, but he helps me along as he tugs down my wet panties. Quick as that, he's grabbing a condom and undoing his jeans.

When he strokes my wetness, his breath hisses. "Look at you. You get so fucking wet for us. For me," he says, teasing my clit, stroking my slickness. "Your pussy is fucking perfect."

I crane my neck to watch the filthy concentration in his eyes. He slides a finger through my wetness, brings it to his mouth. A pulse beats between my thighs as he sucks off my taste.

"Fucking incredible," he says, then he grabs my chin and kisses me roughly. When he lets go, he smacks my ass. "And I'm going to fuck you to remind you who you are before you go to this meeting."

My heart rate spikes. "Who am I?"

He pushes down on my lower back and lines his cock up at my entrance. "You're smart," he says, then sinks into me.

I groan at the sharp, hot intrusion.

"You're clever," he says, sliding out then slamming in.

I grunt as pleasure ripples through me. He slides a hand up my tits, pressing his palm hard against my collarbone but no higher.

"You're strong," he says, punctuating the praise with a hard thrust. "And I fucking need you."

Even though I'm at his mercy, I feel like I have all the power thanks to his grunts, his noises, his feral growls. His bitten off words as he takes me. He's not just showing me who I am. He's showing me how much he wants me, and it's exhilarating.

I drop my head, closing my eyes, giving in to the intensity of his thrusts. He doesn't let up his grip or his pounding, and I'm close when the bedroom door creaks open.

I jerk my gaze to our guest. Hayes is wearing boxer briefs and stubble. He drags his hand through his bedhead as he watches us. "Don't stop on my account," he deadpans, and my breath hitches, my pussy tightening around Stefan as Hayes shamelessly stares at us.

"Why don't you take a picture? Lasts longer," Stefan suggests.

A hot burst of pleasure curls inside me, and I moan.

"She likes that idea," Hayes adds.

"Yes," I moan.

Stefan whispers in my ear. "You want him to, sweetheart?"

"I do. No face though."

He turns his gaze to his friend. "You heard her. She's gonna come soon, so get to it."

Thirty seconds later, Stefan has yanked down the neckline of my cover-up, exposing my tits. Hayes is mere feet away with his cell phone, snapping pictures of Stefan fucking me harder than I've ever been fucked in my life.

Snap. Snap.

I'm up on my toes, my fingers curling around the edge of the counter, my hair a mess. Stefan grabs a breast tight, his other hand snaking between my thighs.

Click. Click.

"So fucking ready to come. Aren't you?" Stefan hisses in my ear.

"Yes, please yes."

Hayes gets closer, snaps another shot of my chest. "Your tits. Your beautiful fucking tits," he rasps out, and then takes picture after picture as exquisite ecstasy rages in my body, storming through me as I detonate.

Stefan squeezes my breast harder with one hand as he shudders on a deep thrust. He pumps one last time, kissing my neck as he goes.

Then, biting me.

I gasp, lifting a hand to my neck, covering it, like it's something I covet.

When he lets go, he pulls me up, eases out. "I picked that red shirt because it'll cover your neck today," he says, sounding devilishly pleased with himself.

"Thanks for the foresight."

"Now, I need you to do something for me, sweet-heart," he says.

I give him a curious stare. "Okay."

He disposes of the condom, then zips up his jeans, tipping his forehead to the man with the camera. "Crawl to him."

"You want me to..." Did I hear him right? And why is my spine tingling? My breath catching all over again?

Hayes sets down the phone on the counter. His eyes gleam, as if he's saying, *Well, what's it gonna be?*

That's a very good question. The last time I crawled was on the ice, in a purple furball costume, when I was being chased by a tiger. But I've never crawled for a man.

Do I want to?

The hair on my arms stands on end. Anticipation bubbles inside me. Slowly, I look to Stefan. He leans a hip against the counter, head cocked, eyes easy.

A man willing to wait for my answer. Maybe knowing it before I do.

Time slows more as I turn to Hayes. He's walking away, heading to the living room, then parking himself on a large gray chair.

Like he knows it too.

"Yes, sweetheart," Stefan says with a sliver of a smile, a man in control as he answers my unfinished question. "I do want you to crawl to my teammate." He closes the distance between us, cupping my cheek, running his thumb along my jawline. "Don't you want to?"

The answer comes in the arousal that shimmies

down my chest. The pull in my belly. The parting of my lips.

"Yes," I whisper.

Stefan's smile is the definition of pleased. "Good. Now show us how well you listen."

He picks up the tumbler as I turn around, then do something I'd never imagined I would. I drop to my bare knees, then my palms. The skirt of my dress is bunched up around my waist. Hayes leans back in the big chair, arms stretched across it, eyes locked on me. His irises blaze with unchecked lust.

I crawl across the cold tile floor. The hard surface bites into my flesh. My knees hurt, but as I go, my heart gallops. My pulse surges. Hayes can't look away. He stares at me like a horse at the gates, raring to go. I crawl over the soft carpet in the open living room, reaching him at last then stopping between his spread legs.

"Such a good girl," Stefan says from the kitchen in what must be his team captain voice, giving orders. "Now, give his cock some attention while I finish my smoothie."

Hayes lifts his chin, his gaze confident, almost daring me. "You heard him, pretty girl."

The way they trade off dominance games makes my mind whirl. I never know who's going to be in charge. I never know who's going to tell the other what to do to me. Judging from the slickness between my thighs, I really like the uncertainty.

I rise up on my knees, peeling down Hayes's boxer briefs. His cock says good morning. He's throbbing already, and a drop of liquid slides down the head. I drop my mouth, darting out my tongue, licking it off reverently.

"Yessss," he says, and leans his head back against the cushion, enrapt.

I swirl my tongue over the head as he curls his fingers around my skull. "That's my girl," he murmurs when I suck him deeper, swallowing his shaft.

He breathes out hard as I work him over, gripping the base in one hand, playing with his balls with the other, and savoring every second of each suck. "You're so good at that," Hayes says.

If I am, there's only one reason. My mouth is full, but I'm compelled to say it. I drop his dick from my mouth right as Stefan says, "Because she loves it."

I meet his gaze in the kitchen with a *you read my mind* smile. Stefan brings the silver tumbler to his lips, but before he takes a drink, he says, "Don't you, Ivy?"

I answer with deeds, licking a long stripe up his friend's shaft, then swirling my tongue over the head as Stefan watches. "I like your cock," I tell Stefan, then give another kiss to the crown of Hayes's dick, but I keep my eyes on Stefan as I add, "And I like your team-mate's cock."

Hayes groans, helpless to my mouth.

"Then finish off the new guy, Ivy," Stefan commands as he downs his kale smoothie while I take Hayes's cock to the back of my throat and suck him like I mean it.

With a grunt and a feral groan, he comes, and I take it all.

Then, I stand. I may have crawled, but every second I was on the floor I had all the control in my hands.

"I need to shower," I say and head for the bathroom. A few minutes later, Hayes is under the rainfall shower with me. "I need to take care of you," he says, sounding desperate.

"If you insist."

"I really fucking do," he says, then he spins me around so I'm facing the wall. From behind, he kneads and strokes my breasts, then bites down on my shoulder. He slides a hand to my stomach then lower so he can stroke my eager clit. Soon, I'm shaking and trembling, chasing another high then flying off the cliff.

When my breathing slows, he turns me back around, then drizzles bodywash on me. As he cleans me up, he segues easily from sex to asking about my day. I tell him about the meeting then ask what he has planned.

"Lunch with my granddads," he says while he washes my hair.

"Bet you're looking forward to that."

"A lot." He kisses my neck, softer than usual. "You'd like them."

I hear what's unsaid—*I want you to meet them.*

And I'd like that too.

As I'm getting dressed, Hayes waggles his phone at me, looking Machiavellian. "See how much I pretended you never told me about the socks and sandals?"

Intrigued, I tug up the zipper on my pants and peer at the screen. It's a text thread between Hayes and his granddads. My heart squeezes as he scrolls past a handful of prior messages about stars and constellations, about what Hayes can see in the San Francisco sky from his rooftop, about how beautifully inky black the night is. It's like he's showing me a piece of himself without having to say as much, and I appreciate the subtle gesture.

He slows the pace of his scroll, stopping at the most recent messages, including a photo of, as promised, a nattily dressed older man and a super-casual one, standing on a beach.

Hayes: That picture hurts my eyes. Why are you wearing socks with sandals?

Ryan: You're saying I can't wear them? That's info that would have been helpful before our vacation!

Bryan: I've been telling you for years. You don't listen to me.

Ryan: Sorry, did you say something?

Hayes: Dudes, I just heard on social that this trend is now officially over. Just wanted you to know.

Ryan: YOU SIT ON A THRONE OF LIES. See you at lunch.

"You tried, at least," I say, patting his shoulder. "Since he saw through it, maybe at least get him some cute socks. Like, with drawings of llamas on them. That's better than plain white ones."

He snaps his fingers. "Yes! That's perfect."

A little later, with Roxy by my side, I head to the door, having been thoroughly fucked by two men, when my phone pings with a text from Simone.

Oooh. What if she's canceling the meeting? I kind of hope she is. But I also don't want her to cancel it, since I need to cover her wedding. I slide the message open, a little apprehensive, then read her note.

I curl my lips. "Ugh. She's bringing Xander."

Hayes takes a sip of his coffee, then looks me up and down approvingly. "And you're walking into that meeting having been fucked so much better than he could ever do."

Stefan sets a now washed-and-dried blender back on the counter with a satisfied grin. "Fucking well is the best revenge."

He's not wrong, especially when Hayes sets down his mug and comes to the door. "By the way, when you're at this meeting, I'm going to jerk off to those pictures of you. So...feel free to picture that."

I drop off Roxy at home, then head to the meeting, certain I'll have a hard time thinking of anything else.

32

THE EX AMBUSH

Ivy

October in San Francisco is one of the hottest months of the year, so here I go, in this sleeveless top. It's the opposite of Simone's retro rockabilly style. I'm very *now*, and I need this fashion armor as I meet her and my ex in a boba shop.

I'd rather not see either one of them, but I'm trying to approach this meeting as a reporter. She's simply someone I'm covering, and so is he. I grab the door handle and prepare to meet the woman who used to be my mentor.

How did I miss all the signs that I couldn't trust her? Or...the man by her side at the pristine white table in the corner of the shop?

Xander's dressed in plaid pants and suspenders and wearing a fake-ass smile to go with his equally fake horn-rimmed glasses.

I stride over to their table, plastering on a faker smile. "Hi, Simone. Hello, Xander."

"Hey, girl!" she says cheerily, waving her bejeweled hand at me, the engagement diamond sparkling like fire. It matches the silvery shade of her headband, holding back all those blond locks. He's the Ken to her Barbie. Well, he's a hipster Ken.

Xander clears his throat. "Hi, Ivy. You're looking very professional."

Can you say *underhanded dig?*

"Thanks," I say evenly as my gaze strays to a...jar on the table that appears to be full of yeast and stuff. "You brought...your sourdough starter?"

He clutches the glass lovingly. "Salinger," he says with obvious pride. There must be a warp in the time-space continuum. Did he actually name that thing he was growing when I was with him?

Xander confirms what I didn't ask. "He needed a name."

And a gender? "The sourdough starter is a *he*? And you carry him around?" I can't not ask.

"It's safer that way for Salinger," Xander says, gripping the jar more tightly. "Simone's cat likes to knock things over."

My stomach twists. What did I ever see in him? I can never date for real again until I diagnose the problem with my taste. I put that on my mental to-do list as I go to the counter to order a brown sugar milk tea. Once Simone and Xander's drinks are ready, too, we sit back down, and I open up a notebook and uncap a pen.

"What do you want me to know about the wedding?" I ask, eager to get down to business. "I'd love to do a preview for my...newsletter and my social." I don't even want to tell them my handle. They'd probably mock me for my paltry number of followers. They'd break out their artisanal ice cubes, drop them in their small-batch cocktails garnished with edible flowers, and laugh at *little me*. And yet, I swallow my pride, then add, "And for you, Simone."

After all, a deal's a deal.

Simone brightens. "Yes, let's talk about the big day." She chatters on about what she'll be wearing, and when she'll reveal it to her one million followers, and I take notes in the purple notebook *my husband* gave me.

That gives me a little zing.

When Simone's done talking, I set down my pen. "That all sounds—"

Xander points at my left hand like I'm wearing a spider. "Your ring. What happened? *How* did that happen?"

Like me being married is differential calculus. And for a second, I hesitate to say anything. But Hayes is wearing his ring, his teammates know, and it's only a matter of time before word gets out beyond the Avengers. It'll happen soon enough at the upcoming golf event.

"Well, I met this guy—"

"I just can't believe you're married *already*."

Ohhh. Right. He can move on while he's with me, but I ought to mourn The Dapper Man till the end of time. I square my shoulders. "Yes. *Already*. It was a whirlwind romance because when you know, you know, right? I'm married to Hayes Armstrong on the Avengers," I say, sitting up straighter, owning it. "My plus-one at your wedding, as a matter of fact. You might have heard of him. The hotshot new hockey star in town."

Xander's jaw drops.

Simone beams.

"You always talked about the importance of *not settling*, so I didn't," I add. *Take that.*

Xander's eyes flash with *clout*. Yup, he's imagining how it'd look to have a bona fide pro athlete at his wedding. Simone grins too. "How wonderful," she says.

He turns to her, squeezes her hand. "So fantastic." He clears his throat, then adds, "And did you know the team captain owns a restaurant?"

Um, yeah. But what does that have to do with anything? "I'm aware."

"Stefan Christiansen," he says—*yes, he fucked me this morning to remind me you never deserved me*—then turns to Simone. "We should invite him too."

What a couple of star fuckers.

* * *

When I leave the shop, I steal a final glance over my shoulder at the pair as they walk into the San Francisco day, Xander clutching Salinger like it's his baby. Shaking my head, I return to my building, a cloud of dark thoughts chasing me as I click to my texts. I'm desperate for a reality check, so I open the thread with Trina and Aubrey.

> Ivy: Question: What did I ever see in Xander?

Aubrey's three bubbles dance.

> Aubrey: You liked that he wasn't a tech bro.

> Ivy: Wow. That's so compelling.

> Trina: And he liked to bake bread.

> Ivy: I mean, I love bread, but was I THAT impressed with someone just...baking?

> Aubrey: Also, he went thrifting with you. You liked that too.

I groan, remembering the things he would say as we shopped. *You can wear this dress when you hit your first 10K. Then get this top for when you go viral.* Once, when I'd shared news of a writing job I'd been offered, he'd said, *Take the assignment. It's going to open doors for you.* It's all so apparent in retrospect—he was trying to change me with his *do this, do that* encouragement. When he gave it, I felt like he was doling out important advice. Like he was a boyfriend who'd legit taken an interest in my career and my life. But now, looking back, I can see that he was always trying to mold me. I just wanted to write about something I loved. I wasn't trying to make gobs of money or rule the online world.

But I'd been fooled by his fake cheerleading as we hunted for secondhand clothes.

I suppose it's no surprise I missed the signs. When I was growing up, it's not like I ever saw a man be truly good to a woman. By the time I was eight or nine, I was looking out for my little sister, keeping her busy when my dad would yell, and then hoping every night and every morning that my mom would kick my dad out of the house.

Annoyed, I put my phone away and drag myself into my building, head upstairs, and shed my shoes as I greet Roxy, who jumps up when she sees me then barks until I give her a daily sock.

Placated, she snags it in her little teeth and scurries off, butt waggling, to deposit it in her secret sock collection in my bedroom.

Well, she thinks it's secret. I've figured her out.

Seconds later, she returns to me, chattering in Dog that it's time for a walk since it's always time for a walk. I fasten on her *burgers or bacon or bust* bandana, then grab her harness and oblige, but I'm still feeling foolish as I go.

On the one hand, Hayes and Stefan aren't anything at all like Xander. On the other hand, I *did* like Xander once upon a time.

What if I can't pick men? What if my taste this time around turns out to be as off as my taste in Xander clearly was? I sigh, disgruntled, until our walk brings Roxy and me to Better With Pockets. Lately, she's been making puppy-dog eyes with the owner's dog. When Beatrix's greyhound mix, Karl, spots my girl from inside the boutique, he trots past the new frocks and out to the sidewalk, stretching his long, sleek frame into a most inviting downward dog. Roxy sashays over to Karl, wagging her lush tail. Karl is easily ten years younger, which puts Roxy squarely in the cougar camp, while Karl's the pool boy.

I never heard back from my email to Beatrix with some ideas for her social, but that's okay. Everyone hates email and most people hate turning other people down. As the dogs *Lady and the Tramp* over a bowl of H2O, Beatrix joins us on the street, snapping a pic of the pups. Beatrix's pixie cut is tousled and silvery today, a fun contrast to her olive complexion.

"Love the new hair color," I say.

She touches her locks, as if just remembering the shade. "Thanks. I nearly forgot what color I did last night." When the dogs stop lapping, she shows me the shot. "Shop Dog and The Flirt. I should post it on the store's social..." She waves a hand. "If I remember."

Hmm. She sounds beleaguered. "Roxy and I would be very honored," I say, then I woman-up and remind her I can help. "And if I can help with your social media marketing, DM me."

Her eyes brighten. "Actually, I keep meaning to follow up with you, but I hate email."

Called it.

"I need some social media work. Someone to write about outfits of the day."

Hello! That's me! "I'd love to."

"I'll DM you later with details. Also, those pants are seriously cute."

"Thanks. They're Zoe Slades. Picked them up at Champagne Taste for seventy-five percent off."

She whistles. "Can you please shop for me?"

"Anytime."

"But you'll only write about the outfits I have here," she says.

I assure her I will and thank her again, then pop into a sock shop next door. Before I go home, I drop off three pairs of socks at Hayes's door. One for him, one for Stefan, and one for Hayes's terribly dressed, but not so terribly dressed anymore, grandad.

Back at my place, I text for a bit with my little sister about her semester abroad, and then I write and research fashion till it's time to head to the arena that night.

* * *

Shortly before the game, I leave the equipment room that doubles as a mascot changing room, and head into the corridor. I'm walking toward the ice when Number Eighteen comes up behind me in his uniform, his eyes traveling up and down my new getup.

"Are you Blob take two?" Stefan asks, incredulous.

I gesture to my gray costume. Just gray. That's all I am. A gray cloud. "I'm...wait for it...The San Francisco fog," I say, trying not to laugh.

"Oh fuck, sweetheart. That's terrible," he says with sympathy. Stefan glances down the hall, then whispers. "I heard you were joining us briefly for a warm-up lap, but they didn't tell us you'd be wearing...*sadness*."

I pluck at the costume. "It is pretty much the fashion manifestation of tears."

"Is there someone here that thinks this mascot costume is a good idea?"

I shrug helplessly. "They were trying to be good stewards of the city."

Seconds later, Hayes joins us, cringing. "Sorry, baby."

My costume is hideous, but I stifle a grin because they're *both* using affectionate nicknames in public, and their pet names for me fit their personalities perfectly. I glance down at my garb. "I mean, wouldn't a foghorn have been better?"

"Yes. Yes, it would," Stefan says, running a hand over his purple uniform. "But does this mean we'll have to wear sad gray fog uniforms? And will we be called The Fog?"

"Only if The Fog is more popular with fans than the next two," I say, and I'm not revealing team secrets since the online voting should be underway any minute.

"It's totally not voter fraud if we manipulate that poll, is it?" Hayes asks hopefully.

"I won't tell if you won't," I say.

"We'll keep your secret safe," Stefan says, then a smile tips his lips as he whispers, "Thanks for the fox socks."

"You kind of remind me of one," I whisper playfully.

"I gathered as much."

"I guess that means I remind you of a star," Hayes

says with a wink in his voice. "Thanks for the star and planet ones. The llamas too."

Their soft expressions tell me just how much they liked the gifts—the same gift that I tailored for each guy. "Just don't wear socks with nothing at all," I tease.

"Noted," Stefan says.

"I knew that," Hayes seconds. He seems relaxed with all of us today. It's so good to see. It's also good to see both of them at work. Initially, I wasn't sure how I'd handle it, liking one guy I worked with, let alone two. But turns out, it's easy to interact with them here in the halls, maybe because that's what we did *before* Vegas. We talked on the rooftop, on the plane, and here in the halls.

"I got another gig today," I say brightly, keen to share. "I'm doing social for a store."

"I told you you're brilliant," Stefan says, his eyes shining with pride as he offers a fist for knocking and I knock back.

"That's awesome," Hayes says, then high-fives me.

Stefan gestures toward the arena. "We should go."

But neither of them moves.

Briefly, doubt fuzzes my head. What strange habits are their biceps hiding? What emotional shortcomings do they possess under their steel bodies? Most of all, how could they hurt me?

My dad hid his anger well for a while, but by the time I was nine, he was getting drunk after work, then screwing other women, then hurling insults at our mom, then telling his daughters we could never trust a man, not even him. It was emotional whiplash till my mom finally kicked him out, and my brother took on the protector role.

Some days, though, I still feel that whiplash in my heart, still hear the echo of his insults in my mind.

And I worry that every man I encounter might be like him eventually. I hate that I still think these things even after these guys have shown their support. Even after they've lifted me up, I *still* expect the worst.

I just don't know how to shake my past with Xander or the way I grew up with my dad.

"Do either of you have a sourdough starter that you named after a writer?" I ask.

Stefan blinks, clearly perplexed. "This feels like a trick question," he says warily, "but I'm going to answer anyway. No. Hayes?"

"I don't even know how to turn on the oven, so that's a big no."

"Good," I say, somewhat mollified. "And good luck tonight."

Hayes gives a chin nod, but before he leaves, he says softly, "Also, I would never stage a blow job pic for a wedding invite. Or any other reason."

Stefan catches on immediately. "And I would never fuck your boss. Your ex is an asshole who never deserved you. Remember that. But if you don't, we'll keep reminding you—you're amazing in every way."

Hayes nods to the ice. "Get out there and go show the city what the San Francisco Fog can do."

"You guys are the best," I say softly, then I head to the ice, fueled by their support.

33

THE ICEMAN

Hayes

"The Avengers were once a crew of righteous vigilantes, protecting the Earth from danger." Or so the story goes, told in a deep, foreboding tone over the loudspeakers and filling the arena as it does before every home game, while purple and blue beams of light sweep across the darkly lit rink.

As I step onto the ice, I leave the day behind. The call from my agent, checking in on my marriage. The texts from my granddads asking how my telescope is working out, and the note from my dad asking me to go ring shopping with him.

They all melt away when I meet the energy of the crowd and the cool, crisp bite of the air.

All that matters is the game ahead, another chance to prove myself to this team.

I take a few laps around the rink to warm up, then

slap the puck into the waiting net as the voice of god regales the crowd with his story of the Avengers. I've heard it enough, but this time, the story shifts...

"But then, the fog rolled in..."

Whoa. There she is, jumping over the boards and barreling across the ice, arms flapping in her gray costume, trying so valiantly to whip up the fans.

The crowd cheers. But then they slow their cheers, like they don't know what to make of that costume.

Poor Ivy. I feel bad that the team picked such a blasé mascot outfit, but she's a trouper, racing across the ice with gusto and spirit. But that's her style—she rolls with the punches and picks herself up. She forges ahead, with her scrappy attitude and her fighting style.

I smile to myself as I glide across the ice, loosely chasing the puck. I like seeing her here. I liked chatting with her before the game. Shooting the breeze with the three of us felt right, then hearing her good news fired me up, just like the twin gifts excited me earlier.

But I try to shake off these fizzy feelings. This is the time when I blot out the world, the buffer between daily life and game time. I zoom in on what lies ahead —winning this match—but as soon as that thought enters my mind, another skates in after it—it'd be fun to keep celebrating wins with her.

Focus, man.

As the pre-game warm-up ends, I head to the players' bench without looking back.

I can't spend this much time thinking about her.

* * *

I'm not on the ice for the face-off against Colorado, but I laser in on the moment when the puck drops. Stefan wins possession, and I train all my attention on the game, watching my team like a hawk as they chase the puck down the ice, Stefan passing to Brady, who aggressively takes a shot on goal in the first thirty seconds.

But the Colorado goalie's glove knocks it down.

When it's time for a shift change, I jump over the boards and fly down the ice with blinders on. There's only room in my head for the game.

I'm in the zone during the first period. Focused, fast, and formidable. This is what I do best. Shut out the world. Been doing it my whole damn life when I get in the rink, and I'll do it tonight, dammit.

As the period draws to an end, I slam a powerful shot on goal. But the goalie blocks it again.

Jaw clenched, I skate off, annoyed I didn't break the scoreless drought, then more annoyed when my attention strays to the stands yet again and finds that giant gray fluff ball clambering down the aisle and onto the ice, ready to fire a T-shirt cannon.

Fuck, she's cute. My irritation burns off, replaced by something...soft as I look her way. I want to introduce her to Ryan and Bryan. To tell them that we're fake married, but shit's getting real.

What. The. Hell.

Now is not the time to linger on feel-good thoughts of Ivy. Game time is never the time to linger on thoughts of a woman. Or a future with her.

Or anything but my mission this year—*stay*.

As Coach prowls the locker room, his resonant voice demanding attention as he talks about how we played too complacently in the first period, my focus slips back to her once again. How did I go from resisting Ivy a few weeks ago to feeling all swoony when I see her before a game? To wanting her to meet my family?

Running into her with Stefan made my stupid heart skip a beat.

I was so fucking excited to see her. She brought a smile to my face, and I hate smiling before games. I hate showing any emotion before games. And during them too.

In college, my nickname was The Iceman for a reason. I shut out the world. That's what I have to do again.

I can't get too comfortable here in San Francisco. The team is changing its identity. Hell, they'll probably toss me out as quickly as they toss out names. That means I can't be the easygoing guy in the halls, hanging with his girl and his buddy. That'll lead to complacency.

And that will see me traded.

* * *

The rest of the game is a blur of skating, shooting, and missing. I don't put a point on the scoreboard for the Avengers. None of us do. Colorado glides off the ice with the victory, handing us our asses in an embarrassing shutout.

Fuming, I stalk to the locker room, pissed at myself. It's one game, and there will be more, but I don't have wiggle room as the new guy. Just because I had fun in Vegas, just because the guys called me Hayes, just because they dared me to get married for fun, and just because Jessie invited Ivy and me to her event doesn't mean I'll get a contract beyond this season.

My goal is to stay with a team, not to stay with a woman. I didn't come to San Francisco for romance, and I can't get caught up in one.

As I leave that night, I turn my phone back on. A message from my dad pops up. Something about Cora. *Of course.*

It's a reminder though. I can't be like him.

My mom is the real iceman, leaving without looking back. Good thing we're heading out of town for a few games. I need a breather. I pack alone that night, and I leave the socks behind.

34

NOT CAPTAIN FOR NOTHING

Stefan

Since we fly to Detroit in the morning, the three of us agreed to take the night off from our festivities.

Shame. But the sex reprieve gives me a few minutes to pop into The Great Dane before it closes. I like to check it out while customers are here to make sure the vibe feels right, like it did when I ate here with Ivy and Hayes.

The thought of her does funny things to my chest. Things I'll have to deal with quite soon. But for now, I swing open the door, say hello to Yasmine, then head to the bar, sitting down next to a guy with horn-rimmed glasses and suspenders. He looks vaguely familiar, so I give a friendly-ish nod and order a scotch.

"Coming right up, Mr. Christiansen," the bartender says and once he gives me the drink, the man next to me turns my way and clears his throat. "Hey! You're Stefan Christiansen. Number Eighteen."

Ah, a fan. That makes sense.

Except, wait.

As I say hello I get a better look at the guy, and he feels awfully familiar—in a *stupid hat* kind of way. He's holding a canvas bag, and he sticks out a hand.

"Xander Arlo, The Dapper Man."

Irritation curls through me at the sight of this fuck-face—the asshat, toxic ex-boyfriend who treated my girl like shit and dumped her for someone with more followers.

I clench my fists.

"I'd been hoping to catch up with you. I see you're a food man," he says, glancing around.

No shit, Sherlock. "Yes. I like food," I say dryly.

He gestures to me, indicating my suit. "And tailored duds."

"Sure," I say, cautiously. Why the fuck is he here?

"Well, I'd love to give you a chance to get in on a great opportunity."

He's come here to pitch me on something?

Oh, this is rich. He slides over the bag, then opens it to show me a loaf of wrapped bread. "It's my special sourdough recipe. I'm going to open a brand-new shop," he says, then makes a camera frame with his hands. "I'm calling it Dough and Duds. It'll sell my homemade bread and my hand-selected bespoke suits. Small batch for what you put on your body and in your body." He slides me a folder with a shiny cover. "There's a presentation in here. I only have a few slots for investors, but I'd love to have you on board."

Is he for real? I barely know what to say to an idea that's so fucking ridiculous. "You're opening a bread and suit shop?"

"Homemade bread," he corrects.

"Pretty sure it's not homemade. It's bakery-made, or what we call house-made in the business."

He taps the wrapped loaf. "Try it. It'll blow your mind. Like I said, I only have a few slots left, but I'll hold one for you."

The chutzpah of this asshole. The motherfucking chutzpah. I'd like to punch his face. Rearrange his nose. Dislocate a shoulder.

But, however momentarily satisfying, those would be career killers.

I take the bread but slide the folder back to him. "I don't need to check out your presentation to know this is a hard pass. And, frankly, so are you."

Oh. Would you look at that? I was a dick after all.

Sometimes it happens.

* * *

On the way home, I swing by a nearby park and walk to the duck pond. Henry's usually here at night. He keeps a tent near the ducks, and sleeps there. The older man comes by the restaurant most nights, and we give him food, when we have extras.

I find him on the bench, doing a crossword puzzle. "Henry. Didn't see you tonight," I say.

Looking up, he sets down the pencil. "This one is hard. It's taking me some time."

"No worries, man. But here's some bread for you," I say, then hand him the loaf.

He leans in to smell it. "Smells good."

Well, at least Xander can bake well. "Enjoy. But don't feed the ducks," I say, pointing to the sign by the pond advising against it.

Henry gives me a look like *are you for real.* "Kid, I know."

I wave, then turn around. "See you soon."

"See you soon," he echoes as I leave with no food waste.

That's one issue disposed of.

But isn't it just the way things go—when you shake off one problem, another creeps up on you. Hayes's mood starts worrying me as soon as we leave for Detroit. He keeps to himself on the plane. That's no good for a guy who wants to feel like part of the team. Before the game, he's all about his earbuds and his rock music. Fine, that's not so strange—every guy has a different way they get into the zone. They do something before a game, then nab a much-needed assist on the game-winning goal, and that becomes their thing. Maybe quiet mode is Hayes's thing.

But I'm not captain for nothing. My job isn't just to look out for the guy I'm sharing a girl with. My job is to look out for the whole team. When a teammate is out of sorts, I've got to either pick him up or kick him in the pants.

I choose the former.

When the afternoon game ends in the early evening, the team jet takes us to Chicago in an hour, giving us plenty of time for dinner. I round up Dev, Brady, and a bunch of other guys and take them to my favorite Chicago pizza spot. The deep dish is approaching ten out of ten levels, but I'd like to think it's my masterminding ways that loosen up my buddy. Over dinner, he and Brady shoot the shit about a home improvement project the new dad is working on, then they trade Netflix recs, with Brady admitting he's a diehard *Bridgerton* fan and Hayes confessing he's a *Schitt's Creek* kind of man.

That's as good a lubricant as any. Back at the hotel, as the other guys peel away to their rooms, I steer Hayes to the lobby bar and a booth in the back. After we trade tips on the formidable Chicago defensemen we'll be facing tomorrow—and whether any are better than Tom or Dimitry on our team—I cut to the chase. "What's really going on with you?"

Hayes tilts his head, like he's shocked I asked. But he doesn't play the surprised game for long. With a heavy sigh, he takes another swig from the beer bottle, though he says nothing.

A year or so ago I might have stayed quiet. Hell, in my twenties, I might never have asked hard questions. But I'm thirty now, and I'm just not interested in miscommunication. Avoidance tactics don't fly with me anymore.

I learned that the hard way. I sensed something was off during the last year of my relationship with Annika, but I never asked her about it. Figured if neither of us said anything, then nothing was truly wrong. But she was missing home, and I didn't realize it. Didn't ask her enough questions. Didn't deal with the way we were drifting apart.

Doesn't matter if this thing with the three of us is temporary. Doesn't matter if there's an end date bearing down on us. Happiness is fleeting, and I'm fucking enjoying it, so I'll fight for it, dammit.

After I swallow some more scotch, I face him, point blank. "You've been quiet ever since Ivy gave us the socks."

The label on the beer bottle must be fascinating because Hayes fiddles with it for a while, then finally looks up and meets my gaze. "It wasn't the socks, man. It was talking to her before the game," he says in a dead voice.

It's like he's already resigned himself to...whatever he's resigned himself to. Concern weighs down my shoulders, but I push on. "And why was that a problem for you?"

"I don't know," he mutters.

"Bullshit."

His jaw is set hard. "Why is that bullshit?"

I level a serious stare at him. "Because you fucking know what's going on. You know what's going on inside you, and you just don't want to say it."

It's a challenge to his competitive side. We need to face this head-on, whatever *this* is. It's easier for Hayes to be quiet. He's an only child. Silence is his friend. I'm the opposite. I need noise, boisterous conversation. "So talking to her before the game set you off?"

He shoves a hand through his hair, still agitated. "I just wanted to see her so badly," he grumbles.

"And that's getting you down?"

"Yes, because I don't have time for something more than sex," he says, seeming desperate. "I don't have the space for this. I can't get involved."

I had an unhappy suspicion that was where this was going. "But you're feeling like that's happening? You're getting involved with her?"

I wish this felt like good news. It doesn't.

He closes his eyes, clearly pained. When he opens them, he says, "I just can't, Stefan. That's the issue. I arrived in San Francisco with one goal in mind—land a contract to stay. You don't get it. You've been with the same team your entire career. I'm just bouncing around."

A new pressure builds inside me. A need to impress on him that he can handle this. It drives me on. "But you've had a great start to the season."

"We've only played six games, man. It doesn't amount to shit."

I'm not going to blow smoke up his skirt when he makes a fair point. "It's better than starting with a run of bad games. You're playing like a rock star. Don't forget that," I say, hoping I'm getting through to him.

"Thanks, but romance is a distraction I don't need." Slumping back in the booth, he drags both hands through his hair. "How am I supposed to handle her, and this, and hockey, and my dad and Cora and a contract and...everything?"

He sounds at the end of his rope already. But maybe if he can see an alternative to disaster, it will help him hang on. Help him climb up, even. Because I can see it so damn clearly. "So what are you going to do? Just walk away at the end of this arrangement?"

Hayes shoots his focus to me. "What are *you* going to do?"

I say nothing. Because what felt like the answer to my empty nights has quietly become more. I suppose that was inevitable. Some people have hurdles. Some have blockades. Me? I just had a few small complications that I relished untangling. The trouble is, once you clear the complications, you open yourself up to new hurts. To fresh wounds.

I didn't see this one coming—wanting so much so soon.

Hayes jumps at my silence. "You're falling for her. I know you are," he says.

It's not an accusation. It's just the truth, the observation of a friend.

I shrug in admission. "Obviously."

He seems to consider that grimly for a beat, then says, "I'm not going to hold you back when this arrangement ends." His tone is heavy. "I know you don't need my permission, but I'd support anything you two choose to do. If you want to go after her, you should. You know that, right?"

Is that what I want? Ivy to myself? The thought weighs me down even more than I'd expected. I guess that's the problem with two men falling for the same woman when only one of you is willing to let himself fall.

I leave Chicago the next day with a loss on the ice, and a problem I can't solve.

35

HEAR ME ROAR

Ivy

Breaking news—the fog was a dud.

But I haven't even been able to talk to the guys about the online poll results. I haven't seen either my husband or my secret boyfriend since they flew back to town.

It's weird, especially after the last several days of regular communication. Of nightly plans.

Okay, fine, their flight landed in the middle of the night. I didn't expect or want a visitor at three a.m., but we didn't make plans for today either. I wrote to them this morning in our group chat and asked if they wanted to get together today or tonight after the game.

The only response? A note from Hayes saying he was taking part in the optional practice, and then a note from Stefan asking how things were going at the store.

I'm heading to the arena now to debut the next mascot option, feeling off, like my clothes are too tight. Possibly I'm reading something into nothing, but their almost silence feels strange.

Maybe this is just the normal ups and downs of an unconventional arrangement? The thing is—I don't know the rules. As I near the arena, I mull over the last few days. I've been busy too. I had a practice yesterday with the Ice Crew. I spent the day today with Beatrix, Karl, and Roxy, shooting videos and photos for the store's social feed. I suppose I wouldn't have been able to see the guys anyway.

But we don't have plans for tonight, and I'm trying not to let that bother me. *Trying* being the operative word. I check my phone constantly as I walk, hoping for a text, a picture, a plan. Something like we've had since we returned from Vegas nearly two weeks ago.

It stays silent, and my gut twists with worry.

When I arrive at the arena, the quiet nags at me even more. Something has shifted. It doesn't feel like how we were before. And you know what? I don't need to put up with it.

They told me I'm smart and fierce, and a smart and fierce woman would ask, *What's your deal*?

I click open our group thread as I push open the door to the arena, then write as I walk.

> Ivy: Hey! Hope you guys are having a
> good day. It feels weird to me that we
> haven't made plans, and I don't like
> feeling this way. I want to see you both.
> Do you want to come over tonight?

I reread it but before I can hit send, Oliver rounds the corner and catches up to me. "Hey, Ivy! Kana is looking for you."

"Brady's wife?" I know who she is. I'm just surprised.

"She's up at the wives' and girlfriends' suite. And boyfriends' and husbands'," he quickly adds. One of the defensemen, Tom, is married to Gilberto from Sao Paulo, the star of the *San Francisco Firefighters Calendar*. They were shipped all over the city when Gilberto attended a game before they started dating.

I volunteer to head over to the suite on my own, but Oliver's too helpful to let me do that, so he walks with me. Along the way, we chat about the poll results, and he whispers, "The Fog was Jessie's idea. I didn't have the heart to tell her it was bad."

I laugh. I get it. "No one wants to tell the boss when she's wrong."

"You get me," he says.

When I reach the suite, Kana greets me like we're old friends. "It's been too long, *Mrs. Armstrong*," she says, then flashes a welcoming grin.

I smile back, but inside I feel unsteady. Mr. Armstrong has barely written to me. Neither has my secret boyfriend. Yes, Kana's in on the fake marriage, but I feel like I'm not in on something now.

I'm not in on my relationship.

Still, I put on a good face, like I know how to do, and I wave to the crew. "Hi there."

Kana takes me under her wing and makes some quick intros and then says, "Brady and I got a sitter next Sunday, and we're having a board game and dinner party. Can you join us?" She gestures to the room. "We'll all be there, and I sent an invite to your brother, and Chase and Trina."

"You'd better be there," a pretty redhead calls out to me. That's Eva, Dev's girlfriend.

"But fair warning—Tom and I slay in Cards Against Humanity." The boast comes from a strapping and devastatingly gorgeous man. He has a light Brazilian accent, but it's the cheekbones I recognize from the fireman centerfold.

I wish I could tell them Hayes and I are aces at something. Until today, I thought our strongest suit was communicating with each other. "I'll consider myself warned." Since I don't even know if Hayes wants me to RSVP, I add, "I'll check with Hayes, but—"

"He'll be good with it," Gilberto says with easy confidence.

I wish I were as certain as he sounds.

As I leave, that feeling of dread creeps back up in me. The second I'm alone I'm going to send the text to them, but when Oliver and I leave the suite, Jessie pops out of hers, smoothing a hand over her blouse and catching my attention.

"You're just the person I need to see," she says in her Texas drawl, then she shoos Oliver away. "This is girl talk."

Uh-oh. Is that code for she knows the truth? And why does that fill me with so much anxiety?

"Sure," I say carefully as Oliver waves goodbye.

Jessie gestures for me to follow her down a quiet hall, and I keep pace until we reach privacy and she spins around, tugging at her cream-colored silk blouse. "What does a full-chested woman do about *this*?"

One more pull and I see the problem. The gap at the boobs.

"All day, I swear," she whispers, "I'm convinced everyone can see my bra."

I've got this. "Charlotte Everly has a line of blouses by cup size."

Jessie's brown eyes widen. "What is this wizardry you speak of? And can I get one in black tomorrow?"

I nod crisply. "I'll bring you one."

"You will?"

"I'd love to," I say, genuinely thrilled at the idea.

"Sold," she says, then like she did in Vegas, she studies me again, peering at my neck. I'm wearing a silver necklace with a skull and crossbones pendant. "The Pirates? The Swords? The Swashbucklers?" Then she rolls her eyes. "Swashbucklers sounds like someone swallowed a belt."

"I won't argue with you there," I say, laughing.

"And what would that mascot costume even look like?" she muses.

"I hope not a blob," I say.

Oh shit, I said that out loud. Is she going to be pissed?

"Or a sad cloud?" She sighs, and I'm relieved she agrees. "That was my husband's idea. Why did I listen to him? I need a cute animal that'll bite your face off."

"That's the new team name litmus test—cute but mean."

She points at me and nods, silently conveying *got it in one,* before saying goodbye. On my way back to the equipment room, I hold my head up high, take out my phone, and send the text to the guys.

I'm not the same girl I was with Xander. The girl who accepted less. I'm the woman giving fashion tips to the powerful owner of an NHL team.

In the equipment room, I change quickly into my costume. This time I'm a polar bear, and I have to say I look pretty fucking fierce. Like a cute animal that'll bite your face off. I set off down the hall toward the ice with my polar bear head under my arm. I hear someone behind me pick up the pace then mutter something that sounds like *fuck it.*

Before I can turn around, a familiar voice whispers, "Hey."

It warms me up. I turn to Stefan, but he's alone. Hayes isn't around.

Stefan's looking at me like that just doesn't matter. And I'm not sure how I feel about that.

"Hi," I say, tentatively.

Is this how it'll be between him and me? But what does that mean when I'm still married to his teammate? And what was he saying *fuck it* to?

"I got your text," he responds.

And???

But I've already turned off my phone, and there's no time to ask what he answered because Dev's booming, "Let's do this, Viking," fills the corridor.

Stefan holds my gaze for a long, weighty beat, then mouths *I'm sorry* before he turns to join his teammate.

What is he sorry for though? The gaze? The poor communication? The apologetic stare that lingered?

They walk ahead of me, and as I pull on my polar bear head, my human one is more muddled than ever.

In the first intermission, I skate circles around the Ice Crew as they sweep the rink. During the game, I whip up the crowds in the stands, urging them to *roar* when the Avengers—or maybe the soon-to-be Polar Bears —score.

The crowds don't just roar. They growl, and hoot, and howl, and that gets the polar bear in me even more riled up. I shake my hips. I shimmy my butt. And I dance until it's time to strap on my skates once more for the second intermission.

I glide across the ice on one furry leg, the other one sticking out behind me.

Laughter fills the arena as I continue my bear antics. When the clock ticks down toward the end of the period, Moses in the Ice Crew chases me with his broom.

But this bear is powerful. This bear is faster. I

outrun him, heading toward the edge of the ice, then spin around and taunt him like we're on a playground. *You can't catch me.*

Then, like we rehearsed, I give him one last chance, and he tries to catch me. Oh hell, does he ever try. I fly down the ice, Moses at my blades, but when I reach the door to the tunnel, he slams into my back.

All the breath whooshes out of me, and I stumble, tripping over my own feet, and landing flat on the ice with a loud *oof*.

My head rings. My wrist barks. My knees scream. Everything aches all at once.

And the next thing I know, my husband scoops me up and carries me off the ice.

36

ON NOTICE

Hayes

The game can't end soon enough. We can't score fast enough. I have to get off the ice and check on Ivy after carrying her to the assistant trainer who was waiting in the tunnel.

I plow through my line shifts during the final period, racing against the clock. If I can just pad this lead. If I can just get off the rink. I fly down the ice, shoulder to shoulder with Stefan, who spots an opening and passes to me.

Just try to stop me, goalie.

I blast that motherfucking puck to the back of the net without thinking twice.

My teammates cheer and the crowd erupts, but I barely feel the usual adrenaline rush. I just want this game to be over.

When I return to the bench with Stefan, he yanks

up his helmet, then says, so only I can hear, "She'll be okay."

"But I hate that she's hurt at all," I mutter.

"Yeah, I know." He pats my back.

How is he so fucking rational?

He taps the boards with his stick. "You can do this," he says, calm and in control.

But I feel like a high-tension line. I've been such an asshole for the last few days. I've fucking ignored her, and I hate that.

And now she's hurt, and she probably hates me. Why the fuck didn't I say more when she texted? Why didn't I text her?

You know why. You're fucking scared.

I breathe out hard, then take this surge of irritation and pour it into the rest of the game, making sure we rack up a win.

When the buzzer sounds, I'm out of there without looking back.

* * *

The second my skates are off, I march into the trainers' room, barking, "Where's my wife?" from the doorway.

Ivy sits on the bench in the corner, kicking her sneakered feet back and forth, drinking grape juice and icing her left wrist while talking to Briar, the yoga instructor who's been contracted to work with the team. "And when she said *you and me*?" Ivy says with a sigh.

Briar, standing by the counter of medical supplies,

clasps her chest like she's swooning. "I was done. Just done. The entire box of tissues—gone," Briar says.

"Same," Ivy says in that tone women use when they're bonding over something romantic said on TV or in a book.

What the hell? Where is the trainer? The assistant trainer? I'm about ready to pull my hair out, and they're discussing romantic quotes?

"What's going on?" I demand, closing the distance to the dark-haired beauty I've missed terribly. "Are you okay?"

Ivy turns to me at last. "Oh. Hi," she says, then waggles the bottle. "This is like candy. Have you had this before? Or is that against the diet rules?"

We're talking about grape juice and diets? She fell and I carried her off the ice, terrified she was hurt badly, and we're discussing drinks?

I'm still in my uniform shorts and pads. My neck is covered in sweat. My hair is a mess. And my heart is beating too fast.

"We won," Ivy says brightly. "It was the polar bear. That got everyone going, right?"

Oh, shit.

I know this Ivy.

This is Ivy's wall. Like in the SUV in Vegas after the wedding when she was too cheery, too upbeat, too happy. She does this when she's hiding something. Afraid of something. And I'm pretty sure I know what she's afraid of now.

Me.

Or more specifically, how frosty I've been the last few days.

My bad behavior wallops me. I shut down. I ignored. I avoided. I was as cold as my ex-girlfriend had accused.

I don't feel cold at all for this woman before me. I feel so much for Ivy it terrifies me. But I face down grown men on the ice who want to body check me, so I can do this. I cup Ivy's cheeks and meet her deep blue eyes, full of the brightness that masks her hurt. "I'm sorry," I say, full of contrition. I hope she hears all of it. "I'm so sorry."

Her eyes swing briefly to Briar. "I just jammed my wrist, that's all," she says, like I'd be silly to think otherwise. "Kelsey was here, but she had to get back to the team. She iced it and gave me the good stuff. Ibuprofen. And Briar found the grape juice. If I'm a good girl, Kelsey said she'd give me goldfish crackers when she checks back in a few minutes. But now, Briar's in charge of me. What do you think, B? Do I deserve crackers too?"

The perky yoga instructor winks at Ivy. "You can have crackers, but only if you send me that link."

Ivy scoffs playfully. "Consider it done."

"What link?" I ask, lost again in their girl talk.

"She needs a dress for a thing," Ivy says.

"I hate shopping," Briar adds with a shudder.

"And I don't," Ivy says. "It works out perfectly. Briar gave me the contraband grape juice, and I'm going to get her a dress for an event."

Fuck.

She doesn't believe me. She doesn't trust me. I run my thumb along her jawline. "Let me take you home," I whisper.

Shaking her head, she meets my gaze, her eyes sharp and shrewd. "I'm fine." She's not being too nice now. She's drawing a line in the sand.

She slides carefully off the table, turning in a slow circle.

My jaw falls. "You should be lying down. Resting. Taking it easy," I sputter.

She waggles her fingers and shows off the ACE bandage on her wrist. "They did an X-ray and nothing's broken. I just need to rest it tonight. Kelsey took care of me, and now I'm literally hanging out with Briar," she says, laying out the facts, crisp and cool. "And I can skate at the game in two days. It was just a fall, and the bear costume helped protect me."

I growl at her. There are lines in the sand and there is also an injured woman I need to take care of. "We're going home. *Now*."

"I need to grab...my water bottle. Yes, that's it," Briar stammers, then exits the room swiftly.

It's just us.

My wife glares at me. "You can't just barge in here and tell me to go home when you've ignored me for three days. That's not how this works."

I reel, shocked at the bite in her words. The truth in them.

"And you can't just come in here and demand to see your wife," she adds.

I drag a hand down my face. I really fucked up.

"What can I do then?" I ask, feeling helpless but refusing to go.

Her fire burns off, leaving only vulnerability. "Just talk to me. That's what I want. That's what you can do."

I wrap my arms around her. "I'm sorry, baby. I ignored you. I practically ghosted you. I just shut down."

She's still at first, then she inches closer to me. "I noticed."

"Of course you did. You always notice."

"I don't like being ignored," she whispers, "by either of you."

I let go and then meet her eyes, speaking straight from the heart now. "Come home with us. Please."

Pretty sure it's the *us* that does it for her. I don't even have to ask Stefan if he wants in. I'm not at all surprised when I look up and spot him standing in the doorway, gazing at Ivy.

He shuts the door and advances toward her. "We were jerks. We don't deserve you. But let us take care of you anyway."

Well, that sums things up nicely.

37

THE OPPOSITE

Ivy

Really, this is too much. But I'll take their *too much* any day. We're at Stefan's place. Usually we go to Hayes's. We've been cautious. But tonight feels different. But there's also nothing wrong with three Avengers staff hanging together after a game. Kelsey checked on me as promised and declared me good to go.

Now, Hayes, Stefan and I are stretched out on Stefan's king-size bed—it's an Alaskan king, and it makes me never want to go back to anything smaller— and he's massaging my neck while Hayes holds the ice pack on my wrist. Roxy's curled up at my feet, keeping a watchful eye on both men, occasionally growling low in her throat while staring at them like *say the word, Ivy, and I'll handle them for you*.

Seriously, we don't deserve dogs.

The guys insisted I take it easy, and so we're

relaxing with an episode of *The Adventures of Mister Orgasm* on the big-screen TV at the foot of the bed. Sometimes an animated show about a superhero dedicated to pleasing women is just what the doctor ordered.

I felt better after their apology. Also, I saw Stefan's text message when Briar brought me my phone in the trainers' room. He'd replied right before the game saying: *I'll be there, and I can't wait.*

But the thing is, I don't know if that means he wants me with or without Hayes—and I don't know how *all in* Hayes is anymore. I glance at the guy on one side of me, wearing a gold band that matches mine. Hayes's dark hair is messy at the top, and his scruff has become scruffier. On my other side, the guy with the lighter eyes and even fairer skin hasn't stopped working out knots in my shoulders and neck.

And yet...

We need to talk more than I need to be coddled.

When the episode ends, Hayes turns to me. "Want another, baby?"

I shake my head, and he turns off the Chromecast. "Want to go to sleep?"

A stupid lump forms in my throat. Annoying thing. I swallow it. "No. I want to know what happened. You guys went radio silent." I hand him the ice pack then gently bat Stefan's hand away.

Hayes sets the ice pack on a towel on the nightstand and drags a hand over his beard. He does that when he gets frustrated with himself. "It's my fault."

"Not true," Stefan corrects.

"It is," Hayes counters.

"Nope."

I roll my eyes. "You're fighting over whose fault it was that both of you shut down?"

"Yeah, but it was mine. I was spinning out the other night. I dragged him into it." Hayes's eyes are full of contrition.

"How so?" I ask Stefan.

But Hayes clears his throat and answers for them. "I said if he wanted to go after you on his own, I was fine with it."

I freeze.

Hayes looks like he just drank battery acid.

I feel that way. Roxy must, too, since she emits a warning bark. *Don't mess with my person.*

"You...said that?" I croak.

Hayes frowns. "I just...I...fuck," he mutters, then drops his head back against the pillow.

Roxy sits up, reading the room, and fires off another warning bark.

My chest aches. I can feel the hurt coming on, the final blow, but I square my shoulders, standing my ground. "If you're ending this, just end it," I say. "I told you I'd tell Jessie. I told you I'm fine with it. I meant it."

Don't mess with my heart.

Hayes straightens, reaching for my forearm, squeezing gently as if he's trying to send me a message. "No, I don't want to end it. Any of this," he says, gesturing to his friend and me. "I just didn't expect to..." He groans again, scrubbing a hand over his scruff once more.

"You're impossible, *Hey You*," Stefan says, rolling his eyes, then turning to me. "He's taken by you just like I am. Okay?"

A joyous laugh bursts from me. "That's it? That's the problem?"

"Yes," Hayes mutters.

"Yes," Stefan says with a laugh.

They're so similar and so different.

I hold up my palm. "Let me get this straight. You ghosted me because you *like* me?"

Hayes nods, resigned to what he did. "Yes. I screwed up."

"We both did," Stefan adds. "Neither one of us was any good at talking to you. He told me what was going on, and I should have pushed him to talk to you, but I didn't. I froze. I didn't know how to do *this* without him."

This. But what is *this*? What are we? Am I pushy to ask? Fuck it. I'm asking. "What are we doing?"

Hayes scoots closer, rubs my arm some more, then shrugs. "I don't honestly know, Ivy. But I know this—I don't want to mess it up. However long it lasts."

"I don't either," Stefan adds, reaching for my hand and linking his fingers with mine.

That seems like something I can get on board with. But Hayes clears his throat, going on. "I'll do better. I promise. I was a callous jerk. I hate that I treated you that way. My ex-girlfriend said I was aloof and distant, and it killed me tonight when I realized I acted that way with you."

I didn't expect that—Hayes confessing all, sharing

past wounds. I watch him, waiting for him to say more, hoping he knows it's safe to tell me.

"We dated in Seattle, and she said all I cared about was my career. Maybe that was true, in hindsight. I felt like a total ass when I was traded to Los Angeles and she didn't even want to try to stay together long-distance. She said I was cold." He blows out a breath. "Maybe I was. But the thing is," he says, meeting my gaze, vulnerability rimming his eyes, "with you, I don't feel aloof. I don't feel distant." Then, like it pains him to say, he adds in a barren whisper, "I feel the opposite."

My heart doesn't hurt anymore. It grows.

"And I don't honestly know what to do about it," he says. His eyes are big and helpless and it's so endearing to see this controlled, intense man a little lost.

"Let's just keep doing *this*," I say.

For a moment, Hayes is quiet, contemplative. Then he says, "Yes."

I turn to Stefan, asking the same. "And do you want that too?"

The man on the other side of me flashes a big, sexy grin. "Sweetheart, I've wanted you from the start. I just want you more now."

I can't fathom more than this, not when I still feel tender, not when I feel softer for them than I ever expected. But maybe for the rest of this arrangement, we can be all in.

We'll have to start with this new wrinkle. "I felt weird tonight at the wives' and girlfriends' and husbands' and boyfriends' suite," I admit.

"Because we're married but not really married?"

Hayes asks, sounding remorseful for putting me in this position.

"Yes, but also because..." I turn to Stefan. "I wanted them to know I'm not just a *wife*." I draw air quotes, hoping it masks the sudden slam of emotion in me. "But I'm also a..."

Stefan drops his forehead to mine. "A secret girlfriend."

Hearing those words from him both thrills me and saddens me. "Yes. Because they invited me to dinner and board games. With Hayes," I add. I pull back to meet Stefan's gaze. His expression is hard to read. There's a bit of a wall up in his eyes. "I want you to go. Is there any way you can?" I ask impulsively.

I haven't worked out the details. I haven't planned this at all. I just feel he belongs there with me. With *us*.

I tell him the date. He thinks on it for a beat, but then he sighs. "Wish I could, but I have a thing that night. A dinner with one of my sponsors."

He sounds disappointed to miss the get-together. I'm sad he can't come too. But at least he knows I wanted him there. It seems a good start to what we're forging tonight.

He strokes my hair. "But the rest of the time, we'll be here. I'll be here," he adds. "Every night we're in town, right, *Hey You*?"

"Fuck you, dickhead," Hayes growls. But when he turns to me, his face softens, and he brushes a kiss onto my cheek. "I won't let you down again."

I still don't know what happens when Hayes takes off that ring—if they'll continue to want me together or if Hayes will walk away. If Stefan will want me to himself. I turn back to my secret boyfriend. "So what did you tell him? When he asked if you'd pursue me by yourself?"

"He said nothing," Hayes answers for his friend.

Stefan flips him the bird now, but to me, his expression fully open and genuine. "Pretty sure you'd be impossible to walk away from."

My heart flips as I let those words wash over me. The strength of them. The passion of them. The promise.

But as good as they make me feel—and they make me melt—I don't know what I want at the end of this arrangement.

What I want right this minute, though, is a little more...*throuple time*. I gesture to the TV screen. "Want to watch something else? You two can pick your favorite shows since I already picked mine."

"*Schitt's Creek*," Hayes says, like he's calling shotgun.

"What's yours?" I ask Stefan.

He just chuckles and shakes his head, saying nothing.

I poke his side. "I really need to know now."

"Yeah, what is it?" Hayes goads. "*Salty Licorice* or *Bicycle Men* or, I dunno, *Viking Thieves*?"

Stefan snort-laughs. "Those aren't shows."

"Bet they are," Hayes says.

"I'll have you know Danish TV is quite excellent."

"I'm not going to let this go," I warn him.

With a beleaguered sigh, Stefan relents. "Fine. But I'll show you."

I give Stefan the remote control. He picks a thriller in a fishing town at the top of Denmark, and then translates the first few spoken Danish lines before adding the subtitles to the screen.

"That was such a flex," Hayes teases.

Stefan turns to me. "Yes, yes it was," he says.

In French.

Then he whispers something else in my ear in that language, and it feels like he's saying, *I'm so glad you're here.*

Me too.

* * *

But in the morning, something nags at me. Something that's been nagging at me since I saw Xander and Simone a few days ago. I try to shake the irritating feeling as I research a post for Birdie. But soon it's an incessant drumbeat and I can't let it go.

38

ONE OF THE GUYS

Stefan

Old-fashioned perfume tickles my nose. Soft, delicate music plays overhead. Ladies shuffle by. That's a department store for you.

When the helpful sales clerk holding a black gift bag strides over to Hayes and me, she flashes a congenial smile. "Here you go, sir."

"Thank you very much," I say, taking the bag.

"Appreciate it," Hayes adds.

Our next stop is the arena, even though it's a day off. As we walk inside the building, I dangle the bag in front of my friend. "Now, can you handle giving this to the boss, or do you need to leave it to the adult in charge?"

"I think I can manage," he says.

Arching a dubious brow, I yank the bag away when he reaches for it. "Let's see. What happened the last time you saw her? Oh, I remember. Your brain froze so you said you were still married, since that made it easier to go to a golf tournament."

Hayes huffs.

"Yes, growl at me. That bothers me so much," I say as we turn the corner to the hallway that leads to the executive suite. "I mean, we could let you try giving it to her and hope that if she, for instance, invites you to dinner, you don't say *great, I just bought a restaurant.*"

He claps my shoulder. "No worries, bro. If she does, I'll say yours is mine. Since, well, we do share."

"Yes. Yes, we do," I say.

There are other things I want to share with him, but now's not the time to marinate on my wishes. It's time to help our girl. She mentioned she needed to pick something up for Jessie, so I insisted she let us do it. She still needs to take it easy.

A few seconds later, I'm knocking on the door to the executive suite. Jessie's assistant answers, but Jessie's right there next to him. "What brings you both here?"

I don't think I've ever come to her office before. There's been no need. "Ivy asked us to bring this to you," I say, offering her the gift.

She blinks. I've surprised the owner. I'm well aware that I'm not the public husband. But I'm doing this with Hayes, anyway, because I want to. *We* want to.

"Thank you," Jessie says, then peeks inside. Instantly, her eyes sparkle. "Oh, yes! Tell her *thank you very much.*"

"We will," Hayes says.

"There's a card too," I add. Ivy handed me the envelope this morning. No idea what it says, of course, since it's sealed.

Jessie peers inside. "Excellent. And see you at the golf tournament next weekend. Both of you. Also, keep winning. I like winning."

"I do too, Ms. Rose," Hayes says.

Jessie gives us one more curious look, like she's trying to puzzle out if there's a reason we're both here, other than us being friends.

But I don't drop any more breadcrumbs. I'm not worried about how she'd handle it. Jessie took Ryker, Trina, and Chase out to dinner when their throuple became public a couple seasons ago. She's an outspoken proponent of loving who you want. I'm not worried she'd have any issues with us.

It's just that timing is everything. And while I'd absolutely pursue Ivy on my own, I want her with Hayes, together. I'm going to need to figure out how to pull that off.

I fully intend to make her mine. But I'm a patient man, and I'm willing to show her that I'm the guy for her.

Or really, one of the guys.

* * *

When we return to the building, a text flashes in our group chat.

. . .

Ivy: I'm at the penthouse. I wanted kale for lunch—early lunch. I made a salad. You can join me.

I give Hayes a look that translates to *salad for lunch? I'm not a rabbit.*

"Food truck," he says, understanding immediately.

Ten minutes later, we head inside with sandwiches from the truck since every hour is mealtime. Ivy's grabbing a fork, and there's a salad on the counter in a large metal bowl. "How did it go?"

"We gave it to her together," I remark casually. I want to plant the seed.

"You did?" There's no uncertainty in her voice. Just curiosity.

"Look, someone had to make sure Hayes didn't tell her his dad owned the department store and wanted to hire her as the spokesmodel," I say.

Hayes smacks the back of my head.

I smack his head.

Ivy laughs, and all feels right in the world. Well, for now. I'll have to take small steps toward the future.

Starting with lunch, and when I open the paper on my sandwich, I'm reminded of something. "I forgot to tell you. Your ex came to visit me the other night."

From across the counter, her eyes bug out. "What?"

"He wanted me to invest in, wait for it, Dough and Duds," I say, and the three of us have a laugh as I tell them about Xander's proposal.

As she takes a bite of the salad, she turns pensive, then says, "It's funny you mention him, because I made a big decision this morning. Something's been nagging at me, and I really want to know what you both think. If it's too crazy or risky."

She sounds earnest and a little nervous.

Please don't say you got a job out of town. I don't think my heart could handle it.

"Sure, hit me up," I say, not giving away that fear.

She sets down the fork. "I don't want to cover their wedding. I think I'd like to turn it down. Or, really, to back out."

"Just not do it?" Hayes asks, but he doesn't sound alarmed. He sounds more like he's reining in a hoot and a holler.

"Yes. I don't want to associate with people who belittle me now or who have in the past. They both did. And if turning this down means I lose a chance at a bunch of new followers and a really click-y piece, I'm okay with that. My mental health is worth more."

I look at the gorgeous, fierce woman across from me. I pretty much have no choice but to fall even harder for Ivy Samuels. "I'm so fucking proud of you."

"Do it," Hayes urges, and a giddy Ivy grabs her phone.

Ten seconds later, she's saying, "Hey, girl, it's Ivy Samuels. Something came up, and I can't cover your wedding."

A pause. "What came up?" Ivy asks, presumably repeating Simone's question.

Another pause. "Oh, just the fact that my doctors have suggested I limit my exposure to all things toxic.

And that'd be you and my ex. Thanks a bunch, though, and best of luck with your blowout bash."

When she hangs up, she lets out a huge, excited breath, then punches the sky. "I did it!"

"You fucking did it," I echo, then stand and wrap her in a hug. Hayes joins me, embracing her too.

Hmm. This hug feels pretty good. Especially when she wriggles against me. Then against him. Then me again. Then she whispers, "I missed...*fucking*."

"And I missed fucking you. But you need to take it easy," I say, but with heat in my voice.

"Don't forget twelve hours ago, your wrist was wrapped," Hayes reminds her. "You need to rest it for a full day."

She peels away and heads to the staircase leading to the roof. "Well, my right wrist works fine."

39

THE ROOFTOP GAME

Hayes

I push through the doors of the restaurant, hellbent on sprinting to the patio this second. I march to the hostess stand, manned by a guy with a handlebar mustache.

"Hey there. Can I grab a soda on the patio?"

Say yes. My jaw is tight with anticipation. Stefan didn't call ahead. I didn't ask him to. We weren't fucking thinking when Ivy said to me, "You've always wanted a show, right?"

Then Stefan said he'd direct.

And yes, yes, yes, I fucking want a show. And I want it now.

The man smiles apologetically, a customer service no. "It's not open right now, sir. We won't open till noon. In ten minutes."

Like I'm on the ice and I've spotted a defender

coming out of nowhere, I switch tactics. After fishing for my wallet, I grab a hundred-dollar bill, then fold it discreetly but clearly. "I just need five minutes to check it out for a party. Can you help me?" I offer him the bill, hoping so hard he'll say yes. Don't want to call Stefan for permission. I want to pull my weight in every way.

The man hesitates, glancing furtively around before he reaches for it. "Of course," he says, pocketing the payola.

I won't tell my buddy I bribed his employee either.

I want to turbo boost out there this second, but I cool my jets as he guides me through the indoor seating to the patio door. After he unlocks it, he says helpfully, "Can I show you around?"

"I can handle it solo." Just like Ivy is doing.

I leave him behind. I march straight to the stone railing, my building in my crosshairs. I bring my binoculars to my eyes and aim them at the roof of my place.

Holy. Fucking. Shit.

Ivy's nearly naked and somehow the white scraps of lace for her bra and panties make her impossibly sexier. She stretches out on the lounge. Stefan's parked in a chair a few feet away, watching her. I can't text Stefan fast enough with one word. *Here.*

He glances at the phone vibrating in his hand, then he says something to her. I catch her smiling.

"Take them off," I mutter, wanting those panties to vanish right fucking now. "Make her take them off."

She doesn't strip though. She slides her right hand into her hair, roaming it through those lush, dark locks. Goddamn, I want that to be my hand. Want to thread my fingers through all that hair. Tug on it, sniff it, play with it.

She turns her head to the side, giving me an inviting glimpse of the column of her neck before she lets go then runs that hand along her throat, over the top of her chest. Stopping at her tits, she turns to Stefan, saying something.

No idea what she says, but I bet she's asking him for permission. I bet he's saying, "Tease him."

Yes, Ivy, fucking tease me.

She flicks her right nipple through the bra, teasing me, indeed. Her lips part.

That's it. That's my girl. She loves her nipple play. She arches her hips higher and higher still before she slides her right hand down her stomach on a sensual, seductive path. Her hips shimmy, subtly rocking the whole time.

I desperately want to draw those tits into my mouth. She's not even showing them to me, not even unhooking her bra, but the way she plays with them drives me wild.

Then her fingers reach the top of her panties, and I'm dying.

Stefan's in view, and he leans back in the chair, fully dressed, urging her on with his words. A nod to her waist. A suggestion, perhaps.

"Show me, baby. Show me how wet you are," I urge.

She doesn't take them off, and I sigh in frustration. But then, I moan when her hand disappears into her panties. When she reaches her wet pussy, her mouth parts in a needy *O*. The look on her face, even from the distance in the binoculars, is so fucking sexy.

She's so aroused. So turned on. So eager to play with herself. She looks enraptured by her own body.

Or maybe she's enrapt by our game—knowing I'm the hawk, watching her every move, and he's the director, moving the pieces on the chessboard. My dick is granite as I stare at the beauty on my roof working herself over.

Hand moving faster.

Hips arching.

Lips parting.

She's fucking her fingers, losing her mind to whatever dirty fantasies are playing out in her gorgeous head, and I can't even see her sweet pussy. She's just taking care of herself under his direction, flicking and feeling and fucking.

Soon she's thrusting into her hand, her head turned to the side. When she rakes her other hand into her hair, it's like she's about to tip over into pleasure.

She tenses. Everywhere. It's beautiful and filthy all at once. The best kind of porn I've ever seen—a live sex show from the woman I'm obsessed with, put on for the two of us. The man on the roof, and the man across the street.

We're her audience. We're her men. And we're so fucking lucky to watch this beauty fall apart. Head thrown back, legs spread, she comes across the block.

I can't hear her, but I swear her cries of pleasure echo in my mind.

I don't lower the binoculars for a good long time. Pretty sure I'll be rock hard the rest of my life.

When I make it back to my place ten minutes later, she's naked, and Stefan's stripped to nothing too.

"Took you long enough," he says to me.

I narrow my brow, suddenly annoyed. "Her wrist. We said no fucking. Nothing rough."

He grins. "Hold her tits. I'm going to fuck them," he says.

I am so jealous and so turned on.

A minute later, he's straddling Ivy. Her hands are stretched above her head. She looks like a long, languid goddess. I move behind her, crouching, and pushing those beauties together so my friend can fuck those gorgeous globes.

He spits, then takes his cock in his hand, slides the makeshift lube over it, and fucks.

A thrust. A pump.

Then, a gasp from Ivy.

And then, from me. My neck is burning up. My dick is iron. My eyes are glued to the scene in front of me.

And I take my job so goddamn seriously. Stefan fucks her beautiful breasts as I hold them in place for him. Soon, slick sounds fill the air, the slap of flesh, the carnal groans, Ivy's sexy little gasps.

Then, a long, strangled moan from Stefan as he spills all over her tits.

I burn up inside. When he slides off, Ivy drags a finger through his climax, then turns my way to slowly, seductively lick it off while gazing at me. I nearly bust a nut.

"Want to come too?" she asks, sounding all dreamy.

I hiss out a breath. "So badly."

In seconds I'm tagging in, and he's tagging out. He gets behind her, cups those beauties, and gives me a perfect tunnel to fuck. She's slick and hot. And I am enrapt by her. By her appetite. By her openness. By her mind, body, and gorgeous heart.

I don't last long, and I don't care.

Soon, my vision blurs and my thighs shake, and I'm coming all over her tits, painting her too.

Then kissing her, slowly and a little desperately before I slide down her body. Stefan leans over and drops a passionate kiss to her lips.

When he breaks the kiss, he drags a finger along her chest, through our orgasms. I do the same. Then, he pushes his finger into her mouth. She opens easily, taking it. I join him, pushing in my finger too. She sucks both, licking us off with a throaty moan.

When she lets go, she says, a little dreamily, "You taste good."

That word—the plural you—echoes in my mind all day.

You.

That's how we feel to me too.

40

OTHER FORMS OF SHARING

Ivy

"Pfft."

That's my grandmother's assessment of the linen pants I show her at Champagne Taste a few days later.

"But you'd look great in them," I urge her, gently tugging on the tawny-colored slacks at the thrift shop.

She arches a brow. "Of course I would. But that's not the point."

I heave a playful sigh. "You can't dismiss everything I show you."

She pats my shoulder. "I can and I will if you keep showing me things that were in and then out of fashion before you were even born," she says, then strolls to another rack at the shop, flicking through blouses that she shakes her silver-haired head at.

"But linen's trendy again. It's this whole—"

"*Trendy grandma look.* I am aware, but I disavow it."

I snort-laugh. "You can't disavow a trend."

"I just did."

I've been having fun with her this morning, but something is pressing at the back of my mind. A little tension. I feel like I'm keeping a secret from her. Only I don't know how to share it as we move through the store.

For now I tuck it away as she waves a hand at another rack. "Why would I go back to something I already moved on from?"

"Well, not to go all cross-examiner, but aren't you dating some guy from high school you met at your class reunion?" I point out. "Hello, second-chance romance."

She spins around again, her eyes ablaze. But her plum-lipsticked mouth is quiet.

"Cat got your tongue, Grandma?" I tease.

She narrows her eyes, crinkling them at the corners, but she stifles a laugh. "Fine, recycling *may* work for men and clothing. But not clothing *trends*," she says as she heads to a nearby row of jeans. "But tell me more about the man in your life before we meet your brother."

I freeze, my hand on soft denim. An uncomfortable feeling slithers down my back. Yes, she knows I married Hayes. Yes, she teased me about it at the time. But she doesn't know there are *men*, plural. Or how serious things have become.

For a brief second, I consider saying brightly, *He's great,* then moving on.

But I did enough covering up of my feelings when I was younger. When my father was yelling at my mother. Insulting her. Putting her down. When I was nine and ten and I hid in my room with my little sister, pretending it wasn't happening. At night then, I'd counted down the days till mom left him. When she finally did, I was the happiest I'd ever been as a kid.

A happy relief isn't how a child should feel. I don't like pretending everything is fine here either.

I push past the queasy feeling in my chest. "Actually, there are..." I stop, glance around the store, not because I'm embarrassed but because this is private. With my chin up, I say, "Men."

My grandmother stops, tilts her gaze my way. "Sounds like we should grab a coffee before lunch."

* * *

Ten minutes later, we're at a nearby café, and I'm telling her the details of my love life. Not the sex details, but the feelings ones, down to the argument, the fall on the ice, the talk that night. "And now, here I am," I say when I finish, nerves skating up my throat.

She's been down this road before with my brother, but still, this is my first time admitting I like two people at once.

She takes a beat, her blue eyes kind. "Sounds like you care for them both, Ivy," she says without a shred of judgment.

"I really do," I say, grateful to have shared this with her at last. But I'm nervous to voice the depth of all my emotions. "A lot. Kind of crazy, isn't it?"

"Not really." She takes a sip of her coffee, her

expression turning thoughtful. "Sounds complicated though."

I drink some of my latte, mulling over that basic truth. She's not wrong. "It feels complicated. I'm not sure what to do next." That's the other issue. Where do I go from here?

"The good thing is you don't have to do anything now," she says, perhaps with the wisdom of years.

"But eventually I will."

"That's true. But sometimes I think we pressure ourselves to make decisions before we're truly ready. Is this even a decision you need to make now? Maybe you need to be in this romance for a little longer to know."

My shoulders relax some more. She's right. I don't have to do anything today. Maybe this is what I needed —just to know that it's okay to exist in my uncertainty.

"Thanks, Grandma. I needed to say all that. And to hear that."

She pats my hand. "I'm glad you knew you could share with me."

"Now, what's going on with the guy you met at your fiftieth high school reunion?" I ask, turning the tables.

But before she can answer, she points to the window and down the street. It's a deflection, but a relevant one. "Oh look, there's your brother. He might know a thing or two about your situation," she says, then lowers her voice and adds with some concern. "Wait. Does he know?"

Nerves race through me as I shake my head. "No. But I want him to."

"Well then," she says, then waves him to our table when he comes into the café.

With a rare smile, Ryker strides to the table and gives Grandma a hug, then me. "Two of my favorite people," he says.

"It's your lucky day," I say.

"Yes, it is."

"How's playing for the team with the worst record?" I taunt. It's easier to trash talk about sports than to crack open my heart.

He growls.

My grandma laughs and high-fives me.

"The season is long," he says, then clears his throat and adds, "How's being a mascot? And being married to a player?"

Goodbye, trash talk. Hello, real talk. "Well, here's the thing. I'm seeing Hayes," I begin, and he gives me a look like *I'm not surprised*, then I hold up a hand and add, "And Stefan."

Ryker blinks, confusion crossing his blue eyes, which is all kinds of ironic. "Wait. Both—"

Before he can say *at the same time*, I say, "Yes."

Five minutes later, he's cracking up, his forehead in his hand. When he lifts his face, he says, "Was it something in the water when we were kids?"

"Clearly," I say.

"Like brother, like sister," Grandma says.

Ryker stops laughing and fixes me with a serious stare. "But if either of them hurts you, I will kill them. Also, athletes can be trouble."

My grandmother snorts. "Ryker, are you a self-loathing athlete? Do you think athletes make terrible boyfriends?"

"No. But imagine how bad it'll be when something goes wrong," he says evenly.

"Bad for team morale?" I ask.

"That. But mostly bad for Hayes's face," Ryker says, his tone so dry I can't truly tell if he's serious. "And Stefan's."

I laugh. But only a little. "You don't mean that."

He drags a hand across his beard, his gaze softening. "Look, I don't trust most people. I especially don't trust guys."

I nod, understanding him implicitly.

"Mom stuck around too long because she was afraid to leave. I don't want that happening to you," he adds, full of concern.

I get where he's coming from. But I have to make my own choices. "I trust them," I say.

That's a little terrifying to say and a little wonderful at the same time.

My grandmother smiles genuinely. "Good. That's what matters most."

So is the fact that I simply don't have to make any decisions about the future of my relationship today. But soon, I will.

41

HER MEN

Hayes

"I need a photo of this. You two look like twins." The declaration comes from Ivy as she enters the kitchen from the bedroom that weekend, smirking at me, then at Stefan.

"We do not," I say, plucking at my newish burgundy golf shirt.

Stefan stares down at his navy one, scoffing. "If we do, it's because you dressed us, sweetheart. You picked out these clothes."

"And I had fun," she says, squaring her shoulders as she closes the distance between us. She bought me this shirt yesterday, since I didn't have one that fit. I've bulked up over the summer and haven't grabbed a new one yet. "And you both look good."

She smooths a hand over the collar of my shirt even though it doesn't need smoothing. I stare at her hand on me. Looks too fucking right. Feels too good. Too bad she stops to tap her finger against her lips. "Maybe I should even do a new post titled *How to find a sexy golf outfit secondhand*. Pretty clothes for—"

She stops short. I can hear *my men* forming on her lips, but then she swallows it.

I glance over at Stefan, and something warm sparks in my chest. Not for him, of course. But for...I'm not sure. Maybe moments like this? With the three of us together? Is that what I'm longing for?

Maybe.

We feel like a team in some strange way, getting ready for the event together. But before I linger too long on that thought, I nod toward the couch where a wrapped gift waits for...*our woman*.

"And since you picked our clothes, we get to pick yours," I say.

"We are excellent at shopping too," Stefan, my partner in crime, adds.

Ivy gestures to the flouncy red dress she's wearing, shooting us a quizzical look. "I already picked my dress. I'm not golfing, so I don't have to wear golf pants."

I step forward, tugging up the skirt of her dress. She's wearing white cotton panties. "Did I say we got you a dress?"

Her lips part. "Oh."

Stefan heads to the living room. "We got you something we can play with later," he says, then returns with a white box with a red bow.

When she opens the box and tugs out a pair of red

lace panties with a tiny wearable vibrator built into the fabric, her breath catches.

"Put it in your purse. We'll tell you *when* to put the panties on," Stefan says, then dips his hand into his pocket, brandishing the remote and handing it to me. "And then we'll decide when to turn you on."

With a glossy look in her eyes, she complies, tucking the gift inside her purse where, I hope, it'll set her on fire all day long.

We leave, and Ivy looks like she's already turned on.

* * *

We arrive together at the golf course, but I feel off. It's strange to step out of my car with my wife and my buddy. I feel like a liar. Well, I *am* a liar. I've been faking everything.

Have you, though, man?

That's the thing. After the valet takes our clubs out of the car, then drives off to park it, we walk to the clubhouse, but I *feel* like I'm faking something. And it's no longer the marriage to Ivy.

It's the truth of who we are behind closed doors. I hate kissing her goodbye at the entrance to the clubhouse when Stefan's not doing the same. This course is owned by Wilder Blaine, who also owns the Renegades football team in this city. The billionaire has a young daughter, so he wanted this place to be more family-friendly and he added a mini-golf course for kids. Since Ivy doesn't play regular golf, she made plans with Trina to play mini golf while we're here, but I feel like shit watching her walk away after kissing her.

This is the opposite of the warm feeling I had in my chest at home. This is something I never expected. Something I'm not even sure how to deal with.

Except...maybe I do know how to deal with it.

Head-on.

I steal a glance at my college friend, the team captain, the guy I've come to know in all the ways. We head on over to the golf carts, where the valet sent our clubs. I glance around, making sure the coast is clear. We're alone on the path. "Stef," I begin.

"Yeah?"

But what am I saying? What am I asking? How the hell do I do this?

We stop on a grassy hill several feet from the carts. "She doesn't feel like just mine," I blurt out, because fuck it, sometimes you just have to rip off the Band-Aid.

He smiles, slow and easy. "That so?"

"She really doesn't," I say, dragging a hand through my already messy hair.

This is so hard, opening myself up. I don't want to be like my dad. Don't want to wear my heart on my sleeve. Don't want to fall and get hurt.

But something shifted when Ivy fell on the ice.

I shifted.

I power through, no matter how uncomfortable I feel voicing my emotions. No matter how much easier it is to be cold, I try to be the opposite. "It's hard to think about this ending tomorrow night. There's no wedding to go to anymore," I point out. That was one of the reasons Ivy and I were staying married. The plan was to peter out after these public appearances, including this one today, then quietly get divorced.

"She doesn't need a wedding date," Stefan says, open-ended, waiting for me to supply the next link in the logic chain.

The first day I met Ivy, I volunteered to be her date. Now, that she doesn't need my plus-one-ing, I feel at loose ends. I feel like I'm wearing the wrong size shoes, but I have to keep walking in them.

"So," I fill in Stefan's blank, "it's this and the game night tomorrow." I want to stop time so I don't have to ask the next question. "What happens then?"

Stefan doesn't answer in his usual rapid-fire style. He pauses, pinning me with a thoughtful gaze, then says, "I think you should ask yourself that question."

Goddammit. He's right. But he's also a good friend, so he adds, "What do you want to happen?"

I'm starting to figure that out. Ideas form in my head, but are they ready to make landfall?

"What about you? What do you want? You're so... chill with everything."

With a laugh, he claps my shoulder. "We're in different places. I've known all along what I want." Hearing it feels like a punch to the jaw. "I just...want it more now."

I wince, rubbing my hand along my beard. Who do I blame for that blow—Stefan, or the realization I have yet to face?

I swallow before I can speak past all the foreign feelings. "I think I do too," I admit.

Damn, that was hard.

But necessary.

Stefan grins, big and broad. "Welcome to the club. Now let's go kick some fucking ass on the course."

He doesn't ask *what's next*, or *where do we go from here*. Sometimes you have to take these realizations in bite-size chunks.

It's time to hit the links.

We're teammates on the course, which seems fitting. What I like best is when we come out ahead at the end and Jessie strides up to playfully chide us. "Don't you know you're supposed to let the team owner win?"

Stefan chuckles. "Somehow I don't think you'd want that ever."

"You're right. I don't," she says, then nods to the restaurant. "Let's head inside."

As we walk there, she says to Stefan, "I hear you're up for Sportsman of the Year for The Sports Network."

"I am," he says.

"I'll be there to see you accept it. It'll be an honor for one of my players to win."

"You do like winning," Stefan says. It's fascinating to watch him hold his own with her. I admire that about Stefan—his ease in any situation. His calmness. His confidence. He's a man who knows what he wants.

"I like winning fairly, so I'll have to challenge you two to another round," she tells him. Then to me, she adds, "Now, let's find your wife."

Your.

That word, like the kiss at the clubhouse, feels off.

Once Jessie and I find Ivy and head inside, Stefan's not at our table, and that seems wrong as well.

It feels wrong the whole time I'm there with Ivy, chatting with Jessie and taking pictures.

It feels wrong as Ivy chats with Jessie's friends and colleagues, then with Trina, Ryker, and Chase.

And it feels wrong when the luncheon winds down and photos are snapped, and Parvati asks if she can post them on social on Monday.

That feels like the worst part of all.

"Actually, I'd like a pic with Stefan in it too," I say.

I don't tell her why. But I collect him for the photo and it feels exactly right. After Parvati takes the picture, it's time for the silent auction, so I turn to Stefan. "Now would be a good time."

He turns to Ivy and whispers in her ear. I watch her breath hitch, then she clutches her purse tightly and heads to the ladies' room.

42

SOME PATIENCE PLEASE

Ivy

I stare hard at the items on this table without really seeing them. My vision blurs, and my neck goes white hot.

I try to focus on...a set of Calloways. They're apparently really good clubs and—

Oh god. The pulse flutters faster between my legs.

I swallow, then grab the edge of the table as the speed picks up, and arousal spikes to the top of my soul.

I swallow my sighs as my body sings.

"I've been wanting to get a new set of clubs," Stefan muses to Hayes. They're both standing across the table from me.

"Me too. But do you like these?" Hayes asks him, and my knees wobble. He must have just hit the remote in his pocket. Now the silent vibrator in my underwear is caressing me like a fucking rock star. I want to close my eyes and moan, but I fight off the onslaught of pleasure.

From over the table, Stefan smiles my way. "Do you like golf, Ivy?"

I breathe out hard, afraid to speak.

"What?" he asks innocently. "I didn't hear you. Can you turn up the volume?"

And Hayes, the fucker, cranks up the speed in his pocket. I rocket to the moon. My legs nearly give out as my panties try to destroy all my control. Pleasure floods every cell in my body. It's so intense, the insistent, delicious buzzing right inside my panties as they play me in the silent auction room.

Guests float by, mingling and chatting, perusing travel and entertainment packages, golf pro lessons, and bottles of wine, all while my mind spins into bliss, my body racing to the edge.

"Did you say you liked golf, Ivy?" Stefan asks innocently.

My thighs clench. A groan threatens to coast past my lips. "Mini golf," I bite out so I don't gasp my pleasure into this room of charity golf attendees.

"So fun, isn't it?" Stefan asks casually, a smirk shifting his lush lips.

"I love to play," Hayes adds as the vibe hits me just so, just right, so damn good.

I want to fall apart in their arms. I want to let go. I want to touch them, kiss them, have them. I want to tell them with my lips and my words and my body how I feel with them.

But I can't.

"I have to go," I blurt out, then seize my chance. I wheel around, racing out of the auction room and heading straight for the ladies' room where I tear off the panties. They're no longer vibrating. Shoving them into my purse, I leave, my skin still tingling, my core still aching.

Down a hall, out the door, onto the course. My heart gallops and my breath comes fast. I march, needing air, needing space, needing to breathe. At the foot of the path, there's an empty golf cart. I slump down into it, whimpering from the aftereffects of almost coming in public.

But more so, from the sheer pressure of wanting to express myself. Wanting to shout and to moan, to writhe and to whimper. I wanted to just...be with them fully.

But I couldn't.

Seconds later, I hear footsteps on the path. Two pairs. "Hey, pretty girl."

I look up. Hayes is here. So is Stefan.

"What's wrong?" The question comes from Stefan. His voice is warm, full of concern.

"Did we push you too far?" Hayes asks in a tender tone.

I feel wrenched apart. "No. I just..."

The issue isn't my limits or whether I reached them.

It isn't about how far my exhibitionist side goes.

It's about the way I want them. "I want to go home. With both of you," I say.

I don't know where home is, but in no time, we're out of there.

* * *

The second we stumble into Stefan's home, everything feels right again. In the foyer, he curls a hand around my throat, pulls me impossibly close. His lips crush down on mine while Hayes crowds me from behind, brushing lush, open-mouthed caresses along the back of my neck, his nimble fingers exploring the bare skin of my arms, then traveling down to my waist.

I'm caught between them—my safe place. Hayes threads a hand up through my hair, tugging on it as he kisses along my shoulders.

Stefan presses his hand against the hollow of my throat as he devours my lips with a new ferocity.

We consume each other, lips and teeth and hands and bodies colliding. We're crashing into each other. Them and me, me and them. I'm touched all over, all at once, by them both.

Lust roars up in me again, an engine revved. Unlike at the country club, I'm free. I hold nothing back. I don't rein in my dirty joy. I'm free to let go, free to give in. Free to be...the woman I'm becoming.

I'm liquid gold under their touch. They melt me with their bruising kisses. Their questing hands. Their strong bodies that feel so right wrapped around mine.

I'm voracious.

I want everything. I want them both to fuck me. And I want it right now.

I wrench my mouth from Stefan's.

My breath comes in ragged gasps as I meet his gaze importantly, then look back at Hayes behind me. I let my body sink against Hayes's chest while I wrap my hands around Stefan's neck. "Fuck me together."

* * *

I'm aroused from the vibrator play, from the kissing, from the sensual touching, but I want to be *ready* because this is brand-new territory.

Hayes grabs a bottle of champagne and brings it into the bedroom as Stefan undresses me then sets me down on the white covers of the bed.

"So fucking gorgeous," he says approvingly as his possessive gaze roams up and down my body, lighting me up.

I'm sitting, and Stefan's taken off his shirt, but he's still in his slacks as he climbs onto the bed, kneels between my legs, and then spreads them open. I draw a sharp breath, full of anticipation.

He's gone down on me before, plenty of times. But the look he gives me—such wicked delight—sends a new charge through me. He dips his face, kissing the inside of my thigh.

As Stefan brushes soft lips along my flesh, Hayes hands me a glass of champagne. I take one drink, then another. The bubbles flow through me, loosening me more as Stefan travels to my pussy.

Then, he French kisses me. A hot burst of pleasure spreads through my body, and I put the flute on the nightstand. I might spill it otherwise, and this champagne is too good. I sink down into the soft pillows, inviting Stefan's exploration.

"That's right. You're doing so well for us." Hayes encourages as he strips off his clothes and comes around to the bed, joining me, kissing me passionately. His mouth crashes on mine as Stefan flicks his tongue against me, then licks a long, tantalizing path up my wetness.

My brain scrambles from the feel-good sensations coursing through me. I'm delirious from them kissing me everywhere. My limbs feel loose and warm. My body is like honey, and my mind is just floaty.

More kisses collide onto my mouth. More land between my thighs. I thread one hand into Hayes's hair as he kisses me. My other hand slides through Stefan's strands. I'm pulling one man to my mouth, the other to my pussy. It's an overload of kissing till I spark, the start of an orgasm rushing into view. Before I know it, I'm gasping against Hayes's mouth, crying out, and coming apart.

My world blurs into bliss, and I break apart.

As I come down, we separate, and I'm panting, tingling.

Hayes glances at Stefan. "Think she's ready?"

With a smug smile, Stefan nods. "Yeah, just a little."

These guys. Their plans. God, it's so much. And I'm so ready, except for one little detail. "I'm on birth control. And I've been tested."

"I've been tested too. Negative," Hayes says.

Stefan seconds him.

I tell Hayes to lie on his back. He complies, his big body a gorgeous invitation with his miles of golden skin, scars, and tattoos. I straddle him, stroking a hand along his thick, throbbing dick. I reach for the lube, then coat his shaft even though I'm outrageously wet. But I need all the extra help I can get as I sink down on his slick cock.

His jaw clenches, then he grunts, "Yesss. You feel so fucking good."

His hands clamp over my hips, and he pushes up into me. I wriggle down, letting the pleasure and the pressure wash over me. For a minute or so, we set a rhythm, then I look behind me. Stripped naked, Stefan is kneeling on the bed, stroking his cock, lubing up.

I draw the biggest breath in the world. "Fuck me too." An electric charge tears through me when I hear my own demand.

"That's my girl," he says, then he grips my hips, angling me up.

I've researched this. I looked up articles on the best way to take two penises in a vagina at the same time.

But really when it comes right down to it, you don't know till you try. Here we go.

I lean closer to Hayes, my chest to his, giving Stefan plenty of room. He doesn't shove his dick into me though. First, he coats his fingers in lube, then takes his time pushing one in.

I hiss in a breath. That's...extra.

"You're doing so good," he whispers, then adds another.

Oh god. It's so tight. It's so much. I tense.

Roaming a gentle hand down my back, Stefan says, "Let me know if it hurts, if you want me to stop."

"I will," I say as I nod. But I want it to feel good. I think it will. "Keep going," I urge. I'm not stopping yet. No way.

He slides his fingers in, then eases them out, fucking me with his fingers while Hayes barely moves his cock. It's painful, for sure. But it's also...*not*.

The possibilities are just out of reach, and I try to move with Stefan as he opens me up. After a few minutes, I'm sweating, and Hayes is a coiled wire of tension under me. But I still...*want*.

I nod, breathing hard. "I'm ready."

"Good girl," Stefan says, then slides out his fingers.

I relax again, but I also feel emptier. Hayes brushes my hair from my face. "You feel incredible," he says, and he's normally the rougher one, the dirtier one, but it feels right to hear him say those words while Stefan nudges the head of his cock against my pussy. Trouble is, when Stefan pushes in an inch, I tense everywhere, locking up. Instantly, Hayes kisses my cheek, whispers against my lips, "Breathe, baby."

I inhale and Stefan pushes in more. Then deeper. "You're doing so good," Stefan praises.

"You're taking us so well," Hayes encourages me.

But it's so tight. It's so much. Sharp spikes of pain radiate through me.

"You okay?" Stefan asks with deep concern.

I bite the corner of my lip, then whisper, "It hurts."

"Do you want me to—"

I shake my head. "Just go slow, okay?"

A kiss to my back. Hands in my hair. Tender touches. They give me time to adjust to the sensations. I close my eyes, breathe in, out, like I'm doing yoga and moving into a new pose. Like yoga, it can hurt, but this hurts so good.

"More," I murmur.

Stefan pushes in gently, giving me time to adjust. I nod again. He sinks a little farther.

Pricks of pain flash in me, but they're followed by tidal waves of pleasure. I feel both at the same time as I take a big, deep breath.

"Look at you," Stefan murmurs. "So fucking beautiful. So fucking gorgeous."

Their praise does its part. It opens me up even more. The hurt starts to ebb. My breath catches, coming up short as my body is stretched to the limit. I'm so full, and I don't know if I can take it. But when Hayes moves a hand down my chest and plays with my nipple ring, I tremble, then gasp his name in a strangled cry.

Like that, Stefan fills me all the way, his cock nestled right against Hayes's. And wow. This is us. This is what I want. The ache fades more, morphing into the first sparks of pure pleasure.

The man under me meets my gaze. "You're so fucking good at taking us, Ivy."

"You look so beautiful stretched like this," the man above me says.

With their words and their touches, with their praise and their adoration, I relax completely, letting myself feel everything.

This pressure.

This new intensity.

These sensations.

Stefan starts to move faster, doing most of the work. With long, luxurious thrusts, he moves me against Hayes, controlling the three of us. With each pump, Hayes kisses me, pets my hair, coasts his hands over my body.

The uncomfortable sensations wash away. And I'm left with this brand-new bliss as Stefan drives us but I feel like they're fucking me together.

It's hard, yes. But it's sexy. It's freeing. It's moving on from the past.

I don't know how long we last because I lose myself to the slap of skin, the grunts of pleasure, the smell of sex, and the feeling of us.

Soon I'm not thinking about time or anything else but the insistent pleasure racing through me as Hayes plays with my nipples, squeezing and pinching, giving me the last piece that sends me soaring. This is the opposite of the golf course, where I couldn't move. Where I had to be quiet. Here I do nothing but writhe and shout, groan and rock.

Here I don't hide who I am, what I want, who I need.

As I give in to the pleasure, I break apart, shattering as they follow me, filling me up.

Sometime later, after we clean up, Hayes returns to the champagne and pours three flutes. We clink glasses, and it feels like a toast to a new and improved *us*.

43

THOUGHT YOU MIGHT WANT TO SEE THIS

Stefan

I feel like a caged lion today.

Ironic since I'm out and about, the city at my feet, free to go anywhere. I wander past the Painted Ladies, snapping photos of the famous Victorian houses on my phone.

This time it is raining, like I'd wanted that night at the start of the season. It's just not raining hard enough to stop me from pacing the city alone.

I stab the focus button, taking picture after picture, capturing the city in its waterlogged mood. As drops fall on my head, I stare hard at the glass, scrolling past the images I took. The screen is wet, though, and I can't slide past them anymore.

I mutter a curse, stalking down the street, huffing out a breath, finally turning into the park across from me. The city is quiet today. The park mostly empty.

That's rare for a Sunday, but so is rain in California these days.

This suits my mood for Kana's *game night*. When Ivy asked me to go I told her I had dinner with a sponsor. That was a lie. I made up an excuse to evade the invite.

I wish we had hockey today. Something to keep me busy tonight. Somewhere to go. Ivy and I walked her dog together this morning, then grabbed smoothies, but that wasn't enough to satiate me. I need to make plans with someone for tonight when the two of them are out. As I weave through the park, aimless again, I take more photos, snapping shots of the tree branches, the tennis courts, the empty playground, hoping that fills the void inside me that's come out of nowhere.

But it doesn't.

And I can't stand being this up in my head, this twisted in dark thoughts about tonight when they go.

I head to my home, avoiding the bedroom as best I can. Yesterday with Ivy already lives rent-free in my head. Don't need it in my face.

I strip out of my wet clothes, dry off, and head to the gym.

I could work out at home. I have equipment there. But I need noise, people, voices. I find it on Fillmore Street at the gym where many of my teammates and other professional athletes from around the city work out. Once inside, I nod a hello to Carter Hendrix, the wide receiver for the Renegades who's curling barbells. I don't usually see him here on Sundays, but I bet he has a Monday night game.

"How's it going?" I ask.

"I can't complain," says the amiable guy. Of course he can't. He's locked up his woman.

Nope.

Not going to indulge in petty jealousies over men who are settled happily in their romances.

I grab some weights, park my ass on a bench, and work on preacher curls. I've done a half-dozen reps when Ledger swings by.

"Aww. Bet you missed me," he remarks as he grabs some free weights too. It's triceps time for the Sea Dog.

"Yes, I came here for you," I say dryly, but then a wave of self-loathing coils in me.

I did come here for company. I did come here to talk. I did come here to find someone to hang with tonight while Ivy and Hayes go to the game night.

Without me.

It's so stupid that I feel this way. I'll just keep playing it cool. Wait for the opportunity to talk about this situation with Hayes and Ivy. Be the patient man I am.

Today's not the right moment. Hayes and Ivy are busy, and I'm...not.

I meet Ledger's dark eyes. "McBride, let's grab a bite tonight. You free?"

He sets down his weights, brings a hand to his chest. "Are you asking me out, Viking? I'm so touched."

I roll my eyes.

"Seriously. And I thought you hated me after the way you ditched me the other week. Now, I'm just a lucky guy," he says, fastening on an over-the-top smile.

"I want in," Carter says from his spot nearby. "I know a great new ramen place. Let's do it, men."

I make plans with the two of them, and that'll keep my mind off my heart, which is too many steps ahead of everything else.

And everyone else.

I shoot the shit with them as I work out for an hour, feeling less like a lion when I leave. But on the way out, an email notification blinks up at me.

From Xander.

Before I even open it, dread whooshes through my veins. The subject line is: *Thought you might want to see this*.

44

IMPROVISATION

Ivy

My outfit looks good, but I'm still not feeling it. I study myself in the mirror, trying to get dressed for game night. It's not the jeans or the floral top. They match. Maybe I need an extra necklace?

I open the jewelry box on my bureau and take out a chain with a moon pendant, adding it to the star necklace I'm already wearing.

As I clasp it on, Jackson pops into my room, whistling his outfit approval. "Don't you look gorgeous, girlie? Where are you going, and why are you never available for me anymore?"

I check him out. He's dressed up and looking fine. "You're busy all the time, too, with the new man in your life."

"And you with your men."

I smile, but it doesn't reach my eyes.

Jackson knows what's going on behind the scenes. He has ever since my Vegas wedding. He's my roommate, and I wouldn't keep that from him as my friend, anyway. But it doesn't feel right to put on my best jeans, some cute shoes, these twin necklaces, and then to head out with Hayes to see the other wives and girlfriends, husbands and boyfriends. Just like it felt wrong yesterday to show up at the golf event as Mrs. Armstrong when I'm not that person.

"I'm going to a game night with Hayes," I answer at last. Yep. Sounds as wrong as it feels.

"Let me adjust those necklaces for you." Jackson straightens them out, and then gives me a kiss on the cheek before looking me up and down with some concern. "Are you okay?"

He noticed. My stomach churns. "I have some things on my mind," I admit, a little relieved to voice it.

"I can tell. Anything I can help you with?"

That's a good question. But I think the answer's coming into view. It's sharpening by the minute. "Thanks, but I think there's something I need to do tonight." I'm nervous, but mostly, I'm certain.

"Can't wait for all the details," he tells me. Then he heads out on his own date, and I return to my bedroom, where Roxy is sound asleep on my bed, lying on her back with all four little legs sticking up in the air. She looks so content with her life. She is who she is, without question.

I move around, and she opens one eye.

"What do you think? Should I do it?" I ask her.

She unleashes a huge yawn then curls into a ball, returning to the land of dog nod.

But really, I know the answer. Yesterday I felt it deep in my soul. Soon, I'll say it out loud.

I finish getting ready, and I'm about to head upstairs to gather Hayes and tell him about a change of plans when there's one loud knock at my door.

Then another.

This knock sounds demanding.

* * *

I'm shaking with rage as I read the email in my living room.

I stare at this stupid note, my thumb cramping, my blood boiling. "I can't believe he sent you this," I say, gripping the phone to keep from chucking it at the wall.

Or, better, at Xander's stupid face. I'm more livid than I was when I learned he was marrying my ex-boss. Than when he dumped me for an upgrade. Than when I discovered he'd been cheating.

This is ten million times worse.

Next to me, Hayes clenches his fists, fuming. He and Stefan had arrived at my door almost simultaneously. "I'm going to find him right now," he grits out.

As much as I relish the thought, I won't let Hayes do that. I grab his arm, trying to settle him with touch. "You're not."

"I want to," he hisses.

"Same here. But it's pointless," Stefan says heavily. There's darkness in his light blue eyes, like looming thunderclouds. But there's fire roaring in me, enough for both of us. *All of us.*

I read the email again as Stefan walks away from the center of the living room, toward the window streaked with rain.

I thought you might be interested in this pic. It prob-ably wouldn't look good for someone who's getting the Sportsman of the Year award to be sleeping with his teammate's wife. Let me know by Tuesday if you want to reconsider that investment opportunity.

He's attached a photo of Stefan and me walking into his apartment building with my dog this morning.

That's it. That's all. But it's clear—Stefan has forty-eight hours to pony up or else Xander's going to claim Stefan's screwing his teammate's wife. That he's not a good sportsman. That he's not worthy of an award he deserves and his family is flying over to see him receive.

I march over to Stefan at the window and shove the phone back at him like it's infected. From her sentry point on the couch, Roxy barks at me with obvious canine concern. I'm concerned too. This is my ex, and I need to fix this, but my god, how many ways can an ex go bad? Is he the worst ex-apple in the ex-bushel?

I wheel around, pacing, dragging my hands through my hair, hunting through options. "We can't let him get away with this."

But maybe he won't get away with anything. This is a perfectly innocent photo. Only his insinuation is salacious. Xander didn't send shots of us on the rooftop. Not that those would have proved anything either. I was with both of them. Xander's completely misunderstanding our arrangement if he's insinuating infidelity.

There's no infidelity when we've all consented.

Yet I'm tired of people underestimating me. I'm tired of people thinking they know who I am. I'm tired of shenanigans.

Fueled by this storm of emotion, I turn to the two men in my life and in my heart and say, "Let's tell our own story."

Stefan leans against the window, a little listless. "You're going to need to elaborate."

With sparkling eyes, Hayes pumps a fist. "Yes, fucking yes."

I haven't discussed a thing with Hayes, but he crosses over to Stefan too, curling a hand around his teammate's shoulder. "What I think she's saying is get dressed. You're fucking coming with us tonight."

But Stefan's not buying what Hayes and I are selling. His eyes are hard. "As your third wheel?" Stefan shakes his head, waves a dismissive hand as he stares back at the city below, dreary from the day's rain. "No thanks."

My heart hurts for my man. He sounds weary and over it.

Hayes and I didn't plan this, but I'm giddy that we're on the same page. The anger I felt over the blackmail note washes away, replaced by the fizzy sense of possibility. I stride over to them, stand between them.

I'm more than ready. I want them both, even if it's temporary. I'm already with Hayes publicly, so why not expand this so they're both my acknowledged partners? I'm not worried how it'll look. Trina paved the way with my brother and Chase. Jessie stands behind them. Their teammates support them. My grandma's firmly in my camp, and so is my mother. My sister too. While the world hasn't shifted, my world has.

"If we're doing this publicly, we're all doing this. We're together. The three of us." It's a declaration, one that'll echo beyond these four walls. "What we are in my home and in your homes is who we are." I point to the window and the city beyond. "No one is going to go out there and say there's any cheating. We're all a part of this."

The distance in Stefan's eyes burns off, leaving curiosity. "What are you saying exactly, Ivy?"

A thrill rushes through me. "The three of us will go to game night together. We're going to go to the Sportsman of the Year awards *together*."

I can't make any promises beyond that. Too much has changed in my life over the last several weeks. Too much has changed at work. But for now I'm going to take control.

I curl one hand around Hayes's strong arm, then the other around Stefan's. "I have a husband and a boyfriend," I say. "We are not a secret. And we're not fake."

Hayes lets out a huge sigh of relief, chased by laughter, and it's so welcome to hear. But the bigger thrill? When Stefan's smile returns. When the clouds drift away. When he becomes my upbeat, happy-go-lucky guy again. "So it's not just a marriage of convenience. It's a...throuple of convenience?" Stefan asks with a curve of his lips and a tease in his tone.

I'm electric at the thought. "Yes."

"Then I need to text Ledger and Carter to cancel our plans for tonight."

After Stefan sends his messages and changes his clothes, we leave the building. Outside on the steps, I set a hand on Stefan's cheek and then kiss him possessively in front of the city. I turn and do the same to Hayes.

We are all dating—at least for now.

45

LET'S MAKE A DEAL

Hayes

Kana swings open the door. Her expression is unreadable for a few seconds, then curious as she roams her inquisitive eyes over the three of us, taking in our body language.

Casual, flirty, comfortable. Theoretically, we could be husband and wife and buddy. But it's not likely, the way Ivy runs a hand down my arm, then Stefan's.

Just so it's clear, I take the lead and say, "Stefan's with us. *With us.* As in, the three of us."

Fuck, did that sound weird? Why did I think it'd be smart for me to go first? I'm not the smooth talker. Stefan is.

Ivy must sense I need her so she jumps in. "What Hayes is saying is..." She casts her affectionate gaze toward me. "This is my husband." Then she looks at Stefan with equal warmth. "And this is my boyfriend."

Calm spreads through me, chased with happiness, with potential.

Kana's lips twitch for a few seconds. Behind her, the guests in the sunken living room have gone starkly silent. My teammates on the couch take a beat, along with their partners. But not for too long. Dev shoots a hand up in the air. "Called it. Pay up, bros."

Brady hangs his head, letting out a long groan. "Damn. I really thought you were all just friends."

I laugh. Stefan laughs harder, breaking the tension. Dev rubs his fingers together. "A hundred bucks from you," he says to Brady, who raises his head and reaches for his wallet.

Trina, Chase, and Ryker are hanging out on the couch. Ryker holds up a hand in surrender. Chase does the same. "I didn't bet. I abstained," Chase puts in. "I already knew it was going on."

Tom whips his gaze to Chase, his deep voice chiding. "Well, thanks a lot for telling me."

"Family secret," Chase scoffs. "Like I'm gonna give it up. Also, you play for our rivals. No way."

"You dated her *with* a rival," Tom fires back.

"And now he's a teammate." Chase nods to the two of us and Trina, smirking. "It's a thing. Deal with it."

In the foyer, Kana just grins knowingly. "It wasn't that hard to figure out. In Vegas you all looked like you wanted to fuck each other."

Ivy covers her face with her hand, cracking up.

On that note, we head inside and settle on the couch, Ivy between Stefan and me.

Kana sits on Brady's lap, roping her arms around

his neck. "I guess this means I'm going to have to take a boyfriend, too, just to keep up with everybody. You don't mind, do you?"

Brady growls. "I don't share."

Eva turns to Dev. "Hmm. What about you?"

Dev drapes an arm around her, tugging her close. "You never know."

Eva's eyes widen. I steal a glance at Stefan, asking silently *do you know something I don't know?* Stefan just shrugs, though he looks intrigued.

But the goalie kisses his girlfriend like she's the center of the world, then Tom grab's Gilberto's hand and declares, "You're all mine."

Gilberto smacks Tom's cheek in a kiss. "Same."

When Dev lets go of Eva, he grabs his beer bottle and lifts it up. "Whatever works for you, right?"

We all lift our proverbial glasses to that.

The three of us get to work on destroying everyone here at game night. As we take them on, I soak in the camaraderie. I figured that *if* I ever felt like a part of a team, it'd be on the ice.

Instead, I found one off it.

There's one little problem though. The expiration date.

Later that night, after Ivy falls asleep, I slip out of bed and catch Stefan's attention on the other side of the Alaskan king. He's still awake and sets down his e-reader. He's reading something in Danish. Figures.

He swings his legs from the bed but so does Roxy, scurrying out from under the covers, checking us out like the policewoman she is. "Shh," I whisper and then scoop her up and carry her, shutting the door and setting her on my lap in the living room.

I point to the bedroom. "Ivy thinks this is going to end at the awards ceremony," I say.

Which is fucking ridiculous.

"Yeah, that's kind of a problem," Stefan says dryly as he sinks onto the couch.

"It's a big problem," I second.

With some amusement in his eyes, he asks, "And why do you say that?"

I flash back to that night in Chicago when Stefan took me out for a drink and asked me hard questions. I didn't know what I wanted then. At the time, he did. He knew he wanted her. He wanted more.

I flash him a grin and admit another truth. "Seems I've caught up to you."

With a grateful sigh, he says, "Yes, and now that you're an official member of the club, we have one rule."

"What's that?"

Stefan leans forward on the couch, eyes sparkling with a plan. Always a plan. "You don't want this to end, do you?"

I scoff like that's the craziest thing ever. "No fucking way."

"That's what I thought. So here's what we'll do," he says, practically rubbing his palms together. "Let's make her fall in love with both of us."

"I'm all in." I offer a fist for knocking.

Operation Win Our Woman begins tomorrow. First, though, Stefan writes back to Xander and asks him to meet us in the morning. And bring several loaves of bread.

* * *

In the morning, Stefan takes me to the duck pond in the park. He's carrying a grocery bag. The name Henry is written on the side. The mallards quack plaintively as we near them. "Don't worry. I'm sure Henry will be here soon," he says to the waterfowl.

"Who's Henry? The duck whisperer? Or is that you?"

He tells me about a guy named Henry who lives in the park, then adds, "So I'm not really a duck whisperer. I'd say I'm more of a...throuple engineer. I got you to come on board, didn't I?"

"You're such a puppeteer."

"And you love it because now you're in love with her too."

He's not wrong. "What's it going to be next? You going to convince the team to sign me?"

"That's up to you, my friend. But I'd really like you to work hard on it," he says sincerely.

"We're on the same page," I say, then shut up as footsteps crunch across the fallen leaves.

I turn to see the fuckface who tried to mess with my captain and my wife. No one does that.

Xander's carrying a bag, with a few loaves of bread

sticking out, and wearing a smile, like we've delivered him the bike he's always wanted on Christmas morning. "You brought along another investor?" he asks Stefan, sounding delighted.

"Oh, he's definitely invested," Stefan says.

Fuckface turns to me, adjusting his bow tie, then offering a hand. I don't take it, so he stuffs it awkwardly in his pocket. "You're Ivy's husband. How fantastic. I hope you'll reconsider coming to our wedding. We'd love to have you two as guests," he says, trying to recover from the slight.

Like I care about niceties or his clout chasing. "Actually, I'd like to introduce you to Ivy's boyfriend."

Xander jerks his head to the side. "Wait. What?" He points at me. "I thought you were married to Ivy?"

I hold up my hand, show him the ring. "I am. And Stefan's her boyfriend. We're both with her, we both take care of her, and no one's cheating. You've got nothing."

Stefan steps forward, stalking closer to Xander, using his size to crowd him to the edge of the duck pond. "And guess what? We're taking her together to the awards ceremony where I'll receive the Sportsman of the Year award."

Xander's lips part in shock.

I step closer too.

He takes another step back.

"You have no leverage for your Dough and Duds." Stefan rips the bag of bread out of Xander's hand and The Dapper Man stumbles. Then, oops.

I, maybe, possibly, body-check him.

Shame.

He falls ass-first into the shallow duck pond. Flat on his back. "Buddy, you're in the way of the ducks. Can you move a little to the right?" Stefan asks politely, as he removes the loaves from Xander's bag and puts them in the bag he brought.

The ducks descend on Xander as he flails to stand up. "You ruined my suit," he cries out, mud dripping over the sky-blue jacket, a piece of weed stuck in his bow tie.

"Too bad. But you can get a new one at Dough and Duds," Stefan offers helpfully while sorting the bread into his own bag.

Once Xander manages to stand, sopping wet, with ducks squawking at him, Stefan looms above him at the edge of the pond, stripping away the sarcasm. "Here's the deal we wanted to make you." Stefan takes a beat to make his point. "Never bother us again. Never go near our girl again."

He stops to let out a breath, and it's my turn. "And never try to fuck with our lives again. Because if you do, the suit won't be the only thing that's ruined."

On that parting shot, we leave, Stefan stopping at a nearby bench to set down the bag. "That's a lot of bread," I say.

"Yeah, it is. But maybe he has friends," Stefan says, then claps me on the shoulder.

Friends. Yes. I hope he does. Not sure what I'd do without mine.

46

THE THING IS

Hayes

That's not the only business I need to wrap up. There's something else I have to handle on my own.

When I arrive at the Avengers arena later that day, I don't look for Ivy or Stefan. I put on my blinders and head to Oliver's office to see if we're still on for the meeting with the big boss I'd set up by text earlier. I told him I wanted to catch up with Jessie before our game tonight and asked him to join us.

"Ready as ever." He's waiting for me at the door. "Is there anything I can do to help in advance?"

I shake my head. "No, but I appreciate you arranging it."

We head to the executive suite, a place I didn't think I'd be twice in a month let alone in a two-week period. This time, though, my gut swirls. I'm not here to deliver a gift.

When Oliver escorts me into Jessie's office, she's finishing up a phone call. Leaning back in her plush chair, she looks powerful and at ease, a smile framing her warm eyes. "That's right, Hannah. At the end of this season you'll be eating crow when my team beats yours. Love you, girl. See you at the next team owners' meeting."

Straightening, Jessie stabs the end button on her desk phone and looks up, a professional grin on her face. "I swear that girl has serious ovaries if she thinks her team is going to beat us."

She gestures to the chairs in front of her. I take one, Oliver the other. "We're seeing a lot of each other, aren't we, Hayes?"

Translation: *why the fuck are you here again*? At least she says it with a smile.

I keep my eye on my task, like when I'm on the ice and in a fight for the puck. The goal today? *Honesty.* "When I saw you in Las Vegas in the elevator, and you congratulated me on my wedding, I wasn't straight with you," I say.

Her brow knits. Beside me, Oliver tenses, vibrating like a Chihuahua who's heard a smoke detector.

"What do you mean?" Jessie asks.

"When I told you Ivy and I were married and that we'd be happy to go to your golf event."

"But I saw you there. At the golf event," she says with shrewd eyes, trying to spot the lie.

It's not really a lie though. It's more like a fuck-up.

But...semantics.

"We got married on a dare. And we were on our way

to get an annulment that morning. And I said we were staying married to impress you and go to your event."

Understanding passes over her face as she nods. "I see."

She steeples her fingers and taps them thoughtfully. I'm about to explain that we're still together, that it's complicated but also not, and that I'm sorry I deceived her then even though it's real now, but her phone rings and she nods to it. "I have to take this. We'll finish this conversation later."

There's nothing to do but say yes and leave, then hope she's not letting me go permanently.

47

BITE YOUR FACE

Ivy

In the equipment room before the game, I wriggle into my new costume as Briar watches me with trepidation. Parvati's here, too, biting her lip.

"Does it look that bad?" I ask Briar.

Briar shakes her head, blonde ponytail swishing. "No."

"Then what's that look for? You're studying me like I'm wearing low-rise skinny jeans." I turn to Parvati, who's bouncing on her flats. "Why is Briar looking at me like I'm a fashion don't?"

Parvati covers her mouth with her hand, but a grin sneaks through. "Because...it's so hot."

I cackle. "Shut up."

"No, swear on it. That is the best costume ever. I can't wait to post pics all over social," Parvati says. But she's always positive. I need the thumbs-up from a gal who doesn't care much about fashion, and that's Briar. Well, she definitely cares about her yoga fashion. Her leggings and sports bras are on point.

I glance down at the tawny fur I'm wearing, the form-fitting waistline, and the lush tail—long, but not so long I could trip on it on the ice.

Briar grabs the head and thrusts it at me. "I'm reserving judgment till we see it all."

I tug the head on, then spin in a circle, anxious for an answer. "Verdict, Briar?"

I stop in front of the yoga instructor, waiting eagerly. Briar taps her lips for a few seconds, then the concern in her eyes vanishes. It's replaced by approval in the form of a confident nod. "It's official," Briar declares. "That does not suck."

I let out a whoop. "Finally!"

"This team has a long history of sucky mascots."

"The polar bear was good," Parvati interjects.

"Good. But not great. This is next level," Briar says with an authoritative tone.

"That's true," Parvati agrees. "It's better than a bear."

I can't wait to check it out, so I head over to the mirror, then smile from the inside. "I look cute but like I could bite your face off."

Just like the owner wanted. And like I suggested when I sent her a card along with the boob-gap-no-more blouse. I still can't quite believe she liked one of my ideas, but here I am, wearing the proof.

* * *

I wait in the tunnel before the game begins, excitement pinging through me. Then, my cue, as the announcer warbles, "And now, fans, get ready to meet...the Golden State Fox!"

Fired up, I hit the ice in my skates, racing across the slick surface, speeding around the oval, one leg stuck out behind me, my fox arms parked coolly behind my back, my tail flying.

The crowd cheers, and after the first lap, the announcer shouts, "And now, tonight's lineup..."

I bring my back leg down, then hold out my furry arms wide, gesturing toward the tunnel, where the Avengers who might become Foxes come racing out onto the ice as I skate off.

Feeling pretty fucking foxy.

*　*　*

During the first intermission, I return to the rink, skating circles around the Ice Crew and their brooms. As they sweep up the surface, I sneak up on them like...

Well, a fox.

They pretend to be scared. By the time we're done, the crowd is cheering and shouting. When the announcer encourages them to vote on their favorite mascot so far, I feel confident the fox won't need to rig a thing.

*　*　*

In the final period, I swap my skates for paw-like shoes to work the crowds in the stands, whipping them up, even though the players hardly need our enthusiasm. Or maybe it does the trick because they beat the Los Angeles Timberwolves six to one.

The crowd goes wild, and I'm pretty sure we'll get a new team name very, very soon.

Later, I'm hanging in the hallway with Oliver and Parvati, huddled over his tablet as we check the early votes. News flash—neither the fog nor the polar bear is winning.

"I knew it," Parvati says brightly, then squeezes my arm.

"You can't argue with a runaway lead," Oliver says, then gives me a thumbs-up.

But leads can change, just like in games, so I won't get too excited. It would be fun to wear that fox costume for the season. Wait. Hold on. I only signed on for the next few months. Why am I even considering the whole season as a fox?

I blink the thought away at the sound of heels clicking on concrete. Oliver, Parvati, and I snap our gazes up in tandem as Jessie strides down the hall, looking fashionable and functional in her Lily Greer pumps.

Her brown eyes meet mine, and she points to her shoes with an approving smile. "Still love them," she says, then stops in front of us. "And the fans loved your idea."

I smile, dipping my face. I hardly want to take credit for it. But Jessie clears her throat. "Ivy Samuels."

Oh, shit. I look up. "Yes."

"It was your idea," she says, staring sternly at me. I came up with several options from wild cats to foxes and listed them on the card I sent her. "Thank you again for your list."

"I was happy to weigh in on the cutest but meanest animals."

My attention briefly snags on a pair of handsome men coming my way, but I try not to get distracted while talking to the big boss.

"Cute but mean?" Stefan asks with sparkling eyes when he reaches us. Hayes is with him, but his expression is more stoic—maybe even concerned. "Oh, you mean the team name?"

Jessie turns to the captain. "Yes. Ivy gave me the idea."

"Yes, she likes foxes." His lips twitch like he can barely hold in a grin.

"I do," I admit, trying not to let on how much.

"So much," he adds, clearly bursting with some kind of masculine pride.

Stefan's mood is light and festive, but Hayes still seems worried. He's unusually quiet even for the quieter one.

When Jessie turns to leave, she says, "I need to head home. But it was good to see all of you."

Like it pains him, Hayes says roughly, "Ms. Rose. I was hoping we could finish."

Finish what? I jerk my gaze to my husband with questions in my eyes.

Jessie's expression is neutral, and I have no clue what's going on. "Yes. Let's finish. I just have one question."

About what?

Hayes nods like a good soldier. "Yes?"

"This marriage dare?"

Oh. My. God. He told her it was a dare? Oliver's eyes widen. Parvati's lips twist in a nervous smile.

"Yes?" Hayes says, remaining steadfast.

"It seems real to me. Was it not?"

Hayes turns to me, his brown eyes full of genuine affection. "Very real."

"And you were very real married." She glances at his ring and then at mine. "And you still are?"

I'm not going to let them have this conversation without me. "We are," I pipe in.

Before I can add something about Stefan, he chimes in with, "And she's with me too."

Jessie doesn't even bat an eye. "I figured as much when you two delivered that shirt." Then she shakes her head, amused. "You men don't surprise me. I've had a feeling for quite some time. Just let me know what I can do in terms of support." She gestures to Oliver and Parvati. "Make sure the PR team knows the proper terms to use. That is, if you want anything posted on social?"

"You're not bothered that it was..." Hayes begins but

stops. He doesn't say fake. Perhaps because it was never anything but real.

Jessie shakes her head. "I'm concerned with running an ethical business and with winning. I'm not concerned with who players love. Keep winning and I'll stay happy."

When she leaves, Hayes looks like he's about to sink down to the ground in relief.

I reach for his hand and tug him close. "You told her?" I ask, but I'm more amazed than anything.

"I did. I didn't want to lie."

I cup his cheek. "I'm proud of you."

"And I'm proud of you for picking a team name," he says.

Stefan clears his throat, comes closer, and slings an arm around me. "I'm kind of proud of me. After all, you gave her a team name I inspired."

With a laugh, I say, "I did. You remind me of a fox."

I kiss his cheek, and when I catch Parvati and Oliver awkwardly slinking away, I call out, "You can post that pic of us from golf if you want. Up to you. Whatever works."

"Whatever works," Parvati repeats, like it's the new mantra.

And maybe it is.

When they're gone, Stefan looks at me again, his blue eyes twinkling. "You might have married him, but you named a team after me. I'll take that."

"And tonight, you two can take me."

"Sounds like a plan," Stefan says.

They execute that plan, all right. And in the morning, I find a note in my planner for a date with my guys to do something I only mentioned once that I wanted to do.

What can I say? My men know how to pay attention.

48

IS THAT A ZAMBONI ON YOUR BUCKET LIST OR IS IT JUST ME?

Hayes

I know it's coming, and there's no way to stop it. Dragging a hand across my trim beard, I groan when Bryan, the older of my granddads, launches into his favorite story while we're seated at the diner in Petaluma on Friday evening.

"And this little guy," Bryan says, ruffling my hair— that's his thing, and always has been, "jumps over the boards with his stick, and his uniform, and his new skates, and he actually challenges the older guys to a *skate-off*. His words."

I drop my face onto the Formica table.

"A skate-off?" Stefan asks, chuckling. "Is that a thing? Like a dance-off on ice?"

"Maybe we should all do that," Ryan suggests from across the booth. "I've got a killer pair of purple skates."

I raise my head and lift a critical brow, eyeing Ryan's

checked flannel shirt. *Tucked in.* "Dude, purple skates are not trendy. Just ask Ivy."

Looking at his husband, Bryan smooths a hand down his sky-blue button-down—classy but stylish, unlike Ryan. "That's what I told you, babe."

At the affectionate nickname Ivy's blue eyes sparkle and she nudges Stefan, then mouths *so cute.*

"I don't know. My skates are pretty sweet," Ryan adds with bravado.

"I can see where Hayes gets his confidence," Ivy says to Ryan.

He nods proudly. "Yup. Now, do you want to see my purple skates?"

"I'd love to. But I also really want to hear the end of the story—what happened with Hayes's dance-off, face-off, skate-off?"

Stefan chuckles and reaches for Ivy's hand. "Yes, tell us everything about the ice-dancing finale."

"Thanks for ganging up on me," I say dryly.

"What are friends and family for?" Stefan asks.

Ivy freezes, like the word surprises her—*family.* Then she smiles as if she turned it over and found she liked it. I hope now that she's met my family, she'll feel as if they could be hers as well. Stefan and I want her to see what it'll be like if she falls in love with us too.

"They exist to reveal all your embarrassing stories, it seems." Ivy props her chin in her hand, looking from Ryan to Bryan. "Now, tell me. How did he do in the skate-off?"

Ryan dives into the tale of my brash, seven-year-old self challenging a bunch of thirteen-year-olds to a shootout, finishing with, "And one by one, he took them down." He squeezes my shoulder proudly.

"At your rink?" Ivy asks.

"That's the one."

"And did you know then that he'd be a star?"

Bryan snorts, and if a snort could be proud that one is. "I knew it before. When he was four and skated like Gretzky."

"Stop. Just stop," I warn him. We're veering dangerously close to the verbal equivalent of naked baby photos.

"Please don't stop," Stefan goads. "I want to hear more about this young Gretzky."

"And I need to see this famous rink," Ivy says.

Well, we'd planned on showing it to her anyway.

* * *

After they give us a tour of the local rink, which is booked up the wazoo—Bryan's terms—Bryan and Ryan take off, leaving us alone.

"You kids can skate all you want. Just shut the door and lock it when you're done," Bryan says.

Ivy shoots me a curious look. "They don't mind us using it?"

Stefan and I laugh. "We booked it tonight," I say.

"Oh," she says, then smiles so wide my heart beats a little harder for her.

We lace up, and the three of us skate for a good long time, all alone in the rink, under the lights, blasting rock music. When we've raced around the ice enough, I check in with Stefan. "Ready?"

"Absolutely."

Skating backwards, I tug on Ivy's hand. "Want to ride on a Zamboni?"

Her blue eyes pop. "Yes!"

* * *

We take off our skates, and after I show her the basics of driving the big blue beast, I let her take it for a spin while I ride shotgun and Stefan watches from the edge of the rink. After a lap or two, she's breathing hard and her cheeks are red—steering one of these is a workout. She stops the machine in the middle of the ice and lets out a contented sigh.

Stefan walks over and stands at the open door. "New career path as a Zamboni driver?"

"Imagine how valuable I'd be to hockey teams then. From mascot to Zamboni driver in a single bound." She pats the metal edge of the machine. "Seriously, this was so fun. Are you guys trying to be the best boyfriends ever?"

It's a dead-serious question.

I catch Stefan's gaze, grinning like she's caught on to us. I like, too, that she calls us boyfriends. She's not making distinctions in titles anymore. We're both her boyfriends.

"Yes," Stefan answers her. "Is it working?"

Ivy's smile is coy. "Kind of, but I'm not convinced yet."

"Woman, what's it going to take?" Stefan teases.

Ivy climbs out of the driver's seat and onto my lap, patting the other seat for Stefan, who hops up where she's indicated. There's not much room for any one of us, but who needs room when my woman has dirty deeds flashing in her eyes? She manages to straddle me, rocking subtly against my dick. I'm not even hard, but that changes quickly, especially when she dips her face to my neck. She kisses me there while reaching toward Stefan's face, running her knuckles down his cheek and over his stubble as she rocks against me.

My dick salutes hello, and my mind hums with possibilities. Stefan's thinking fast too. He blows on his hands, warming them up, then slides them under her sweatshirt, touching her belly, the curves of her breasts.

She gasps, then breaks the kiss to lock eyes with me then him.

"I like taking turns," she says with slow, tempting thrusts against me while she turns and stretches to kiss him.

She's kissing him while dry humping my cock as the Rolling Stones' "Start Me Up" plays on the ice rink's sound system.

My mind pops. It whirs with lust and excitement. The chilly air feels supercharged. I never expected *this* when I accepted a trade to San Francisco. Never imagined a moment like this. And I don't want to lose sight of what it means.

Fun, but intimacy. A risqué evening but trust, as well. Our sex is wild, but it's also soul deep, even in an ice rink. All alone, in the cool air, we get to work taking care of Ivy's needs. As she kisses Stefan again, I warm my hands then fiddle with the waistband of her leggings, pushing them down to slide my fingers over her belly button and inside her panties so I can tease her clit.

With a shuddery gasp, she breaks the kiss, letting her head fall back. "Oh god, yes."

"You dirty girl," I rasp out. "You're already turned on from humping my dick."

"I am," she says as I maneuver a hand down to where she's slick and hot.

She trembles, then a longer moan escapes those lush lips. Stefan reaches for her mouth, offering her his fingers. She draws one, then two past her lips as she rocks against my hand.

"She likes that," Stefan says, like he did the first night we all hooked up in a chapel in Vegas, when we talked about her as we played with her.

"She loves it when we fuck her in public," I say, stroking her more.

"Let me check," Stefan says, like he's just casually curious.

I grab her hips and lift her up a few inches, giving him room. He drops his fingers from her mouth, slides them inside her panties, and strokes her. She's gasping, panting, and curling her hands around my shoulders to hold on.

With a rumble, he smiles, then brings his finger to his lips, sucking off her taste. "She gets so fucking wet, doesn't she?"

"I love it when she's dripping for us," I say. "You need to fuck, don't you baby?"

"Yes. Now please," she whimpers.

Stefan tucks a finger under her chin. "Let's get these leggings off you. I want to watch you fuck your husband right here on a Zamboni."

Ivy shudders, and it's clear that even though we're both her boyfriends, she still loves the idea of being a hot wife. Of her husband sharing her.

I do, too, and so does Stefan. Terms are terms, words are words. We both know we're in this together, all of us. We know, too, that sex is one of the things she needs a certain way—an overload of sensations.

Handing off roles.

Everything between us shared.

As he helps her push down her leggings, I unzip my jeans and free my cock.

Ivy stares wantonly at my dick, at attention and ready for her. Wrapping a hand around my shaft, she strokes up, then down.

"Get on him now, sweetheart," Stefan says, lifting her back over me, and with her panties pulled to the side, I offer her my dick. She looks heavenly as she sinks down onto me, and I shudder down to my bones.

Yes. Fucking yes. She's so snug and warm. My arms come up to her face, and I hold her as Stefan leans back, parks his hands behind his head and just...watches.

"My favorite view," he says, admiring her.

She locks eyes with him as she rides my dick. "You like it when I fuck him, don't you?"

"Love it, sweetheart," he says.

"Why?" Her voice catches, filled with a new vulnerability.

Reaching forward, he slides a hand down her cheek as she rises up and down on my cock. "Because of how your cheeks pinken. How your lips part. How your eyes glass over. It's fucking breathtaking to watch you get turned on."

"I like looking at you when I fuck him," she says, and the temperature in me shoots to the sky.

"I can tell. I can see it in your eyes," he says in a sensual voice that excites her so she fucks me faster, more recklessly.

She drags her teeth across her lip, gazing at him as she rises up on me. I'm burning. I'm a furnace as she fucks. "Hayes likes it too, Stef. I can feel his cock getting thicker in me."

I groan like an animal. She's taking a page from our playbook, talking about me to him. It's so fucking erotic, so ridiculously sexy, I don't know if I can last.

"He fucks me deeper when I look at you," she adds.

Stefan drags a thumb across her lower lip now. "You like that, sweetheart?"

"Love it," she gasps, her voice breaking. I can hear the emotions and the heat, twining around each other. I want to wrap myself in them.

I grip her hips as she owns my cock and my whole damn heart. Lust slams into me, obliterating my thoughts. I can barely speak. I'm so fucking turned on. "Baby, I need to come. Let me get you there," I warn and beg at the same time.

She looks to me, her eyes wide and filled with passion and something brand new: a new openness, like she's letting us in further. "Don't hold back. Stefan will finish me."

This woman has me by the goddamned balls. I shudder and come inside her, the world going black and mind-numbingly good.

After I empty myself, she eases off me. Stefan's ready, cock out, and then she's taking him inside her then using his dick for her release.

It's the sexiest thing I've ever seen, watching her reach new heights as she comes on my friend on a Zamboni.

Later, after we've cleaned up everything—rink, Zamboni, and ourselves—and headed for the exit, she stops at the door, looking back with affection and maybe even the start of nostalgia. "That was a bucket list item for sure." She turns from me to him. "Or a dream come true."

As she makes for the car, I hang back with Stefan, giving him a look that says Operation Win Her Over is working.

It's also making me fall even more in love with her.

The next day, I invite my dad and Cora to my hockey game. Then I take them out after it for a late dinner.

When she goes to the ladies' room, he checks to make sure the coast is clear. "I'm asking her this weekend."

"That's great, Dad."

I mean it this time.

I might not connect with him the way I do with my granddads. I might not love hanging out with him. I might have put up walls when I saw him hurting when I was younger. But my mom left, and he didn't, and that has to count for something.

Mostly, though, I think I finally understand him a little more. Sometimes you'll just risk your whole damn heart for a woman.

49
___

THE SWEETNESS OF LIFE

Ivy

In the morning, I sit on Stefan's back deck, with a cup of coffee and my legs tucked under me, watching my dog roam the yard.

She sniffs every blade of grass like she belongs here. I tilt my head, studying the little lady. What would it be like to feel so at home here? Like this place was mine, with the guys and with Roxy?

They treat me that way. But doubt still chases me, nagging at the back of my mind.

What if I could let go of some of it? Would I feel like Roxy, raising her little face to the November morning, embracing the sunshine on its own terms? She's not thinking of her past in Florida. She's not remembering the sad days. She lives for the here and now. Rolling in grass, bathing in the sun, soaking in the sweetness of life.

My planner lies on the table, but I don't open it. I sip my coffee and stare at the yard, but my thoughts are elsewhere. They travel to the great and terrifying unknown of the future until the door slides open, bringing me back to now.

Stefan emerges, but he's not alone. Hayes is with him in a rare morning appearance. They both look sleep-rumpled and sexy as they join me at the table.

"Hey there," Hayes says in a gravelly morning voice I don't hear often.

"Why are you awake at this early hour?"

He scratches the back of his neck. "Going to work out soon. Gotta stay hockey ready."

"And I have to make sure he lifts all the heavy weights," Stefan says on a yawn.

I smile, loving that they look out for each other on the job. And for me, since Stefan asks what I'm up to today. I tell them about a piece I'm working on for Birdie. She's been sending me a story a week to write for *Your Runway*, and I'm loving all the pieces I get to pen for her.

When I'm done, Stefan taps the planner. "We added something to it. Our next date. This coming weekend. Sticks and Stones with the crew."

I love that they organize dates in my planner. They usually write "TOC night out," for Throuple of Convenience. I imagine this weekend they'll pull out all the stops like they did the other night at the rink. "You guys are doing so much for me," I say, but my tone's a little heavy, like my heart this morning. "Why?"

The question feels vitally important, but Hayes

scoffs like it's nonsensical. Maybe it is. "I like doing things for you," he says adamantly, then he glances at Stefan. "We both do."

He says it like there's no two ways about it. It's just an *is*.

"You're worth it. You have to know that," Stefan says, just as emphatic and certain. This isn't our usual flirty vibe. It's weightier, more emotional.

"I think I do," I say softly. Then, even though something hurts inside my chest, I push past that tangled knot to say, "It's just...it's hard for me."

Stefan's expression is gentle as he asks, "Because of Xander?"

I shake my head, flashing back to years ago. To the things I heard in my own house. There are knives in my throat when I think of how my father treated my mom. "And my dad."

I haven't told them much about him. I don't like to talk about him. But they need to know why I hold back. "He hurt my mom so much."

Hayes sits up straighter, his brow knitting, protective instincts kicking in. "Physically?" He sounds ready to kill.

"Verbally. He was a drunk. He put her down, insulted her, cheated on her." I pull my knees to my chest and wrap my arms around them as the reel of my childhood flashes by, too familiar, too painful. "I used to go to my room with my little sister and turn up the music so we wouldn't hear. We did fashion shows for each other. That's how I protected her from him. I tried on all my clothes, dressing up to entertain her," I say with a hard lump in my throat and tears pricking my eyes.

"That was courageous of you to take that on," Stefan says, his tone warm, his hand even warmer as he reaches across the table to squeeze my knee.

"I was just trying to entertain her so she wouldn't hear. She's five years younger. So maybe it worked— she seems happy enough."

"What's she up to now?" Hayes asks. "You've mentioned her a few times. She's in New Zealand for school?"

I smile, thinking of Katie. Of the ways Ryker and I have looked out for her. Of how upbeat and buoyant she is. "She's studying marine biology, and every time we text, she's having a blast. She's like Roxy." I gesture to the dog, who's flat on her side, sound asleep. "Sucking the sweetness out of life."

"So you helped," Stefan says.

"Maybe I did. I learned it from my brother, who did that for me." Then I close my eyes and breathe deep, my fears nipping at my heels.

I try to push past them. Truly I do, but they're still swirling around me.

When I open my eyes, I look to both men, listening attentively, trying to become the center of my world. I want to let go of my past, but I can still feel the pain of those childhood moments. It's taken me years to learn new ways of living. "I want to trust all this," I say, gesturing from them to me, speaking from the heart of my hurt. "I want to believe it all. I don't want to be wrong."

Stefan takes my hand, presses a kiss to it. "Take your time."

Hayes reaches for my calf, rubs it. "There's no rush, baby. We're going to be here for you. In a week, in a month, longer."

The awards are in a month. The reason we said we'd do this—be a throuple of convenience.

But it hardly feels like a romance of convenience.

It feels like it's becoming the real thing, and that scares me even more.

50

KARMA IS TWO BOYFRIENDS

Ivy

A week later, I duck behind the front counter of Better With Pockets, where Beatrix studies me intensely as I gather my planner and my purse, ready to take off for the evening. I've been in her shop for a few hours, snapping pictures of outfits for her social, some that she wears, some that I wear.

But she's still staring at me when I sling my purse over my shoulder.

"Is everything okay?" I ask with mild concern.

She taps her chin, then points to my Zoe Slade pants, which she knows are secondhand. "Hear me out. What if we have a thrifting section of the store. A consignment section. But we take in clothes for consignment that I once sold?"

"Don't get me excited, Beatrix," I say.

"I thought you might like that idea. I'll look into it, and we can add it to our marketing and promos."

"Love it. I'm your girl, whatever you need."

That's who I've been for her for the last few weeks. She's become a regular client of mine, right along with Birdie at *Your Runway* and a couple other publications that I've started writing for again. But I'm still doing my own thing online for Your Scrappy Little Fashionista, posting fashion rules and suggestions for outfits of the day, as well as tips on recycling clothes. Somehow, along with my side gig as a fox, I've cobbled together enough work from enough places to cover my bills. The hustle takes up a lot of energy and focus, though, and I don't want to backslide into relying on only one person, like I did with Simone. I want to make sure, too, that I can trust my own instincts as I work on my passion.

"Great," Beatrix says in that no-nonsense tone that I've grown accustomed to. She shifts gears, nodding to the planner in my arms. "Got something fun planned for tonight?"

I sure do. Hayes and Stefan are quite proficient at scheduling. "As a matter of fact, I'm going out with my guys."

I haven't mentioned them to her before, and for a few seconds, a flurry of nerves races through me, wondering how she'll react.

She arches a brow. "Two guys?"

I square my shoulders. "I have two boyfriends," I say, doing my best to own it. To keep telling my own story.

I can see the gears turning in her head as what I've

said registers. Then, she just shrugs. "Well you know what they say—karma is two boyfriends. I guess you have really good karma."

I recall the two weeks since we went to game night at Kana's and Brady's. Nights and days and dates. Work and play and games. Them traveling, us FaceTiming, all of us texting.

I smile, agreeing wholly. "I do."

I'll put that karma in my pocket as I head out with my guys that night.

They played Vancouver at home last night—and lost, which sucks—so they have tonight off before traveling tomorrow.

As per the planner, we're going to Sticks and Stones with a bunch of friends. Trina, Ryker, and Chase will be there, and so will Jackson and his boyfriend. Dev is going, and Ledger is supposed to be there too. Stefan told me they're buddies, which doesn't surprise me since hockey guys hang with their own. I've met Ledger through my brother, but Stefan is close with him, as well, so it'll be fun to get to know him in that capacity. Aubrey and the guy she's been seeing are also coming, so I'll get to check out the allegedly fabulous hair on Aiden.

When I head home to shower, Roxy greets me at the door with happy yips. She's wearing a black bandana with oranges on it.

Hmm. I don't think that's the one that I gave her this morning.

But she barks so excitedly that now's not the time to check it out. Now is the time for socks. I remove one and give it to her. "Here you go, girl," I say, and she snaps it up, then trots off to hide it.

Well, probably to set it on the floor by my bed, but she thinks it's hidden.

With her daily sock duty done, she returns to slather me in kisses as I harness her up.

As we walk, I peer at her accessory more closely. Is that a QR code on the tag? "Who gave you this bandana, girl?"

But Roxy doesn't say a word, just waggles her cute little butt.

On a street corner, I scan the code. I walk a few feet more then I come to a full stop on Fillmore Street when I see what the code is for.

Roxy's Playroom.

I clasp my hand to my mouth. I can't believe it. I can't believe they really did this. And I can't stop the tears from falling down my face.

I bang on the door to Hayes's apartment, my makeup streaked, my face a mess. When the door swings open, both guys are there, grinning like they've pulled off a heist.

"I'm going to have to redo all my makeup," I sob, holding my dog and the bandana, evidence of their generosity.

Stefan just shrugs. "Sorry not sorry."

"Such a shame," Hayes deadpans.

"You guys are too much," I say between broken breaths. "I can't believe you did this. I love it."

Before we'd even gone to Vegas together, back when we hung out on the rooftop, I told them about my dog and my dream to someday make a big donation to her rescue in Florida. To build a space for other foster dogs who needed homes and call it Roxy's Playroom.

They did it, then got a bandana, then dressed her in it.

"Now all these other little dogs will have homes because of you," I say.

"It's really because of you. It was your idea. We just made it happen," Hayes says.

I shake my head, denying that. "You guys did this, and I love it so much."

My heart is in my throat. It's tight and full of all the emotion I feel for these two men. The more time I spend with them, the more I start to let down my guard. And the clearer I can see beyond the Sportsman of the Year awards.

Maybe I *can* trust myself. Maybe I don't have questionable taste. Perhaps I have the best taste of all.

I bring them in for a big, tearful embrace.

"Glad you like it," Stefan says softly.

Tucked in the crook of my arm, my little critter whimpers, a happy sound of love. She's not alone in that. "I love it. You guys are really outdoing yourselves."

When I break the hug, Stefan gives me a look of pure satisfaction. "That's the plan."

* * *

At Sticks and Stones that night, they introduce me to Gage, who's behind the bar. His green eyes twinkle, and after we say hello, he turns to Stefan and Hayes. "It's the bone structure she likes, right?"

"It sure fucking is," Hayes says, patting his cheek with a cocky grin.

I roll my eyes. "Yes. That's it entirely."

When we head to the poolroom, I greet friends who feel like family. And new ones, too, like Hollis. He's a recent addition to the team. "It's the newest new guy," I say, teasing the guy with the surfer smile and laid-back vibe, who's had a few good games so far.

"And I don't mind taking the title away from Hayes," Hollis says.

"Funny, I don't mind it either," Hayes says, and it's nice to see Hayes so at ease at last. "Just don't play better than me," he warns Hollis.

"But do play well," I add. "We want a cup."

"Fuck yes," Hollis says. "That's the goal."

"Let's make it happen," Hayes adds.

As they chat I join Aubrey and meet her new man. Aubrey hasn't had the best of luck on the apps, so maybe Aiden will be the change she wants.

Her brother, Garrett, is here as well. I've never met him before, but lots of the guys have, since he's a sports agent and reps both Dev and Ledger. He's friends with them both, too, so...small world.

Aubrey and Aiden are off in the corner playing a game of Ping-Pong as Garrett rubs chalk on a pool cue and I rack up some balls.

"What do you think about that guy?" Garrett asks Dev, tipping his forehead toward Aiden.

Dev scoffs. "You want me to comment on your sister's man?"

"Yeah, I do."

"Ask Ledger," Dev says.

With amusement, I ask Dev, "Are you passing the buck?"

"You bet I am. I'm not stupid."

"Me, neither," Ledger says, then taps his pool cue to the felt. "Let's play a round instead of playing watchdog over your sister."

Garrett growls but acquiesces, and I file away the fact that Aubrey's big brother is very protective.

Then, I watch my guys with admiration as they begin a round of pool.

Yes, it's the bone structure, but it's really the size of their hearts that's making me fall in love with them every day.

51

SURPRISE SHOOT

Ivy

I'm pretty good at taking care of my guys too. One evening in early December, as Hayes is undressing me for Stefan, slowly, sensually taking off my white bra, kissing my shoulders as he goes, a delicious idea pops into my head.

The next morning, while Stefan makes double kale smoothies for the two of us in the kitchen and we talk about the day ahead, I tell him my idea.

Stefan grins wickedly. "You're a mind reader. He told me the day we shopped for your vibrator that he wanted that."

"That so?"

"Yes. You know him well."

"And I know a photographer," I say, smiling at him like *that's you, babe*.

Stefan checks his watch, as if it contains a calendar.

"He's got dinner with his agent tomorrow night after the game, I think he said. Why don't we surprise him when he comes home?"

My heart flutters. I love that Stefan not only showers me with affection, but he looks out for Hayes too. I melt a little more from that knowledge.

That feels a lot like family.

There's that word again. It's true—these men are starting to feel like family. Instead of elated, I'm suddenly terrified. Terrified of falling harder.

* * *

That next night at the arena, I zip up my fox costume and hit the ice for the first intermission.

"And now," the announcer booms. "Your Golden State Fox, also known as...Foxy."

I chuckle inside my costume—the mascot officially has a name. The fans voted for it. As Foxy, I race around the ice, heading straight for the T-shirt cannon. Then, I fire T-shirts into the crowd.

Dogs, planners, and operating a T-shirt cannon— some things just make you forget your fears and just feel happy.

* * *

Nighttime and lace are two of those things. At Stefan's home that night, as Roxy curls up on the fluffy red dog bed the guys got for her, I slip into a pink, demi-cup bra and matching bikini panties. I roll a pair of stockings up my thighs, then slide into white heels with ribbon straps that Stefan ties at my ankles.

"Ready?" he asks as he runs his hands up my legs.

"So ready." I stretch out on the big Alaskan king bed that we share most nights.

Stefan arranges me on the pillows and then adjusts the lights. He picks up his Nikon, and when Hayes arrives home from his dinner, calling out to us as he climbs the stairs, Stefan begins the shoot.

"In here," I answer as the photographer snaps the first photo.

Hayes turns the corner, enters the bedroom, then unleashes a rumble that makes my skin sizzle. "Wow."

I give him a pout, my lips red and glossy, my eyes full of desire. "You wanted a boudoir shoot of me. Come watch," I say, inviting him into this gift.

Stefan carelessly gestures to a chair we set up in the bedroom with us. "Take a seat."

"Hell, yes." Hayes tugs on his tie and sinks down, staring as Stefan takes pictures of me in all sorts of lingerie and lace, satin and silk, undressing me layer by layer throughout the shoot. Sometimes I look at the camera. Sometimes at the spectator. Sometimes at neither.

Soon, I'm down to only my panties and heels. Then, I shimmy off the panties too, and turn to my side, the angles and the lights keeping the pictures on the artistic side of nude.

Stefan comes around the bed, getting close, snapping a few more shots of me that don't show too much but enough to make my man very satisfied.

He sets the camera on the nightstand and turns to his friend in the chair. Hayes looks like a lion who's been watching its prey, waiting to make its move.

"Did you save room for dessert?" Stefan asks.

"I fucking did," Hayes rumbles.

"I'll take two," I say.

"Then spread those thighs," Stefan orders.

I comply, but he tugs me down the bed, then widens my legs. He undoes the ribbons on my ankles and ties them to the bedposts.

I'm at their mercy, my legs in a *V*. Like that, I welcome Stefan between my thighs.

He groans savagely as his mouth comes down on me, then he laps me up noisily, curling his arms around my ass, yanking me impossibly closer to his sinful mouth. He kisses my pussy with a filthy sort of reverence. I claw at the sheets, writhing against the restraints on my ankles as Hayes joins us on the bed. With hungry lips, he sucks and bites my nipples as he plays with my tits.

I gasp and groan, arching my hips, begging for more. I can't move my legs, but I take everything they give me with their mouths and hands and boundless appetites. I cry out in bliss as Stefan sends me over the edge, but they don't give me a chance to come down from that first high before Hayes prowls between my thighs, rubbing his beard against my flesh, nipping at my skin, and then flicking his tongue against my pussy.

I'm overstimulated, but that seems to be my life these days.

And maybe, just maybe, it will become my life for longer.

* * *

In the morning, while they're gone at the gym, I return from walking the dog and find an email icon blinking for my attention. It's a ticket to the Secondhand Fashion Show in Los Angeles next weekend.

Well, it's three tickets and a night at a luxury hotel.

And I know. It's time to break out my planner.

52

MAKE HER AN OFFER

Ivy

We make the most of our one-day holiday between hockey games, visiting Santa Monica, taking pictures along the pier, posting them on social.

We do Los Angeles Hayes, Stefan, and Ivy style. *Together*.

A little shopping, a little eating, a little private time.

On Friday afternoon in our Venice Beach hotel, I get ready for the fashion show I've always wanted to attend. I pick out my favorite vintage dress, a Charlotte Everly that I found at Champagne Taste, then a pair of cute ankle boots. My guys dress up in tailored slacks and button-down shirts, and they take me to the event at a nearby boutique hotel.

The venue is trendy and cool, teeming with fashion writers, influencers, and designers. The best part? Neither Simone nor Xander are here. Jackson told me he saw on social that their wedding was a bust. Hardly anyone covered it or posted pics or shared stories. That's even worse than bad publicity. But I don't feel bad for them. Because I don't care about them anymore. I care about the people here, who love fashion for the reasons I do—a chance to express yourself in new ways, and, sometimes, to do so without producing more stuff. I weave through the crowds, pointing out rising star designers to my boyfriends, then hotshot fashion trendsetters too.

I'm giddy over the clothes, and the shoes, and the fabrics, and the colors, and the desire to do right by our planet. I drink it in, my mind popping with ideas for posts and articles, for outfits of the day, for fashion rules, for...well, everything.

When it's time for the fashion show itself, I head into the roaring twenties-themed ballroom with its emerald lamps and speakeasy vibe. It oozes vintage charm.

My guys take me to the seat in the front row, and I feel glittery everywhere. "I've always wanted to see this," I say.

Then I kiss Hayes's bearded cheek, and Stefan's lightly stubbled one as Stefan says, "We know."

Those words reverberate in my mind. *We know.* For the last month they've shown me how deeply they know me, how well they listen, how much they want this. I've taken my time, tried to be patient, and worked through some of my past hurts.

I've also tried to listen to my head, but my heart knows what it wants.

I know how to tell them, and I plan to later tonight before we go home to San Francisco. For now, I enjoy the show, feeling both peace and excitement that I'm finally ready to say *I know* too.

* * *

When the show ends with Birdie Michaels thanking everyone for attending, I clap and cheer with the crowd, and we make our way out of the ballroom. I didn't come here to see Birdie. This wasn't meant to be a networking trip, but when we're milling about in the lobby, I catch her striding my way. There's determined focus in her keen eyes, which are lasered in on me.

My pulse skitters. She's become something of an idol to me in these last few months of working together.

She looks exactly like her photos, rocking a flowy maroon dress, with long hair curled in lush waves. She's in her late thirties, and she radiates warmth and energy, but efficiency, too, as she comes right up to me. "Ivy Samuels? I thought that might be you."

"It is me. Nice to meet you," I say.

"I was thrilled when I saw you on the guest list. Any chance I can steal you for a quick drink?"

I blink. I wasn't expecting that. Stefan gestures gracefully to the nearby hotel bar as if saying *feel free*. "We've got some things to take care of anyway," he says, paving the way.

A few minutes later, I'm swirling a metal straw in a frosted iced tea glass at the hotel bar as Birdie says, "We're expanding *Your Runway* and producing more content on recycled fashion, vintage clothing, and secondhand trends. It's some of the most popular content with our young readers, and frankly, the biggest growth area right now in fashion media. We want to run with it and stake a claim. I'd love to have you move to Los Angeles and take a lead on it."

Wait. What? All the air whooshes out of my lungs. That isn't what I came to Los Angeles for.

"And here's what I'm prepared to pay you." She tells me, and it's double what I make on all my jobs together.

I leave the bar a little later feeling woozy even though I didn't touch a drop of liquor. Nearly speechless with shock, I return to the room and unlock the door in a daze. The guys are waiting for me, curious and expectant.

"She just made me an offer," I say, still flabbergasted, "to move to LA."

53

TABLES TURNED

Stefan

What. The. Fuck.

The next morning, after we return to San Francisco, I pace the weight room at the gym on Fillmore Street. "We can't let her go," I say, dragging my hand through my hair.

"We can't tell her what to do, either," Hayes says as he hoists a barbell in a dead lift.

I've never seen him so calm. So laid-back.

"How can you take it like this?" I'm so agitated I can't focus. I can't exercise. I don't know how the fuck I'm going to skate tonight.

I couldn't sleep after she told us about the offer. I said all the right things. *You should consider it. It's a great opportunity. You'd be amazing at it.* Now I'm both exhausted and wound the fuck up.

What kind of shitty boyfriend would I be not to

support her? But fucking hell. I'm going to tear my eyes out. "What can we do?"

"To stop her?" Hayes asks evenly as he pulls the bar up to his chest again. A Nirvana tune blasts through the gym. We're the only ones in the free weights section at the moment.

"Yes!"

"You can't, man. That's not how this works."

I park my hands on my hips. "How do you know?" I'll pick a fight over anything evidently.

Setting the weight down, Hayes stares at me like he's the cool, in control older brother. "Because I've been here before. I've been traded."

"She's not being traded," I bite out. "She has a choice."

"And I did too. I could have turned down an offer and, oh, gee, not had a career." He frowns. "This is huge for her, man. Don't you get it? This is something she has to think about. By herself. *Without us.*"

I burn inside. No, I seethe. I'm not mad at Ivy though. I'm mad at Birdie. I'm mad at myself. I'm mad at the world. "You know she doesn't have to work. We could support her," I say, grasping at straws.

Hayes laughs in my face and rolls his eyes then turns dead serious. "Dude, listen to yourself. She's an independent woman."

"But we could." I'm desperate to keep her nearby. I can't stand the thought of her going to Los Angeles.

Hayes stabs his sternum. "You think I don't want to keep her? You think I want to watch her move to another fucking city?"

"I don't know," I say, scrubbing the back of my neck with my hand. "We need to do something. Can't you think of anything?"

He grabs my shoulders. "The thing we have to do is support her. That's what she needs."

"How? How can we do that?"

"It's LA. It's not that far. We can do this," he says, patting my shoulders, trying to reassure me.

How the hell he can be the calm one, I don't know. But I'm glad he is because I'm a wreck. "How?" I ask again.

He lets go, breathes out hard, then paces for a minute. Then he stops, turns, and says, "I've got an idea."

He does.

And it's brilliant.

The next day, Ivy asks us to meet her at The Great Dane before work. I reserve a table, and Hayes and I bring the gift we have ready to show her we support her.

She gets to the restaurant ahead of us, and when the hostess shows us to the table, it looks like Ivy has had the same idea.

54

ALL THE WAYS

Ivy

Aubrey curls a chunk of my hair into a loose wave.

"Beach waves," she says with pride. "You look so good like this."

"Thank you," I say, more calm than I'd expected to feel, given what I've planned for tonight.

"There's nothing quite like getting a blowout before you pour your heart out," she says.

"Good hair really sets the stage for everything, doesn't it?"

"I've been saying that for ages. Finally, someone's listening."

I look into the salon mirror. I feel ready. Certain. And most of all, *changed*.

Nearly three months ago, when I grabbed Jackson's binoculars and checked out a naked man on the roof of my building, I had no idea that it would upend my life.

I had no idea that it would lead to me marching into a job I'd thought I loved and flipping all the tables. That it would send me into the arms of not one amazing man, but two.

But life is surprising. When Aubrey's done, I stand and then give her a hug. She lets go first and shoos me to the door. "Go. Report back tomorrow."

"Promise." I leave Aubrey's salon, fueled by confidence and great hair. When we returned from Los Angeles the other night, the guys told me not to make a decision about the job right away. To take my time.

I told them I would.

But really, *I knew*. I didn't need to run to my grandmother when I landed. I didn't need to wring my hands and ask her plaintively what to do. I didn't need to wander along the water or walk across the city or play emo music until the answer came to me in a bolt of lightning from the heavens.

The answer's been inside of me since the night the guys and I went to Kana's and Brady's house and declared ourselves together. I knew then, somewhere inside me, what I wanted. It just took a few more weeks for that voice to grow louder, to turn into a Greek chorus in my heart, to become its own anthem, guiding me to a wide-open door.

That door leads to The Great Dane tonight. I suppose it's fitting. Stefan wasn't here the night I spotted Hayes, but I learned later that he'd swung by a few hours after. He told me that he'd come here, stared off in the distance, and plotted a course to reach me. So, it seems fitting that we'd meet here now.

I arrive early. Mid-December is not rooftop weather. The warm fall has burned off, and the chilly temperatures have rolled in. I'm wearing jeans and a sweater that slopes down one arm, my waves curling over my shoulders.

Right on time, two handsome hockey studs walk toward me from across the restaurant. I spot the vulnerability in their eyes, but the confidence too. I also notice the planner under Stefan's arm and give it a funny look.

When they reach me, Stefan dips his face and brushes a kiss onto my cheek. It's a kiss that says *you're mine*. Hayes does the same, his lips saying *this was meant to be*.

They sit across from me at our table for three.

Yes, this is what I want. *I know*. But I am curious what they have. "Is that a planner in your pocket or are you just happy to see me?"

"Both." Stefan slides it across the table.

Normally, he sets the agenda, but Hayes jumps in. "We made you something. Open it to today."

With excited fingers, I open the book to December, finding the date. They filled in dinner at The Great Dane. Then tomorrow's home game. A few days from now, there's a night in at Stefan's house. Then Christmas together. But January gets more interesting. They've filled in their hockey schedule, where they'll be, and when they can get away to see me in...Los Angeles.

And when I can fly up here.

Wow. They've done it for every month through the end of hockey season. When the summer months come, they've blocked out all their days and nights in Los Angeles.

My breath catches.

I'm floored by their declaration. By their plans for me.

"Ivy, if you want that job, we'll make it work," Hayes says, intensely serious, his eyes locked on me.

"We plotted it all out," Stefan adds. "How to see you. How to do this." He's calm but full of emotion. "Whatever you need, we'll make it happen." Then, he grabs my hand, squeezing it desperately. "I love you so much. I'll do whatever it takes for you. *We'll* do whatever it takes for you."

Hayes grabs my other hand, the three of us squeezing hard together. "I'm so in love with you. I love the way you are with your dog. I love how you take care of her. I love how you look out for your friends and treat them like family."

Stefan locks eyes with me and continues, taking the baton. "I love spending mornings with you. Talking about our days. Making smoothies and coffee, answering your questions and then asking a million more."

"I love that you understand what I need before I even need it," Hayes says, taking his turn. "I love that you've supported me from the day we met. I love your confidence, and your energy, and your eyes that just make me fucking melt."

He draws a big breath, and Stefan takes over. "And I love that you stand up for yourself. You tell people no when you need to. You don't take any shit. I love that you're tough and resilient, but so damn tender in your heart."

"And I love how you look out for both of us," Hayes adds, then shifts his gaze briefly to Stefan, who smiles back. An appreciative smile from both of them.

A knot rises up in my throat, climbing sky-high. I'm bursting with emotions, with joy, with...this overload of feelings.

That's what I've always felt with them—so very much. I shake my head, amazed, awed, and wildly happy. "I love you," I blurt out simply. How can I compare to that beautiful ode to all the ways they love me? I can't, and that's okay. It's not a competition for their love or mine. Both are boundless. "I love both of you. I need both of you. *Together*. This thing we have? It's better as three. I can't imagine us any other way. I love you both so much, and I'm not taking the job. I want to be here in San Francisco with my friends and my family and my growing business—and with the two loves of my life. So I turned it down." My voice cracks at the end, my heart overflowing.

"Thank god," Stefan says, relaxing in his chair, laughing with joy.

"I'm so fucking glad," Hayes seconds.

These guys. I love them so. "And look...great minds." I take out my planner, the one where they mark our dates, and I flip it open to show them what I did.

I point to a date a week or so from now. The Sportsman of the Year awards. It doesn't say TOC. It says JT.

"What does that mean?" Stefan asks tentatively.

"It means we're not a Throuple of convenience. We're just...throuple," I say, then swallow past the emotions clogging my throat. "We're just together. No end date. Just...a wide-open future."

"It worked," Stefan says, sounding on top of the world. "We've been trying really hard to get you to fall in love with us, and you did."

I laugh, delighted to hear his confession. "News flash: I was already in love with both of you."

"Good. I was going mad thinking about you leaving," Stefan admits.

Hayes cracks up. "He really was."

But then they both stop laughing. Stefan cups my left cheek. "You're staying," he says with relief.

Hayes takes my hand and squeezes it solemnly. "This is us."

I nod as tears slip down my cheeks. "This is us," I repeat, then purse my lips together before taking one more chance. "I was thinking...what if we all moved into Stefan's home?"

Stefan pops up from the table and taps his watch. "Yes. Now. Let's go."

We don't go right away. We stay and eat and drink and laugh. Then, we get my dog and make plans for the three of us—well, the four of us—to make a home.

EPILOGUE

A NEW HOME

Stefan

It doesn't take long for my place to fill up. Hayes brings his telescope and sets it on the rooftop balcony, since, yes, I have one too. We'll definitely make ample use of that for stargazing and other nighttime activities. Daytime activities, too, come to think of it.

Ivy brings all her clothes, and I have to make room in the main bedroom closet for them, adding a new hanging rack, which gives me the chance to break out my toolbox, which gives Ivy the chance to watch me hammer.

She stands in the doorway, studying me with eager eyes.

"So you like your men to wield hockey sticks and hammers?"

"Yes. Yes, I do," she says.

"Good. I'll keep doing both."

We bring over Roxy's collection of bandanas and set up a cubby for her by the front door. Then, I indulge and buy her a literal fuck-ton of beds.

Yes, it looks much more like home with a dog bed in every room. But the little critter still manages to sleep on the Alaskan king every night. Smart girl. It's just more fun to stretch out in a big bed.

Once Ivy's out of her apartment, Jackson's boyfriend moves in, and I know it makes Ivy happy that her friend wasn't left hanging with the rent. As for Hayes's place, I'll find someone to lease the penthouse to soon. With that rooftop garden, and all the opportunities it affords for naked sports, it'll go fast.

For now, when I come home from the arena after games with Hayes and Ivy, my house no longer feels empty. Neither do my nights or my days.

ANOTHER EPILOGUE
THREE OF A KIND

Ivy

"What do you think?"

I show my shimmery, ruby-red dress to my trusty fashion sidekick.

Roxy watches me eagerly from her spot on the floor in the main bedroom, probably with the hope that I have a secret burger stashed somewhere. Her tail twitches, a telltale sign where her heart really is.

"Fine. I'll take your silence as two paws up."

She wags her tail harder. Wow, she really thinks I have food for her, the cute little beggar.

I gather the silky-soft material of my dress and bend to give her a scratch under the chin. But she offers me a tongue in return. Okay, maybe she did want a kiss.

"I love you too," I coo, giving a soft kiss to her even softer little nose. Then I rise and let the dress fall against my legs, the material swishing as I leave the bedroom in my gala finest, my girl trotting beside me, decked out in her red-and-white holiday bandana with illustrations of dog bones on it.

Before I even reach the living room, though, I hear the debate.

"You are the raccoon on meth," Hayes accuses.

With a confident chuckle, Stefan says, "No. It's Ivy."

I stop and listen, my lips twitching in amusement.

"No. She's organized. You just appear to be," Hayes says.

"Pfft."

"Just admit it."

I stifle a laugh.

"I admit nothing," Stefan says, and I imagine he's leaning back in a chair, casual and easy, holding a tumbler of scotch.

Hayes is relentless though. "In every home, there's one person who stacks the dishwasher like a Scandinavian architect and the other like a raccoon on meth."

"Obviously, I'm the architect. Isn't that what I've been all along?"

Stefan makes a good point, and it sounds like *case closed*.

Roxy and I proceed, and when we turn the corner, warmth flows over me. My men look so good, relaxed at home. They're both wearing tailored suits. Stefan lounges on the couch, decked out in a dark blue suit that matches his gorgeous eyes and hugs his strong frame. In one hand, he holds a tumbler of amber liquid. Hayes, dressed in a dark charcoal suit, leans against the mantel where stockings are hung with care. Roxy barks a hello, announcing our presence.

In tandem, the men turn to me and jaws drop.

"Wow."

"Gorgeous."

"You look..."

"Incredible."

Their praise feels like champagne bubbling through my body, but I hold up a hand. "I have a confession."

Concern flashes in Hayes's dark eyes. He stares hard at me, asking silently, *Are we doing this right now?*

But I need to set the record straight. "I'm the raccoon on meth," I say pointing to my chest.

Stefan's grin stretches across his handsome face, and he looks pointedly at his teammate. "Told you so."

Hayes shakes his head like he's disappointed in me. "I stand corrected."

"It seems we have two architects and one feral trash panda," I say.

Hayes's expression softens. "But you're our trash panda."

"I am."

Stefan pauses to linger his gaze on me. "And you look absolutely stunning, sweetheart."

"I don't know how we'll last all night at the gala," Hayes adds in a gravelly rasp, his eyes not leaving my body.

They look like they're about to upend all of our plans this evening and take me here on this couch instead.

"Just think of tonight like foreplay," I suggest. I'm helpful like that.

"Fair enough." Stefan sets down his glass and gestures to the door. "Should we go?"

Not so fast. We have a surprise for him.

I turn to Hayes, anticipation bubbling up in me. I give him a quick nod, and he crosses to the U-shaped couch. Roxy's sitting on the floor next to me. "Actually, Ivy and I have an early Christmas gift for you," Hayes says as I scoop up the dog and set her on the couch.

Stefan furrows his brow, but amusement coasts across his lips. "Is that so?"

Hayes and I taught Roxy a new trick. He reaches into the pocket of his pants and takes out one, new Christmas sock with illustrations of presents on it. It's weighted down in the toe.

He gives it to me. I dangle the sock before the dog. "Roxy, give the sock to Stefan," I say.

She takes it.

Stefan startles. His expression grows more curious as Roxy trots across the cushions to him, the sock in her mouth.

I'm bursting with excitement, giddy before he can even open it. I meet Stefan's eyes. "I love you both so much, and I don't want a husband and a boyfriend. I want both of you as my partners."

Stefan's eyes glimmer with wild hope. My marriage to Hayes was a legality, born from a late-night dare that had me married to one man while I fell equally for two.

With us all living together now and sharing our lives, I don't want the distinction anymore. Hayes doesn't either. Distinctions might exist in the eye of the law, but we can make our rules for our world.

"Hayes and I got new rings. Three of them. They match," I say, my voice trembling with emotion.

Stefan parts his lips, but he can barely speak. "I... wow...I'm..."

"Open it," I say.

Stefan reaches into the sock, takes out the box, and opens it. When he sees three gorgeous, matching platinum bands, his eyes glisten. But he's stoic—a hockey player after all. He swipes his cheek like there was simply dirt in his eye.

"Let's do this," Hayes says to his friend, intensely serious.

Stefan stares at the rings for a long, weighty beat then says, "Yes."

Like if he said more, all the tears would fall.

He takes out the bands and turns one over, then the other, then the third. Studies each inscription on the inside. They're all the same.

Home.

He looks up at us, his eyes full of love. He stands and holds out his hand to me. With reverence, I slide the band on his ring finger. Then I hold up my hand for him to see I'm no longer wearing my gold ring from Las Vegas. Hayes does the same. His finger is bare.

I slide another band onto Hayes's finger.

Then they take the last one and together, they slide it onto mine.

A little later, we walk into the gala, three of a kind.

* * *

During the awards ceremony, I sit with Stefan's family from Copenhagen, chatting and getting to know his outgoing parents, his friendly brothers and sisters, and then watching and cheering the loudest when my man receives the Sportsman of the Year award that he so deeply deserves. An award that no one could ever take away from him.

Afterward, when the photographer asks for a picture, Stefan brings Hayes and me to him. We pose together with me in the middle, our matching bands visible for all the world to see.

On the way out of the hotel, I stop to say goodbye to Trina, showing her the rings, then telling her about the gift.

"You beat me to it," she teases.

"Your day will come soon," I say, and I'm a fortune teller evidently, since a few months later, Chase and Ryker propose to her on Valentine's Day. And she says yes. It looks like we'll be having a busy season of triad weddings.

Until then, I keep busy with work, doing what I've been doing. Turns out, my side hustle as Foxy is hard for me to give up. I love whipping up the crowds at home games for a sport I adore. During the days, I keep writing articles for Birdie and a few others, including my own channels, as well as working for the store. Oh, and I have one more new client—Jessie hired me as her personal stylist.

Looks like I picked the right name, because I am definitely a scrappy little fashionista. One with a devoted canine sidekick, who likes hanging out with me as I work.

At the end of the hockey season—the best of Hayes's hockey career—the team offers him a new contract, and he says yes so fast. He loves being part of the Golden State Foxes.

It's a relief to him, but not a surprise to me at all. I believed in him from the start, and I'm glad he started to believe in himself more as the season went on.

That summer, the three of us host our friends and family in a private wedding ceremony in our San Francisco backyard, where we pledge our love to each other.

We aren't the only ones going on a honeymoon though. Aubrey is too, but it's not what she expected. It's...complicated. Well, double honeymoons are, and I'm sure I'll get all the details when she returns.

When we arrive at our hotel in Tuscany, I shut out thoughts of everyone else, and so do my guys. Once the door to the honeymoon suite closes, Stefan turns to Hayes and says, "Question for you."

"Hit me up," Hayes says.

Stefan moves behind me, pushes my hair to the side of my neck, then presses a kiss to my nape while looking at Hayes. "Do you want to fuck my wife?"

With a smile, I lean back against one of my husbands.

The look on my other husband's face is magic. Kind of like how I feel with both of them.

Trina's spicy MFM roomies-to-lovers + sweet revenge hockey romance DOUBLE PUCKED is FREE in KU!

Can't get enough Ivy, Hayes and Stefan? Scroll below for access to an exclusive bonus scene of their life together!

Mark your calendars for THOROUGHLY PUCKED in January when Aubrey's runaway bride + brother's best friends, double honeymoon romance with Dev and Ledger comes FREE to KU!

* * *

Click here for the Puck Yes Bonus Epilogue! Or scan the QR code!

If you've already devoured Double Pucked, you'd likely enjoy the spicy, fake-dating-ish romance PLAYS WELL WITH OTHERS, available for free in KU.

BE A LOVELY

Want to be the first to know of sales, new releases, special deals and giveaways? Sign up for my newsletter today!

Want to be part of a fun, feel-good place to talk about books and romance, and get sneak peeks of covers and advance copies of my books? Be a Lovely!

ACKNOWLEDGMENTS

I am so grateful to so many amazing people for their insight into this story.

First, thank you to Sharon Abreau, AKA the hockey goddess. Sharon is a life long hockey fan and she graciously read the entire book TWICE and checked all the hockey details. Any mistakes in hockey are entirely my own.

Thank you to Lo Morales for her guidance on diversity, and her fabulous opinions on words and dirty talk. Thank you Rae Douglas at Bookink Services for her eyes on the schmexy times, the kink and the relationship dynamics. Also, on lube. Rae, let's make *throuple of convenience* a thing! Gratitude as well to April Gaisford for her insight into polyamory and MFM. I so appreciate her thoughts.

Roxy's rescue in Florida was inspired by Pawlicious Poochie Pet Rescue. I adore this rescue so much — it's run by one woman who has made it her mission to save little senior dogs who need her help! I love to support this rescue and if you're ever looking for one to check out, I highly recommend it!

Big gratitude to Melanie Harlow, who encouraged me to pursue this book's particular path as I saw it unfolding, to Laurelin Paige who offered her invaluable insight too, and to Corinne Michaels, who was right from the start. You told me so.

I am indebted to KP Simmon for her tireless support and early reading and feedback. She also knew what this book was supposed to be!

Thanks to Kim Bias for her eagle eyes and deep thoughts. I am grateful to Lauren Clarke for taking this over the finish line, and for Rosemary Clement for the polish. Kara Hildebrand, Sandra Shipman, Claudia Fosca, and Virginia Carey were immensely helpful with eagle eyes and eager spirits.

Huge kisses to Kayti McGee for her creativity and eyes, and to Anthony Colletti for his acumen and guidance. Thank you to Sarina Bowen for hockey insight.

Thank you to Kylie Sek for a dream cover and her endless patience in getting it just right.

Thank you to Sarah Pederson for the inspiration for the book club scene.

Most of all thank you to my family for their support, to my husband who supported all my wild ideas for this book, and to my dogs for their big, big, big, furry love.

But last and certainly not least, I always and forever more grateful for YOU. The readers. Thank you.

MORE BOOKS BY LAUREN

I've written more than 100 books! **All of these titles below
are FREE in Kindle Unlimited!**

Double Pucked

A sexy, outrageous MFM hockey romantic comedy!

Puck Yes

A fake marriage, spicy MFM hockey rom com!

The Virgin Society Series

Meet the Virgin Society – great friends who'd do anything
for each other. Indulge in these forbidden, emotionally-
charged, and wildly sexy age-gap romances!

The RSVP

The Tryst

The Tease

The Dating Games Series

A fun, sexy romantic comedy series about friends in the city
and their dating mishaps!

The Virgin Next Door

Two A Day

The Good Guy Challenge

How To Date Series (New and ongoing)

Four great friends. Four chances to learn how to date again. Four standalone romantic comedies full of love, sex and meet-cute shenanigans.

My So-Called Sex Life

Plays Well With Others

The Anti-Romantic

It Seemed Like A Good Idea At the Time

Boyfriend Material

Four fabulous heroines. Four outrageous proposals. Four chances at love in this sexy rom-com series!

Asking For a Friend

Sex and Other Shiny Objects

One Night Stand-In

Overnight Service

Big Rock Series

My #1 New York Times Bestselling sexy as sin, irreverent, male-POV romantic comedy!

Big Rock

Mister O

Well Hung

Full Package

Joy Ride

Hard Wood

Happy Endings Series

Romance starts with a bang in this series of standalones following a group of friends seeking and avoiding love!

Come Again

Shut Up and Kiss Me

Kismet

My Single-Versary

Ballers And Babes

Sexy sports romance standalones guaranteed to make you hot!

Most Valuable Playboy

Most Likely to Score

A Wild Card Kiss

Rules of Love Series

Athlete, virgins and weddings!

The Virgin Rule Book

The Virgin Game Plan

The Virgin Replay

The Virgin Scorecard

The Extravagant Series

Bodyguards, billionaires and hoteliers in this sexy, high-stakes series of standalones!

One Night Only

One Exquisite Touch

My One-Week Husband

The Guys Who Got Away Series

Friends in New York City and California fall in love in this fun and hot rom-com series!

Birthday Suit

Dear Sexy Ex-Boyfriend

The What If Guy

Thanks for Last Night

The Dream Guy Next Door

Always Satisfied Series

A group of friends in New York City find love and laughter in this series of sexy standalones!

Satisfaction Guaranteed

Never Have I Ever

Instant Gratification

PS It's Always Been You

The Gift Series

An after dark series of standalones! Explore your fantasies!

The Engagement Gift

The Virgin Gift

The Decadent Gift

The Heartbreakers Series

Three brothers. Three rockers. Three standalone sexy

romantic comedies.

Once Upon a Real Good Time

Once Upon a Sure Thing

Once Upon a Wild Fling

Sinful Men

A high-stakes, high-octane, sexy-as-sin romantic suspense series!

My Sinful Nights

My Sinful Desire

My Sinful Longing

My Sinful Love

My Sinful Temptation

From Paris With Love

Swoony, sweeping romances set in Paris!

Wanderlust

Part-Time Lover

One Love Series

A group of friends in New York falls in love one by one in this sexy rom-com series!

The Sexy One

The Hot One

The Knocked Up Plan

Come As You Are

Lucky In Love Series

A small town romance full of heat and blue collar heroes and sexy heroines!

Best Laid Plans

The Feel Good Factor

Nobody Does It Better

Unzipped

No Regrets

An angsty, sexy, emotional, new adult trilogy about one young couple fighting to break free of their pasts!

The Start of Us

The Thrill of It

Every Second With You

The Caught Up in Love Series

A group of friends finds love!

The Pretending Plot

The Dating Proposal

The Second Chance Plan

The Private Rehearsal

Seductive Nights Series

A high heat series full of danger and spice!

Night After Night

After This Night

One More Night

A Wildly Seductive Night

Joy Delivered Duet

A high-heat, wickedly sexy series of standalones that will set your sheets on fire!

Nights With Him

Forbidden Nights

Unbreak My Heart

A standalone second chance emotional roller coaster of a romance

The Muse

A magical realism romance set in Paris

Good Love Series of sexy rom-coms co-written with Lili Valente!

I also write MM romance under the name L. Blakely!

Hopelessly Bromantic Duet (MM)

Roomies to lovers to enemies to fake boyfriends

Hopelessly Bromantic

Here Comes My Man

Men of Summer Series (MM)

Two baseball players on the same team fall in love in a forbidden romance spanning five epic years

Scoring With Him

Winning With Him

All In With Him

MM Standalone Novels

A Guy Walks Into My Bar

The Bromance Zone

One Time Only

The Best Men (Co-written with Sarina Bowen)

Winner Takes All Series (MM)

A series of emotionally-charged and irresistibly sexy standalone MM sports romances!

The Boyfriend Comeback

Turn Me On

A Very Filthy Game

Limited Edition Husband

Manhandled

If you want a personalized recommendation, email me at laurenblakelybooks@gmail.com!

CONTACT

I love hearing from readers! You can find me on TikTok at LaurenBlakelyBooks, Instagram at LaurenBlakelyBooks, Facebook at LaurenBlakelyBooks, or online at LaurenBlakely.com. You can also email me at laurenblakelybooks@gmail.com

Printed in Great Britain
by Amazon

29337100R00255